Bı.

Murder on the Edge

Detective Inspector Skelgill Investigates

LUCiUS

Kindle edition first published by Lucius 2014

Paperback edition first published by Lucius 2014

For more details and rights enquiries contact:
Lucius-ebooks@live.com

Cover design by Moira Kay Nicol

EDITOR'S NOTE

Murder on the Edge is the third mystery in the Detective Inspector Skelgill series. It is a stand-alone novel, although its events take place immediately following those described in *Murder in School.*

Absolutely no AI (Artificial Intelligence) is used in the writing of the DI Skelgill novels.

THE DI SKELGILL SERIES

Murder in Adland

Murder in School

Murder on the Edge

Murder on the Lake

Murder by Magic

Murder in the Mind

Murder at the Wake

Murder in the Woods

Murder at the Flood

Murder at Dead Crags

Murder Mystery Weekend

Murder on the Run

Murder at Shake Holes

Murder at the Meet

Murder on the Moor

Murder Unseen

Murder in our Midst

Murder Unsolved

Murder in the Fells

Murder at the Bridge

Murder on the Farm

1. WASDALE HEAD

Monday, early morning

'Fancy a stretch of the legs, Jones?'

DS Jones pirouettes proficiently, crunching loose car park gravel beneath her flat rubber soles. She squints into the bright morning sun beyond Skelgill's silhouette.

'Oughtn't we get these under lock and key, Guv?' She refers to the loose bundle of documents cradled against her thorax.

Skelgill does not reply immediately. He casts about and sniffs the fresh dewy air. Then pointedly he glances at the sturdy piebald dog that stands obediently at his side, seemingly unconcerned by the fraying length of rustic yarn threaded through its collar.

'I think you're outvoted, Jones. Cleopatra's up for it.'

DS Jones frowns. 'What exactly did you have in mind?'

Skelgill casually flaps a hand in an easterly direction, towards the silvery grey bulk of Great Gable, its flanks attractively dappled with irregular sliding shadows cast by small fair-weather cumulus. 'I was thinking we might stroll over to Gladis's at Seathwaite.'

Now DS Jones's voice takes on a distinct note of exasperation. 'Guv – that's miles – we'd be hours.'

Skelgill beams generously. 'Trust me – I know a short cut. We'll be there by eight.'

'But what about my car, Guv – and all this evidence?'

Skelgill shrugs. 'Lock it in the boot. Leyton needs to take a statement from his lordship. He can bring a DC to drive your motor back to the station this afternoon.'

'And how will we get from Seathwaite to Penrith?'

'Leyton can fetch us. It's just down the road for him. I'll text him now.'

DS Jones continues to protest. She tries a different tack. 'Guv – I know the case is cracked – but won't the Chief want to see you first thing – to congratulate you?'

Skelgill scowls. 'That'll be the day.'

'Oh, come off it, Guv – you'll be her blue-eyed boy this morning.'

Skelgill patently affects diffidence. He stoops so that he is at eye-level with the dog.

'If I am – which I doubt – but let's say you're right – then now's the time to take advantage of our magnificent surroundings.'

'You mean breakfast, Guv.'

Skelgill looks up with an innocent twinkle in his eye. 'You're getting to know me too well.'

DS Jones shakes her head resignedly and pops open the car boot with her remote.

'After all, you just ate a bacon sandwich – why wouldn't we go to a café?'

Skelgill rises and does a little skip, to which the dog responds with a playful sideways bound of its own.

'Mountain air will do us good. I'm still seeing double from Copeland's sloe gin. Come to think of it, you're probably over the limit, anyway.'

DS Jones carefully places the documents into the vehicle, leaning away from Skelgill as if to conceal the rueful grin that plays at the corners of her mouth.

'We'd better not lose Cleopatra, Guv – doesn't she count as evidence, too?'

Skelgill deftly wraps the dog's improvised lead in a clove hitch around a footpath marker-post adjacent to their parking spot.

'I bet she could tell us a thing or two.'

Now DS Jones squats to stroke the affable creature.

'What *will* become of her, Guv?'

Cleopatra gives out a little whine, as if she detects the tenor of their conversation. Skelgill does not reply, and instead turns his attention to retying the laces of his trail shoes.

'Still got your trainers in the car?'

DS Jones stands and puts a foot forward for him to inspect. She wears what are ostensibly training shoes, but in fact they owe a lot more to fashion than to function.

'Think these will be okay, Guv?'

Skelgill narrows his eyes and cranes his head sideways to get a look at the sole.

'You'll do – it's dry now – there's a good path. Take it easy, though – you don't want to sprain your ankle in the middle of the fells.'

DS Jones has evidently given up trying to talk her superior out of his scheme. Her response is more benign. 'I thought you had a hotline to the mountain rescue, Guv?'

Skelgill flashes a reprimanding glance. 'That would be just too embarrassing. I'd rather cart you out myself.'

'In that case I shall watch my step.'

Skelgill raises his eyebrows, and looks momentarily irked, but before he can devise a retort a scraggy border collie slinks between them and stops a yard short of Cleopatra.

'Tha' a pit-bull?'

The voice belongs to the gnarled shepherd – or *ex*-shepherd – who, for the second time in as many visits, has surprised Skelgill with his stealthy approach.

'Bullboxer. Staffie cross.'

'Yourn?'

'Just minding her for me marra.'

DS Jones appears mildly astonished by Skelgill's hitherto undisclosed canine knowledge (or it could be his sudden descent into Cumbrian dialect). She reaches down, perhaps out of politeness, to pat the matted collie, but Cleopatra selects the same moment to inspect this reticent visitor. With a sudden lunge she summarily snaps her leash, causing the poor creature to dart away with his tail firmly between his legs. Skelgill snatches up the trailing end of string, but it breaks again the moment he applies limiting force.

'Tha' wunt wuk. Tek this, lad.'

The old man rummages in a pocket of his baggy trousers and philanthropically presses upon Skelgill a hank of faded but effectively unbreakable blue baler twine.

'Dunt want 'er spookin' t'yowes. Yon Copeland's keeper's a reet trigger happy b–'

Evidently the next, unfinished word is not *bloke*, for the old man stops his sentence dead in its tracks. This is presumably in deference to the presence of DS Jones, whom he now paradoxically takes the opportunity to eye somewhat salaciously, as if it is his entitlement for such gentlemanly consideration.

Skelgill restrains Cleopatra and, employing the baler twine, fastens a slip-knot onto her collar. He has a slightly chastened air about him, as if there is a small public humiliation in being upstaged by the decrepit farmhand.

'I normally keep a reel in my wagon – but I came with–'

Now it is Skelgill's turn to dry up. Holding out a palm in her direction, he seems unprepared as to how he should describe his relationship to DS Jones. Whether this is at a personal or professional level is not clear. Notwithstanding, with regard to the latter, the elderly herdsman will soon receive an official visit from DS Leyton, and as yet is unaware of Skelgill's true interest in his locale. Understandably, therefore, Skelgill might be reluctant to reveal what have been the clandestine motives for his cordiality.

However, the old man seems to make up his own mind, and cackles something colloquial and largely indeterminate – but possibly along the lines of, 'Women? Can't live *with* them... can't live *with* them' – a hackneyed Saturday night thigh-slapper from Skelgill's own book of beer-inspired and inadvertently sexist maxims. Then, perhaps not wishing to overstay his welcome, he takes a last leering look at DS Jones and limps away in the direction of his cottage.

'What did he say, Guv?'

'It was something about the dog – I didn't quite catch it – they speak their own version of English out here.'

'Think he was he serious about Copeland's gamekeeper?'

'Can't be too careful. Farmers are within their rights to shoot – if a dog worries their sheep. And you know what divvies townies can be.'

DS Jones nods. 'I once had to write an essay about the pros and cons of calling the Lakes a National Park. The word *park* being the source of contention.'

Skelgill purses his lips. 'I'm torn, myself. We've got the rescue services pulling idiots off three-thousand-foot fells dressed like they've just been to Bondi beach. But, right now, you and I can pick our own route to Gladis's without fear of his lordship unloading a couple of barrels in our direction for trespassing.'

'So long as we keep Cleopatra in check, Guv.'

'On which note – shall we make tracks, ladies?'

They set off into the bright sunlight, the cool air jangling with the song of larks and pipits and the mewing of a buzzard as it rises upon a thermal over the slopes of Lingmell. Skelgill glances surreptitiously at his companions, and he must wonder about their relative capacities to deal with the cross-country hill walk ahead. Certainly, the athletic-looking DS Jones should not be too challenged, but Cleopatra seems better equipped for exercise of a more muscular nature – such as bringing down a sheep or two.

*

There are no doubt some official restrictions concerning dogs and cafés, but on the Hope family's isolated farmstead such rules may be considered flexible, especially when it is a long-acquainted policeman that is bending them. In any event, Skelgill has already introduced Cleopatra to the assembled breakfasters as a 'sniffer dog in training', implicitly endowing her with access rights in common with guide dogs, and – much to the amusement of Gladis Hope – facetiously crediting the canine for

11

leading him and his colleague to 'the best fry in the North of England' (and by definition therefore the *whole* of England). Cleopatra, of course, is well schooled in petitioning for titbits – her former owner saw to that – and keeps a diplomatically low profile as she moves undercover from table to table.

'So, Guv – doesn't this place disprove your ten-minute claim?'

Skelgill produces an inquiring look over the rim of his mug. 'Come again?'

'The other night – you said, on your patch, you're never more than ten minutes from a meal.'

Skelgill ponders for a moment, and then replies, 'Depends where you start from.'

'Ha-ha, Guv.'

'Anyway – it's ten minutes from Keswick the way Leyton drives.' Then a thought obviously enters his mind and he asks, 'Jones – at the station – have you heard me and Leyton referred to as the *North Lakes Sweeney*?'

DS Jones looks suitably perplexed. Skelgill is adept at divining untruths uttered by the crooked mouths of criminals, but is more susceptible to white lies that emanate from fairer lips, so she probably considers herself on fairly safe ground.

'Don't think so, Guv – why?'

Skelgill immediately appears disinterested, as if it is now inconsequential.

On such an apposite cue, however, from an open window comes the sound of a vehicle grinding to a sharp halt, followed by the harsh ratcheting of a handbrake and the heavy-handed slam of a door.

DS Jones glances knowingly at her superior, who is forced to respond with a raised eyebrow.

'The Sweeney, Guv?'

Skelgill tuts and checks his wristwatch. 'He's earlier than I expected – he must be on the scrounge for breakfast.'

This might be considered an ironic statement coming from Skelgill, and one that proves to be inaccurate too when DS Leyton's rather harassed visage appears at the said window.

'Got a minute, Guvnor? Something's come up.'

Skelgill nods reluctantly and rises from his chair.

'Jones – settle up with Gladis, will you?'

DS Jones blinks obediently.

'Make sure she takes the money.'

'Sure, Guv – but what about Leyton?'

'Better get him a takeaway burger.' Skelgill lingers for a second or two. 'Make it a couple – never know where I'll be for lunch.'

DS Jones grins widely and shakes her head, while the incorrigible Skelgill fishes abstractedly in his pocket for Cleopatra's makeshift leash. He snares the dog and leads her out into the enclosed farmyard, where DS Leyton loiters uncertainly, his expression somewhere between one of bewilderment and distaste.

'Blimey, Guv – it don't half pen – it's enough to put you off your Becks and Posh.'

Skelgill shrugs nonchalantly. 'I've just ordered you a burger – but never fear, there's a good home waiting if you can't face it.'

DS Leyton eyes the dog suspiciously, but decides to let Skelgill's ambiguous threat pass. More pressing is the official business that has disrupted their arrangements.

'What it is, Guv – there's been a climbing death reported this morning – on a fell to the north of Keswick.'

Skelgill looks annoyed, as though this is no reason to be troubling a Detective Inspector over his breakfast. 'And?'

'The body was discovered by a couple of elderly walkers at about seven this morning. PC Dodd attended the scene. Apparently he does a bit of rock climbing himself – he called in to suggest that you should have a butcher's before they move the body.'

Skelgill frowns. 'So, what's he saying – there's something suspicious?'

DS Leyton appears a tad browbeaten by his superior's intolerant manner. 'I guess so, Guv – I've only got the message indirectly. Apparently HQ have been trying to phone you for the last hour.'

Skelgill is now further irked. A regular observer of his habits, such as DS Leyton, might suspect he is planning to take advantage of the hiatus that follows the successful conclusion of the Oakthwaite case by disappearing on a fishing trip this morning. Certainly he has the excuse of reinstating his boat to its familiar berth. Skelgill pulls out his mobile and affects to check the screen.

'No signal on my network, Leyton.'

In fact his phone has been turned off since he and DS Jones left Wasdale Head an hour and a half since.

'How do you want to play it, Guv?'

Skelgill taps the toe of his left foot against the rim of a large dried cowpat. Then he watches as a swallow hawks for a clegg and disappears into the darkness of a low byre.

'Look, Leyton. My car's still down at Peel Wyke. It's as quick that way to Wasdale. Drop me there and I'll head back to this incident. You take Jones. She can give you a hand with the statements and then recover her own motor.'

'Right, Guv.' Now DS Leyton becomes a little apprehensive. 'What about the dog, Guv?'

They both glance down at Cleopatra. She produces a baleful stare that suggests she grasps the insinuation inherent in DS Leyton's question, and disapproves accordingly. The sergeant takes half a pace backwards.

Skelgill shortens the leash by winding it a couple of turns around his fist. 'I guess she starts on her first case.'

2. SHARP EDGE

Monday, mid-morning

Skelgill can't be surprised to hear that the unfortunate male victim he is en route to inspect lies crumpled below the notorious Sharp Edge, a vicious saw-toothed spine of rock that strikes out from the black cliffs of Foule Crag, itself the cantle of Blencathra's 'saddleback' massif. This locus has been the scene of numerous tragedies down the years, but for all that, he is also probably wondering why the episode is being described as a *climbing* accident. While, to the layman, the distinction might seem academic, to the outdoorsman there is a wide practical gulf between *climbing* and its devil-may-care cousin, *scrambling*. And Sharp Edge – in summer at least – is probably the Lake District's most popular scramble.

Sharp Edge's notoriety stems not from its degree of difficulty (it rises barely above the horizontal, and is classed only as a Grade 1 scramble), but from its exposure. A slip on – or, rather, off – Sharp Edge holds the very real risk of a fatal fall. Indeed Skelgill's literary idol Wainwright serves up this very same warning, and remarks that the sight of the undertaking ahead can cause its beholder to forget even a raging toothache. Amusingly, he adds that, for the faint of heart, there is the alternative threat to one's tender parts – for those who opt to cross the most razor-like sections of the ridge in the safety-first style known as *à cheval*.

Driving from the west, Skelgill takes the first though not the shortest point of access, parking just before Scales on the A66, brushing breadcrumbs from his lap, and setting off on a gently rising traverse into Mousthwaite Comb. As the crow flies, his destination is precisely one mile away, though it involves a curving and steepening ascent of some twelve hundred feet. The general public picture the police screeching up to the scene of an investigation amidst a cloud of tyre-smoke and the wailing of sirens, but in rural areas this mode of approach is frequently unavailable (and helicopters few and far between). Thus, while Skelgill might question the statistical bias that sees him dealt more than his fair share of off-road assignments, it is an inequality with which he is content. And no doubt his ego is boosted by its implicit recognition of his obscure if opportune expertise. It might be an inverted busman's holiday, but at least he's a busman. Indeed, as he overtakes a small gaggle of fifty-something hillwalkers, they exchange pleasantries regarding the weather, and the thought can't occur to any of them – seeing his lived-in outdoor attire, and his dog trotting eagerly beside him – that he is a Detective Inspector heading for a nearby corpse.

Skelgill pushes himself, and is breathing hard as he crests the rim of the corrie that holds the indigo waters of Scales Tarn. Over to his right is the smooth grassy shoulder that leads the walker up onto the arête. At the base of the scree below this ridge, adjacent to the rocky shoreline, he spies a small gaggle of men who appear to be skimming stones. There's a triumphant shout of 'thirteen!' and a little war dance from the thrower.

Then one of the group notices Skelgill, and over the next few seconds they gradually assume the collective demeanour of a gang of schoolboys caught smoking behind the bike sheds. There are apprehensive glances cast at the evidence of the receding ripples on the tarn, like the last telltale drift of smoke from hastily stomped cigarette ends. A shirt-sleeved PC Dodd numbers among the conspirators (indeed he is responsible for the most recent, seemingly record-breaking, attempt). Self-consciously he reaches down for his cap and carefully folded duty vest, which items he dons before breaking away and picking a path towards the approaching Skelgill.

'You winning?'

'Sorry, sir?' The young constable looks too embarrassed to wipe away a bead of sweat that trickles from his brow and finds its way onto the tip of his nose.

'I hope you're not letting that bunch of layabouts beat you.'

16

'No, sir.'

Skelgill articulates at the waist to get a look past PC Dodd. Though his expression is stern he raises a palm – and the three remaining confederates each keenly acknowledge him likewise. He knows them all – indeed is a member of the same voluntary mountain rescue fraternity to which DS Jones referred earlier – but his arrival in an official police capacity has him ranking above them, and he shows no inclination to engage further for the time being. The men, perhaps relieved at escaping a reprimand for their inappropriate high jinks, turn their attention to readying their equipment – a stack of bulging rucksacks from which protrude various aluminium struts and poles.

Skelgill eyeballs the anxious-looking PC Dodd. 'Right, where is it? You've pulled me off an important job.'

PC Dodd points to a spot about fifty yards away, where the rough scree beneath Sharp Edge tumbles into the waters of the tarn. 'You can just see the blue clothing, sir.'

Skelgill squints, taking in the lie of the land.

'Has the body been moved?'

'I don't believe so, sir. The chap who reported it – he's a retired doctor. He said he could tell instantly the man was dead. Made his wife feel ill – so he pulled her away. He called 999 and they were waiting at the top of the footpath when I arrived.'

'And no identification?'

'Not that I could find, sir.' PC Dodd swallows, as though the act of checking has left an unpleasant taste in his mouth.

Skelgill nods. He takes a step in the direction of the corpse, but then stops, realising he has Cleopatra on the leash.

'Hold this, Dodd – in fact, take her over for a drink, will you?'

'Yes, sir.'

PC Dodd tentatively slides his hand into the loop at the end of the string.

'Don't worry, Dodd – that's baler twine – virtually unbreakable. You should always carry some.'

'Yes, sir.'

He strides away, leaving PC Dodd fighting to haul back Cleopatra; she seems determined to stick close to Skelgill.

Eventually she yields, and reluctantly allows herself to be led to the shoreline.

Very soon, Skelgill can be heard swearing. Since he is alone at the death scene, the others – PC Dodd especially – must find this behaviour rather disconcerting. Indeed, as Skelgill comes storming back towards him, his face like thunder, the poor PC must be wondering what he has done wrong. It can only be that he has wasted the time of this senior officer, a man known about the station for his fiery temper and intolerance of incompetence.

PC Dodd stands rooted at the edge of the tarn, like a petrified Greek messenger awaiting his fate. Skelgill closes in and raises an accusing finger.

'Dodd – you should have the courage of your convictions, son.'

Though Skelgill hisses this through gritted teeth, there is just the hint of hope for PC Dodd in the content of the message.

'Sorry, sir?'

'You knew there was something wrong, didn't you?'

'Well, sir – I just thought what with there being a climbing rope...'

'And his clothes?'

'Yes, sir – that as well – plus the footwear...'

'Exactly.'

'Yes, sir.'

PC Dodd still appears somewhat disconcerted, his tall gangly frame stretched to attention. At this juncture Skelgill is near enough for Cleopatra to butt his knee with her formidable snout. He glances down at her and seems to be distracted by a moment's reflection.

'Okay. So no great loss. At least you didn't let that bunch of clowns take the body away.'

'No, sir.'

'You did right, Dodd.'

'Yes, sir – thank you, sir.'

Skelgill points his index finger again, though less aggressively. 'Next time don't wait for the likes of me. Take a flyer.'

'Yes, sir.' PC Dodd looks mightily relieved. Perhaps he tries to convey this gratitude to Skelgill through his body language, though he is probably thinking that taking flyers is no doubt how Inspector Skelgill has earned his reputation – as a maverick who is frequently unpopular with the powers that be.

'How's your radio signal?'

'Good, sir.'

'Get a scene-of-crime team up here pronto. They're looking for any signs of interference – before or after he died. And make sure someone tracks down Dr Herdwick – I want to know everything possible about time, cause and location of death.'

'Will do, sir.'

'And you can probably stand down the rescue crew – no point them skiving off work any longer. Our boys are not going to be finished until late this afternoon, at best.'

'Okay, sir – I'll tell them to go.'

'What's the griff on the couple who found him?'

'Doctor and Mrs Lumsden. They're staying for the week at the Coledale at Braithwaite, sir. Live at Todmorden. I asked them to return and wait at the hotel until we'd sent someone to speak with them.'

Skelgill nods; he is evidently content with PC Dodd's simple, quiet efficiency.

'I'll call in. It's on my way.'

PC Dodd probably does not think to analyse this statement, but if Skelgill were meant to be heading to police HQ, Braithwaite is certainly not on the way. Indeed, it lies 180 degrees in the opposite direction along the A66, just a two-minute drive from Skelgill's mooring beside Bassenthwaite Lake. In any event Cleopatra creates a minor distraction by making a sudden lunge at a grey wagtail that has been working its way boldly towards them around the water's edge. The little bird flits away, while PC Dodd is almost pulled off his feet.

'Whoa!' He recovers his balance and meets Skelgill's amused gaze. 'Spirited dog, sir. Is she the one from Oakthwaite?'

Immediately a wary frown creases Skelgill's features. 'That didn't take the jungle drums long.'

PC Dodd grins contritely. 'She's taken a shine to you, sir.'

'Well, Dodd – that makes a change, I can tell you.'

PC Dodd raises his eyebrows, but diplomatically chooses not to comment.

Skelgill, meanwhile, stoops and picks up a smooth mudstone pebble. With an easy flowing left-handed action, he sends it skimming across the flat surface of Scales Tarn. PC Dodd turns and watches over his shoulder, his lips moving as he silently counts the skips, until a little crescendo of splashes marks the stone's eventual and inevitable descent into the water – but not before it has almost doubled the best score achieved in the mini-competition that was in full swing before Skelgill's arrival.

On this triumphant note, Skelgill winks at PC Dodd, takes Cleopatra's lead, and sets off briskly in the direction whence he came, neither pausing nor glancing to see what approbation his feat has drawn from the surely watching trio of rescuers. His parting words are reserved for the dog as, almost fondly, he murmurs, 'Come on lass – we've got a boat to catch.'

3. BARRY SEDDON

Monday, midday

At ten minutes before noon Skelgill is having a swift fish upon Bassenthwaite Lake, no doubt convincing himself it's only right to confirm his boat is shipshape and none the worse for its overnight mid-water abandonment in the cause of duty. Simultaneously, some twenty miles to the east, in the parking lot of one of Penrith's supermarkets, Barry Seddon eases his battered builder's pick-up into a vacant space. Pocked and scarred with dents and patches of rust, its tailgate livery is just legible, *Seddon & Son Scaffolding*. Fifty-four-year-old Barry is the said son and sole surviving proprietor.

Alighting from the vehicle, he checks the time on his wristwatch. Purposefully he strides into the store and makes a beeline for the kiosk. He purchases twenty cigarettes and a newspaper. Then he joins the short queue in the nearby open-plan cafeteria, dispensing a black coffee from the self-service machine. From the checkout he carries off his tray and places it upon an empty table in one corner of the seating area. Instead of settling down, however, he casually threads his way across to a door marked 'toilets', through which he passes. A minute later he reappears, and walks directly out of the store, leaving his coffee untouched.

Returning to his van he rounds to the near side and unlocks the door. Leaning in, he opens his wallet and extracts a wad of notes, from which he counts and pockets two hundred pounds. He returns the balance to the wallet, and secretes it along with his mobile phone among the discarded flotsam of crackling snack wrappers and clanking soft-drink cans that laps about in the passenger footwell. Next he breaks open the cigarettes and lights one up, inhaling tenaciously. Re-locking the vehicle, he stoops to check his appearance in the dust-streaked wing mirror, at the same time surreptitiously placing the keys out of sight beneath the front wheel-arch. He flips up the hood of his grey sweatshirt. Rather more furtively now, he glances about, and then vaults the low dividing wall that separates the car park from the adjacent highway.

Head bowed and hands tucked into his kangaroo pockets, he sets off in a northerly direction, preceded by short puffs of smoke and his truncated shadow, cast by the high noonday sun. He slinks past a parade of run-down shops – newsagent, bookmaker, hairdresser, off licence – but does not glance up until he arrives at a junction some two hundred yards beyond, whereupon he slows to check the street sign. It is marked 'Ullswater Place'. He turns purposefully into this narrow thoroughfare, which is lined on each side by a low terrace of red brick pre-war houses. Their front doors open directly onto the pavement, and most have net curtains in varying degrees of faded decay shrouding their ground-floor windows. There is no regular position for the house numbers (indeed some owners evidently rely upon their neighbours for the identification of their own address for postal purposes). Seddon's eyes flick left and right as he proceeds, and it would appear he is unfamiliar with the precise location of his destination.

About half way along the street there is a distinct slowing of his pace, but then he spies a young woman hurriedly pushing a double buggy towards him. Avoiding eye contact he steps off the kerb, and does not respond to her somewhat abashed thank-you. Instead he continues to the end of the terrace – it terminates in a patch of waste ground and a row of run-down lock-up garages with graffiti on their doors – where he wheels around and hesitates as though he has forgotten something. Seeing that the street is now empty, briskly he retraces his steps towards the mid-point. Without breaking stride he gives notice of some impending action by discarding his half-smoked cigarette into the gutter, and indeed he stops abruptly to press the bell of the house marked thirty-seven. Almost immediately the peeling red front door opens and he is admitted without pause for introduction.

*

His boat anchored just forty-five yards out from the wooded slipway at Peel Wyke (where Cleopatra is safely tethered in the cool shade, in reach of the shallows), Skelgill appears to be dozing off. Having removed the forward thwart he has made himself comfortable in the bow, a threadbare *Barbour* for a pillow, while one hand rests limply on the rod that – with its desiccated and likely ineffectual dead-bait cast shoreward – pays lip service to the act of angling. Sleep has been an unreliable visitor in the past week or so, and its scarcity, allied with the balmy conditions (another prized commodity, in Lakeland) may be conspiring to drive out whatever thoughts wish to occupy his mind regarding the disagreeable scene he has just witnessed upon the slopes of Blencathra.

For there is some thinking to be done. Even before the results of any autopsy or forensic examination of the locus, it is clear to Skelgill that this is no climbing accident. As was recognised by PC Dodd, the deceased was clad in 'street' clothes – black zip-up ankle boots (recently polished), stressed blue jeans of a designer label, and a leather bomber jacket; there was not an outdoor brand logo to be seen. His pockets yielded no clues as to his identity. Then there was the incongruity of the climbing rope. Who would carry such an item without the accompaniment of the one other significant and obvious accessory – a climbing partner? Apart from the unlikely need for an emergency abseil, a rope is of little utility to a lone person. Climbers work in pairs. The leader takes the rope, progressively anchoring it as he ascends, while safely belayed by his second below. At the end of the pitch he finds a secure stance, and in turn belays his second, who gathers the protection as he comes. The only other circumstance in which a rope could feasibly be employed is the method known as Alpine short-roping, commonly used by mountain guides, in which the members of a team are literally tied together. The operative word here is *team*. Thus, as was immediately apparent to Skelgill upon assessing the context of the 'accident', more questions were raised than answered by the presence of a rope.

In any event, it was wound tightly around the victim's neck.

*

The blonde who admitted Barry Seddon to number thirty-seven Ullswater Place has now discarded a flimsy satin ankle-length dressing gown to reveal what might be described as the outfit of a dominatrix, and is presently fastening broad *Velcro* cuffs around his wrists and ankles. While his pile of cash lies on the bedside cabinet beside a tube of lubricant and an eye-watering collection of sex toys and attachments, he lies supine and naked upon a black PVC sheet, stretched tightly around the entire king-size mattress. The small interior bedroom is effectively devoid of natural light, and candlelight flickers upon the unevenly *artexed* ceiling as the woman goes about her work.

'These won't leave any marks, honey.'

Seddon is prevented from replying as she presses a ball-gag into his mouth and slides her hands behind his head to tie its retaining straps. Next she returns to check and adjust the spread-eagling restraints, forcefully applying maximum tension to each, stretching his limbs and ligaments to their limits.

'An hour with the two of us, honey, wasn't it?'

Seddon grunts his approval.

'It won't take that long.'

The woman's somewhat cryptic comment sees Seddon's eyebrows narrow, perhaps in mild protest. From the arm of an easy chair she picks up a pair of elbow-length latex gloves. Her hands must be a little damp with perspiration, and it takes a minute of pressing and pulling to achieve a snug fit over her fingers. Seddon watches with anticipation. As yet she has not touched him in what might be the expected titillating manner – especially now that he is helpless – but it is clear that he is becoming aroused.

24

'I'll just see if my sister's ready.'

Seddon makes an affirmative hum through his nose as the woman rises from the edge of the bed and opens the door a fraction.

'That's it.'

A second woman enters immediately, as though she has been waiting outside on the landing. She is considerably taller than her sibling, younger, her figure less comely, her hair dark, though there is a marked facial resemblance. Perhaps 'lesbian sister dominatrices' is an honest and truthful marketing description, if not quite legal and decent. Her outfit is similar: thigh-length wet-look boots and a skin-tight basque.

In one gloved hand she carries a coil of rope.

The pair settles side-saddle on either flank of Seddon; he initially fixes his attention on the newcomer, squinting in the gloom as if to satisfy himself she represents the goods as advertised.

She meets his gaze, and her expression is stern.

'You're here to be punished.'

Though the phrase sounds more like a statement than a question, Seddon nods eagerly in response, literally champing at the bit.

'Do you remember me, Barry?'

If Seddon's limbs were not extended to their maxima, then perhaps at this moment there would be a visible stiffening of his body. Instead it is just his features that freeze. In making his appointment, he has scrupulously avoided revealing his identity, not even his first name – and he has brought nothing about his person that might indicate the same.

'How about me, Barry?'

It is the first woman who now speaks, though her voice has lost its formerly soothing tone and has acquired a harsh edge.

Seddon stares, his eyes widening. He glances from one to the other in bewilderment.

'No one knows where you are, do they Barry?'

Seddon is clearly confused – and frightened – but too late he realises his error, for when he begins vigorously to nod, as if to say, 'Yes, they do', the action is unconvincing. Indeed, the only record of the address is in his head, supplied to him in a call he made from a public telephone shortly before his arrival at the supermarket.

'Perhaps you remember me now, Barry?'

The brunette pulls off her wig to reveal short-cropped fair hair beneath. Beads of sweat are breaking out upon Seddon's brow and beginning to stream down his temples like proxy tears. The blonde meanwhile reaches to open a drawer of the bedside cabinet. She extracts what appears to be a creased *Polaroid* and holds it in front of his increasingly terrified face.

'Don't worry, Barry. Even if you've forgotten, we haven't.'

The rope is lying beside the brunette. It is thick and firm and of the climbing variety and she easily slides one end between his neck and the PVC sheet, whence her partner draws three arms' lengths through in climbing fashion. Then free ends are exchanged so that the rope is now crossed over at Seddon's throat.

'You always liked ropes, didn't you, Barry?'

*

The sudden tautness in the nylon line, contingently wrapped around Skelgill's wrist, rouses him from his pleasant waterborne slumber. He jerks upright and scrambles for his rod, which is threatening to disappear overboard. Fortunately he has positioned it to lie in the port rowlock, and this device now acts as a brake of sorts and affords him the opportunity to grab the last couple of inches of the butt. Though while he might belatedly get a grip, the pike – for that is what it must be – gets away. Too slow to strike effectively, he finds himself lashing loose line and spray into the air above his head – by the time he has regained contact, he can tell that his quarry is gone.

'Wakey, wakey, Danny,' he mutters, although not as bad-temperedly as might be expected when such a fish has slipped from his clutches.

Perhaps on reflection he acknowledges that he can't be expected to strike in his sleep – although this acceptance has not in the past prevented him from claiming (after a few beers) that it is exactly what he *has* done on many a late-night-early-morning expedition. Methodically he reels in to inspect the bait for damage – but it is gone: a double getaway. He shrugs phlegmatically and settles back down into the accommodating curvature of the hull.

4. LEE HARRIS

Tuesday morning

'**G**uv it's me.'

'Leyton – where are you?'

'HQ, Guv. Reckon we might have an ID on that body you went to see yesterday.'

'Aye?'

'Name of Lee Harris – ring any bells, Guv?'

This is a common question asked by DS Leyton of his superior; Skelgill being a local man while the former is an exiled Londoner.

'I've got a plug called Harris.'

'Come again, Guv?'

And this marks the beginnings of a typical exchange between the two, in which Skelgill can be (perhaps intentionally) obtuse, abstruse and antagonistic, while the long-suffering DS Leyton does his best to roll with the punches.

'Plugging, Leyton – it's a method of pike fishing.'

Skelgill's *Harris* is not an official brand of angling equipment that can be purchased in a tackle shop, but in fact a home-made item that he has fashioned from a paintbrush handle of the same name; nonetheless it is one of his most productive lures.

'Oh, right, Guv.'

DS Leyton seems to have been knocked out of his stride. After a short pause it is Skelgill that speaks.

'So why should I know of him?'

'He'd be about your age, Guv – our age. Late thirties.'

'Mid thirties.'

'Yeah, Guv – sorry – mid thirties, I mean.'

Skelgill ponders for a moment – perhaps contemplating how much longer thirty-seven-going-on-thirty-eight will indeed qualify as mid thirties.

'He doesn't sound local. Where's he supposed to be from?'

DS Leyton clears his throat.

'We've had a call from an employer – motorbike joint in Kendal. Geezer who owns it heard the description we issued on Radio Cumbria this morning – says it sounds a bit like a mechanic who's not turned up for work this week. Hasn't phoned in and they can't raise him.'

'Biker boots.'

'Sorry, Guv?'

'The dead guy was wearing biker-style ankle boots.'

'Sounds promising, then, Guv?'

'What time is it?'

'Er... eleven-twenty, Guv, give or take.'

'Meet me at Tebay at twelve. Bring a photo – one that doesn't show the rope marks.'

'Sure, Guv.'

'If you're there first, get me the all-day breakfast, will you?'

'Roger.'

DS Leyton's sigh of resignation goes unheard, since Skelgill has cleared the line.

*

Motorway service stations have a special place in Britain's contemporary folk history. Watford Gap, for instance, is cherished by the over-fifties as a symbol of freedom and discovery, having been opened concurrently with the nation's first motorway, the M1, in 1959. Today, its curious name mystifies many a motorist, suggesting some association with Watford – a large town lying sixty miles and twelve junctions due south in Hertfordshire (and north of which 'soft southerners' are reputed never to venture). There is no connection, and the 'Gap' refers to a low point between two hills near the tiny Northamptonshire *village* of Watford.

Tebay service station is another such institution. Likewise gaining its epithet from its proximity to an ancient hamlet, for the vast bulk of the vacationing British public (roughly ninety percent of whom live to the south) Tebay embodies a panoply of emotions and sensory experiences. It is the culmination of a long traffic-bound journey; the first moment of exposure to the sounds and scents that infuse the moorland air – from the song of the skylark to the sour reek of sheep dung; and paradoxically in its mini-mall a last oasis of urban familiarity, before diverting from the wide motorway comfort zone into the claustrophobic single-track lanes and winding passes of the Lake District (to the west) or the Yorkshire Dales (to the east). More prosaically, in its homophonous name it really could have been put there by the bluff northerners to welcome their southern cousins, taking simultaneously the opportunity to proclaim an indigenous proclivity for the traditional beverage: it literally is a 'tea bay', and this notion appears to have passed into popular folklore.

And it is along such lines that Skelgill is a not infrequent visitor. On this occasion, as DS Leyton foresaw, he casually ambles through the servery, no doubt confidently predicting that his trusty sergeant will have taken care of the eating arrangements. He pauses, however, at the cutlery section, to pocket a handful of sachets of *HP* sauce. Then he deftly sidesteps a small child who charges at him brandishing a ray gun.

The accents reaching Skelgill's ears as he weaves between occupied tables are a mixture of home counties (less pronounced than DS Leyton's cockney brogue), midland (mainly Brummie), north-western (Manc and Scouse) and indeed Scots – this peculiar combination a result of the fact that, while he and DS Leyton are heading south to Kendal (the next motorway junction down the M6), they have rendezvoused on the northbound services. This apparent paradox – and indeed navigational conundrum – is explained in the knowledge held by most policemen, that such institutions can always be accessed via service back-roads that provide practical and necessary short-cuts for delivery vehicles and staff. Thus when Skelgill suggested to DS Leyton that they should meet at Tebay, the latter took it as read that they would do so at Skelgill's preferred northern side. Ostensibly this might seem to be due to its reputation for better food, although on reflection – as Skelgill would be first to admit – this attribute is ranked no better than third in his list of priorities, well below volume and speed of service.

Skelgill might be a tad late, but his timing is perfect. DS Leyton has only just queued, paid and sought out a quiet spot in a distant alcove, insulated from the screeches emanating from the kids' soft play area and the general hubbub of the holidaying hordes. Indeed, this very table is one of their many regular haunts dotted about the county. Now DS Leyton glances uneasily at his plate as if he is wondering whether to begin. Skelgill has not yet come into sight, but will surely reprimand him for not waiting. His gaze drifts out through the great plate glass wall beside which he sits. There is an expansive view of the rising fells, hidden beyond which lies Windermere, and – contrastingly close at hand – a murky ornamental pond that washes right up against the foundations of the building. In comic fashion, swimming like an Egyptian, a moorhen jerks past, pursued by a brood of tiny fluffy black chicks with oversized bills that scrabble across the surface like windblown cotton bolls. Further out, a swarm of house martins swoops and dives for insects that mate or lay or hatch – any of the above an unfortunate moment to become an impromptu meal.

'Hey up, Leyton – still off your food?'

DS Leyton looks across from his reverie, surprised. Then he cocks his head to the outdoors.

'Nah, Guv – I was just watching those birds catching flies – amazing how they can do that.'

Skelgill takes a seat, a slightly superior expression crossing his features.

'I've hooked a swallow more than once. They especially go for hawthorns.'

DS Leyton looks suitably impressed.

'Tuck in, Guv – before it goes cold.'

Skelgill scrutinises the fare on offer. 'Been waiting long?'

'Just sat down, Guv. Thought I saw your jam jar in the car park when I pulled in.'

Skelgill keeps his eyes firmly fixed upon his food and feels for his knife and fork. Deftly, he assembles a large forkful.

'Must be a doppelganger.'

This is an unlikely coincidence, given the idiosyncratic long brown estate with its distinctive replacement aerial: a wire coat-hanger fashioned into the shape of a fish.

DS Leyton nods, though not with great conviction. More likely Skelgill was waiting for him to get the food in – or poking around the place on some clandestine business of his own.

After an initial minute or so of silence, punctuated only by the hungry clatter of cutlery, DS Leyton introduces the subject of their inquiry, the late Lee Harris (if it proves to be he).

'I spoke to forensics before I left, Guv – nothing doing so far.'

'In what way nothing?'

'The crime scene – assuming we're calling it that, Guv – no trace of blood or disturbance, no stones freshly turned over, no vegetation crushed.'

'What about Herdwick?'

'Couldn't raise him, Guv.'

Skelgill tuts and swallows.

'Spoke to his assistant, Guv – that dolly bird student they've got in – she was a bit cagey. Managed to get her to say that there were no superficial injuries, cuts, breaks, bang to the head, whatever. Doesn't look like it took much of a fall to kill him, Guv.'

Skelgill snorts. 'Leyton – there's no way he fell. Not a chance.'

DS Leyton gives Skelgill a wide-eyed look. 'What makes you so sure, Guv?'

'How long have you got?'

Skelgill breaks off to stare at a middle-aged man in an olive-green fleece and tan walking trousers who has come to stand beside them bearing a loaded tray. The interloper is alternately eyeing the spare table nearest to the detectives, and glancing back in the direction whence he came, presumably waiting for his accomplice to catch up with him. Skelgill fixes his unwelcome presence with an unwavering glare. After about thirty seconds no one has appeared, and Skelgill's offensive tactic bears fruit. The man swivels away with a shake of his head and apparently goes in search of his companion. Skelgill returns his attention to DS Leyton.

'For a start, the body was yards from the foot of the slope.'

'Couldn't it have rolled, Guv?'

Skelgill shakes his head dismissively. 'Too rocky. Anyway – like the lass in the lab-coat says – he'd be smashed up. Instead he looked more like he'd settled down to sleep.'

'Could have been moved, Guv?'

'Except you're telling me forensics found no signs of disturbance.'

DS Leyton raises a fork in acknowledgement of this contradiction.

'So what, Guv? What did happen?'

Skelgill is chewing, and doesn't hurry his mouthful. 'Which one of my dozen hare-brained ideas do you want to hear first, Leyton?'

'Take your pick, Guv – I'm clueless.'

Skelgill suppresses a grin that begins to form about his lips. 'We're not so far apart, Leyton. But what I do know is you don't generally get togged up as if you're off to the pub, then grab a rope and head for the hills.'

DS Leyton gives the impression this might be how he would dress in such circumstances – like many people, not being in possession of the requisite outdoor gear.

'Well – I take your point about the rope, Guv.'

Skelgill's eyes narrow, as though he detects DS Leyton's reservation. 'And what climber takes a rope on his own? You climb with a partner.'

'Maybe he went on his own, Guv – topped himself?'

'He'd be dangling, Leyton. There was nowhere to dangle. And why yomp a mile up to Scales Tarn when all you need is a coat hook on the back of your bedroom door?'

DS Leyton fidgets uncomfortably in his seat.

'Could he have just strangled himself with the rope, Guv – on the spot, like?'

Skelgill frowns, and looks momentarily annoyed at this suggestion.

'Bizarrely, Leyton, that happens to be my least hare-brained explanation at the moment.'

'Oh.'

DS Leyton looks pleased with himself – although that soon becomes an expression of apprehension, as though he is worried about having usurped one of his boss's ideas and might be punished accordingly for attempting to steal some of the limelight.

Skelgill seems to detect his sergeant's quandary. 'Look, Leyton – we're clutching at straws here. Until we get cause and time of death, we can speculate until the cows come home.'

DS Leyton nods, encouraged. 'And the ID, too, Guv.'

'True, the ID.' Skelgill checks his watch and throws his napkin onto his empty plate.

DS Leyton pushes back his chair, and looks expectantly at his boss.

'If you're volunteering, Leyton, I reckon there's just time for tea and a fruit scone.'

5. KENDAL

Tuesday afternoon

'Aye – that's Lee right enough.'

Skelgill is watching closely the garage owner's reaction as DS Leyton holds the mortuary photograph at arm's length before him. He is small and wiry, and looks as though he might be almost completely bald beneath a faded navy-blue engine driver's cap, though he sports several days' grizzled stubble on his chin and throat.

'What happened to him?'

'Looks like a climbing accident, sir.'

The man shakes his head. He continues to stare at the photograph; his expression is more one of curiosity than horror.

'How well did you know him, sir?'

Now the man looks up at Skelgill and digs his hands deeper into the pockets of his grease-smeared boiler suit. He shrugs his shoulders somewhat indifferently.

'I've got eight mechanics, part-timers. They come and go. Mostly in their twenties and thirties, like Lee. Didn't know he wo' a climber.'

The man could be in his early sixties, and the suggestion of an arm's-length relationship with his younger and itinerant employees is not unreasonable.

'How long had he been with you?'

'Eighteen months, twenty maybe.'

'We'll need to trace his wife, girlfriend, next of kin – that sort of thing.'

Skelgill stares at the man as though this is an instruction, and indeed the latter drags open the top drawer of a grey metal cabinet that dominates one corner of the tiny office. He lifts out a small card-index box and places it upon a desk covered with oily thumb-printed invoices and curling triplicate pads. His stout craftsman's fingers, ingrained with engine grime, work with surprising dexterity to extract the sought-after record. He hands it to Skelgill.

'That's your lot, cous.'

Printed in uneven capitals in black biro is the name Lee Harris and, beneath, the address of a flat in Kendal and a mobile phone number. Skelgill turns the card but its reverse is blank. He appears for a moment as though he is about to cast it disdainfully away, but then he squints at an out-dated certificate of employer's liability insurance pinned above the filing cabinet. The man seems to sense disapproval: that his approach to human resources management leaves something to be desired. He inclines his head in the direction of the workshop, which can be glimpsed through a cluttered hatch in the wall.

'Happen some of yon lads might be able to fill you in – personal life, like.'

Skelgill nods patiently.

'I understand you last saw him on Friday, sir?'

'Aye – then we got four smash repair jobs brought in over t' weekend.' The man is now trying harder, and his local accent becomes more pronounced. 'Lee's gey tidy wi' Hondas. I was trying to raise him from first thing yesterday, and again this morning.'

'You rang this number?' Skelgill flaps the card like a fan.

'Aye.'

'And?'

'Woman's voice – a recording, like – kept saying t' person were unavailable.'

'Was there anything in his behaviour lately that struck you as unusual?'

The man's beady eyes narrow, giving him a guarded ferrety appearance. 'I thought it wo' an accident he died of?'

Skelgill remains impassive. 'Like I said, sir – it looks that way.'

There's the faintest hint of inflection placed upon the word *looks*, and the man nods slowly, as though he is now wondering if the police are unofficially taking him into their confidence.

He shrugs once more. 'Any road, like I said – I divn't have owt to do wi' lads. Ars twice their age – more. I just oversee t' wuk and pay 'em's wages.'

'Pay cash, do you, sir?'

'It's all above board.' Now the man is back on the defensive. 'Payroll clerk comes in Thursdays – that's when they get their wage packets.'

'So was Mr Harris paid last week, sir?'

The man nods, perhaps a little grudgingly, although it seems unlikely that his erstwhile employee was remunerated in advance. 'Aye – he did more or less a full week. He weren't short of ackers if that's what tha' wondering.'

Skelgill does not reply directly. Instead he slips the address card into his jacket pocket and checks his wristwatch.

'We shan't detain you any longer, sir. If you could supply us with contact details for any of your staff that are not here – and if you'll bear with us my sergeant will just have a quick chat with each of those present. Then we'll be out of your hair.'

*

Leaving DS Leyton to interview sundry swarthy mechanics, Skelgill sets off on foot to seek out Lee Harris's apartment. However, for the capricious police inspector, the small Lakeland town of Kendal (population circa 28,500) holds several imminent distractions. Not least is its renown for the eponymous mint cake – in fact a high-calorie peppermint-flavoured concoction of sugar and glucose, enjoyed by mountaineers the world over, and reputedly eaten by Hilary and Tensing atop Everest in 1953. Skelgill professes to possess both a savoury and a sweet tooth, and generally justifies a bar of Kendal mint cake on the grounds that it is entirely fat free. Indeed his propensity to snack is driven on the one hand by his pastimes of fell-running and fishing (the latter usually involving an energy-sapping row on his beloved Bassenthwaite Lake), and on the other by his general disregard for normal hours of work, which often finds him arriving home to a desolate fridge and the realisation that all neighbourhood takeaways have long ago closed for the evening. Right now the hour is fast approaching three o'clock, and thus, as he makes his way through the bustling town centre, he must run the gauntlet of spectacular window displays of local confectionery, compounded by the drifting aroma of scones baked to waylay tourists susceptible to the temptation of afternoon teas.

However, there is a third enticement that exerts even greater magnetism as far as Skelgill is concerned, and that is the River Kent. Neatly bisecting today's enlarged urban area – it flows north to south, with much of the old town on its west bank – it is the principal game fishing river in the south of the county. As Skelgill lingers upon the Nether Bridge his antennae are clearly twitching, no doubt at the thought of the potential double-figure sea trout that may be passing under his very nose, and perhaps the added frustration that between here and Victoria Bridge is a one-mile stretch of free angling. The water level is arguably a little low, following three or four days of dry weather, but nonetheless he scrutinises the gently rippled surface for signs of aquatic life below. A fine drake goosander sails briefly downstream, its glossed green mane glinting as it twists about and returns to fish the depths between the piers. Skelgill watches in admiration while it dives and then surfaces, a staring minnow secured in its long red saw-bill; a magnificent bird, sleek predator of fast-flowing waters, though little appreciated by human fishers.

Skelgill has taken a significant detour to indulge his craving and, finally dragging himself away from the allure of the Kent, he heads back into the old town, north along Kirkland. For a main street it is a narrow thoroughfare, lined by an irregular miscellany of two-and-three-storey buildings, mainly stores and public houses, in grey limestone or white-painted stucco. He almost breaks stride as he encounters a fishing tackle shop he has forgotten about, but the road is busy with traffic, and deters him from crossing. Indeed, this is the A6, the old London-to-Carlisle coaching route (taking in Leicester and Manchester), the one-time slow road to the Lakes – before the M6 motorway laid a slick swathe of grand prix tarmac over Shap's peaceful summit. In any event, shortly he ducks away from the noise and fumes, into a tight cobbled ginnel (in Kendal referred to as a *yard*) innocuously squeezed between a cheque casher's and a financial advisor's.

More stealthily now he passes silently beneath the property above and out into the open space beyond. While many of these yards once ran down to the river, and are of great antiquity, this one is truncated, blocked by unsightly and angular modern additions of obscure function. Indeed, unlike some of the town's famous yards, which are picturesque and photogenic and visited for such purposes by tourists, the air here is permeated by the stale smell of urine, and an unsightly heap of black bin bags lies torn open by scavenging cats or gulls. The heat from the high June sun isn't helping, and Skelgill responds to the stifling atmosphere by inhaling through gritted teeth.

The dwelling he seeks – there appear to be four numbered properties in the yard – is a basement flat, which he reaches by descending a flight of worn stone steps, its diminutive *area* crowned by a rusting iron balustrade. If anything, the bad odour is worse in this dank stairwell and Skelgill, not one to be bound by protocol, checks about for CCTV and promptly breaks in.

'Hello – police.'

This precautionary introduction proves unnecessary. The pile of mail and newspapers behind the door tells Skelgill no one is home. A dampness that pervades the empty property deadens his voice. He makes a quick tour to satisfy himself there is no imminent threat – or, perhaps, indeed, no corpse awaiting discovery. From a tiny hall off which open a toilet and separate shower cubicle, there are only two rooms to speak of, conjoined: a kitchenette-diner and a bed-sitting room. The ceilings are low – maybe only seven feet – and the place has the air of a typical cheap rental apartment: poorly fitted linoleum, worn nylon carpets, badly hung curtains, and furniture randomly discarded and acquired.

Now Skelgill begins a more thoughtful, if ostensibly haphazard perusal of the contents. Taking care not to disturb anything of potentially forensic significance, he has the bemused manner of a visitor to a gallery of modern art – one who is trying to work out whether the mundane household exhibits displayed around him are actually of any merit. His features seem to be fighting disappointment as he casts his eyes over the fat-spattered electric cooker hob and its accompanying chip pan. A small refrigerator seems relatively well stocked (certainly by Skelgill's standards), and if truth were told he might reflect that the general level of disarray is probably inferior to that of his own domestic domain.

Several bloated chocolate cereal rings float in the kitchen sink, and there is an open packet of the same variety on the little dining table. Alongside it is an empty milk carton, but no suicide note propped against either. The milk has a best-before date of last Thursday but, as Skelgill knows from personal experience, you can't read a lot into that.

Broadly speaking, there is little to indicate that the flat's occupant departed with anything other in mind than to return in the near future. The wardrobe and dresser are crammed with clothes, and a newish flat screen TV and a rather dated games console in the bedroom are in standby mode.

Where Lee Harris's home differs from Skelgill's is in that an inspection of the latter would quickly reveal its occupant's interests: various items of tackle and gear, spilling from shelves and cupboards, and – out of sight of the casual visitor (but not so hidden as to avoid detection by anyone so chosen) – trophies and certificates and framed photographs testifying to outdoor and sporting exploits. Moreover, though not a reader as such – fiction does not register on Skelgill's radar – he has an extensive collection of maps, manuals and climbing guides (his prized set of *Wainwrights* at the heart of this), and an assemblage to match covering all methods of angling known to man. Then there are years' worth of specialist magazines – climbing, fishing, fell walking – with useful articles marked by bent corners or *Post-it* notes (indicating Skelgill's as yet unfulfilled intention to scalpel out and file these pages).

So it would not require Sherlock Holmes to deduce what sort of person Skelgill is, to which clubs and societies he might belong, where he could potentially be found in his leisure time, and with whom he may associate. Not so Lee Harris. Other than the computer games console beside which is stacked the stereotypical array of bloodthirsty killing games (perhaps suggestive of an immature personality, a lack of social engagement, and – in Skelgill's analysis – a totally incomprehensible wish to be indoors when you could be outside) – apart from this – there is little flesh of biographical detail upon the sparse bones of his existence. In other words, there is not a lot for the police to get their teeth into.

Skelgill soon finds himself back in the hallway. A washing machine is a considerable obstacle. He notices that a display light is blinking, and with what must be considered a small flash of inspiration (given his limited aptitude for matters domestic) he stoops down and jerks open the clear plastic door. Inside the drum is a sodden but apparently laundered navy serge boiler suit.

Perhaps encouraged by this find, he gathers up the now crumpled mail that impeded his entry through the front door a few minutes earlier. He places the items on top of the washing machine and sifts through them. The letters are exclusively bills and circulars, pre-printed postage-paid envelopes that offer no clue to the date of their delivery. But there is a local advertiser. Skelgill flattens this out. Beneath the masthead is the slogan 'Free Every Saturday'.

The leading article concerns flood defences (the River Kent is notorious for its impromptu visits to the high street) and Skelgill lingers a moment over this. Then he begins to flick through the pages of parochial events and poorly composed display ads. A more professional full-page advertisement for a broadband service seems to hold his attention – indeed it seems to prompt him to turn away and stride decisively back through the kitchen-diner and into the bedroom.

Clearly he has something in mind. He works his way around the walls and, after a short search, he finds what he is looking for. Behind a small bedside cabinet is a telephone socket, and beneath it upon the carpet a wireless router. A blue light winks at him. He examines the settings on his phone and sure enough the signal is detected. Then he squats down and takes a photograph of the account and password details printed on the rear of the transmitter. So the flat has *Wi-Fi*, but there is no trace of a receiving device.

Now Skelgill departs, checking carefully that he has not damaged the rudimentary pin tumbler lock in gaining entry. He seems to be in two minds about pulling the door shut behind him, and casts about in the gloom of the stairwell. There is a worn fibre doormat that resembles hedgehog road-kill, many times run over. On impulse he peels it from the step to reveal a rusty key. With a little effort it proves to fit the lock.

Skelgill pulls a remorseful face to nobody, pockets the key and jogs up the stone staircase, squinting in the bright sunlight that pulsates about the enclosed yard. The chirrup of sparrows creates a restful atmosphere, and he seems immediately infected, yawning and lingering aimlessly as if wondering what to do next. After a few moments he walks across and rings the bell of one of two doors opposite Lee Harris's flat. There is no reply. He moves on to the next, but the result is the same. He steps back and regards the properties: on reflection they could be vacant, perhaps recently refurbished and awaiting occupation.

There is one other apparent residence, a kind of half-basement dwelling with its door set down a short flight of steps. A vagrant *Buddleia* springs gaily from a crack at the angle of wall and ground. The flat's one grimy window is hung with what looks suspiciously like sackcloth. There is no number or bell, but as Skelgill approaches he becomes distracted by something beneath his feet. Much of the yard is unevenly cobbled, but here is a level rectangle of concrete hard standing. More or less at its centre is a circular black stain, extending to about a foot in diameter. Skelgill squats and wipes an exploratory finger over the oily substance, but as he does so something catches his eye. The window-drape has twitched.

He rises and makes his way tentatively down the steps, but before his hand reaches the bell the door jerks open, at least, to the extent that an internal chain allows. In the crack between the jamb a small wizened face appears at a child's height, but then Skelgill must quickly realise this is a cat. There is a waft of musky air – in fact a quite overpowering aroma of pets – with acrid undertones of something worse.

'What d'yer want – poking about?'

From behind and above (though not far above) the uncomfortable-looking feline, a second face pitches forward from the darkness. This one is human, albeit somewhat wanting in humanity. The sullen features are lined and pinched, and a considerable mass of matted greying hair is the main impression imparted. It is an old woman, and her accent, spoken in a strained, creaky voice, seems to hint at Merseyside origins, long left behind.

Skelgill takes a step closer and holds out his palms in a gesture of cooperation. Something less than a sixth sense tells him this is not a moment to declare his profession.

'I'm looking for Lee.'

'Who's Lee?'

Now he jerks a thumb over his shoulder. 'Lee. He lives across the yard.'

'Lee.'

The woman says this as though she is a foreigner trying out the word for the first time.

'Do you know him?'

'Who?'

'Lee – Lee Harris.'

'I know everything.'

The old crone's expression becomes conspiratorial, though she reveals no inclination to share her wisdom.

'Have you seen him?'

'Who are you?'

'Er... we were at school the same time.'

'You're not taking me cats.'

'Pardon?'

'I know their tricks.'

Skelgill seems to get a hint of what she's driving at. 'I'm not the council, love – I'm looking for Lee. I don't want your cats.'

'You're not having them. You're not coming in.'

Now Skelgill brings both hands to his chest. 'I love cats. That's a nice tortoiseshell you've got there.'

This is rather more than a white lie, since Skelgill is engaged in a running battle with a gang of neighbourhood moggies who nightly deplete his holding pond of small roach and dace. In any event, his placatory words fall upon stony ground, for the woman's mind seems made up about his mission.

'The last one they sent didn't get in neither. He said he came to read the meter. But I recognise you. You ain't getting me cats.'

'Look – can you tell me – please – when did you last see Lee from across there?'

'There's no Lee.'

'I think he was home at the weekend. You just noticed me – surely you've seen him?'

The woman screws up her face and lifts the cat up to her chin. The animal looks like it would dearly love to make a break for freedom, but is restrained by a claw-like grip. Now the woman grimaces, revealing few teeth and plentiful gaps.

'Witches took him.'

'What do you mean?'

'I saw 'em.'

'When?'

'Night time.'

'What – last night?'

'Some night.'

'Recently?'

'Disguised, they were.'

'Was Lee with them?'

'Who's Lee?'

44

At this moment Skelgill's phone rings. He pulls it from his back pocket and looks at the display. An expression of relief spreads across his troubled features.

'Beam me up, Leyton.'

*

'What was that all about, Guv?'

Skelgill has scrambled into the car as DS Leyton holds it momentarily on the double yellow lines of the main street, and now is pressed back against the seat as his sergeant guns the small engine and swings the vehicle back into the traffic.

'Steady on Leyton, this is Kendal, not Brands Hatch.'

'Sorry, Guv – there's a flippin' great truck up me jacksie.'

'Unlucky truck.'

Skelgill shrugs himself into the seat belt. Then he notices a half-eaten packet of crisps that DS Leyton has placed in the dashboard cubby and begins to help himself.

'Some mad woman lives opposite – completely batty – I made the mistake of asking if she'd seen Harris. She insisted I was the council come to confiscate her cats. Then she tried to tell me he'd been abducted by witches.'

DS Leyton chuckles.

'More likely she saw a hen party caught short, I reckon.'

'That could have been interesting, Guv.'

'Behave, Leyton.'

DS Leyton looks like he is still trying to picture the scene, and rather loses concentration, failing to move away as the lights at which they wait turn to green. The lorry that has been tailgating them gives a long blast of its air horn.

'See what I mean, Guv? You tell me to slow down and everyone else gets uppity.'

'Well, *up* theirs.'

To DS Leyton's evident consternation, Skelgill now finishes off the crisps by tipping the remnants of the bag into his mouth and munching pensively.

'No one at home at the flat, I take it, Guv?'

Skelgill swallows with some difficulty. 'Neither alive nor dead.'

'You got in?'

Skelgill pats his breast pocket. 'I found a key hidden outside.'

DS Leyton glances across; there's a hint of suspicion in his eyes, which is not assuaged when Skelgill declines to produce the claimed item.

'That was handy, Guv.'

'I reckon he was last there on Saturday morning – going by the newspapers and breakfast stuff lying about.'

'Oh, well – that's good to know, surely, Guv?'

'Is it?'

Skelgill's tone is harsh, and DS Leyton looks momentarily crestfallen.

'Well – at least we can rule out anything dodgy at that workshop.'

'It still leaves the best part of a two-day gap until he was found on Monday.'

'Perhaps he went away for the weekend, Guv?'

DS Leyton seems to be mulling over this possibility when Skelgill raps sharply on the dashboard.

'Anyway, no need to dawdle, Leyton. Get a shift on and we'll have time for a little something back at Tebay before you knock off.'

6. PENRITH HQ

Wednesday morning

'Morning, Guv.'

'Jones. You're up with the lark.'

'I'm taking a leaf out of your book, Guv – there's more to the Oakthwaite case than I expected.'

Skelgill invites her to join him by unceremoniously dumping his empty breakfast plate on the next table. He eyes her *Tupperware* container of fresh fruit rather dubiously as she sets it down.

'That's not a leaf out of my book – I don't know why you're eating diet stuff.'

DS Jones smiles demurely, an indication that she accepts the oblique compliment. Her reputation for superior admin skills has seen her delegated to tie up the deskwork for Skelgill's last case. Since this task can be undertaken entirely from HQ she has adopted a comfortable outfit of jeans and sweatshirt – in contrast to recent nightclub assignments when striking and oft more revealing attire was *de rigueur*. Nonetheless, her stretch denims are figure hugging, and her slender form catches Skelgill's eye as she settles opposite him.

'Got an ID on the climber yet, Guv?'

Skelgill makes a *so-so* head movement as he appraises her over the rim of his mug.

'We're pretty certain he's called Lee Harris. From Kendal. He's no climber, though – at least, it wasn't a climbing accident.'

'Really? What do you think happened?'

'At the moment I'm in limbo. Until I get something concrete from Herdwick I'm just guessing. Let's just hope it's a *domestic* – preferably suicide.'

DS Jones nods – she understands Skelgill's point: if, like most such deaths, the incident is a self-contained event, then the investigation can be conducted at leisure. If not, however – and there is a killer on the loose – then time may be of the essence.

'Struck lucky on that toffs' school job, I hear, Skel.'

The voice – in the plaintive Mancunian tones of DI Alec Smart – emanates unexpectedly from behind, and Skelgill momentarily flinches. Despite the disciplined fisherman in him, he continually strains not to rise to the bait of DI Smart's provocative banter. But experience has taught him such verbal skirmishing is not his forte, whereas DI Smart is a master of goading put-downs and mocking one-upmanship. Taciturn at the best of times, in situations of stress Skelgill becomes even more tongue-tied. He is a man of action. Many a criminal opponent – cockily believing they were engaged in a verbal stand off – has been taken painfully unawares by the detective inspector's trademark left hook. This form of escalation being currently off limits, by way of a displacement tactic Skelgill takes a long, slow swig of his tea.

DI Smart insinuates himself effectively between them, coming to stand at the head of their table. Then he leans back to perch nonchalantly against that to his rear. He fixes a lingering gaze upon DS Jones.

'Alright, Emma. Not used to seeing you with so many clothes on.'

'Morning... sir.'

DI Smart pulls a face of mock surprise: that she should address him formally, when he clearly considers they have a familiar relationship. She looks uncomfortable, caught as she is between a rock and a hard place – for now she has to tread a delicate path of diplomacy, littered with obstacles of rank, duty, etiquette (or DI Smart's lack of) and her own personal feelings.

Skelgill does his best to conceal a pained expression. He clearly wants to intervene, but in the end only does so by conceding a compliment to DI Smart.

'Looks like you're dressed to impress, Smart.'

DI Smart does not squander this opportunity to preen. He thumbs his lapels and then opens his jacket to reveal a designer logo stitched onto the inside pocket.

'Pretty sharp, eh? *Armani* – pure merino. Picked it up in a new boutique in Manchester. Just near my flat.' He winks at DS Jones. 'Next time we're working down there I'll show you around – leaves the West End standing, you know.'

DS Jones nods obediently and then steals an apprehensive glance at Skelgill, whose expression is blackening by the second. At this moment, however, respite appears in the shape of George the Desk Sergeant. He pops his distinctive bald pate around the door of the canteen to announce that DI Smart's lift is waiting at reception. DI Smart dismisses him with a self-important flap of the hand.

'I'm giving evidence up in Glasgow. Bunch of Jock gangsters I nailed last year, trying to muscle in on my patch. I shall enjoy seeing them go down.'

'Don't let us keep you.'

DI Smart begins to walk away without a goodbye, but then he returns to their table. He taps the side of his nose in conspiratorial fashion and puts a hand on DS Jones's shoulder.

'I've had a word with the Chief. The drugs case could be back on. I've requested you as my number two. That would be a step up for you. We make a good team, Emma.'

DS Jones watches him closely as he saunters across the canteen. Skelgill's eyes are fixed upon his sergeant, perhaps narrowed possessively.

'If Manchester's so brilliant, why do all the tourists drive straight past and come to the Lakes?'

DS Jones levels a sympathetic gaze upon Skelgill.

'Take no notice, Guv.' Then she giggles.

'What is it?'

'He's got a dollop of tomato ketchup from your plate on the seat of his pants.'

*

Skelgill is not in the best of humours – evidenced by the way he kicks open the door of his office – as he arrives bearing a plastic cup of machine tea. DS Leyton, seemingly loitering behind the said door, jumps to attention, rather in the manner of a schoolboy caught inspecting the headmaster's private display of photographs. Indeed, he cradles a black plastic trophy crowned by a rather garish silver-plated figurine of a cricketer.

'Didn't realise you got *man-of-the-match* while I was away, Guv. You kept that one quiet.'

Skelgill steps over a pile of ring binders and gains the far side of his cluttered desk. He looks for a space to deposit his drink, but in the end is forced to continue to hold it as he takes a seat. As he sips he inhales to cool the hot liquid.

'You know me, Leyton. Don't like to blow my own trumpet.'

'Course, Guv.'

Now there is a pregnant pause – before DS Leyton suddenly realises he should inquire how Skelgill was awarded the accolade.

'Did you score a century, Guv?'

'Leyton, I'm a bowler.'

'Right, Guv – what then, a hat-trick?'

Skelgill smiles contentedly. 'I did, as a matter of fact. First one since 1948 in the Carlisle challenge, and that was by a Lancashire ex-pro. I took seven for eighteen in under five overs.'

'Well played, Guv.'

DS Leyton's knowledge of cricket's arcane terminology does not extend much beyond the basic clichés, and now – perhaps to avoid blotting his thus-far clean copybook – he changes the subject to the object of their meeting. He leans over and pats a document in the centre of Skelgill's desk.

'There's the interim autopsy report, Guv. Herdwick says he'll have more detail this afternoon.'

'What's with him – has he taken up golf or something?'

DS Leyton replaces the trophy on Skelgill's filing cabinet and sits opposite his boss. 'Maybe he's getting distracted by that new assistant, Guv. She's turning a few heads about the place.'

Skelgill grins cynically. 'Maybe we should arrange a meeting – so you can see what all the fuss is about.'

DS Leyton pulls a face indicating some indifference. 'Word is that Smart's already asked her out.'

Skelgill, on the other hand, appears discomfited. But rather than respond further to this apparently unwelcome information he scowls and points a gun-finger at the report.

'Have you read it?'

'Er... yeah, Guv.' DS Leyton sounds unsure as to whether he should have done so in advance of his superior. 'While I was waiting for you to finish with DS Jones.'

Skelgill leans back in his seat. 'Fire away, then.'

'Right, Guv.' Now DS Leyton rubs his temples, as though this will help to bring the details to the front of his mind. 'There ain't a whole lot, really. No injuries or signs that he was involved in a struggle...'

'I thought we knew that already?'

'Just confirmation I suppose, Guv – and this covers internal as well as external.'

Skelgill nods grudgingly.

'Nothing untoward in his blood or urine – alcohol, drugs, poison. No indication of any illness or disease.'

Skelgill looks like he is getting bored with the growing list of negatives, but his attention level rises as DS Leyton suddenly gets to the crux of the matter.

'Cause of death asphyxiation by strangulation. Possibly but not definitely self-inflicted. Probably but not definitely by the rope found around his neck.'

Skelgill thumps his desk in a gesture of obvious annoyance, and to remove any doubt about his feelings accompanies the blow with a choice expletive.

'What's Herdwick playing at? That's no use to us – possibly... probably – I think you're right, Leyton – I'd say *definitely* he's taken his eye off the ball.'

Skelgill reaches for the handset of his telephone, but in his enhanced state of displeasure he manages to knock it off the cradle and onto the floor on DS Leyton's side of the desk. The amply proportioned sergeant grunts as he bends forward to retrieve it.

'There is one thing, Guv – time of death – between noon and midnight on Saturday.'

'What?'

'It says they're ninety-five percent confident about that.'

Skelgill glares at DS Leyton. 'Why didn't you say that at the start?'

'Sorry, Guv – I was just going through the points in the order I could remember 'em.'

Skelgill declines the handset that DS Leyton is still holding out to him, rises and crosses to the window. He hauls up the venetian blind and stares out across the car park towards the woods and rising fields beyond. Rain has returned to Cumbria, and a low blanket of grey stratus is coating the county with a fine precipitation.

'So it's murder.'

DS Leyton looks expectantly at his superior, but Skelgill seems preoccupied with the view.

'Murder, Guv?'

Skelgill spins around. For a moment there's an expression of impatience upon his face, but then he softens and stalks back around his desk to his seat.

'If he died on Saturday, Leyton, it wasn't at Sharp Edge.'

'What makes you so sure, Guv?'

'No way could a body have lain there in plain sight and not be spotted from above. Weekends this time of year it's like Clapham Junction. Not a chance, Leyton.'

DS Leyton nods reflectively. 'I suppose he *was* found early doors on Monday, Guv.'

'Exactly my point – the very first people out on the fell saw him – and they'd not even climbed the ridge.'

And now the puzzling dilemma – with which Skelgill has no doubt already been wrestling – dawns upon DS Leyton:

'But, Guv – if someone put him there after he was dead – how did they do that?'

'How, Leyton? And why?'

The detectives both sit in silence for a minute or so. Then DS Leyton stands up.

'I'll get us some fresh teas, Guv.'

Skelgill nods distractedly. If there is an irony intended in DS Leyton's statement – given Skelgill had arrived bearing only one cup – it is not conveyed in his generous intonation. When he returns shortly, Skelgill is poring over an Ordnance Survey map covering the north-eastern quadrant of the Lake District.

'It's a mile from the nearest road, Leyton – and, more to the point, Scales Tarn is the thick end of two thousand feet above sea level.'

DS Leyton places the steaming drinks on the window sill and then extracts the autopsy report from beneath the edge of Skelgill's map. He scans its contents.

'Says he weighed sixty-seven kilograms, Guv.'

Like most fisherman, obsessed by record weights, Skelgill's brain is quick to convert this statistic.

'Ten and a half stone.'

DS Leyton, who weighs in at a good fifty percent more than this figure, self-consciously adjusts his jacket.

'What are you, Guv?'

'About twelve.'

'Right.'

'What are you thinking?'

'I have enough of a job carrying one of my kids up to bed, Guv – if they've fallen asleep watching the telly, like. Eldest can't be above five stone. How would you have got Harris all the way up that hill – never mind without anyone noticing?'

Skelgill purses his lips. He shrugs.

'I once did a bit of climbing in the Himalayas, Leyton – Annapurna. I remember following a *Tamang* porter – five foot two if he was an inch – carrying a load of steel scaffolding poles strapped on a frame across his back. We overtook them – a gang of labourers – but they caught us up at our camp by the end of the day. Guess the weight.'

'Dunno, Guv – I suppose you're going to tell me ten stone.'

'Twenty.'

'Blimey, Guv – so what are you saying?'

Skelgill opens out his palms in a non-committal gesture.

'All I'm saying, Leyton, is I've seen a guy half your size wearing flip-flops lug more than your weight up a five-thousand-foot mountain path.'

'A good bit above my weight, Guv.'

'Whatever.'

Though for DS Leyton this is rather more than a matter of splitting hairs, he opts not to pursue the distinction.

'Surely it would take at least two people to shift a corpse, though, Guv?'

'Be easier, sure.'

'It's still a load of trouble to go to, Guv – and then *not* hide the body.'

'It was left on display, Leyton.'

DS Leyton's eyes widen at this suggestion. 'What – for *us* to find?'

Skelgill shrugs. 'There's got to be something symbolic here, Leyton. Why strangle him with a climbing rope and then take him to a popular scrambling site? Most bodies end up dumped in the nearest convenient ditch.'

DS Leyton nods, though his features remain puzzled.

'What I still don't get, Guv, is – if he were murdered – how come it looks like he died peacefully in his sleep? He wasn't drugged, he wasn't drunk – and, as you point out, suicide doesn't fit the facts.'

'Like the old woman said, Leyton – maybe the witches did it.'

DS Leyton chuckles, but Skelgill has made the remark out of frustration rather than an attempt at humour, and he does not join in with his sergeant's mirth. Once more they sit in silence, like delayed passengers in a waiting room, unsure of when the awaited train of inspiration might draw haltingly into the station.

After a minute DS Leyton begins to fidget, and then he pipes up, 'I wouldn't mind being abducted by a hen party, Guv – if you had to meet your maker, I can think of worse ways to go.'

Skelgill glowers at him, but does not respond.

'Thing is, Guv – it's all we've got to go on at the moment – what that old girl told you.'

'She's not my idea of a reliable eye witness.'

'Think we should pull her in though, Guv?'

Skelgill looks alarmed. 'Rather you than me, Leyton.' Then he shakes his head. 'She's a crackpot – she doesn't know anything. You'd get more sense out of the cats.'

'Well, where do we start, Guv?'

Skelgill places his elbows on his desk and folds intertwined fingers beneath his chin.

'We need to go to work on Lee Harris. What he did on Saturday – where he went. Whatever there is to know about him. There'll be relatives somewhere, maybe a friend or two. Local shopkeepers, hairdresser, dentist, pub landlord. He paid bills; there'll be a lease on that flat, a bank account. There's loads to go on.'

DS Leyton is nodding. Skelgill begins to count off his fingers.

'Other things, Leyton. One: check with the workshop – I reckon he had a motorbike – where is it now? Two: see if we can track any activity on his phone before it was switched off. And, three: where's his laptop? There was *Wi-Fi* in the flat, but no sign of a computer.'

'Right, Guv – I'll draft out an action plan.'

'And organise a full forensic inspection of the property.'

Skelgill stands up and lifts his jacket from the back of his chair.

'I'll go and break the bad news to the Chief – before she starts allocating all the best staff to Smart. We need bodies, Leyton.'

7. STRIDING EDGE

Wednesday morning

It is just after eight-thirty a.m. when Skelgill returns from his mission upon high, to find DS Leyton standing anxiously in his office. Judging by Skelgill's thunderous expression it does not appear that his request for extra personnel was acceded to.

'Why are you still here, Leyton?'

'Sorry, Guv – it's this. Someone just rang the incident room.' DS Leyton flaps a single sheet of paper. 'I think you tempted fate, Guv.'

'What are you talking about?'

'When you said *bodies* – there's been another one found.'

Skelgill stares uncomprehendingly. 'That's not what I meant, Leyton.'

'No – I know Guv. I'm just saying, like.'

'Well – what is it?'

'Sounds similar to Harris, Guv. Looks like a climbing accident – beneath Striking Edge.'

'There's no such place.'

'That's what it says, Guv.'

'*Striding* Edge, Leyton.'

DS Leyton holds the page at arm's length and squints long-sightedly. 'Maybe it is, Guv – Striking, Striding – this handwriting's pretty rommel.'

'How long have you lived up here, Leyton?'

'About seven years, Guv.'

'And you've not heard of Striding Edge?'

'Don't think so, Guv.'

'It's one of the best-known landmarks in the Lake District – everyone's heard of Striding Edge.'

'I'm not really a great one for the hills, Guv.'

'You don't like water; you don't like hills – why didn't you stay in London, Leyton?'

DS Leyton is beginning to look browbeaten.

'We thought it would be a better place to bring up the kids, Guv.'

DS Leyton says this somewhat sheepishly, but the honest altruism inherent in the statement must penetrate Skelgill's bristling exterior; and of course it can only ring true with the deep and fierce pride he harbours for his lifelong surroundings. He continues to scowl, but there is a more subtle concession in his general body language.

'Well – I'll give you that.'

DS Leyton knows this is as much as he'll get by way of apology for Skelgill's bad temper, and diplomatically he doesn't press home this moral advantage. Instead he makes it easy for his boss.

'Apart from the dodgy accent they're getting, Guv.'

'Hark at Mr Kettle.'

'Queen's English, I speak, Guv.'

'Pearly queen's, aye.'

'Least neither of us sounds like Smart, eh Guv?'

DS Leyton is on safe ground with his mutually jingoistic observation. England's regional rivalries are both complex and irrational, and it is a curious happenstance that finds a Cumbrian and a Cockney in this particular alliance against their abrasive Mancunian colleague.

'Anyway, Leyton – Striding Edge – you were telling me?'

'What it says, Guv – an outward-bound school party from the youth hostel at... Glen...'

Again he stretches to read, but is thwarted by either the hastily scrawled script or the unfamiliar pronunciation, or indeed perhaps the wish to avoid a second *faux pas*.

'Glenridding.'

'That's it, Guv – Glenridding. They set off early this morning – spotted the body just before eight o'clock. The kids have been brought back down to the hostel. The group leader's waiting up there – called Graham.'

At the mention of this name Skelgill's eyebrows flicker, but otherwise he does not react.

'How do we know it's *not* a climbing accident?'

'We don't, Guv – but the duty DC who took the call thought we should be informed straightaway – just in case.'

Skelgill purses his lips, and swivels to face the window. From his seated angle it is a uniform rectangle of grey and he stares into infinity rather like a lost mariner willing land to appear on a distant horizon. Then he spins around and decisively brings both palms down on the desktop.

'Get your cagoule on, marra – now's your chance to learn everything you need to know about Striding Edge.'

*

The picturesque settlement of Glenridding nestles in a small bay at the southern reaches of Ullswater, and on any occasion its waterside setting makes it a desirable destination. This is especially true for Skelgill, and particularly when he is chauffeured. For eight miles, the winding road from Pooley Bridge (itself just six miles from Penrith) hugs the lake's western bank, affording excellent eye-level observation and thus prospecting for future fishing forays. A regular raider of the water's healthy population of wild brown trout, Skelgill spends much of the journey exhorting his sergeant to slow down. For DS Leyton, on the other hand, the main attraction of the route is its snaking trajectory, and the challenge presented to his driving skills. However, he is continually obliged to bow to his superior's demands, and – much as the significance of rising fish is lost upon him – he becomes enlivened when Skelgill points out the famous 'steamer' plying its course, its rippled wake gently creasing the mercury-like surface. Indeed, the entire scene to their left is one of tranquillity, a sense of serenity curiously enhanced by both the mist that wreaths the distant fells and the blur of drizzle in the still air. There are few water-users abroad, a couple of oared craft and a becalmed dinghy; motorboat owners are deterred by today's pedestrian speed limit – a far cry from the time in 1955 when Sir Donald Campbell burned up a measured mile at over two hundred miles per hour.

For those reaching the hamlet on foot, the hike to Glenridding youth hostel has something of a sting in the tail: there is no hostel. Glenridding is not solely a village, indeed it is first and foremost a geological feature – a glen (the old Celtic word for valley). Steep-sided and bordered on its northern flank by formidable screes and crags and disused mine workings, the 'valley overgrown with bracken' was carved by ice and water, and now harbours a post-Ice Age remnant in the form of the fast-flowing Glenridding Beck. This cool clear creek darts beneath Rattlebeck Bridge and rushes through the village with considerable haste, to feed Ullswater just beyond. Working back from this point of confluence, the youth hostel is situated the best part of two miles upstream – a height gain of five hundred feet – much to the dismay of the hungry hillwalker.

Nowadays, of course, many patrons are long in the tooth and longer out of their youth, and travel from hostel to hostel by car – a practice that was once considered as hiking sacrilege. However, in keeping with the times, the Youth Hostels Association now permits such indolent means of arrival, and indeed has accommodated it at this particular location via a bumpy access track. This adds a further dimension to DS Leyton's novel driving experience in the deceptively powerful pool car.

'Blimey, Guv – glad this ain't my motor.'

'Aye.'

Skelgill's unforthcoming response does not reflect displeasure, merely the pragmatic expedient of clenching his teeth to avoid a bitten tongue, as the vehicle pitches and rolls over the rutted rocky surface.

'You wouldn't want this to be your drive to work every morning, Guv.'

'I reckon most of the staff live in – apart from the local instructors. They come up according to whatever course is on.'

59

'We did an outward bound jaunt to North Wales when I was a schoolkid, Guv – we only lasted two days.'

'Get high on the fresh air?'

'Nah, Guv – we were banned – sent home in disgrace. The smokers caused a forest fire, the drinkers got nicked in the local boozer, and the pranksters put a sheep in one of the teacher's dorms.'

Skelgill eyes his sergeant with a mildly approving grin. 'And which category did you fall into?'

'Whoa, *Silver!*' DS Leyton swings the wheel to avoid an especially vicious pothole. 'You know me, Guv – good as gold – always kept my nose clean.'

Skelgill shakes his head. He cranes out of the side window to get a look at the cloud base. 'No one's going to be starting a forest fire today – this weather's set.'

DS Leyton frowns rather apprehensively, as if suddenly reminded of the task that lies ahead. They are now approaching a cluster of dour grey former-mining properties of which the youth hostel is part. Their altitude is nine hundred feet, and only a short distance beyond these bleak habitations the speckled fellside dissolves gently into the mist. To their left, Glenridding Beck is strewn with jagged boulders, its black waters foaming white as it swells with the steady accumulation of run-off from Helvellyn's eastern watershed.

'Shall I take the statements at the hostel, Guv?'

'Not so fast, Leyton – if this is another murder – you need to absorb the atmosphere.'

'I reckon I can do a pretty good job of imagining it, Guv.'

'Try imagining yourself getting promoted, Leyton.'

'If I must, Guv.'

*

Striding Edge, though not exactly a stroll in the park, is for the average able-bodied person (and in fair weather conditions) a fairly undemanding traverse, requiring no special equipment or skills. An impressive arête with spectacular views, it lacks the deadly exposure of Sharp Edge, and as such is a favoured route to Helvellyn. Thousands of people of all ages cross it each year, and mishaps are few and far between. For many youngsters – as was intended for those led back to Glenridding youth hostel this morning – it forms a memorable initiation to walking in the Lakes.

It is not an area, however, that offers much in the way of excitement for the rock climber (or even the scrambler), and Skelgill would be somewhat surprised to hear of a genuine climbing accident in this vicinity. Callouts with his mountain rescue hat on have tended to be of the twisted ankle variety, injuries generally self inflicted by impetuous tourists who have set off to climb Helvellyn wearing inappropriate footwear.

'*Helvellyn* – that sounds Welsh, Guv.'

Skelgill glances back at his partner, with a shadow of the exasperation that accompanied their earlier discussion concerning DS Leyton's ignorance of the existence of Striding Edge.

'Aye – that's because we all spoke Welsh, once – even down in your neck of the woods.'

DS Leyton takes a lungful of air.

'Come again, Guv?'

'When the Romans invaded – the blue-painted reception committee lined up on the White Cliffs of Dover spoke Welsh – or near as damn it.'

'I'll take your word for it, Guv.'

They march on in a silence punctuated by the heavy panting of DS Leyton and the occasional crack of a stone dislodged by a stumble. Skelgill has kitted out his sergeant in a miscellany of spare gear from the back of his car – including footwear one-and-a-half sizes too large (supplemented by two extra pairs of socks), waterproof trousers a good few inches too long, and an old orange cagoule that DS Leyton has just about managed to zip around his bulk. His arms, however, are caused to stick out by this arrangement, and he has more than a hint of the penguin about his gait.

Skelgill must surely be pleasantly surprised by his sergeant's performance. Despite the sweat that drips from the latter's heavy brow (it can't be drizzle, for his hood is up), his continuous asthmatic gasping for breath, and the blisters that are likely forming upon his ill-shod feet, he manages to keep pace with Skelgill's (albeit moderated) stride pattern. It appears that what DS Leyton lacks in physique and fitness, he more than makes up for in dogged determination. Moreover, he does not complain – and it is this quality that is perhaps most atypical, for he is usually quite adept at finding a subtle way of informing his irascible superior when he is unhappy.

From Glenridding youth hostel there is a direct path to Red Tarn, a roughly circular pool suspended high in the corrie bounded by Striding Edge, Helvellyn and Swirral Edge. This mountain lakelet is their destination. The deceased is reported to lie near the shore just beneath Striding Edge: a symmetry with the Scales-Tarn-and-Sharp-Edge combination that cannot have escaped Skelgill's notice.

They cover the mile-and-a-half in less than thirty minutes, and as Red Tarn suddenly appears dark before them Skelgill lets out a piercing whistle. The sound fills the heavy air all about, its echoes suggesting the presence of the invisible amphitheatre that surrounds the water. Almost before the strains of this summons have died down, a long piping reply, six times repeated, comes from their left. It is the recognised mountain distress signal.

'That must be that Graham bloke, Guv.'

'Aye.'

'Do you know him?'

Skelgill is already moving in the direction of the whistle, but he turns briefly to raise an inscrutable eyebrow at DS Leyton. Then rather curiously he pulls down his hood, and with both hands rakes his fingers through his hair, and wipes the dew from his face. And then he is away, picking a rapid path along the shingle at the water's edge. DS Leyton falls in behind him, but has to trust that Skelgill keeps to this course, for his superior quickly disappears into the mist.

Indeed, when DS Leyton suddenly comes upon Skelgill and a smaller red-cagouled figure, his eyes widen at the sight of what can only be the unhurried detaching of a seemingly affectionate embrace.

'Leyton – this is Jenny Graham.'

DS Leyton approaches rather self-consciously, as if he is unsure of whether or not to replicate Skelgill's style of greeting – clearly his superior knows the woman (and perhaps rather well) – but until now has not taken the trouble to share this information. In the event he settles for a rather clumsy handshake, forced as he is by his undersized overgarment to turn sideways to complete the manoeuvre.

'Leyton's desperate to climb Helvellyn – I promised we'd nip up when we're done. Seeing as we're so close.'

The girl – for she can be no more than mid-twenties – smiles a broad white grin; she might even be a touch star-struck in Skelgill's presence. She is pretty, with thick lashes and long dark hair that she now gathers into the hood of her jacket. She doesn't seem particularly fazed by the circumstances: some two thousand feet up in the fells, amidst inhospitable conditions, for the best part of an hour she has been standing sentry over a corpse. But when she leads them to its location, there is at least a partial explanation for her sanguinity. Beside a substantial rucksack she has erected a portable survival shelter, and visible within are a down sleeping bag and emergency blanket, a two-way radio, along with a gas burner, kettle and mug. As leader of the party of youngsters, she came well equipped. Any casualty would have been in excellent hands, and – in the meantime – she has made herself comfortable.

'Nice little set-up, Jen – thought you'd have a brew ready for us, though.'

Now the smile becomes a little coy. 'Not sure I've got enough sugar for you, Danny.'

Skelgill's high cheekbones are already rosy from effort and exposure – but now they surely take on a deeper hue. DS Leyton, who is perhaps feeling something of a gooseberry, sidles across behind Skelgill and walks the six or seven paces to where the body lies.

'Blimey – have a butcher's, Guv.'

Skelgill seems content to receive this summons. He crosses to gaze at the supine figure.

'I take it you've not moved anything.'

The girl joins them, understanding that this question is for her. They stand in line like a bowing royal party politely examining some ghastly tribal exhibit.

'Danny – I could see he was dead before I even got close – look at the eyes.'

Skelgill nods. The eyes are open and staring, though abnormally opaque.

'I just don't see how he's got the rope tangled round his neck like that.'

This is the girl's observation, and DS Leyton shoots a sideways glance at Skelgill. But Skelgill shows no flicker of reaction.

'He's not exactly dressed for it, either.'

The man is clad in scuffed rigger boots, worn cargo trousers, and a hooded grey sweatshirt.

'You don't recognise him, Jen?'

The girl presses her full lips into an arresting pout. She shakes her head slowly.

'I've been down at Coniston for the last three days – but he's not from the hostel – that school party's taken the whole place.'

Skelgill goes on bended knee and, as best he can, with minimal interference, pats down the dead man's pockets – but to no avail – they appear to be empty. Reluctantly, he rises.

'Did the kids see the body?'

Now the girl turns to face him. For a moment her smooth features are creased with anguish, as though her upbeat positivity has been mere bravado, and he has suddenly pierced the brave façade.

'I turned them straight around before I scrambled down – Pete took them back the way we'd come up.' She looks at DS

Leyton and lifts her hands to her breastbone. 'I'm a fully qualified rock-climbing instructor – and a first aider.'

DS Leyton nods vigorously, as though it's not for him to question her decision-making.

'They just got a glimpse from the ridge – there was a break in the mist – it was by fluke that I spotted him, really.'

Skelgill gazes up the steep stony bank as far as the limited visibility will allow. At the moment there is no view of Striding Edge above.

'And you didn't see anyone else?'

'Not a soul – neither here nor on the path. I guess most folk are waiting indoors to see if it clears.'

'They've got a long wait.'

The girl concurs. 'It's thicker now than an hour ago.'

Skelgill begins to turn away from the body. He takes the girl's arm above the elbow and gently shepherds her back to her little encampment.

'We've got a uniformed officer about ten minutes behind us. He'll keep watch until the whole crew gets here. Do you mind leaving your gear for a while?'

The girl looks momentarily surprised: she realises she is being dismissed from the scene. But she cooperates willingly.

'No problem – make yourselves at home.'

'You head down to civilisation – get yourself dry – have some breakfast. We'll need a statement later. In the meantime...'

She seems to know what is coming, and is nodding earnestly before Skelgill completes his request.

'... until we know the cause of death – we'll be reporting it as a climbing accident – so if you could keep the gory details to yourself.'

Now her ring of confidence returns. 'You know me and secrets, Danny.'

She offers a tentative high-five to Skelgill, which he reciprocates, and she beams a farewell at DS Leyton and turns away. In thirty seconds she has vanished into the mist. Skelgill waits in silence; he seems be listening to the diminishing crunch of her footsteps as she rounds the edge of the tarn and picks up the path. After a minute or so more he turns to DS Leyton.

'It's exactly the same rope, Leyton.'

DS Leyton nods, understanding now that Skelgill did not want to share this conversation with the girl.

'You certain, Guv?'

Skelgill shrugs. 'I've seen a lot of rope, Leyton.'

'I guess forensics will tell us for sure, Guv.'

Skelgill clearly disapproves of his sergeant's questioning of his judgement.

'A tenner says it's from the same original piece.'

DS Leyton takes a half step backwards and puts up his hands in a placatory gesture.

'I'll go with you, Guv.' With some difficulty he reaches inside the hood of his jacket and scratches his head. 'But do you mean it's been cut up?'

'That's exactly what I mean. Both pieces are about fifty feet.'

'And a hundred's the norm?'

'Two hundred.'

DS Leyton folds his arms and blows out his cheeks. After a moment's exaggerated deliberation he says, 'That leaves enough for two more, Guv.'

'That's what I'm worried about, Leyton.'

8. PENRITH TRUCKSTOP

Wednesday afternoon

'I thought you were joking about Helvellyn, Guv.'

'When do I joke, Leyton?'

DS Leyton stirs a heaped spoonful of sugar into the mug of steaming tea that has been set before him.

'Wasn't so bad, really, Guv. I thought it'd be miles to the top from that lake.'

'Tarn.'

'Sorry, Guv – tarn.'

'Third highest mountain in England, Helvellyn – only Scafell Pike and Sca Fell are higher. Tell that to your kids tonight, Leyton.'

'Pity there wasn't a view, Guv. My selfie could be anywhere.'

Skelgill shrugs. 'You'd never get out if you let the weather decide for you.'

'I'm amazed you found the way, Guv.'

Skelgill frowns. 'We were following a path, Leyton.'

This is not strictly accurate, although the improvised route was no doubt a path of sorts on Skelgill's mental map of the fells. He had announced – upon PC Dodd's arrival at the improvised base camp at Red Tarn – that he and DS Leyton were 'going to recce the surroundings', and promptly marched his disoriented sergeant up the steep northern flank of Striding Edge. Within fifteen minutes they had gained Helvellyn's main ridge, the boundary between the old counties of Westmorland and Cumberland. Here the low cloud was probably a blessing in disguise, rescuing DS Leyton from a potentially agonising exposition of the many peaks ordinarily visible. Instead, with little to look at but a cairn, a cross-shaped dry-stone shelter, and a trig point, they did not linger. Skelgill had briskly led the way onto Swirral Edge, to descend by the southern slopes of Catstye Cam, and rejoin the path that had originally brought them to Red Tarn. Here, however, DS Leyton *was* subjected to a lecture. Evidently the *schelly* – a curious black-finned freshwater herring, one of Britain's rarest fish – frequents the tarn and just three other Lakeland waters. While this piscine eulogy was largely wasted upon the fast-flagging non-angler, his ears did prick up at Skelgill's seemingly unselfconscious pronunciation of the name as 'skelly' – a homonym for a disliked nickname used by his colleagues.

DS Leyton shakes his head in bewilderment at this information – that they followed a path. He attempts to take a swig of tea, but it has been served in the scalding fashion of the truck stop. Yet he will need two or three more of these sizeable mugs to reinstate his normal level of hydration. Of course, it is possible that his disbelief also relates to Skelgill's congratulatory promise to buy a late lunch, for which they have diverted to a popular lorry drivers' retreat on the western outskirts of Penrith.

'Fit-looking girl – that Jenny, Guv.'

DS Leyton's uninflected observation sounds quite innocent (and to have literal intent), but it may be a subtle invitation to Skelgill to open a door on the patently familiar acquaintanceship.

'You would be, doing her job Leyton.'

There's a finality in Skelgill's retort that suggests the portal is going to remain firmly closed. Perhaps in laddish, beer-fuelled company he might be more forthcoming, or at least feel obliged to join in with the salacious guffaws when some wag mentions her sobriquet of *Spinning Jenny*. (Or maybe it is this thought that disturbs him.)

'Guess so, Guv. Is she in your mountain rescue team?'

Skelgill leans sideways and peers beyond DS Leyton, as if he is trying to see if their order is on its way. His reply has a ring of disinterest.

'Most of the local instructors are affiliated. Gives us a bigger pool to call on.'

'She seemed pretty competent, Guv.'

Skelgill pauses, perhaps to frame a reply. Again he casts about the transport café, surveying its scattering of mid-afternoon patrons: mainly lone drivers whiling away their compulsory break times, mechanically sipping from mugs of tea, heads buried in their red tops.

'You don't mess with the Grahams.'

This oblique reference to the feared tribe of English border reivers (who had their wayward heyday in the sixteenth century) holds no great significance for DS Leyton – he can only assume it is a contemporary family of dubious repute. Skelgill could mention – but evidently opts not to enlighten DS Leyton – that his mother's maiden name is Graham, and that he doubtless hails from the outlawed clan himself.

'It was the Kray family round our manor, Guv – but you'd know that, obviously.'

Any droll observation that Skelgill might wish to make about DS Leyton's provenance is pre-empted by the arrival of two plates laden with the mountainous all-day trucker's breakfast. To the sergeant's surprise, his boss had earlier eschewed the offer of similar at Glenridding youth hostel – despite its glowing reviews. He might now suspect that Skelgill wished to avoid further contact with the girl – but it is also a fact that the portion size was unlikely to have matched the fare now set before them.

'Blimey, Guv – I shan't manage my tea – and the missus gets well brassed off if I leave anything.'

'Can't you have it later?'

'She likes it on the table for six so the kids can eat with us.'

'I can take your sausages off your hands, if it helps.'

DS Leyton now wavers, a mildly pained expression troubling his features.

'Thing is Guv, they're my favourite – can't beat Cumbrian sausages, I'll give you that.'

'Cumberland.'

'Right, Guv – Cumberland.'

But the sergeant continues to gaze mournfully at the said local delicacy.

'So – do you want them, or not?'

DS Leyton sighs. 'Then she complains I'm putting on weight and it's bad for my health.'

'You just climbed Helvellyn, Leyton – you're quids in on the calorie front.'

'How many do you think I used on that walk, Guv?'

Skelgill ponders his colleague's plate. 'Maybe two sausages' worth?'

'How about you take one then, Guv?'

'Done.'

Skelgill swoops with his fork, impales the sausage and bites off half, as if to insure himself from a change of mind. He chews and nods approvingly, while DS Leyton, still with an expression of regret, begins to tuck in. There now follows a few minutes of industrious consumption, before Skelgill pauses to speak.

'So – what's it all about, Leyton?'

'Come again, Guv?'

'Two murders – let's assume they both *are* murders – near as damn it identical: the rope, the location, the timing. What's he trying to tell us?'

'*He*, Guv?'

'The killer, Leyton.'

DS Leyton sinks forward onto his elbows, as though fatigued by the effort of eating.

'I can't quite get my head round it, Guv. I mean, I know you saw that Sherpa carry a load of metal pipe – but lugging a body up there in the dark doesn't bear thinking about.'

Skelgill stares thoughtfully at his partner. 'It could still be done, though, Leyton. Park-up beyond the youth hostel. Ground's not so bad underfoot. Fireman's lift.'

'But why's he gone to all the bother of making them look like climbing accidents?'

Skelgill shakes his head. 'Thing is, they don't.'

'On the face of it, though, Guv?'

'Aye – but if you were going to stage an authentic fall, these are not the places you'd do it. And one glance at the victims' clothes tells you they're not walkers or climbers. They look like they've been plucked off the street.'

'Maybe some geezer's got a grudge, Guv.'

Skelgill can't help a scornful laugh. 'What, like a gamekeeper who strings up dead crows on a fence?'

'Why not, Guv? Some eco-warrior nutter – or a sheep farmer gone off his trolley. Had enough of the hillwalkers trampling everywhere.'

'Mind what you say, Leyton – you're one yourself now.'

DS Leyton looks a little alarmed at this notion.

'There'll be all hell breaks loose when this hits the papers, Guv.'

Skelgill nods ruefully. The entire Lake District economy is underpinned by outdoor tourism. The public panic that could be provoked by the scandal of a random strangler at large cannot have escaped his thinking. And, at some point in the next few days, the police will be obliged to come clean with this news. Perhaps mulling over the prospect, and the attendant pressure that, predictably, will become heaped upon his shoulders, he falls silent and readdresses his meal.

In due course DS Leyton gives up, defeated by the sheer volume of food (and, perhaps in addition, by some unpleasant domestic hallucination). He excuses himself to pay a visit to the washroom. Skelgill snatches the opportunity to scavenge the best of the forsaken morsels from his sergeant's plate.

As DS Leyton comes wandering back he is listening to his mobile phone. His features are creased with concentration, and indeed he stops short of Skelgill at a vacant table and pulls out his pocket notebook. Trapping the handset between shoulder and ear, assiduously he writes down details of the communication. When he rises, his expression tells he is the bearer of news of some import.

'Guv – looks like we might have a lead – person reported missing – fits the description of the Glenridding body.'

Skelgill appears unimpressed; if anything his features take on a negative hue. Not one of nature's followers, in a bloody minded way he makes hard labour of others' candid enthusiasm.

'Miracles never cease.'

Phlegmatically, DS Leyton resumes his seat. There is a mild flicker of his eyebrows when he notices his plate has been looted, but he straightens the cutlery and slides it to one side. He flips open his notebook upon the flat surface and reads verbatim from his neatly printed if rudimentary script.

'Barry Seddon. Age fifty-four. Jobbing scaffolder – self-employed. Lives at Aspatria. Reported missing by wife. Last seen Monday morning when she left for work.'

'Monday?' Skelgill's interjection has the ring of distrust.

DS Leyton flinches, as if the idiosyncrasy in the evidence is his fault. 'That's what the report says, Guv.'

'So he's been gone for two nights before she gets in touch?'

Skelgill finishes off his tea and bangs the empty mug angrily upon the chipped *Formica* table top.

DS Leyton ventures an ironic grin. 'Maybe she wasn't missing him all that much, Guv.'

Skelgill does not reply. Something seems to have triggered a thought in his mind, and he folds his arms in concentration.

'Perhaps he was working away, Guv?'

Without obviously switching back into sentient mode, Skelgill places his hands on the table and with an urgent jolt pushes back his chair.

'Let's go and ask the question. B5305, James.'

He rises and tugs his waterproof from the seatback. He shakes it vertically as though he is weighing its contents.

'Damn it, Leyton – I've left my wallet in my other jacket in my car. I got sidetracked sorting out that gear for you.' This way, he contrives to make it sound rather like DS Leyton is responsible.

The sergeant's stoical expression reveals no hint of surprise. He pats his hip pocket.

'I'll get it, Guv.' Then he looks sadly at the substantial leavings on his plate. 'Feel like I ought ask for a doggy bag.'

'Ah! – well remembered, Leyton – I need to buy some dog food – I'll nip into that petrol forecourt next door while you sort the tab.'

'Right, Guv.'

There is now something of a pregnant pause, and neither officer moves from their station. Skelgill is looking at DS Leyton as though his subordinate ought to know what the delay is all about.

'Guv?'

'Lend me a fiver, Leyton.'

9. ASPATRIA

Wednesday afternoon

'**M**rs Seddon, we can't be certain, but – going by this picture – we believe that a body found this morning could be that of your missing husband. You may have to prepare yourself for the worst.'

DS Leyton sounds uncharacteristically solemn as he delivers these words, and seems to find it difficult to meet the woman's inquisitive gaze across the small, neat sitting room. He and Skelgill crowd a compact two-seater settee, and appear uncomfortable in such close proximity, while the woman is perched precariously on the edge of a plain wing-back chair. There is a tray of so-far untouched tea and biscuits on a low 1970s style coffee table. The photograph, she has produced following a minute's rummaging in the drawers of an oak dresser – it is a strip of three identical images of the type used for official applications, such as a passport or driving licence. One glance has confirmed to Skelgill what he needs to know, and the item has been handed on to his subordinate accompanied by a none-too-subtle elbow in the ribs – thus the delegation of the task of breaking the bad news.

'He's not my husband.'

'I'm sorry, madam?' Now DS Leyton does look up.

'He's not my husband – Barry's my cousin.'

'So, you're not actually Mrs Seddon?'

'Most people call me Hilda. Hilda Seddon. I never said I was *Mrs* Seddon.'

DS Leyton appears confused – or perhaps he is embarrassed by the corollary: a personal question at this time of bad tidings. But Skelgill has no such inhibitions and he intervenes, to avoid confusion using the Christian name she has volunteered.

'Hilda, so you and Barry – you're not a couple – that's what you're telling us?'

The woman shakes her head – meaning the affirmative – and frowns disapprovingly at the suggestion.

'Barry's my lodger. He's got his own room.'

The woman sounds local, though her accent is mild, if unrefined. In her early fifties, she is small and wiry and shares something of the pinched features that characterise Barry Seddon's passport photo. She wears a knee-length overall rather like that of a hospital orderly, and has the ascetic demeanour of the B&B landlady that is cloned throughout the Lakes and beyond – though this is no B&B as such. The property is scrupulously clean but sparsely furnished; indeed there is a Spartan, waiting-room feel – hard-wearing loop-pile carpets, venetian blinds rather than curtains, few ornaments, and no photographs, paintings or houseplants.

'And you last saw him on Monday?'

Though the tone of Skelgill's question does not hint at criticism, her brows knit defensively.

'I didn't know he was missing.'

'Is it unusual for him to be away overnight?'

'Not since the building trade went bad. He does jobs all over. Reckon he sleeps in his van.'

'Did he say where he was working?'

'He never did.'

'How long's he been your lodger, Hilda?'

She sucks in her already hollow cheeks by way of thinking. 'Ten years or more.'

'What brought him here?'

'He stayed with his old ma over Whitehaven way. She only had a corporation house. When she died he had nowhere to go. He never wed or had kids. So he got in touch – I hadn't hardly seen him since we were teenagers.'

'Has he been in any kind of trouble – a job gone wrong, money problems?'

The woman shakes her head abruptly. 'Always has plenty of cash. Pays his board and lodging regular.'

They must all be aware that they are still referring to Barry Seddon in the present tense, as if he might arrive at the front door at any moment. Perhaps it is an easier state of affairs, and they continue in this mode. It may be that, were the woman to acknowledge Seddon's death, her fragile façade would crack and leave her incapable of continuing with the interview. Skelgill is staring at the biscuits – not avariciously, more likely elsewhere in thought – but the woman notices with a start and jerks forward to pour out milk and tea into the three assorted mugs. She hands round the plate of digestives. DS Leyton politely declines. Skelgill takes two. Perhaps he senses this is a good moment to ask a more probing question.

'What was he like, Hilda?'

'You wouldn't want to be married to him.'

Her answer comes without pause for consideration, as if she is accustomed to trotting out this line over shopping bags in casual neighbourly conversation.

'Oh?'

'He's just interested in himself. Doesn't wonder how food gets on the table, nor washing and ironing done.'

Skelgill nods. The woman has the inured look of someone long starved of recognition. But if the relationship has survived for a decade or more, there surely must have been some symbiotic return for her.

'Does he have any friends?'

'He works late most days – sometimes drinks on his way back. Weekends, if he's home, he's usually watching the racing through in the back, or along at *William Hill.*'

'What about the weekend past?'

'Aye, he was here the whole time. Never even went out of doors on Saturday. I had to wake him off the couch come bedtime.'

DS Leyton is unobtrusively taking notes, and Skelgill glances to see that he registers this point.

'Does he have hobbies, Hilda – climbing, for instance?'

'He's a scaffolder.'

'No – I mean, like mountaineering.'

The woman looks blank. 'Never known him do that.'

Skelgill dunks a biscuit into his mug and just manages to pop it into his mouth before it collapses upon him. He washes it down with a swig of tea. Then the woman catches him eyeing the plate and she offers him another.

'Don't mind if I do, thanks.'

'You're welcome.'

Skelgill forces a smile, but his lips remain compressed. 'Hilda, it's possible that Barry was murdered. Can you think of any reason why someone might want to do that?'

Her features contract further with concern, although there is no real sign of the horror that might be expected at such a revelation.

'He's not one to speak about his business.'

Skelgill stares at her – he is probably just framing his next question – but she must find his pale grey-green eyes disconcerting, and visibly she shrinks away.

'It weren't me – if that's what you're thinking. He's never done nowt to me. Now I've lost his money.'

Her denial, though convincing in its simple repudiation of the major motives for murder, lacks any real impression of underlying grief.

Skelgill attempts to convey his sympathies through an understanding grimace.

'How about girlfriends – is there anyone at the moment?'

This question seems to bruise her pride, and in a small way she bridles, her knuckles blanching around the mug she clasps.

'He's not had a girlfriend while he's stayed with me. Least not that I've known of.'

'What about before?'

She shakes her head rather vacantly.

'He's never mentioned no one.'

'Does the name Lee Harris mean anything to you?'

'Can't say I've heard of her.'

The negation comes without a delay, and Skelgill does not trouble to correct the mistaken gender.

'Hilda – you mentioned Barry's van.'

'Aye, that's right.' Instinctively she glances towards the window.

'Where does he keep it?'

'Outside, ont' road.'

'So his van's missing?'

She nods unconvincingly, as though this is beyond her remit.

'But he took it – when he left on Monday?'

'It were gone when I came back lunchtime.'

'From work?'

'I clean at the hospital at Wigton, seven till one.'

'Do you drive there?'

'Never learnt. I get the bus.'

Skelgill places his mug carefully on the coffee table. He stands up and with a groan straightens his back. Then he casts about the room.

'Well, you keep a tidy place, Hilda – I could do with a landlady like you. I should think Barry didn't know how lucky he was.'

'Happen.'

Her bleak expression, in the way of a woman unused to compliments, seems to reject this little tribute, though there is something in the softening of her body language that tells otherwise. Skelgill presses home his advantage.

'If you don't mind, I'd just like to take a quick look at his room – while Sergeant Leyton gets a few formal details from you – no need for you to get up, love.'

She is about to rise, but dutifully obeys his downturned palm.

'It's the front bedroom – there's only two.'

Skelgill nods. 'We'll need to send a couple of chaps along – but this'll save me another trip out, you see.'

The woman nods and watches meekly as Skelgill leaves the parlour, patting his sergeant encouragingly upon the shoulder as he squeezes past him. It might be a signal meaning 'keep her occupied'.

*

'She's relieved, Leyton.'

'What – that we're gone?'

'No – that Seddon's gone.'

DS Leyton does not seem so sure. He turns to stare through the open driver's window at the house they have just left. Aspatria, an inauspicious former market and mining town, can be found in the nondescript swathe of no-man's land between the Lake District National Park and the Solway Coast, and sits astride the old Roman road that once linked forts at Maryport and Old Carlisle. Fronting onto this ancient thoroughfare, Hilda Seddon's end-of-terrace property is of lesser though indeterminate age. There are modern-style PVC replacement windows and unsightly water-stained 1950s harling, but an undulating roof of weathered hand-cut slate hints at more primitive origins. A poorly constructed low wall of ornamental concrete-blocks rather pointlessly encloses a bare rectangle of uneven slabs. In common with many of the homes along the street, the ubiquitous grey satellite dish juts out half way up the rendered wall, sucking in signals that are the methadone of the square-eyed masses.

'Look, Guv.'

As they watch, the venetian blinds of the sitting room tilt in unison and then snap shut. They might assume this is a response to their continuing presence, but a minute later the curtains above in what was Barry Seddon's bedroom are pulled to. While it is late afternoon, dusk is still many hours away: Hilda Seddon is at least paying lip service to mourning.

'What did you say to her about a public announcement?'

'Just that it would be on the news, probably tomorrow.'

'What did you get?'

DS Leyton lets out an exasperated sigh. 'I reckon she'd know more about the private life of her cat – if she had one. No idea where he drank, whether he'd got any pals, where he'd been working. She hasn't got a mobile herself, and doesn't know his number. Not a lot of communication passed between 'em, Guv.'

'That would be the life.'

Skelgill does not elaborate upon this somewhat cryptic remark, so DS Leyton is left to make of it what he will.

'She did say he normally carried a fairly hefty wad around with him – his board and lodging was a ton a week. I get the impression he did most of his business in cash, Guv.'

Skelgill nods in a rocking fashion, as if this corresponds with his own assessment. 'I couldn't find sign of a bank account.'

'What – in the bedroom, Guv?'

Now Skelgill grins cynically. 'Bedrooms.'

'Right, Guv.'

'I believe her story – looks like they kept to themselves upstairs as well as down. He's obviously well into horses – gets the *Racing Post*. No trace of a phone, or wallet, or his keys. Limited wardrobe – no climbing gear.'

'I just don't get this rope business and whatnot, Guv.'

Skelgill becomes pensive. 'We need a break here, Leyton. Two loners dead – and that's all they've got in common. Loners. And dead. Not very helpful.'

DS Leyton suddenly notices that his mobile, perhaps inadvertently switched to silent mode, is now ringing. With a jab of a stubby index finger, he accepts just in time.

'Leyton.'

There is a short pause while he listens.

'How do you know?'

Again a pause.

'We're on our way.'

He ends the call and turns to his superior.

'A break, Guv? We've found his van.'

'Are we sure?'

'Apparently it's got his name painted on the side, Guv.'

10. DI SKELGILL'S OFFICE

Thursday morning

'Jones – you'd better speed-read these while we talk – bit of multi-tasking.'

Skelgill hands over a file that contains the autopsy report on the late Lee Harris, and a provisional, fast-tracked summary of the post-mortem relating to the similarly departed Barry Seddon. DS Jones nods efficiently, observed with some admiration by DS Leyton. The three officers are gathered to review the evidence to date: while Skelgill is battling with limited success for additional troops, he has at least ensured that DS Jones remains under his command for the time being. Possession being nine-tenths of the law, he figures that while she wraps up his Oakthwaite case, she can provide intellectual support in relation to these perplexing mountain murders.

'My missus is like that, Guv.' DS Leyton chimes in with his usual cheerful London brogue. 'She'll be on the old dog and bone, rabbiting ten to the dozen, watching *Eastenders* – and stone me if she's not doing the ironing as well.' He regards his colleagues in wonderment. 'I mean – imagine talking to the mother-in-law, watching the telly *and* ironing!'

Skelgill frowns cynically. 'Imagine ironing, Leyton.'

'Fair point, Guv.'

'Glad we have our uses.' DS Jones makes this quip without looking up from the document she holds.

'Leyton's got his uses – I just haven't worked out what they are yet.'

Skelgill seems to be in relatively bright spirits. Not one to hide his feelings from his subordinates – as DS Leyton will readily testify – he might be excused this morning for labouring beneath more gloomy skies. He has two unsolved murders on his watch, and very little to go on. The silver lining from his perspective – albeit a temporary one – must relate to the conclusions of the post-mortem on Barry Seddon. It appears he was killed some time on Monday *("...death probably occurred between the hours of 10:00 and 14:00...")* – only shortly after the discovery of the body of Lee Harris, and before it had been established that the latter was murdered. Thus the police can hardly be accused of failing to react in order to prevent the second crime. Skelgill crunches the chewing end of a biro and taps it on the blank writing pad upon his desk.

'Circumstantially, and MO-wise, there's categorically a connection between these deaths.'

'The killer, Guv?'

'But that's about it, Leyton – the killer. At the moment there's nothing else to link Harris and Seddon. We know what they died of, and roughly when, but we don't know how, or where, or why.'

Now DS Jones glances up.

'Perhaps forensics will get a match on fibres on their clothes, Guv?'

Skelgill screws up his nose doubtingly. 'How many carpets are there in Cumbria?'

'What if the killer owns a rare breed of dog, Guv?'

While DS Leyton chuckles at his own joke, Skelgill appears uninterested. He casts a hand back in DS Leyton's direction.

'Leyton – run us through what we know so far – for Jones's benefit.'

DS Leyton shuffles a sheaf of papers that represent the collated efforts of a small team assigned to background desk- and leg-work, until a summarising page of his handwritten notes surfaces.

'Harris – not a lot. A couple of local shopkeepers have recognised him from the mugshot, but don't know anything about him. No acquaintances identified as yet. No joy tracing his mobile – the number was for a pay-as-you-go SIM. Nothing on a bank account – perhaps he didn't have one. His work paid cash, as you'll recall, Guv. The only contract on the address is broadband, and that's in the landlord's name. He's been traced. There's no tenancy agreement – he owns half a dozen properties and collects the rent himself in cash. Harris was up to date. Landlord doesn't bother with references. Evidently by the look of him you wouldn't trust him – nor double-cross him neither.'

Skelgill is moved to bristle at this. 'Good enough reason to pull him in, Leyton.'

DS Jones looks up from her reading. 'Sounds like this Lee Harris was living under the official radar, Guv. I take it he's not an *illegal* or using an alias?'

Skelgill glances expectantly at DS Leyton.

'Pretty certain he's British, Guv. His workmates – if you can call them that – reckoned he was from the Midlands. Apparently he supported Leicester City.'

Now Skelgill raises an eyebrow, but does not elaborate upon its meaning. However, in England, the following of a non-fashionable football club is often a reliable indicator of where a person spent their formative years.

'We need to bottom that, Leyton. What about the motorbike?'

'One of the mechanics thought he was fixing up an insurance write-off.' He checks his notes. 'Honda CBR600 – if that means anything to you, Guv.'

Skelgill nods in a rather superior fashion. 'Sports bike. Registration?'

'We got a plate number, but the DVLA system shows a Certificate of Destruction against it.'

'There was fresh oil beside his flat, Leyton. And no helmet indoors. Unless that old bat belongs to Hell's Grannies, that bike must be somewhere.'

'The lad at the garage didn't reckon it was roadworthy, Guv.'

'Since when did that become a criteria for riding?'

DS Jones glances up briefly, as though she is tempted to correct Skelgill's grammar – but silently she resumes her study.

'I've got an alert out on it, Guv – hopefully a warden will spot it.'

'Sooner rather than later.'

This sounds like an instruction – not that the outcome is in DS Leyton's power, but he nods vigorously all the same.

'Better fill in Jones on the latest on Seddon – the van.'

DS Jones moves as if to give her undivided attention to DS Leyton, but for a moment some detail on the page detains her and it is a couple of seconds before she raises her eyes.

'We found his truck yesterday in the superstore car park on Scotland Road. His mobile and wallet were locked up inside – looked like he'd put them out of sight. There was £150 in the wallet, and the phone hadn't been used since Friday. Recent calls all appear to be to and from contacts in the building trade. Monday's racing newspaper was on the passenger seat. Keys had been left under the wheel-arch.'

'Could he have gone into the store?'

DS Leyton is nodding. 'We're going through the CCTV at the moment – it's slow work though.'

'If he bought the paper there, they ought to have an electronically timed record – they can't sell all that many copies.'

'Fair point Jones.' Skelgill's interjection is a little terse. 'But let's see what the CCTV brings first.'

DS Jones nods compliantly. With the back of one hand she taps the reports.

'What do you think about the time interval, Guv – I mean between the murders and the bodies being discovered?'

Skelgill nods sagely, although his reply does not suggest any private intelligence. 'What are you driving at?'

'Assuming the bodies were dumped in the early hours before they were discovered – it means they were each kept hidden for the best part of a day and a half. There must be an explanation for that. It might tell us something about the killer.'

The trio sits in silence for a few moments, metaphorically (and DS Leyton literally) scratching their heads, until DS Jones, who perhaps already has a theory up her sleeve but has been exercising diplomacy, speaks up.

'I was on a forensics course a little while ago, Guv. Rigor mortis sets in three to four hours after death. Maximum stiffness occurs after about twelve hours, and then it dissipates from about twenty-four hours.'

Skelgill seems engrossed by this thought, and it takes DS Leyton to respond in the vernacular.

'You wouldn't get a stiff in a saloon car boot, or even a hatchback – it'd take a big estate like yours, Guv.'

'I'll remember that, Leyton, next time you're paralytic after a police night out.' Skelgill projects a reprimanding frown at DS Leyton. 'Carry on, Jones.'

'You'd need transport to get a body to the foot of the fell. Kill someone during the day. You can't move them until it's dark and the neighbours have gone to bed. But on the first night, you're too late – rigor mortis means the body doesn't fit in a small car, if you could even move it. So you have to wait until the next night.'

Skelgill is cupping his chin between upturned palms. He stares hard at DS Jones. 'So, your *something* about the killer – he lives in a built-up area, probably residential.'

DS Jones averts her eyes apprehensively. 'It's just an idea that corresponds to the facts, Guv.'

'It's good thinking.'

DS Jones shrugs modestly. 'But it does mean keeping a corpse in your house – that has its complications.'

'What if they were killed in an outbuilding, or a garage?' This is DS Leyton's contribution. 'I've been wondering if they went to buy something, Guv.'

Skelgill sits back in his chair. 'Leyton – I agree – nine times out of ten we'd be looking at drugs – but this pair seem as clean as whistles in that regard. And Seddon's wallet was stuffed with cash.'

'So why did he leave it, Guv – and his phone?'

Skelgill shrugs.

'Strikes me, Guv – you can't be mugged of what you ain't got.'

Skelgill considers this proposition. 'I've obviously led a more sheltered existence than you, Leyton.'

'But say he just took the amount of cash he needed? If it were for some dodgy deal, he'd maybe think he couldn't be double-crossed. Look at Harris – his phone and wallet are gone, there might be a laptop missing, and no trace of his motorbike.'

Skelgill seems uncomfortable with the notion of petty robbery as a motive. His features agonise as he takes a deep breath, inhaling and exhaling, before he speaks.

'Easy enough to lose a bike in a lake, Leyton.'

Again there is a hiatus, before DS Jones raises another question.

'And no sightings of vehicles near the disposal sites, Guv?'

With an inclination of his head, Skelgill refers her inquiry to DS Leyton.

'They were all spark out at the youth hostel. The staff bunk down early because they have to be up first thing – and you know how hard it is to wake teenagers once they're asleep.'

DS Jones looks rather amused by this statement.

'That's me, still.'

'Lucky you – wait till you've got some little 'uns bouncing on your head at six in the morning.'

DS Jones glances at Skelgill, but his expression is inscrutable. DS Leyton continues.

'The other place – to get up to Sharp Edge by the shortest route – it's along a tiny back road to nowhere. There's a rough parking area for hillwalkers. A car left overnight wouldn't look especially out of place – and the chances of anyone passing in the early hours are ten percent of nothing. We're checking with local farmers, but no takers so far.'

DS Jones leans back and crosses her legs – it is warmer today and she has opted for just a short skirt and ballet-style pumps, with a sleeveless t-shirt top. She must notice that she has drawn the gaze of both of her colleagues, for she self-consciously places the papers on the edge of Skelgill's desk and reaches forward to clasp her hands around her uppermost knee.

'It seems a heck of a lot of trouble – to take a body into the hills.'

'That's what's bugging us, Jones.' Skelgill stretches skywards and rests his hands for a moment behind his head. There are fresh droplets of sweat spotting the armpits of his shirt. 'It's the crux of the case.'

'In what way, Guv?' DS Jones strives to maintain eye contact.

'There's a message here, for someone – us, maybe.'

Skelgill's subordinates unite in a respectful silence to acknowledge the gravity of his statement. After half a minute it is DS Jones who finally voices a thought.

'When is the news going to be released, Guv?'

'There's a conference at one.'

'Are you involved, Guv?'

Skelgill scowls and leans back and stares at the ceiling. 'I feel a puncture coming on.'

DS Jones glances surreptitiously at DS Leyton, who raises an eyebrow as if to say 'upon his own head be it'. They know well Skelgill's antipathy to journalistic gatherings, but the Chief will be expecting him to be present – if not to address the press pack directly.

'It might flush something out, at least, Guv – as far as the victims are concerned.'

Skelgill sits forward again and with a flourish of his pen casually scrawls four rough circles on his desk pad.

'What worries me, Jones, is that the killings are random.' He marks a cross between the circles. 'If they are, even their unabridged autobiographies won't help us.'

Again a silence pervades the office. Skelgill has the window ajar, and the song of a blackbird quite close at hand fills the temporary void with its melodic mourning lilt. All three detectives appreciate only too well the spectre Skelgill has raised: there is a certain type of serial killer for whom only one thing makes them stop – and that is getting caught.

DS Jones clears her throat and her colleagues glance her way.

'What do you think about there being an accomplice, Guv?'

'Quite possible.'

Skelgill's instantaneous reply catches DS Leyton by surprise.

'Really, Guv?'

Plainly it is news to him that his boss is thinking along these lines – when Skelgill has thus far been determined that a single person could transport the bodies. DS Leyton remains wide-eyed but he does not protest further – the idea of one person hauling the dead weight of a grown man has clearly been at odds with his estimation.

'Stands to reason, Leyton.' Skelgill springs to his feet and snatches up the car keys that rest on top of his towering in-tray. He strides out of the door with a parting shot. 'Takes four fit blokes to stretcher a casualty off the fells – and that's downhill. You'd want certifying to take the weight the other way.'

11. SHARP EDGE

Thursday, midday

At the parking place along the 'tiny back road to nowhere' (as DS Leyton put it), Skelgill, who has changed into outdoor gear, is methodically loading stones from a collapsed wall into a large army surplus backpack. He has lined this with a sturdy woven rubble-sack, and chooses with care, weighing each boulder in turn, rejecting some as either too light or too heavy (or perhaps too angular), before lowering them into position. The rucksack stands upright on the flatbed of his estate car, about a foot from the rear sill. The car's suspension creaks a protest with each new addition. On the face of it, he might be making a collection for some gardening project – a rockery, perhaps.

But, no. When the bag is almost full, he tightens the drawstring, buckles down the hood, and turns to sit with his back against it. He shrugs his shoulders into the straps and adjusts them to fit. Without further ado – other than taking a deep breath and bearing his teeth in a fearsome grimace – he pitches forward, pivoting at the hips and levering the burden from the car. As he intimated to DS Leyton, it is a method he has marvelled at when employed by diminutive *Tamang* porters – lifting huge composite bundles of trekkers' rucksacks held only by a head-strap or *naamlo*. On occasion it takes a giggling gaggle of kinsmen to raise one man to his feet and set him in motion.

Without such assistance Skelgill staggers drunkenly, alarmingly in fact, and only the close proximity of a wooden farm gate prevents him from toppling over and ending up on his back, kicking like a stranded beetle. Swearing colourfully, beads of perspiration breaking out upon his brow, he clings on to the uppermost bar of the gate until he steadies himself. But this is no time to dwell. He wrenches up the bandana that he wears around his neck to form a sweatband, and, bent over like the crooked man of the nursery rhyme, unsteadily retraces his steps to his car. He drags his walking poles clattering from amongst the untidy debris of assorted tackle. Using one of the poles he tries to snag the hank of baler twine – Cleopatra's makeshift leash – that hangs from one of the rear coat-pegs. This proves tricky and he is almost defeated, but at what might be the final attempt he manages to hook it and transfer it to his back pocket. Finally, reaching up blind, with outstretched fingertips he just obtains sufficient purchase to wrench down the tailgate. Then he produces a short piercing whistle.

'Come on, lass.'

Belying her age – which is currently uncertain, though undoubtedly well into maturity in doggy years – Cleopatra springs through the gap in the wall from the pasture she has been exploring. A matted wad of blackish silage dangles from one side of her muzzle rather like a half-smoked cigar, complementing her Churchillian demeanour. However, the similarity ends here, for the great wartime leader was not known to eat his Cuban coronas. She circles Skelgill, probably rather too closely for comfort, and gets a poke in her sturdy rear from one of his poles. He can't now bend to tie her onto the twine, but she seems to know his mind as, obediently, she trots ahead, leading the way across the lane to pick up the worn path that is their route to Scales Tarn.

From here the ascent, relatively short in terms of distance, breaks into three distinct stages. First, there is the climb up through Mousthwaite Comb, an increasingly steep valley that accounts for roughly half of the required height gain. Second, there is the respite of a traverse across the north-eastern flank of Scales Fell, where the gradient rises imperceptibly. And third is the sting in the tail, a short, sharp five-hundred-foot haul up beside Scales Beck to its source at the tarn of the same name.

Ordinarily, Skelgill would deal with this degree of difficulty without breaking sweat or straining his capacious fell-runner's lungs. Even carrying a regulation fifty-pound backpack, sufficient to sustain him for a week in the hills, tent, food and all, he would set a brisk pace and spend his time admiring the scenery. Not so today. Walking flat-footed and bent almost double beneath the extraordinary (and yet only human) weight, and despite the mountainous incentive to get the crazy masochistic experiment over and done with, Skelgill does rather exude the appearance of one on his last legs. He is not assisted by the warm, muggy conditions and the fact that the entire route is in the lee of the hill to his left, sheltered from the day's light westerly breeze.

Nonetheless, there is a limit to how slowly a person can actually walk and, inch by inch, step by step, he makes steady if unspectacular progress. At one point he is overtaken by a group of hurrying hikers, four well-equipped and lively sounding young guys who look like they know what they are doing. Their conversation wanes as they pass him, perhaps recognising something of his ordeal, and – when their chatter resumes a few moments later – they can be heard speculating in awed tones whether he might be an SAS trooper in training. Perhaps hearing this spurs a flagging Skelgill on and, one hundred minutes after setting out, several litres of body fluid the lighter, he sheds the rucksack and throws himself full length and fully clothed into the cold, clear waters of Scales Tarn. As he submerges his burning muscles, his already lofty estimation of Nepalese porters has surely soared to Himalayan heights.

He surfaces to find himself face to face with a rather bemused-looking Bullboxer. Cleopatra has waded out to join him, and now seems dismayed that he has failed to produce whatever prey item it was that he dived for so eagerly. Skelgill blows a spout of water out over the dog; amusingly she makes a leap for this, and as he follows her trajectory a splash of pink up on the fell catches his eye.

Then he hears the faint cry for help.

Struggling to his feet he extends a downturned palm to the dog. She seems to understand this command and immediately stiffens, watching him avidly. Skelgill pulls off his bandana, for it is causing water to trickle down his brow. He stares hard, shielding his eyes with his left hand from the brightness of the sky above the dark line of the ridge. The plaintive exhortation comes again. Someone is in trouble on Sharp Edge.

Without further hesitation he wades to the shore and jogs past his abandoned rucksack and poles. He could loop around and pick his way along the arête, but instead he opts for the direct route, three hundred feet up the steep southern flank, over loose soil and scree and smooth slabs that slope at a dizzying sixty degrees. But Skelgill, his wet clothes sticking to his body, swarms up like a bedraggled *Spider-Man* refusing to be vanquished. Perhaps an equally remarkable sight, though, is the faithful hound at his heels – what the sturdy creature lacks in finesse she more than makes up for in dogged determination. Skelgill might reflect that four feet and sixteen claws have their uses where gravity is concerned.

The cries – they are of a woman – are becoming increasingly desperate, and Skelgill pauses to bellow that help is at hand and the stranded person should hold on for another minute. But when he gets within about thirty feet he sees that she is in fact a small girl – perhaps aged seven or eight. The explanation for the vocal mismatch becomes clear when he pulls himself up beside her – he realises there is another female beyond and below, a youngish woman who clings to the upslope halfway between them and the walker's path that shadows the scrambler's route.

The girl is ashen faced and perched astride the very crest of the arête, frozen with fear and rightly so, for the drop to Scales Tarn is not easily survivable; recorded deaths on Sharp Edge number in double figures. In mountain rescue parlance, she is *cragfast*. Skelgill wedges himself into a crevice so he can't go anywhere, and reaches out and takes a grip on one strap of the denim dungarees she wears.

'It's alright, lass – you're safe now. What's your name?'

The girl's lower lip turns out, and tears begin to stream down her cheeks – but no words are forthcoming.

'She's called *Rhian* – her name's *Rhian*!'

Skelgill glances down at the mother – or aunt or cousin or whatever relation or otherwise the woman might be.

'Get yourself back down to the path and stay there!'

Skelgill's bark is fierce, but he knows Sharp Edge's marginally less formidable northern flank has taken its share of casualties down the years. The woman holds out her hands despairingly. There is fear in her dark eyes but she begins to comply with his order. He watches with concern.

'Take it steady – keep a firm grip with both hands each time you move a foot.'

As all mountaineers know, twice as many accidents happen on the descent, when momentum, restricted vision and fatigue unite to summon ill fortune. But the woman is at least athletic in her movements, and with the prescribed care she makes it back to the narrow mudstone shingle ledge that is the path. Now Skelgill turns his attention to the girl.

'Right, little lady – think you can climb down with me?'

The girl shakes her head.

'Rhian – is that your Mum?'

She nods once.

'You're a better climber than her, aren't you?'

Another nod.

'So you can do better than she just did.'

A blank stare.

'Look – I'll go first, just ahead of you. If you slip – I'll catch you.'

As soon as he has uttered the word *slip* Skelgill must inwardly curse his own slip of the tongue – she shrinks away from him and clutches more desperately at the rock in front of her. In the explosive wake of this embedded command her confidence plummets away like a landslide. Only once has he experienced vertigo brought on by fear of falling – but he knows that if the girl is similarly struck then all her instincts will be screaming at her to cling on for dear life.

For a moment he looks at her as if he's sizing up the possibility of making a grab and taking her down over his shoulder. But in their exposed position there is a risk that the girl will panic and kick herself free. Then an idea must come. Still holding her in his firm grip, he casts about for sight of the dog – but in the interim the inquisitive Cleopatra has descended to investigate the other stranger, and is providing moral support of a fashion as mum, on bended knee, anxiously watches proceedings above.

'Do you have a dog, Rhian?'

A slight but perceptible shake of the head.

'When we get down in a minute, I'm going to have to put my dog on a lead. That's because if she chases sheep, a farmer could shoot her. We wouldn't want that, would we?'

Now a more discernable shake.

'Do you think you could hold the dog's lead for me?'

A slight nod.

'She'd like that. Her name's Cleopatra.'

'We've done Cleopatra at school.'

Bingo. Or so must Skelgill be saying to himself.

'Well, *my* Cleopatra – just like the Egyptian queen – can be a bit naughty. But I reckon you can manage her, eh?'

'Aha.'

'Okay then, here's what we'll do.'

With his free hand Skelgill reaches into the damp recess of his back pocket. Slowly he draws out the hank of baler twine.

'Cleopatra's a Bullboxer – that means she's very strong. So I have this special unbreakable string – that's what I use for her lead. It'll keep her safe.'

The girl stares curiously at the bright blue twine.

One-handed, Skelgill shakes out the twine and presents a tied end. A little pink hand tentatively reaches forward and small fingers close around the loop. He lifts up the other end, which also has a knotted loop. He clenches his fist around it with a gesture of import.

'In one minute, this will be Cleopatra.'

He winks, and the girl winks back.

Together, jerkily, painstakingly at first, and then more easily, with Skelgill a yard below and the magic baler twine dangling loosely between them, they begin to scramble down. In the dry conditions it is not so difficult; the girl has her mother's innate agility, and it really does just take a minute to cover the thirty feet or so in order to gain the protection of the path.

As might be anticipated, mum envelops daughter in a great hug, the former's eyes brimming with tears of relief and thanks as she gazes at Skelgill standing close behind. He reaches out to place a palm on the little one's head, but the woman intercepts and gives his fingers a long hard squeeze. He looks somewhat sheepish held in this pose. But quickly he turns to practical matters. With the thumb of his free hand he indicates the dangers of the steep downslope.

'Let's get off here – we'll stop beside the tarn.'

Mother nods and detaches herself from her daughter. At this point Skelgill skilfully renegotiates the plan, suggesting that they allow Cleopatra free to lead them to the water, where the girl can take her for a drink, and after that hold her on the leash. This finds agreement, and in Indian file they cautiously retrace the steps the small family party made before going astray.

Soon the narrow walker's path swings over the broadening ridge to merge with the scrambling route, and widens out as it dips down to the tarn and the outfall of Scales Beck. Though they are well above the treeline, Skelgill manages to find a stick – a splinter of charred kindling discarded by a wild camper – which he tosses ostentatiously into the shallows. Cleopatra needs little encouragement to retrieve the item, and in no time the girl is having great fun in repeating the procedure.

Her mother and Skelgill stand rather self-consciously a few yards away and a couple of paces apart, their attention somewhat artificially fixed upon the boisterous game. After a longer pause than must be comfortable for either of them, it is the woman who breaks the silence.

'I'm Liz, by the way – Liz Williams.'

She reaches across the hiatus and this time holds out a formal hand.

Skelgill seems reluctant to accept – there is a moment's unnatural delay – but he realises he must reciprocate.

'Dan.'

'Are you local?'

'Aye.' He stares at her – then realises he should make conversation. 'How about you?'

The woman smiles contentedly, as if she senses his awkwardness and feels comfortable in taking the lead. She is very attractive and presumably knows it: there is something oriental in her full lips and rich nut-brown eyes and matching hair pulled tight into a pony tail; a small, slim figure has its curves accentuated by the skin-tight gym outfit she wears. In answer to Skelgill's question she shakes her head.

'When I was a kid – for a few years we lived in Keswick – but we're here on holiday from South Wales, just Rhian and me. I've taken her out of school early to beat the crowds.'

'That's something well remembered.'

She laughs. 'We'll certainly remember today.'

Skelgill seems to relax, and lowers himself down to sit on a dry slab of rock. He inclines his head towards girl and dog. 'Looks like we're here for the duration.'

Now facing him, the woman takes the opportunity to appraise his appearance. As she moves to sit beside him – quite close as the rock only seats two – there's a lively glint in her eye.

'You're soaked through.' Her inflection carries an inquiry.

'It's a long story.'

'If we're here for the duration...'

Skelgill throws her a sideways glance, the sort of stoic gesture that recognises the capacity of women to get their way.

'Let's just say I was cooling off.'

'Do you always cool off fully clothed?'

'Just as well that I was.'

The woman's smile is honeyed. She is amused by their banter and perhaps too the comic prospect of being rescued by someone akin to the Naked Rambler. But it is Skelgill who speaks next.

'Liz, tell me – what the heck were you doing on Sharp Edge?'

Now she is the one to nod ruefully.

'We do a lot of hillwalking at weekends – we're only an hour from the Brecon Beacons, you see?' There is suddenly a strong Welsh lilt in her words. 'When I was a girl, a little older than

Rhian – when I lived in Keswick – I was a member of an outward-bound club – I don't recall too much, but this was one of the places they used to bring us to.'

Skelgill tilts his head from side to side, as if assessing the wisdom of such a policy.

'It's an interesting spot – so long as you know what you're doing.'

The woman presses the tips of her fingers together like she might in prayer. Her hands are slim and her long nails coloured to match the rose pink of her lips.

'The instructors used to tease us that they'd make us climb Sharp Edge if we misbehaved – like walking the plank. I think my friend and I only joined because we fancied some of the boys – and the instructors, I suppose – it was more of a youth club really – I've still got my scrapbook and photographs somewhere – they had a climbing wall at the farm where it was based – and they used to do quad-biking and clay-pigeon shooting for corporate events.'

Skelgill's antennae seem to become alert as she completes this description.

'Was that over at the back of Threlkeld, near the lead mine?'

The woman turns out her bottom lip and shakes her head apologetically.

'My memories are hazy – I would only have been eleven or twelve. My parents used to drive us. It had a queer name.'

'Knott Halloo?'

'Of course – that's right – so it was.'

'That place burned down the thick end of twenty years ago – went out of business – I heard talk it was arson.'

'Really? I'm surprised *you're* old enough to remember.'

Skelgill immediately looks both embarrassed and flattered by this engineered compliment. If he is correct about the incident at the climbing centre, he would have been in his late teens, which would make his present companion some seven or eight years his junior – and now around the thirty mark.

'It sparked a bit of news at the time – especially if you moved in climbing circles, I suppose.'

'You obviously do – that was brilliant how you talked Rhian down.'

Skelgill's chest swells a little more.

'You could hear?'

He makes this question sound as though he had not intended to broadcast the exchange.

'Only some of it.' The woman backtracks a little, responding with appropriate diplomacy.

'Climbing's ninety percent confidence – that's why there's such a thing as a *confidence* rope – you wouldn't trust one to break your fall – but it works wonders for climbing ability.'

'And you had a confidence *string*.'

Skelgill grins at her joke. 'Baler twine – never without it.'

For a second he looks like he might wish to own up about the shepherd's recent good advice in this regard, but vanity evidently gets the better of him and he allows the woman to nod admiringly.

'It certainly did the trick.'

'Obviously you'd never belay anybody like that – but belaying wasn't an option. I figured I'd catch her if she slipped – it was just a matter of getting her moving.'

'You're quite the expert – you must have a way with women.'

Skelgill affects to adjust one of his laces, though he must feel her gaze upon him. Then he glances fretfully at his wristwatch. The woman immediately responds.

'Dan – you mustn't let us keep you.'

Skelgill shrugs. 'It's no problem – what are you planning to do?'

The woman stretches, curving her back and running her hands over her glossy scalp, emphasising the contours of her breasts beneath the taut fabric of her sports vest.

'I think we should head home – have an ice cream to recover from the shock. We're staying at the caravan site at Braithwaite – just Rhian and me.'

It is the second time she has mentioned her lone parent status. As she rises, the movements of her lissom figure draw Skelgill's eye; she catches his absorbed gaze and, turning to face him crosses one leg over the other, emphasising its toned musculature. He hauls himself to his feet, and pulls rather self-consciously at his own damp attire.

'I could walk down with you – that way your daughter gets to lead the dog like I promised.'

'That would be nice.'

'Where are you parked? I didn't see a car the way I came up.'

'We're near a pub, I think.'

'Scales.'

The woman shrugs and grins helplessly.

'I'll find it.'

'I know we can rely on you – you're our hero.'

And suddenly she steps forward and embraces him – at first with a sob but quickly she lifts up her face and reaches with both hands to pull down his head for a kiss. It is a prolonged kiss and not easily interrupted.

'Mummy!'

*

When Skelgill wakes, the ceiling above him is out of focus and unfamiliar – it is the inside of the roof of his car. His phone – switched to silent – vibrates loudly beside him, drumming in bursts upon the steel of the flatbed. He lies in a narrow channel between untidy banks of tackle, his bare feet protruding from the vehicle, the tailgate open to the half-clouded heavens. As he sits upright with a pained groan – the beginnings of delayed onset muscle soreness – the inquiring face of Cleopatra rises beyond his long bony toes.

He checks his watch – it is approaching four o'clock, less than an hour since he left the rescued mother and daughter at their car, waving them away with the woman's entreaty ringing in his ears and, hot in his pocket, her mobile number on a scrap of paper.

He shuffles forward onto the rear sill of the estate. His shirt and trousers had largely dried out on the walk down. Not so his boots, which lie still sodden where he kicked them off. His socks appear suspiciously gathered together and one shows signs of having been lightly gnawed. The probable culprit sits to attention, keenly awaiting their next adventure.

Skelgill licks his dry lips.

'Want a drink, lass?'

The dog seems to know the word, and dunts his knee approvingly with her broad snout. He rises, emitting more groans, and turns to dip into the debris, dragging out a plastic storage crate. He carries this to the dry-stone wall adjacent to the car. With a clank he extracts a soot-blackened *Kelly Kettle* and gives it an experimental shake. Removing the cork bung he reaches for the pan of an equally worn *Trangia* and pours into it a measure of water. While the thirsty hound laps at his feet, he digs for the kettle base and places it upon a suitably flat rock. Next he takes a handful of finely chopped kindling and arranges it in a lattice inside the aluminium base. From a *Sigg* bottle he sprinkles sparkling violet methylated spirits over the wood. He settles the kettle on the base, checking its balance before completely letting go. Finally he rummages in the crate for matches, strikes one, and drops it through the kettle's internal chimney. With a whoosh the meths ignites, and flames lick from the mouth of the eccentric contraption.

It takes under two minutes for the water to boil, and within another he is sitting with his back to the wall, sipping tea contemplatively from a tin mug (still containing two tea bags and floating flecks of undissolved powdered milk). He is seemingly oblivious to the temperature of both the scalding liquid and the mug itself. His exertions have perhaps created the right conditions for involuntary musing. And certainly he has plenty to consider.

As his mind appears to drift, his pale eyes become oddly glazed. Their pupils contract and he ceases to blink. Of course, he could be playing out some scenario involving the attractive divorcee, whose lithe *Lycra*-clad form has no doubt left its impression upon his primeval instincts, and whose further acquaintance remains an open invitation. But Skelgill's mind is a mystery even to its owner, and perhaps duty is the stronger drive right now. The enigmatic subconscious can solve a conundrum long before it makes public such success. It does so by piecing together seemingly disparate facts, making connections that defy linear, logical thinking. And, though scant clues there may be, vague forms that lurk in the shadowy recesses of the brain, experience has told him that in later hindsight their significance will be sharp and bright and tangible. Perhaps already he has everything he needs. And now, in his semi-trancelike state, Skelgill is apparently mouthing the stanza, *'Harris Honda, Seddon Scaffolding.'*

His reverie is interrupted by the buzz of his phone. He presses a palm above his heart, as if to suppress the vibration in his breast pocket. But it persists, and he rips up the flap.

'Leyton.'

'Guv – you missed the press conference – the Chief's spitting feathers.'

'Let her spit – I've just done a rescue.'

'A *rescue*, Guv?'

DS Leyton's tone is not so much incredulous as exasperated.

'Behave, Leyton – I'm being dead serious – I just got a seven-year-old kid down off Sharp Edge.'

DS Leyton sighs. 'Yeah, but what it is, Guv – I told her you had a flat tyre.'

Skelgill is silent for a moment.

'Oh, well – can't be helped – good work, anyway, Leyton.'

'What were you doing up there, Guv – was it an emergency call-out?'

'I needed to check something.'

'Right, Guv.'

DS Leyton knows better than to interrogate Skelgill when he produces this kind of bland explanation. Now he is silent for a moment.

'You rang me?'

'Ah, yeah, Guv – we've got some progress – reckon we've found Seddon on the CCTV tapes – midday Monday.'

Skelgill takes a mouthful of tea, perhaps to aid his thinking.

'He was supposed to be dead by then.'

'Exactly, Guv – at least, it must have happened not long after – between ten and two, according to the PM.'

'Where are you, Leyton?'

'Still at base – I thought you'd want to come.'

'I'll swing by and get you on the way – be outside in twenty minutes.'

12. PENRITH TOWN CENTRE

Thursday afternoon

'Y ou alright, Guv?'
'Like I said, Leyton – I got involved in a rescue.'
'You look like you've done your back in, Guv.'
Skelgill glares disapprovingly across the roof of his car. Nonetheless, he tries to adjust his posture, but the effect is stilted and military. And it is with restricted freedom of movement that he stoops to check the interior – Cleopatra has already scrambled into the driver's seat, and gazes forlornly through the two-inch gap by which he has lowered the window.

'Shan't be long, lass. Sit tight.'

He has parked in the shade at the side of the store, in a bay marked *'Deliveries, Keep Clear At All Times'*. He rounds the long estate car and follows DS Leyton, who is noticeably hobbling towards the entrance of the building.

'You're not exactly the spring chicken yourself, Leyton.'

'Cor blimey, Guv – you ain't kidding – my old pins feel like they've been run over by the Mile End bus.'

'You need to get out more, Leyton – buy a dog – do your kids a favour.'

DS Leyton glances suspiciously at his superior. It is unlike Skelgill to be showing a concern – or even an interest – in his wellbeing and domestic life. Perhaps he suspects an ulterior motive, such as the provision of ad hoc boarding for the challenging canine recently acquired.

'The missus reckons she's allergic, Guv.'

Skelgill waves away the objection. 'Get yourself one of those Labradoodles – they're all the rage apparently.'

'Pricey, though – so I've heard, Guv. Then there's insurance, vets' bills, feeding 'em.'

Skelgill nods pensively. 'Reminds me – I'd better stock up on a few tins of *Chum* while we're here.'

DS Leyton winces, presumably in anticipation of being tapped up for a further instalment on his credit facilities.

*

'Decent scran, this, Leyton – for a supermarket.'

DS Leyton, who has succumbed to a chocolate brownie, nods agreeably as Skelgill tucks into a large plate of sausage, beans, fried eggs and chips. Skelgill has already pointed out that not only did he miss lunch in the line of duty (although no doubt DS Leyton strongly suspects he was walking the dog in lieu of attending the media conference), but also that it is tea time – five p.m. – when, by tradition, working-class British families have their main meal of the day (sometimes called *high* tea by cafés to differentiate it from the more genteel *afternoon* tea, which is an upscale and often extravagant cake-centred snack indulged in between luncheon and evening dinner). Of course, Skelgill eats whenever he can – on the principle that often he can't – and doesn't generally display any obligation to justify himself to DS Leyton – unless perhaps the latter is footing the bill.

'So, this is the same table as Seddon, Guv.'

Skelgill nods and chews and points with a fork in the direction of the washrooms, presumably to indicate Barry Seddon's direction of egress. They have spent the past half-hour with the store manager and the detective constable assigned to interrogate the CCTV records. Once Seddon was spotted, it had been a relatively straightforward task to examine the contemporaneous tapes from other cameras and piece together his movements. While these records do not extend to the car park, it is clear that he entered the store at ten minutes to twelve, and left five minutes later, having briefly visited the cigarette kiosk, the cafeteria and the toilets. Both of the female shop assistants who served him have been interviewed. Although neither have shed any particular light on the matter, the buxom and somewhat scatterbrained young girl from the cafeteria claims to remember him as 'a bit pervy' – evidently he stared overlong at her breasts. They did not attempt to establish what would have been a reasonable period of observation.

'Why do you reckon he bought a coffee, Guv – and then never touched it?'

Skelgill finishes his mouthful of food and takes a gulp of tea, draining his mug.

'I'll need another of these, Leyton, I'm parched.'

'Have mine, Guv – I just finished one before I left the station – I'm tea'd out, truth be told.'

Skelgill shrugs indifferently and pulls his sergeant's brimming mug to within comfortable reach.

'Maybe he thought to use the gents' you have to buy something.'

DS Leyton does not respond – it is obvious from Skelgill's tone that this is not a serious suggestion. In any event, Seddon had already paid for cigarettes and a newspaper.

'Perhaps he didn't fancy it, after all, Guv.'

Skelgill stops eating and, with unusual decorum, places his cutlery amidst the work in progress on his plate.

'Leyton – if you were meeting someone – what time would you make it?'

'I'm not with you, Guv.'

'Well – say you were going to arrange to meet DS Jones later to discuss this case?'

DS Leyton looks perplexed. But he glances uneasily at his wristwatch and shrugs. 'I dunno – what – six o'clock?'

'Precisely.'

'You sound like the Speaking Clock, Guv.'

'Ha-ha, Leyton – but watch my lips: six o'clock – *on the hour.*'

'Ah.'

'You make appointments on the hour, don't you? Not eight minutes to six or eleven minutes past – even if that suits you better.'

Now the penny drops.

'You reckon he was meeting someone at twelve, Guv?'

'And if he was, Leyton, he wasn't going far.'

*

Their respective meals consumed, Skelgill and DS Leyton stroll replete across the store lot to the parking bay where the scaffolder's pick-up had been located before it was removed for forensic examination. The muggy afternoon is turning into a brighter evening; the sky has cleared and the sun is still respectably high in the west, with plenty of heat to spare. Skelgill cranes his neck to watch a group of swifts that screams and swarms overhead before diving twisting and glistening to skim the slate rooftops of the old town centre beyond the busy road. Though the supermarket is quiet, there is plenty of traffic on the move – folk that are not home are heading whither for their tea. Skelgill sits on the low wall that divides the car park from the sidewalk. With a casual flap of the hand he beckons to DS Leyton to do the same.

'So, Leyton – the sixty-four thousand dollar question – did he walk, or did he get in a car?'

'Maybe someone picked him up, Guv – he parked a long way from the shop. He could just nip over this wall.'

Skelgill glances over his shoulder.

'Double yellows, though.'

'Wouldn't stop you, Guv.'

'Aye – but why come into the town centre? There's plenty of easier meeting points out by the motorway.'

'Well, maybe he did go on foot, Guv.'

Skelgill ponders for a moment.

'I think it's more likely – but why not park outside wherever you were going?'

Again, Skelgill's question sounds like he already has an answer in mind.

'Well – like you just said – yellow lines, meters, no spaces, whatever – supermarket's a good place to park free. I do it myself, Guv.'

'It's one reason.'

'What are you thinking?'

'His name was painted on his van.'

DS Leyton nods – evidently he grasps Skelgill's line of thought. He stands and looks both ways along the road behind Skelgill.

'There's a bookies up there, Guv. Maybe it *opens* at twelve?'

Stiffly, Skelgill rises and stares in the direction indicated by DS Leyton. There is an arcade of shops and the bookmaker's sign stands out clearly. In his line of sight a fake-tanned twenty-something pair of females are approaching, quite briskly. The taller of the two is dark, and by a few years the younger, though it is her accomplice that wins Skelgill's attention, her scanty outfit of hot pants and sleeveless t-shirt winning over against the other's more modest attire. His gaze is drawn to the scarlet straps of her bra, which don't quite line up with her vest-top. Then he catches her partner's disapproving eye, and switches his attention a little ostentatiously to his wristwatch. He examines it, frowning, and carefully adjusts the outer dial on its face with a series of clicks.

'Let's go see, Leyton.'

The couple are past, perhaps on their way to the grocery store's pedestrian entrance. Gingerly he straddles the wall. The shorter, heavier DS Leyton struggles over, swearing under his breath.

'Remember his cousin Hilda said he was into betting, Guv? It could explain why he left his wallet in the van. And he'd bought the *Racing Post*.'

Certainly this logic is quite compelling: if Seddon didn't want to advertise his presence in the turf accountant's, the supermarket car park would be a handy alternative. And, by leaving the balance of his funds in his vehicle, the temptation to lose everything would have been mitigated. However, Skelgill's stern features reveal little trace of enthusiasm, and indeed when the pair reach the gambling emporium he strides right past without breaking stride.

'Guv – what's the score?'

'Keep walking, Leyton.'

DS Leyton scuttles to catch up, hampered by sore thighs.

'Where are we going?'

'Search me.'

'What about the bookies?'

'On the way back – right now I'm timing us.'

'Come again, Guv?'

'If he came this way – and fifty-fifty he did – he probably had three or four minutes to get somewhere for twelve.'

They have to halt for a moment as a car indicates to turn into the side street that interrupts their smooth progress. It is called Ullswater Place. As they cross Skelgill glances along its twin banks of terraced houses, but his gaze is not especially critical. They gain the opposite pavement and continue onward.

'Thing is, Guv...' (Skelgill is setting a brisk pace and DS Leyton wheezes a little) '...that assumes he was punctual.'

Skelgill scowls. He does not reply and instead checks his watch. They walk on for what must be another minute before he wheels around. The supermarket is now shielded from view by other buildings, though its liveried sign is still recognisable, perhaps four or five hundred yards to the south.

'There's only so many routes he could have taken, Leyton. We need to plot them on a map and get some boots on the ground. Door-to-door, starting with a five-minute radius. And talk to anyone who's out and about either side of twelve.'

'Right, Guv.'

'Better ask his cousin if she knows of anywhere in Penrith he might have had an appointment – something he might have wanted to keep under his hat – doctor, accountant, lawyer.'

'Hairdresser, Guv.'

Skelgill shakes his head unsympathetically at DS Leyton's attempt at wit. Indeed, he falls silent as they retrace their steps, and now seems content with a casual gait – which finds favour with DS Leyton. They become visibly more alert as they reach the betting shop; however, the hypothesis that Barry Seddon might have paid a noon visit begins immediately to unravel: on the door is a sign advertising opening hours from nine a.m.

They enter a plain windowless shoe-box of a room, presently devoid of punters, with plastic chairs lined up against one long wall and a bank of television screens high on the other, displaying horses that race or recover or parade in silence. Overhead, naked fluorescent strip-lighting creates a clinical brightness, though the place is shabby and lacks the modern fast-food feel of the big chain bookmakers, where placing a bet is as easy as buying a burger. Beneath the row of screens, pages from today's *Racing Post* have been rudely fixed with masking tape onto the distempered plaster. Below these is a long shelf, on which are placed at intervals jam jars crammed with small ballpoint pens, and little stacks of betting slips. At the far end is a screened counter, whence a small elderly woman eyes them benignly from behind thick-lensed round-rimmed spectacles.

DS Leyton approaches and makes their introductions. He establishes that she is the manageress and has been running the business single-handed for the past two-and-a-half decades, no less. He explains their purpose and slides a photograph of Barry Seddon beneath the screen.

'Ah hav'nae seen him since April the seventh.'

Her accent hails from across the border, but probably this side of Glasgow; perhaps Larkhall, a hundred miles up the motorway.

DS Leyton is nonplussed. In a case that has so far produced vague intimations and doubtful connections, her reply is bizarrely specific.

'You recognise him?'

The woman nods once, patiently.

'April the seventh – that's over two months ago.'

His intonation infers doubt into the accuracy of her recollection.

'Aye – it was the Grand National on the fifth. He collected his winnings on the Monday. Twenty-fives – not many folk napped it.'

DS Leyton looks a little relieved that there is a less-than-supernatural explanation. With a rank outsider winning the year's big steeplechase, it had generally been a good Saturday for the bookies – and also a reason to remember those few, if any, successful punters.'

'Hope he didn't have too much on it.'

Now DS Leyton sounds sympathetic.

'A ton.'

'Ouch.'

'I laid it off – backed it at thirties wi' *Bettoney's*.'

DS Leyton chuckles. This discrepancy in the odds means a tidy profit, whatever the outcome. He might wonder at this paradoxical situation: bearing more than a passing resemblance to Mrs Goggins from *Postman Pat*, the woman looks substantially out of place in this rough-and-ready establishment; but her cunning replies tell him she is more than up to the job.

'So, after the Grand National – that was his last visit?'

'He disnae bet on the flat – prob'ly willnae be back 'til Wetherby in October.'

DS Leyton glances sideways. Skelgill remains inscrutably silent. DS Leyton gathers that he is to continue in the present tense.

'Does he have any associates – pals he meets here?'

'Not as ah ken.'

'Is there anything else you can tell us about him?'

The woman's eyes flicker, but it is apparent that her attention is becoming divided between the plain-clothes policemen and the five-thirty maiden fillies' stakes at Haydock, which is just reaching its climax on the screen nearest to the counter. Her shrewd gaze dwells only long enough to take in the *1-2-3*, whereupon she seems to relax, suggesting a successful outcome for the house book. She exhales and focuses once more upon DS Leyton.

'He kens whit he's dae'in' – disnae stay to watch a race. Puts on a bet and he's awa' – he's nae one fae small talk.'

DS Leyton nods. He looks again to Skelgill, who gestures with an inclination of the head that they should leave. He hands over his card printed with his contact details. But as he steps away, Skelgill closes in upon the counter.

'You seem pretty observant, madam.'

'It helps tae read a face in ma job.'

'Any new faces lately – last couple of weeks?'

'There's always one or two – we get some passing trade – especially this time o' year.'

'You'll remember if we need to come back?'

The woman grins conspiratorially. She points beyond her shoulder.

'It's all on film.'

She says film in the Scottish way, *fill'um,* and Skelgill takes a moment to interpret the extra syllable. She means there's a CCTV system, though it is not apparent on cursory inspection of the rear wall. After a moment he nods, and begins to back away, raising an approving thumb. Then he, too, grins.

'Any tips, before we go?'

'Tips for in here – or tips for taking money off ma competitors?'

Skelgill laughs. 'Aye – the latter.'

The woman purses her lips and squints. 'There's a lot of interest in a colt running at Newmarket tomorrow – the four o'clock. Anything above threes is worth taking. Y*ou Stupid Boy.*'

'That's got my name written all over it.'

*

'It was good of you to humour her, Guv – about that tip.'

'I'm deadly serious, Leyton – horse with a name like that.'

'My old uncle was a tic-tac man for a bookie – he reckoned only mugs bet on horses with names they liked.'

'Leyton – *You Stupid Boy* – have you forgotten who said that?'

'Er... no, Guv – it was Captain Mainwaring, wasn't it?'

'To?'

'Oh... I get it – *Pike.*'

'Exactly. The mountain, if not the fish.' Skelgill slaps DS Leyton between the shoulder blades. 'Now if you could lend me a tenner, Leyton, I'll split the winnings with you on Monday.'

111

13. DS JONES CALLS

Thursday evening

S kelgill is inexpertly arranging his damp hair, squinting critically into the film of dust that coats a little-used vanity mirror. From amongst the jumble of clothes on his bed his mobile rings. Naked, and rather pale but for his head, neck and forearms, he braces himself with one arm and rummages to retrieve the intrusive device. He frowns at the display, his lips compressed. The bright screen tells him the same caller has tried three times in the past ten minutes. Then he jabs at the handset with his left index finger.

'Jones?'

'Sorry to bother you, Guv...'

'No problem.'

The flat tone of Skelgill's reply hints at something of the opposite sentiment.

'What it is, Guv – I've had some thoughts on the case.'

'Aha?'

DS Jones is silent for a moment; perhaps she has detected his reticence and is recalibrating her approach. Her response is somewhat tentative.

'Well... I wondered – are you free – for a drink... or something?'

Skelgill hesitates. He casts about the room – though it appears for nothing in particular. He picks up an angling magazine from his nightstand and gazes blankly at the cover, which he holds upside down.

'Where are you?'

'Er... outside, actually, Guv.'

*

Only two minutes have passed when Skelgill ducks into the passenger seat of DS Jones's car. His downward angle of entry causes his gaze to fall naturally upon the area of her lap. She has changed out of the daywear in which he last saw her, into a short black skirt with a floral lilac and pink print, and a simple figure-hugging black t-shirt. Her smooth bronzed legs – slightly parted by accelerator and clutch – are naked but for a pair of black open-toed sandals. There is a subtle, but heady perfume in the air, and he seems momentarily transfixed as he settles himself beside her.

'Nice shirt, Guv.'

She says this earnestly, but Skelgill creases his features in reprimand.

'Very funny, Jones.'

The garment, in the style of the season, is one that he acquired with her encouragement.

She beams warmly. It is apparent that he has just showered; from him there is even a competing hint of after-shave. And his smart-casual attire has more emphasis upon the *smart* than might normally be encountered. Not a dedicated follower of fashion, as a rule his gear is generally a good few years behind the times; and he wears unashamedly what is most suitably technical for the task in hand – fishing, motorcycling, fell-walking. Now, in an open-necked short-sleeved shirt, stressed jeans and polished brogues, he looks a shade outwith his comfort zone.

'You were quick, Guv.'

Skelgill harrumphs.

'Aye, well – that depends if we're talking about quick on the scale of male-getting-ready, or quick on the scale of female-getting-ready.'

Ds Jones bats her eyelashes contritely.

'I thought you might be out with the dog, Guv – I tried your phone a couple of times. But as I was driving this way...'

Skelgill shakes his head.

'No need tonight – the neighbour's babysitting her for me.'

DS Jones glances away, as if this fact raises some incongruity in her mind, and indeed Skelgill uncharacteristically supplies further superfluous details.

'Turns out she's a part-time dog-walker – does it for a living. I barely knew the job existed. She's mentioned it before, but I thought she was joking – you know, like people call themselves domestic engineers. She's got an Alsatian of her own – he's taken a bit of a shine to Cleopatra – good company for her.'

DS Jones, her exuberance seemingly a fraction bruised, contrives a grin.

'I hope his intentions are honourable, Guv.'

'I'm assured he's had the snip.'

Skelgill makes an affected shudder, in solidarity with members of his gender. He inhales as if to speak, but then holds in the breath; he stares for a moment directly through the windscreen. He might be expected to ask what has brought DS Jones out of her way (when a telephone conversation would surely have sufficed) – and to turn up at his house on spec – but perhaps he decides such information is now irrelevant. He exhales and slaps his thighs purposefully.

'Have you eaten?'

'Well... not to speak of, Guv – not since morning break.'

Skelgill stares at her with mild incredulity. In his geography of the day's meals, she might as well be stranded on the far side of the Grand Canyon.

'Can you find *The Yat* at Gatewath?

DS Jones closes her eyes and lays neatly manicured nails gently on the steering wheel, as if she is driving an imagined route in a dreamlike state.

'Is that by the motorway, Guv – just off the old A6?'

'That's it.'

'I always get lost around there – you can't cross the river for miles – it feels like you're taking a massive detour.'

Skelgill looks pleased with himself. He taps his temple with an index finger.

'I have an inbuilt maps app. Start by making a u-turn.'

*

Their destination is a smartly whitewashed, low slate-roofed two-storey building with contrasting black window surrounds. It reveals its antiquity as a coaching inn through its worn stone mounting-block, today an inconspicuous seat for a trough of scarlet geraniums. The main door is open and boisterous chatter spills out. They enter to find a cheerful throng, presumably enticed out by the fine summer's evening. There is a mix of tourists and locals: a distinction that is seemingly evident to Skelgill, for he nods casually to expectant faces here and there. In turn the newly arrived couple attract some interested stares as they squeeze through to the servery, with most eyes lingering upon DS Jones. It is difficult to discern if this is because she is in tow with Skelgill, or simply a product of her looks in their own right – but maybe it is a combination of both. This latter conclusion is perhaps reinforced when the comely blonde landlady greets Skelgill with a hawkish leer. Her features are aquiline and her eagle-eye is quick to take in DS Jones, scanning its quarry with a single penetrating yet sufficiently respectful sweep. As her gaze returns to meet Skelgill's it carries a curious glint, both inquisitorial and yet triumphant, as though she is intrigued by the unexpected, and secretly approving of the incorrigible.

Skelgill introduces DS Jones as 'Emma' – which must seem a rarity to her – and she responds with a generous smile. The landlady reciprocates, reaching a hand across the counter, chirping, 'Veronica, alright my love?' Skelgill orders drinks and, while he makes no mention of food, Veronica tilts conspiratorially towards them, dividing her ample bosom with a *Jenning's* handpump.

'I could have saved you that corner table.' She gestures with an inclination of her head towards the large inglenook fireplace. Her accent is southern – she says *tie-bol* – like a moderated version of DS Leyton's, perhaps suburban Essex. 'But I thought the bar might be too rowdy – so I've put you in the alcove in the back room – a bit more intimate. Go on through and Julie will bring your drinks.'

Skelgill nods once, his features inscrutable. He had, rather covertly, sent a brief text message during their journey. He did not mention its purpose and there was apparently no reply. Perhaps this exchange provides the explanation. DS Jones follows him, looking somewhat perplexed; a sight that draws a knowing grin from Veronica as she turns her charms upon some newly arrived prey.

*

'It's funny, Guv – how in the local dialect *yat* means gate.'

Nose in pint, Skelgill raises a mildly interested eyebrow. Encouraged, DS Jones continues to muse.

'So this place is technically *The Gate* at Gatewath.'

Skelgill screws up his face in a comic manner.

'Ivver sin a yow lowp a yat?'

DS Jones laughs at his sudden lapse into Cumbrian. She thinks for a few seconds while she translates the vernacular.

'Ever seen a sheep jump a gate?'

'You do too many crosswords, Jones.'

'Just for mental agility, Guv – it's good brain gym for solving complex problems.'

'My brain doesn't need a gym – it's got a mind of its own.'

She chuckles again. Only Skelgill can come out with these seemingly oxymoronic truisms, stated in all seriousness.

'Anyway, Guv, it beats listening to DI Smart when you're trapped for hours on a stakeout.'

'I'll give you that one, Jones. Stick to your crossword. Especially if it mithers him.'

'You can be sure of that.'

Skelgill appears to approve of her stance, but now he shifts back in his seat as their meals arrive: sea bass and green salad for DS Jones, a hefty portion of home-made steak-and-ale pie for him, garnished with carrots and chunky fries. He has already emptied a basket of its mountain of rustic wholemeal bread, generously buttered, but shows no sign of a diminished appetite as they both tuck in while the food is piping hot. After a minute or two it is DS Jones who speaks, only now taking the opportunity to raise the subject of work.

'I saw DS Leyton's email about the CCTV, Guv. And the betting shop.'

Pensively, Skelgill takes a sup of beer.

'Treat the bookie's as a bit of a red herring.'

'Think the owner was telling the truth, Guv?'

Skelgill shrugs.

'No reason to suspect otherwise. She virtually offered us her own CCTV records. I don't think Seddon was there on Monday.'

DS Jones nods acquiescently.

'Just the supermarket, then, Guv.'

'And not a lot from that, either. Went back to his van. Dropped off his phone and wallet and the newspaper. Then disappeared into thin air.'

'Surely we'll get a sighting, Guv – once we start asking? Especially if he went on foot. It's not as though we're talking Windermere, packed with tourists.'

'Let's hope so. It's our only serious line of enquiry at the moment.'

'Was he working in the area, Guv – or maybe on his way to do an estimate?'

'But why not just park at the building site?'

DS Jones frowns.

'I know, Guv – that doesn't really make sense.'

'Based on the calls we've traced from his phone, last week he had a job at Langwathby. He'd put up a scaffold for a big roof repair at a private house. Looks like that was all his kit out on hire. The roofers hadn't finished on schedule – what with the rain we've had. So he was probably a free agent until they gave him the call to dismantle it.'

'Still, Guv – at least we've got twelve noon nailed down. Quite possibly he was killed soon after he left the store – if you take the mid-point of the estimated range for time of death.'

There is a candle burning between them, its golden flame steady just below eye level. In the low light of the ancient hostelry DS Jones's smooth tanned complexion is dark, and her striking features appear as sculpted shadows and highlights, hinting at an ancient and noble physiognomy. Skelgill stares broodingly at her before he speaks.

'You said you'd had some thoughts.'

DS Jones, too, pauses before she replies, like an explorer coming unexpectedly upon a fork in the path.

'On the case?'

Her question hints at an invitation for him to suggest otherwise. But Skelgill sticks to the straight and narrow.

'Aha.'

Rather distractedly she shifts the untouched rice on her plate to make a space for her cutlery – which she places at five-twenty-five to indicate she has eaten sufficiently. Then she straightens her back and looks directly across at Skelgill.

'It could be nothing, Guv – it's just a minor detail.'

Skelgill frowns, and gestures with open palms to their surroundings, as if to indicate it has brought them here, and she ought to be forthcoming. She leans forward compliantly, lowering her voice a little.

'The post-mortem report on Barry Seddon states that his underpants were on back to front.'

Skelgill is stern-faced.

'You noticed that this morning?'

DS Jones nods.

'I thought I'd wait until I could speak with you.'

Skelgill clears his throat.

'Were you worried Leyton would make a joke of it?'

'Something like that, Guv.'

Her reply implies it perhaps wasn't only DS Leyton about whom she harboured a concern. After a moment's consideration, Skelgill pontificates.

'Truth is – there's nothing unusual about that, Jones. Standard procedure for the second week of wear.'

'Guv!'

She knows he's ribbing her, and indeed now his features relax.

'Then turn 'em inside out – get a couple more weeks' use, front and back.'

'That's an awful thought.'

Skelgill shrugs indifferently.

'If you were marooned on a desert island, why not?'

'If you were on a desert island, Guv, you'd be surrounded by water – you could wash them.'

Skelgill gives a couple of seconds' consideration to this proposition.

'Depends who you were marooned with.'

DS Jones shakes her head, smiling resignedly.

'I think you're proving my point, Guv.' She refers to her earlier reticence in raising the matter whilst outnumbered by male company.

Skelgill has a mischievous glint in his eye.

'Don't be shy, Jones – come a few years and you'll be lording it over the likes of Leyton... and me. You should have the Chief in your sights.' He drains the remainder of beer from his pint pot. 'Okay – so what's your real point?'

DS Jones sips from her water and replaces the glass carefully upon the table. She rotates it and stares into the clear liquid as a fortune-teller might interrogate her crystal ball.

'What if he were dressed *after* he was killed?'

Skelgill places his elbows on the table and intertwines his long fisherman's fingers beneath his chin. He blows softly at the candle, guttering the flame without extinguishing it.

'Continue.'

DS Jones watches the candle recover its form, and then meets Skelgill's gaze with a hesitant glance.

'Guv – if it were a... sex game – gone wrong?'

Skelgill stares at her for a few moments, holding his breath. His eyes are steely and his expression sceptical. Then he sits back and exhales, forcing his breath through closed lips. The candle flickers in response.

'We're looking for a male suspect, Jones.'

Gently her eyebrows rise in a gesture that suggests, 'It's the twenty-first century.' Skelgill is still frowning.

'Jones – *one* accidental fatality – I could buy that. We've had it before. Curate's wife comes home – finds the vicar wearing her bra and knickers, strung up like a chicken on the back of the bedroom door. She can't face the public humiliation – so she calls the verger for help – they stage it like he got snagged by the rope in the belfry.'

DS Jones looks mildly intrigued by Skelgill's imaginative narrative.

'You should write *whodunits*, Guv.'

But now Skelgill is not willing to be drawn into banter.

'*Two*, Jones – two identical, accidental deaths?' He shakes his head. 'Impossible. And both bodies put on blatant public display.'

DS Jones does not appear perturbed by Skelgill's antipathy. She presses her palms together in an attitude of prayer.

'But, Guv – it would explain why the victims show no sign of a struggle. We know they weren't chemically incapacitated. It looks every inch like they let it happen – at least, until it was too late. And in a dark room it would be easy to get the underwear the wrong way round.'

Skelgill does not respond. He watches her delicate hands as she rhythmically flexes them, fingertips together, like a beating heart.

'Guv, I appreciate we have to explain why there were two murders – and why the killer, or killers, put the bodies in the fells – but how else can we account for the actual nature of the deaths?'

Skelgill raises an index finger, as if he is about to respond with a counter point, but then his phone, lying on the surface of the table, illuminates briefly to indicate an incoming message. He glances down and picks it up, but instead of opening the text he drops the handset into the breast pocket of his shirt. He seems distracted and looks over his shoulder uneasily. Then he pushes back his chair and indicates with a jerk of the head that he intends to pay a visit to the washroom.

'Jones – you read the reports more thoroughly than I did – well done for that.' (She nods once, obediently.) 'But remember they also say there were no traces of sexual activity – neither Seddon nor Harris.' He rises, and as he turns away he quips, 'If it's any consolation, Leyton thinks it's a lunatic farmer with a grudge against hillwalkers.'

DS Jones watches Skelgill pick his way between occupied tables and duck beneath a low oak beam into a narrow corridor marked for the toilets. The hint of a frown creases her normally smooth brow. The absence of such forensic evidence, of course, does not necessarily undermine her theory – a fact that ought to be obvious to Skelgill, despite his devil's advocacy. When he returns from the gents' he remains standing, taciturn, and rests his hands on the back of his chair. DS Jones looks up expectantly.

'The waitress asked if we want a dessert, Guv – she recommended sticky toffee pudding with rum butter and double Jersey ice cream.'

Skelgill forces a smile. It would not be like him to eschew this local delicacy, but he appears already to have something else on his mind.

'I need to make tracks.' He looks pointedly at his wristwatch – an anachronism that must be for DS Jones's benefit. 'I told the neighbour I wouldn't leave the dog too late. And she'll want to chat before I can escape.'

DS Jones's gaze falls away, her long lashes signalling disappointment.

'Sure, Guv – it took us less than twenty minutes to get here.'

Skelgill ignores what might be a plaintive invitation to linger. Instead he pinches out the candle's flame, before making his way through to the bar.

*

Indeed it is precisely twenty minutes later that DS Jones deposits her superior on the grass verge outside his house, and slowly drives away.

And it is only ten minutes after that when Skelgill's long estate car slides out of his drive, turns in the opposite direction, and roars off into the darkening night. His chosen route will pick up the A66 westbound, and pass possible destinations such as Threlkeld, Braithwaite and Peel Wyke.

14. LINDA HARRIS

Friday morning

'I got you a Rosy Lea and a couple of bacon rolls, Guv – so we can get a shift on.'

Skelgill tosses his jacket onto the back seat of the pool car, slams the rear passenger door, and slumps into position beside his sergeant. Immediately, he reaches for the brown paper bag on his side of the dashboard and critically inspects its contents. DS Leyton engages first gear and pulls away, ducking towards the windscreen until he finds the wiper control.

'Shame about this rain, Guv – apparently it's due to clear south of Manchester.'

'There's a surprise.'

'That'll be just over half way, I reckon, Guv – journey's about two hundred miles.'

'Warwickshire.'

'That's what I thought, Guv.' DS Leyton has sensed Skelgill's poor humour and is being diplomatic. 'Turns out it's Leicestershire.' With his left hand he indicates a couple of sheets of typed notes that are folded into the central console between two takeaway tea cups. 'Have a butcher's, Guv.'

Skelgill yawns and settles back into his seat. For once he doesn't tuck directly into the motorway services breakfast his sergeant has thoughtfully provided for him.

'Tell me as we drive. How long do you reckon?'

'The satnav's showing three hours, Guv – nearly all on the M6.'

Skelgill, dangling the bag between his knees, closes his eyes. They have rendezvoused at Tebay southbound, subsequent to a lead that developed yesterday afternoon and was conveyed overnight to Cumbria. Among the many responses to the

123

televised appeal for information concerning the deceased persons, one seems especially promising. An anonymous neighbour has identified a 'Linda Harris' (resident of a Midlands town called Hinckley) as the estranged foster mother of a 'Lee Harris' – the latter being of an age to match the description of the reported victim of the same name. Local police have investigated and established that these facts do indeed stack up, and a preliminary cross-check of dental records corroborates the identification. DS Leyton was alerted upon his early arrival this morning. Skelgill proved harder to track down, and it was about eight-thirty a.m. before he responded to his sergeant's umpteenth call. In the background, there had been various indeterminate noises, which could have been birdsong, human voices or perhaps a radio programme. The inspector himself had sounded tired, terse and relatively disinterested.

'I'll take over the driving at Knutsford services.'

Skelgill is still resting his eyes.

'Fine by me, Guv.'

*

'This tea's stone cold, Leyton.'

'You've been asleep, Guv.'

'No I haven't.'

'Guv – we're past Sandbach.'

'Don't wind me up, Leyton – we're still north of Lancaster.'

Skelgill blinks and squints through the windscreen, as if somehow the unchanging motorway stretching out before them will confirm his erroneous claim.

'We've been going two hours, Guv.'

About a mile ahead there is a blue junction sign. They are closing on it rapidly and plainly this will settle the dispute. Skelgill must know the odds are against him. He tries a different tack.

'I only wanted forty winks – you were supposed to wake me at Knutsford.'

'Guv - you were out for the count. I thought it would be better to let you catch up on your kip.'

Skelgill is plainly irked that he has nodded off, and appears to be in denial about any such sleep deficit. His temper shows no indication of having improved, despite his extended catnap, and he now resorts to a sustained bout of swearing, peppered with words to the effect that DS Leyton should not take it upon himself to decide if and when his superior might require a siesta. This irrational argument, doubly unreasonable in light of DS Leyton's considerate approach, rouses the normally phlegmatic sergeant to respond in kind; he is certainly Skelgill's equal in the creative use of Anglo-Saxon terminology, and on this occasion justifiably gives as good as he gets.

Skelgill, of course, is not one readily to admit he is wrong – but DS Leyton has known him long enough to understand that behind his infallible exterior there will lurk a painful shadow of contrition, wishing for a glint of daylight. Thus, while something of a truce breaks out in the form of strained silence – Skelgill naturally having had the last (swear) word – DS Leyton points out that he has placed the brown paper bag of bacon rolls in the cubby box of the central console, to keep them from becoming stale. Skelgill grudgingly investigates, and then begins to work his way pensively through what can only be an unsatisfactory meal, washing it down with the cold tea. Meanwhile, signs for Stoke-on-Trent come and go.

'Decent rolls these, Leyton.'

DS Leyton grunts an acceptance of Skelgill's oblique apology.

'Forty minutes to go, Guv – that's us well into the Midlands.'

*

The Midlands is very much an English as opposed to a British definition, for the actual north-south midpoint of the island of Great Britain corresponds to Windermere in the Lake District, just sixty miles short of the Scottish border. Indeed, Scotland has its own midlands, more generally referred to as the Central Lowlands. That said, the landlocked foxhunting county of

Leicestershire certainly has a claim to being the historical heart of *England*, not least as it sits upon the once great Roman junction known as High Cross, where the ancient trunk routes of the Fosse Way and the Watling Street intersect. These days they are known more prosaically as the A46 and the A5 respectively.

It is just three miles north of High Cross that DS Leyton swings the car briefly from the motorway onto the Watling Street, before immediately turning into the outer suburbs of Hinckley. A former hosiery town, it is known as *'Tin-Hat'* to its locals, who themselves are distinctive for their disproportionately northern-sounding brogue. At a latitude where the Brummie twang might be expected, the ubiquitous greeting for friend and stranger alike is 'Ay up, me duck?' ('How are you, my Duke?'), and the place name itself is pronounced 'Inkleh'; indeed the initial letter 'h' is foreign to most townsfolk. Apart from its friendly, good-hearted yeoman stock, the town itself does not have many claims to fame. In 1834 the original Hansom safety cab was developed here, while almost a century and a half later there was a brief frisson of publicity when one John Hinckley Jnr shot US President Ronald Reagan. Given the unusual shared spelling, there was speculation that the would-be assassin was in some way a descendent of the eponymous settlement.

Ten minutes more finds Skelgill and DS Leyton parked near the older centre of the town, in a long narrow sloping street of mainly red-brick terraced houses dating from as early as 1900, which matches the satnav's designation as Queen's Road. Some of the properties are variously harled and painted; some have low barriers of brick or block or timber enclosing improbably tiny front areas, while others give directly onto the pavement; some have a bay window and others a decorative canopy above the door. Only the satellite dish is an omnipresent constant, but insufficiently so to counteract the overall impression of incongruity. The detectives prise themselves stiffly from the car, and for a moment stand stretching and yawning in the midday sunshine as sparrows chirp unseen from a nearby rooftop. Purposefully, a mongrel dog trots past; while from the sidewalk opposite two small children interrupt a fight to eye them suspiciously.

'Cor blimey, Guv – if this is Queen's Road I shouldn't like to see Pauper's Avenue.'

Skelgill scowls as if to disagree. 'What did you expect, Leyton – the Champs-Élysées?'

'I thought Leicestershire was supposed to be all quaint villages and *tally-ho*, Guv.'

Skelgill moves towards the door of the house.

'Let's hope we're on the right scent, then.'

There is no bell and he rattles the aluminium flap of the letterbox. After a few moments there is the scrabbling sound of a chain being released and the door swings inwards to reveal the dressing-gown-clad figure of a woman in her late fifties.

'I've bin expectin' yer.'

Before Skelgill can make introductions the woman turns slowly, beckoning with her head for them to follow. They see she has a stick with a rubber foot, and she leans heavily to one side as she limps. The front door opens directly into a sitting room. There is a staircase to their left and, on the far side of the small parlour, what appears to be a kitchen. Strains of a local radio station and the smell of a stew cooking percolate from this vector. She indicates with the stick two chairs that back on to the net-curtained window. Skelgill picks the nearest, leaving DS Leyton – after carefully closing the front door – to squeeze past him to the second. Recognising Skelgill as the senior officer, the woman fixes him with a somewhat lopsided stare.

'Like a mash, me duck?'

Skelgill is about to reply – undoubtedly in the affirmative – but the woman continues.

''ow about some snap – I can put yerrup a cheese cob?'

'Perfect, thanks, madam.'

She rotates at the hip, her weight pivoting on the stick, and shambles through into the kitchen. Skelgill looks perplexedly at DS Leyton, but the sergeant spreads his palms and pulls a face to indicate he has no idea what the woman said. The sound of a kettle being filled and the clinking of cutlery emanate from the kitchen. The detectives occupy themselves with looking about, though there is not a lot that would strike the professional investigator as significant: the usual complement of television, coffee table and gas fire; a pair of wooden candlesticks and a moulded brass *three-wise-monkeys* on the mantelpiece; knitting-in-progress and a copy of *The People's Friend* protruding from a magazine rack; and, beside DS Leyton, a square leather pouffe with a round fur stole or hat upon it. DS Leyton absently reaches out to touch the item, and then recoils with a small yelp as it turns out to be a sleeping tabby cat, now awakened. The cat flashes him a malevolent glare and resumes its slumbers, tucking its head out of sight amidst its loins. After a minute more the woman returns bearing a tray. She has abandoned the stick and approaches awkwardly. Skelgill rises to assist, and conveys the tray onto the coffee table. Meanwhile the woman gingerly lowers herself into an upright chair.

'*Branston* alright foryer?'

The proprietary pickle had better be alright, since it is already generously layered on top of thickly cut Red Leicester cheese inside the two large white 'cobs' (local parlance for bread rolls) that she has 'put up' for them.

'My favourite, madam.' Diplomacy aside, Skelgill is difficult to disappoint when it comes to snacking on the hoof.

'There yergo, me ducks.'

The woman leans forward and turns the handles of two mugs of tea in the respective directions of Skelgill and DS Leyton, and gives each side plate a small push accordingly. She lifts her own mug and eases herself back into the seat.

'I just 'ave it black – cozzer me MS – they say it's best to avoid dairy.'

'I'm sorry to hear that, madam.'

The woman shrugs. 'Kern't be 'elped.'

Both detectives gaze at her, momentarily sharing a collective pained expression. The woman is fleshy without being overweight; her pale skin has a sickly pallor that contrasts against a black mop of wiry shoulder-length hair. Her pupils are dilated, making her dark eyes appear deep-set between heavy brows and half-moon shadows, and her facial muscles languid – perhaps a product of her unfortunate affliction. She has the look of one who lacks exercise and sleep and exposure to daylight.

Skelgill reaches for his roll across the hiatus. He takes a substantial bite, catching an explosion of crumbs with his free hand, and simultaneously turning to DS Leyton with an inquiring look. DS Leyton realises this is a cue to speak, and tugs the briefing notes from his jacket pocket.

'Thank you for seeing us, madam – I appreciate it can't be an easy time.'

The woman does not appear distressed, and watches him calmly, if a little unsteadily. He takes this as approval to continue. He taps the sheaf of papers with the back of one hand.

'We've got the details passed on by your local police – that you fostered Lee in 1988 and that he left you in 1994 when he was sixteen. What we're trying to find out is whether there's anything in his background that might help us explain what has happened to him.'

'Din't 'e 'ave a wife or nowt?'

The woman speaks from one side of her mouth; her face is rather expressionless – though her tone is noticeably forlorn.

'We don't believe so, madam. As yet we've not been able to trace any acquaintances other than the people in the motorcycle workshop in Kendal.'

''e always were a bit of a loner. Though 'e were a nat'rel wi' engines – used ter meck a packet fixin' stuff fer folks roundabout.'

'You must have been proud of him – a young kid doing that.'

The woman's eyes flicker between the detectives before coming to rest again upon DS Leyton.

'It were 'is mam as bought 'im to me.' She uses the vernacular 'bought', meaning *brought*. 'It weren't official, yer know?'

'You mean he wasn't officially fostered, madam?'

The woman gives something between a shake and a nod of the head.

'I used ter work in the 'osiery wi' 'er – it were a bad situation she were in – 'er old man were a drunkard – used ter knock 'em about – Lee were startin' to get outer control – she were worried 'im and 'is little sister'd be put in care – she used ter give us a few pounds 'ere and there – but I mainly paid for 'im me sen.'

'What became of the family?'

'They moved away to Earl Shilton and I never 'eard no more of 'em.'

'How far is that?'

'Coupler miles, I shouldn't wonder.'

DS Leyton looks momentarily nonplussed: that such a small distance of separation could constitute permanence.

'What was the family name?'

'Atkins. Lee's mam were called Janet.'

Skelgill has finished his cheese cob, and now he interjects.

'Madam – Linda – alright if we call you Linda?' (Again the woman produces the ambiguous head movement, which Skelgill takes as a yes.) 'Linda – did Lee return to his original family?'

'Far as I know he din't never 'ave owt to do wi' 'em after. Kept my surname.'

Skelgill nods. 'What about with you, Linda – what kind of contact has there been?'

'Last I saw of 'im were in the summer of ninety-four when 'e went to Skeggy.'

'Skegness?'

'Ar.'

'Why there?'

'Reckoned 'e'd got a job fixing dodgems on the pleasure beach.'

'So this was when he was sixteen?'

'Just turned.'

'And after that?' Skelgill opens his palms, and then widens the air-gap between them to indicate whatever extended period she may wish to comment upon.

'Sent me a few postcards – but they dropped off after a while.'

'Were they all from Skegness?'

The woman closes her eyes briefly, and looks as though she is nodding off to sleep.

'Robin 'ood's Bay, I remember – and Appleby.' Her expression fleetingly lights up. 'That's where they 'ave the 'orses, in't it?'

Skelgill smiles and nods in agreement. The annual Appleby Horse Fair takes place only twenty miles from Penrith – although of course there is also the matter of twenty *years* between Lee Harris's flight from his home town and his ignominious coming to rest beneath Sharp Edge.

'Perhaps he'd hooked up with a travelling fair.'

'Lee always loved the fair – they used ter 'ave it in Queen's Park – 'e'd 'ang around fer 'ours watchin' the rides.'

'Did he have any other interests?'

She thinks for a moment. ''e quite liked football – used ter 'ave posters of that Gary Linklater on 'is bedroom wall.'

Skelgill must recall that this Leicester City connection had been mentioned by one of Lee Harris's workmates. However, it is merely a stepping stone to a potentially more pertinent question.

'Was he interested in hillwalking or climbing, Linda?'

Now there is a glint of amusement in her eyes.

''ave yer seen it round 'ere?'

Skelgill nods, perhaps a little reluctantly. It hasn't escaped his eye – accustomed to the vertical nature of the Lake District – that this part of the Midlands, with its sprawling fields of rape and wheat, is about as horizontal as the proverbial pancake. He changes tack.

'What about girlfriends, Linda – did he leave a sweetheart behind?'

'Kern't say as 'e did. 'e were too wrapped up in 'is old motorbike. 'e'd spend 'ours teckin it apart through in the back kitchen.'

'How about his pals – you mentioned he was a bit of a loner?'

''e were a shy lad – 'e got picked on at school – sagged off a lot. And it wun't teck nowt ter start 'im blartin' if I ever told 'im off.' She sighs and shakes her head, a rueful expression troubling her pallid features. 'At 'ome 'e'd 'ave got a good beltin' yer see – an' I reckon 'e always expected that off've me at first. Like a poor maltreated dog, he were.'

Skelgill drains the last dregs of tea from his mug and replaces it carefully upon the tray.

'Is it possible he kept in touch with anyone in the area? Maybe someone connected with the motorbikes?'

'I wunter thought so – if 'e weren't bothered about me – why would he bother wi' anyone else?'

The woman stares for a few moments into her half-empty mug. Then tears well in her sad eyes and silently trickle down her sallow cheeks.

*

'What is it, Guv?'

Skelgill indicates his reason for loitering with a slight inclination of his head. The house opposite to that belonging to Linda Harris is undergoing some renovation. A rudimentary scaffold frames its narrow frontage, and as they watch a bronzed youth wearing only rigger's boots and cargo shorts swings down gibbon-fashion and drops to the pavement. He flashes a gap-toothed grin at the watching detectives and calls, 'Yoright?' before disappearing through the open front door.

'No safety harness. No helmet. Probably no insurance.'

'Small wonder there's so many accidents in the building trade, Guv.'

A crooked signboard advertises the fact that the firm is local – the usual father and sons trade name – though Skelgill seems more preoccupied by the Heath Robinson structure itself, as if he is assessing whether he could scale it bare-handed.

'Think it's an omen, Guv?'

'I think it's time to find that café, Leyton. What did she say, again?'

'Left at the top of the road, cross over, and it's down the first *jit* – whatever that means.'

15. WALTER BARLEY

Friday afternoon

As the detectives run the gauntlet of the Friday afternoon rush that converges upon Birmingham's infamous *Spaghetti Junction*, Skelgill retrospectively decrees that they should have taken the M6 toll or indeed the A5 past Tamworth, Lichfield and Cannock, as if this collective failure of foresight is entirely DS Leyton's doing. Thus ensues a colourful argument over the cause of their current jammed predicament. Meanwhile, back in the calm of their traffic-free Cumbrian constituency, sixty-four-year-old retired agricultural labourer Walter Barley is about to begin a different kind of journey.

Presently, however, he roams distractedly about his cottage. A small border collie, accustomed to various set routines, seems to sense this vacillation, and anxiously trails his master's every move. In the narrow hallway the man spends some moments uncharacteristically checking his appearance in a mirror. He is clean-shaven and dressed in a sports jacket and slacks that are normally reserved for semi-formal occasions (rare though such may be), and which are slightly too big for his wiry but still vigorous frame. His receding hair, mousy in hue, is combed over sideways in the style sometimes known as a *'Bobby Charlton'*, and he leans forward in a vain effort to inspect his thinning crown. Then, when he might normally be expected (at least, by the dog) to unfasten the door-catch and depart, he returns instead to the sitting room, where a laptop is open upon the surface of an oak dresser. He extracts a pair of reading glasses from his breast pocket, and touches the trackpad to waken the screen from sleep mode. A rather lurid image materialises: two scantily clad though masked females titillate an equally anonymous pimply male slave. He stares hungrily at this for some time, his breathing becoming more frequent and faintly wheezy. Then he clicks through a sequence of related photographs, pausing longer on some than others, before eventually exhaling heavily, checking his wristwatch and closing the lid of the machine. On this cue the collie, which has been watching intently (the man, not the screen), excitedly circles the room before trotting into the hall to wait expectantly at the front door. But the dog is disappointed. Its owner, patting his jacket pockets to confirm the presence of miscellaneous personal effects, takes an opposite route via the kitchen and exits through and locks the back door. Against a downpipe leans an old boneshaker of a bicycle, and as its rider freewheels away the forsaken hound is left to watch him out of sight, its snout pressed somewhat forlornly against the smeared pane of the sitting room window.

Walter Barley's Victorian stone cottage squats at the periphery of a straggling farmstead on the lower slopes of Blencathra. A quarter of a mile further uphill there is a main farmhouse, and an assortment of sheds, barns and outbuildings of various sizes, ages and states of repair. Not far beyond these the fences and walls give on to the open fell, where ruined nineteenth century mine-workings tell of a time when ores of barium, copper, iron, lead and zinc were raised from beneath the great mountain. All in all, the quasi-industrial appearance of the whole enterprise is not one that complements the spectacular wild backdrop.

From this locus first a rough track and then a narrow metalled lane leads down to Threlkeld. The topography is such that Walter Barley has no need to pedal as he sails under the influence of gravity towards the village. Threlkeld once lay directly upon the main east-west Penrith to Workington coaching route, and had its own railway station, but today it is bypassed, and the trains, with their regular ebb and flow of passengers, are long gone. Nowadays a quiet backwater, this Friday mid-afternoon sees Walter Barley ride sedately and apparently unnoticed into the midst of the becalmed settlement.

With a squealing protest from his brakes, he grinds to a halt near one of the village's public houses, dismounts and wheels the machine around into the deserted patrons' car park. There is a thick beech hedge running at right angles to the perimeter wall, and he jams the bicycle into the junction where stones meet foliage, largely concealing it from the eye of the casual observer. He returns to the public highway, and the nearby bus stop. He consults his wristwatch, and – although it has now ceased to rain – he chooses to wait inside the rather dilapidated wooden shelter provided for passengers and courting couples.

The weather is indeed clearing from the south-west, as it has been doing progressively during the day across the whole of England and Wales. Shafts of sun are beginning to strike the immense angular bulk of the Blencathra massif, bringing life with light and shadow to its spectacular buttresses. Of these, Gategill Fell towers above the village like an immense russet pyramid shorn of its apex, while a pair of ravens circles above the silhouetted rocky outcrop known as Knott Halloo. Many a walker down the years has alighted at the bus stop and immediately reached for their camera to capture this striking scene, but for Walter Barley it must seem like old wallpaper – for, as his transport arrives, he does not trouble to cast a glance upon the hills that have watched his life come and go.

The bus draws away towards the east, heading for its scheduled stops at Troutbeck, Penruddock, Stainton and Rheged en route to the terminus at Penrith. First it disappears from sight. Then the rumble of its engine fades. And, finally, the breeze disperses the sulphurous reek of diesel fumes. As if he has been waiting for confirmation from his senses of the all-clear, a small boy – perhaps aged about twelve – drops elf-like from the leafy lower branches of a sycamore, crunching the gravel of the car park beneath his new-looking trainers. He casts about – but no soul stirs. Hands in pockets, he saunters casually up to the spot where the rear wheel of Walter Barley's bicycle protrudes from its beech cover. He reaches in and carefully pulls the machine out by its seat. It is large for his pre-pubescent frame, but he confidently mounts and propels the bike in one smooth motion. Now he takes a few turns about the car park, building up speed with each successive lap. On the fourth of these, instead of passing the gateway, he stands in the pedals and rides out onto the road. Then he, too, disappears from sight, albeit in a westerly direction.

*

Having eventually emerged from the choked West Midlands bottleneck, Skelgill and DS Leyton have enjoyed a short spell of relatively open road. However, just when they might breathe easily, brake lights have begun to signal trouble ahead, and it is not long before the motorway is once again at a crawl. On Friday afternoons this Cheshire stretch of the M6 is troublesome at the best of times – as residents of the sprawling Manchester metropolis commute home – but in summer the rush is compounded by an exodus of weekend tourists bound for the contrasting charms of Blackpool and the Lake District. When these forces combine, caravans and all, the great north-south artery becomes inexorably clogged, and radio traffic news presenters resort to the catch-all expression 'sheer weight' by way of scant consolation for their captive audience.

Thus a unilateral decision is taken to bide a while at Sandbach services. Once inside the cafeteria, Skelgill quickly darts away on the pretence of 'saving a window table' (though there are plenty to be had) leaving his subordinate to queue at the counter and obtain the requisite refreshments. DS Leyton's protests that he needs to get home for his own tea have been waved away by his boss, on the grounds that teatime would be spent in a line of traffic. Skelgill argues that they may as well sit out the jam, and resume their journey once it has cleared. As usual, he treats regular mealtimes as an entirely moveable feast, so to speak. In the way of the lone wolf, he scavenges opportunistically rather than when hunger calls.

'The missus'll go crackers if she delays tea and I don't eat it, Guv.'

Skelgill frowns at the two crowded plates of cakes that DS Leyton slides onto the table between them.

'Well, I'll have yours if it's going to be a problem, Leyton.'

As has been witnessed, this is a familiar scenario. Customarily, Skelgill is responsible for placing them in a predicament whence overindulgence might ensue; and, typically, DS Leyton remonstrates about such an outcome. Skelgill then rails against any suggestion that it is somehow his fault, and threatens to consume DS Leyton's portion; at this point the latter generally yields. Unfortunately, his metabolism (and, it must be said, his inactive lifestyle) means that excess consumption tends to head for the waistline, while Skelgill seems ever unaffected.

'I'll try the blueberry muffin, Guv – and see how I get on.'

The hint of a grin creases the corners of Skelgill's mouth. He flaps a hand at the lines of northbound traffic that crawl beneath their vantage point.

'Beats being stuck in that lot – imagine having to put up with this every Friday.'

DS Leyton nods agreeably as he bites into his muffin.

'You should see it round the M25, Guv – when we go visiting the mother-in-law, there's always gridlock – the kids are bouncing off the roof – total nightmare.'

Skelgill slurps at his tea. 'You ought to get her to come up on the train.' Then he notices the alarmed expression upon DS Leyton's face. 'Maybe not, then.'

'Jams it is, Guv – least it gives us an excuse to get away early on the Sunday.'

Skelgill raises an eyebrow sympathetically. They eat in silence for a minute or two, each drifting with their own thoughts, their heads turned to watch the noiseless vehicles below. It is DS Leyton who speaks in due course.

'What did you make of Linda Harris – don't think we got much really, Guv?'

Skelgill shrugs noncommittally and takes a bite of a scone in lieu of replying. DS Leyton is left to develop the conversation.

'Reckon she was being straight about not hearing from him?'

'I reckon she was being pretty straight altogether, Leyton – she's not in a good way – why would she withhold anything?'

DS Leyton is silent for a moment.

'Think we should track down the birth family, Guv?'

'Aye – on Monday, see if we can get the local plod onto it – if nothing else we can get a DNA sample to confirm the ID.'

'Makes you wonder if they'll even remember him, Guv – no great surprise that he turned out to be a loner as an adult.'

'Could fix bikes, though, eh? Spoke his own language.'

'He must have been under age, Guv – if he were riding one himself.'

Skelgill shrugs.

'Stick on a helmet – so long as you look big enough, nobody knows.'

What Skelgill does not add, is that he talks here from experience, having clandestinely 'borrowed' an elder brother's motorbike on numerous occasions as a young teenager.

'Looks like he bolted at the first opportunity, Guv – I suppose when you ain't got no proper home, it's easy to take to the road.'

Skelgill nods pensively.

'His problems started early, didn't they?'

DS Leyton looks momentarily agitated. He sits upright and folds his arms determinedly.

'Think someone came after him, Guv – someone from his past?'

'What kind of someone?'

'Well – I don't want to cast aspersions – but there's geezers among that travelling crowd you wouldn't want to cross – I mean, look at the bare-knuckle fighting, badger-baiting, pit bulls and all that. And we've not long had the Horse Fair, Guv.'

Skelgill is staring penetratingly at DS Leyton.

'Aye – that's all very well, Leyton – but where does Seddon come in? To the best of our knowledge he's been putting up scaffolding all his working life. Why would they be after him?'

DS Leyton looks a little crestfallen. Certainly there is no obvious link in this regard.

'Maybe he owed money, Guv?'

Skelgill looks doubtful.

'In his line of work, he'd be the one that was *due* money – he was a one-man band, remember.'

'What about gambling debts, Guv? There's a lot of unofficial stuff goes on – great wads of bangers-and-mash change hands over horses at Appleby.'

Skelgill grimaces and takes a swig of tea.

'It doesn't fit, Leyton. Where's the climbing connection? Where's the rope?'

DS Leyton suddenly starts and looks momentarily alarmed.

'Cor blimey – that reminds me Guv.' He fumbles for his mobile. 'When I was paying I noticed an email come through from DS Jones – it's about the rope, I think.'

Skelgill pats his pockets.

'Left mine in the motor. Think it's out of gas.'

'Here we go.' DS Leyton licks crumbs from an index finger and wipes it on his shirt. 'Let me just get it bigger so as I can read it. Me old mince pies ain't what they used to be. Comes to us all, eh, Guv?'

'Speak for yourself.'

Skelgill looks at the palm of his hand, lifting it improbably close to his eyes, as if to demonstrate his point.

'Right, Guv – they've got some of the tests back – both pieces definitely from the same original rope – consecutive – the cuts match exactly. The section used to strangle Harris was an end piece, and the one for Seddon a middle piece – you were spot on, Guv – there's some missing.'

DS Leyton glances up, but Skelgill still seems to be checking his focal length.

'They've traced it to an American manufacturer that was founded in 1992 – so that's the maximum age it could be – there's a sample on the way to them to see if they can be any more specific. American, Guv?'

Skelgill purses his lips doubtingly.

'Could be a red herring, Leyton – most climbing ropes used in Britain are made abroad – that's long been the case. Both of mine are Swiss. And they're not cheap, so there's a big second-hand market.'

'Money for old rope, eh, Guv?'

'Very funny, Leyton.' Skelgill allows himself a smile. 'Another thing – if it's a rope that's been passed around, think how much foreign DNA there's going to be on it. I lose some of the skin off my hands every time I climb.'

DS Leyton nods. He scrolls through the message, his features assuming a mask of progressive concern.

'Anything else?'

'That's about it, really, Guv.' The sergeant swallows apprehensively before he continues. 'DS Jones mentions the Chief's been trying to get you for an update – says she's expecting some good news for a Friday afternoon.'

Skelgill's expression becomes one of severe irritation. While the long trip to the Midlands has not ostensibly been productive – like most of the leads they have followed thus far – there is something about his general offhand demeanour that suggests he at least *feels* they are making progress. As he is wont to point out, the knack is to know which pieces of jigsaw belong to the puzzle you are trying to solve – often they come to hand at an early stage, but are simply not recognisable as such. Skelgill's approach to this recurring conundrum is a mystery even to himself – but what he does know is that the connections *will* snap into place: when either a critical mass has been reached, or some unforeseeable catalyst short-circuits the process. Either way, this is not a paradigm that may easily be forced – much to the frustration of his senior officers. The Chief wants results – which is understandable given a baying media pack and a panicking general public – but Skelgill is not a machine but a mere mortal. And, right now, matters of mortality are about to take a turn for the worse.

*

Walter Barley alights at the bus station in Penrith and heads north on foot through the town centre. He seems to know where he is going, and keeps up a steady pace. He does, however, take a small detour to a public telephone kiosk, where he extracts a slip of paper from his wallet and makes a brief call. Shortly after, he passes the supermarket on Scotland Road, and thus approaches the little arcade of retail businesses. He interrogates his watch, and draws to a halt. Rather self-consciously he wanders over to the first of the premises, a newsagent's. For a minute or so he window shops, hands in pockets, but then he digs for change and pushes through the door, emerging a minute later tearing at a packet of chewing gum with his teeth whilst also clenching between his fingers a black comb in a clear plastic sleeve. He pops a pellet of gum into his mouth and then slides the comb from its case. Peering again into the shop window he uses his faint reflection to style his equally meagre hair. Once more he checks the time – but still it seems there are some minutes to kill, for now he takes his wallet from his pocket and flicks through its contents. Then he steps purposefully towards the entrance of the next emporium, the bookmaker's.

16. GRASMERE

Saturday morning

'It's getting like a police state – that's what it is.'

'No worries, Guv – I've got my purse.'

Skelgill does not appear mollified by DS Jones's generosity.

'There's no escape – you can even pay by credit card or mobile. Bloody disgrace.'

DS Jones beams encouragingly. 'Come on, Guv – maybe one day these cameras will catch us a criminal.'

Skelgill harrumphs.

'Pity the rope murderer didn't have the bright idea to come here.'

'Exactly, Guv – think these cameras operate at night, as well?'

Skelgill's features are creased into a cynical scowl.

'Pound to a penny – where there's money involved.' He shakes his head. 'How to make your visitors feel welcome.'

He kills the engine and climbs from his car. He stands for a moment and glares at the number plate recognition cameras that guard the public car park. Gone are the days of the Lakeland stone honesty box. Then he rounds to lift the tailgate and release a relieved looking Cleopatra. The dog tumbles onto the uneven surface, performs a couple of her customary sideways dodges, and then picks up a scent and trots off into the nearby bushes. Skelgill busies himself with his gear, hauling out a jangling rucksack and a pair of walking boots.

'Think we'll need waterproofs, Guv?'

'Is there water in the Lakes?'

Perplexed, DS Jones squints at the largely clear blue morning sky. Skelgill, pulling on extra socks, glances sideways at her – she appears reluctant to take his advice, and indeed she wanders casually away from the vehicle towards the parking payment machine. Skelgill is about to close up the car – then at the last second he reaches in and grabs her cagoule, and stuffs it into one of the side pockets of his rucksack. He swings the heavy bag onto his back and sets off, bisecting DS Jones and the dog, which has reappeared and is mooching about in some long wet grass.

'Walk this way, ladies.'

Skelgill must, however, be in reasonable fettle; as for a brief moment he goose-steps to accompany his command. A grinning DS Jones hurries across to catch up with him, while the Bullboxer falls in a few yards behind.

'It says we pay when we leave, Guv.'

'They'll be taxing fresh air next.'

The country path begins to weave between clumps of willows and alders, and shortly leads them across a footbridge over a wide though shallow stream into sessile oak woodland. From high in the canopy the energetic trill of a wood warbler, invisible to the eye, attracts Skelgill's attention – though he does not remark as they stroll beneath.

'Think Cleopatra will be okay off the lead, Guv?'

Skelgill stares reflectively in the direction of the dog, which has now gambolled ahead.

'Aye – that's why I chose here – no sheep to worry about.'

'Where are we going exactly?'

'There's a decent walk – circuit, more or less – up Loughrigg and back beside Grasmere.'

'Decent for you, Guv – that could be a marathon for me.'

'No – three miles, at most.' Skelgill glowers somewhat woodenly. 'I've got to get back for an exercise up at Honister this afternoon.'

DS Jones seems momentarily dismayed by this news, and perhaps it prompts her to be forthcoming with a question she has put off twice already: first when he called her earlier, and subsequently when they rendezvoused in a hotel car park in Grasmere village.

'So I was wondering, Guv – to what do I owe the honour of being asked along?'

Skelgill does not reply immediately, but stares unblinkingly ahead. Then he jabs at the rucksack with his left elbow, producing a response from its metallic contents.

'I'll explain when we stop for a brew.'

DS Jones shrugs phlegmatically. Then, just as she inhales as if to speak, from around a bend in the woodland path there suddenly appears the incongruous sight of a party of Japanese tourists. It is quite a crowd, and must represent the contents of an entire coach. There is no obvious group leader, and at the head is a smiling couple of student age – although the demographic spectrum stretches from the youthful to the positively venerable. Clutching mobiles, tablets and cameras, they are all smartly dressed, and – blinking and somewhat bewildered by their surroundings – they look more like they have lost their way in an airport concourse and have somehow ended up in the woods by mistakenly following a fire escape. As the human snake winds towards them, Skelgill and Jones step aside onto the raised bank. Skelgill bends down on one knee, and takes hold of the dog by her collar, to pre-empt any over-zealous lunges. Now it seems every last one of the Japanese wants to practise their English, and each goes to some lengths to enunciate a stilted greeting. Trapped as he is, Skelgill looks progressively troubled by this predicament – reciprocating twenty-five or thirty 'good mornings' severely tries his patience. DS Jones, on the other hand, is highly amused, and can't help herself from giggling as each couple insists upon having their hello. But eventually the last one passes and they are able to resume their walk.

'I think they would have liked to take our photo, Guv.'

Skelgill looks relieved that they did not. 'How come?'

DS Jones hesitates. Perhaps she is searching for a diplomatic answer, when the true response might be that they would have liked to take *his* photograph. The combination of his threadbare country attire, rucksack, boots, windswept hair and weatherbeaten features – complemented by the fierce-looking hound – probably confers the appearance of exactly the kind of authentic 'wild' local that foreign visitors would hope to spot in these woods.

'Well – I mean Cleopatra, really, Guv – she's quite a novelty breed, isn't she?'

Skelgill frowns, as though he is not entirely convinced by this explanation.

'So long as they don't dump any litter, they're welcome to photograph whatever they like.'

'They won't leave litter, Guv – did you see the Japanese football supporters on the news the other night – they stayed behind after their match to clear up all the rubbish in the stadium.'

'Good for them.'

'Think England will ever win the World Cup again, Guv?'

This enquiry seems to fall on deaf ears, for Skelgill does not respond, and marches on in a rather gloomy silence. After a minute, however, he stops, and cranks out an arm to bar DS Jones's path beside him.

'What is it, Guv?'

'Look.'

He points to the undergrowth on one side of the path. A butterfly rests in a splash of sunlight upon the filigree surface of a fresh green fern leaf. Slowly it opens and closes its wings to reveal an attractive chequered pattern of pale spots and false eyes upon a chocolate brown background.

'Speckled wood.'

'That's beautiful, Guv – pity we can't show our visitors.'

Skelgill shrugs.

'They'd photograph it to death. That's the trouble when you walk round with a camera – snap everything and see nothing.'

He sets off quickly and DS Jones has to scamper to catch up. The undulating ground begins to rise more sharply now, and for a few minutes they walk on without speaking. Soon the dappled shade of the oak wood comes to an end, and they pass through a gap in a dry-stone wall and out onto a steep fellside, blanketed in rampaging bracken, fern's delinquent cousin. Skelgill sets a steady pace, and while he does not appear troubled by the exertion, DS Jones slips off her cardigan and ties it around her waist. Cleopatra, meanwhile, seems to know that she is in the kind of open country where it is expedient to stick close to her master, if she wants to stay off the leash. After a moderate pull the gradient eases and they begin a traverse of the airy bank known as Loughrigg Terrace. Skelgill pauses beside a bench where the view north over Grasmere is perhaps at its best, but instead of admiring this he cranes his neck to look skywards. An insistent shrieking birdcall has alerted him, and he raises an outstretched arm to indicate its source to his companion.

'Peregrine.'

DS Jones shades her eyes anxiously, but in due course locates the majestic falcon, a soaring, circling, scything silhouette. Then without warning it drops into an arrowing stoop, homing in upon some unsuspecting prey, to disappear behind a shoulder of the fell.

'Wow – that's impressive.'

'Fastest animal on the planet.'

Skelgill says this rather proprietorially.

'How can you tell it's a peregrine, Guv?'

He purses his lips. 'It just is.'

'You're quite the naturalist – you could be a tour guide in your spare time, Guv.'

Skelgill looks askance – they both know he wouldn't have the patience, though his reply is ostensibly at odds with this.

'I've thought about fishing guiding more than once.' But then he sets his features grimly and shakes his head. 'Ruin it, though.'

DS Jones nods sympathetically, her expression sharing his pain. She turns back to face across the valley.

'Amazing view, Guv.'

Skelgill is pensive. Certainly the vista is idyllic, a chocolate-box Lakeland scene, dappled by shadows of wandering clouds; the diminutive Grasmere set like a sapphire jewel amidst green velvet folds of rippling fells. Though twice the size of neighbouring Rydal Water, it is still one of the smallest lakes – a

146

mere fraction of nearby Windermere, whose waters both of these minnows share through the sometimes rushing River Rothay.

'Seen enough?'

Skelgill does not wait for a reply, and sets off once again. Soon he leads them back into woodland, this time more mature and with less undergrowth than down in the valley. A mix of deciduous and conifers, it has that cathedral-like sense of calm, where dust motes float in shafts of light that penetrate stained glass – though in this green-hued arbour it is flies that hover like tiny angels, pinned in space by sunbeams. To pause is to allow midges to pounce, but the heady pine-scented ambiance subdues their urgency, and they amble to the accompaniment of an avian choir: the liquid warbling falsetto of a blackcap, a faltering, chuntering chiffchaff and, high above in a larch, the faintest cork-on-glass soprano of a diminutive goldcrest.

They reach a gate and with a metallic clang the spell is broken. Skelgill digs in his pocket for the baler twine that is now Cleopatra's regular leash. It is tied at each end and he slides it beneath her collar and feeds one loop through the other, forming a slip-knot. The free loop then goes over the wrist.

'Like to take her?'

He holds out the lead to DS Jones, who turns from fastening the gate.

'Sure.'

Their route now runs along a narrow tarmac lane, bordered on the downhill side by a well-maintained stone wall. Periodically they pass a residence – sometimes close to the road, while others are tucked away more or less out of sight – these are a mixture of holiday cottages for rent, and full-time homes for those fortunate enough to lead a life that enables desirability to prevail over practicality in the battle of location. They walk on in silence for maybe half a mile – though DS Jones seems happily occupied engineering whatever glimpses she can of the properties. Soon the view on their right opens out, with meadows beyond the wall running down to Grasmere. Just as they approach a woodland brake that will interrupt this prospect, Skelgill draws to a halt.

'We have to improvise here.'

He inclines his head towards the wall.

'Climb over, Guv?'

'Aye.'

'What about the dog?'

'Pass the parcel. Want to go first, or stay this side?'

DS Jones sizes up the wall. It is about shoulder height to her. Then she eyes Cleopatra. The dog, though medium-sized, is nothing if not stocky, and probably weighs in at fifty pounds.

'I don't know if I could lift her, Guv – especially if she makes a fuss.'

Skelgill grins. He crouches down beside the wall and forms a stirrup by interlocking his fingers.

'Up you go then, lass.'

DS Jones duly gets a leg up, and scales the wall without too much difficulty, despite her tight jeans. However, balanced precariously on the line of coping stones, she hesitates.

'It's further down this side, Guv.'

'That's the slope. Just stay there a mo.'

Without prior warning, Skelgill stoops and grips the startled canine with his long fingers spread on either side of her broad thorax, and with a grunt he heaves her up onto the ridge of the wall. She scrabbles anxiously for a foothold.

'Hold her there – grab her collar.'

Cleopatra is clearly not happy and begins to whine, but DS Jones gets a sufficient grip while Skelgill swarms over the wall – almost as though there is no obstacle. He drops down easily into the pasture. Rising, he swivels and reaches out to cradle the dog, but this invitation proves too much, and she leaps prematurely, striking him full in the chest and pulling a wide-eyed DS Jones with her. As Skelgill begins to topple backwards – drawn by the weight of his backpack – Cleopatra springs over his shoulder and flies a short distance before coming to rest on all fours. But DS Jones's momentum is irreversible and she can only scream and crash onto Skelgill, and the pair of them go down in a flailing, slightly comic, embrace, a landing thankfully cushioned by the long dewy grass.

For a few seconds they lie entwined, and who knows what might happen next – but Cleopatra intervenes, darting in to lick faces that can only have been placed at ground level for her enjoyment. DS Jones rolls away spluttering and protesting – and laughing, too – for she must be able to tell that Skelgill is unharmed. She rises to her knees and balls her fists on her hips.

'You did say improvise, Guv.'

Skelgill pushes himself up into a sitting position. He wipes his face on his sleeve and glares with exasperation at Cleopatra, who is now waiting expectantly on her haunches for the next round of this new jumping game.

'I forgot she was called the canine cannonball.' He manipulates his head between his two hands, as if to check all is in place.

'You okay, Guv?'

'I'm fine – it's the *Kelly* I'm worried about.' He jiggles the rucksack, but seems reassured by the clanking and sloshing of water. 'Mind you, it's pretty indestructible – no moving parts. I've fallen a lot further than that with it on my back.'

'Maybe not with a dog and another person on top of you?'

'The dog's a first.'

DS Jones flashes him an expectant look, as though she hopes he might elaborate. But Skelgill's thoughts apparently remain fixed upon his equipment.

'Anyway – we'll soon find out – I could murder a cuppa.'

He extends a hand and they exchange a grip on one another's wrists, pulling together to raise themselves to their feet. Grasmere lies just a stone's throw away, and meeting the lake they veer in a southerly direction, back towards their point of origin. A sandy path now hugs the shoreline. To their left the water is calm, for this is the west bank and the breeze drifts in from their right. Skelgill's pale eyes dart about, watching the surface for traces of aquatic life. Cleopatra trots along the water's edge, pausing occasionally to lap. She disturbs a small piebald bird from a rocky perch. It bounds airily into a gnarled hawthorn tree. Skelgill stops and shakes his head reflectively.

'What is it, Guv?'

'A pied wagtail – but I was looking at the haws.'

'Excuse me?'

DS Jones's tone of voice is intentionally scandalised, but Skelgill does not play along.

'H-a-w-s.' He spells it out. 'Seems like only last week the May was blooming. Now look at the berries – they're almost ripe.'

'Doesn't that mean we're in for a hard winter, Guv?'

'It's about as good a way of forecasting as any.' He screws up his features contemptuously. 'Where's the barbecue summer the boffins promised us?'

'Actually, it hasn't been that bad, Guv – we had that hot spell in June. And it's nice today.'

Skelgill raises a sceptical eye to the heavens. Although the sun is still shining there is a distinct build up of nimbostratus in the west, and he shrugs cynically.

'Better make hay, then.'

DS Jones raises her eyebrows. Skelgill sees this gesture, but turns and marches on. After about ten minutes' steady walking, they emerge from beneath shady bankside alders onto a broad stretch of pale shingle, extending perhaps fifty yards or so to the neck where Grasmere's outflow, the River Rothay, slips beneath a footbridge. For the time being, they are the sole occupants of this tiny haven.

'A private beach, Guv.'

DS Jones's voice has the ring of an excited child; Skelgill looks pleased with himself for providing such a surprise.

'Can we paddle?'

'I'd have brought my bathers if I'd known you were so keen.'

She flashes him an impish look.

'I could always dare you, Guv.'

Skelgill flinches, presumably at the thought of his underwear appearing on public display.

'I'll leave the water sports to you – I've got work to do.'

He swings the rucksack down onto the stones and begins to unpack its contents. DS Jones picks up a stick and – much to the unbounded joy of Cleopatra – tosses it into the shallows.

This quickly develops into a game of fetch – and it is hard to tell which of them is having more fun. Skelgill observes for a moment, perhaps reflecting that the nimble DS Jones is not so long out of girlhood to have lost this basic hedonistic aptitude – or maybe he considers that she has an unusually good throwing action for a female.

She catches him watching; he pretends to busy himself with firing up the *Kelly Kettle*. He has brought supplies of newspaper, kindling and methylated spirits, two enamel mugs and the requisite components for tea. As the contraption begins to spit and boil, DS Jones skips back from the lake's edge, Cleopatra trotting beside her. Skelgill eyes the dripping canine apprehensively, as though he anticipates a shake coming on.

'You'll be pleased to know I've carried four pints of fresh water – especially for you.'

'What other kind of water is there, Guv?'

Skelgill inclines his head towards the shore.

'Aw, yuck – what about all the ducks?'

Skelgill shrugs.

'It's never done me any harm – it all gets boiled.'

He taps a knuckle against the battered aluminium cylinder and then lifts it from its smoking base. He has drilled the mugs into the shingle to prevent them from toppling over. His *Barbour* is spread out as a crude picnic blanket, and he indicates to DS Jones that she should make herself comfortable.

'You sure, Guv?'

By way of reply he digs into the rucksack and produces a roll of foam, which he flattens into a sit-mat for himself. Next he pulls out a small tin that formerly held a well-known brand of tea, and flips open the lid.

'Flapjack? It's home-made.'

'Thanks.' DS Jones nibbles a corner of the rustic treat. 'It's good.'

'Cheers.'

Skelgill munches a piece himself, and they are silent for a few moments.

'Make it yourself, Guv?'

'Er... no – my neighbour.' Perhaps Skelgill was going to claim the credit, unless asked. 'I took Sammy out last night.'

'Sammy?'

Her question carries a forced inflection, as though she is trying to moderate her curiosity.

'Her dog – he's pals with Cleopatra.'

'Oh – that's right – you said.'

'Whacking great Alsatian – so she claims. Looks half-wolf, to me.' He waves his flapjack wistfully. 'My kind of dog, actually.'

'Poor Cleopatra.'

Skelgill shakes his head briskly, as if to dismiss any suggestion of a comparison.

'She's a one-off.'

As if to confirm his admiration for the quirky Bullboxer he snaps the flapjack and offers half to her. It must be noted that she has shown great restraint thus far – perhaps Skelgill's regime is tempering her penchant for scrounging. He pats her heartily and dips so she can lick his ear.

'There's no accounting for taste, Jones.'

DS Jones observes him contemplatively.

'No, Guv – there's not.'

Absently she tries her tea, but recoils. Made with only powdered milk it is far too hot for all but Skelgill's asbestos-lined digestive tract. She returns the mug to its niche in the shingle and settles back upon the jacket, placing her cardigan as a pillow. The sun is strung between clouds, and closing her eyes she stretches out luxuriously to absorb its warmth. Skelgill's gaze falls upon her trendy plimsolls and slowly travels north: trainer socks encircle slim ankles; white stretch denims sheathe her legs and accentuate their athletic musculature; she wears no belt, and the hipsters are loose about her slender waistline, a glimpse of white underwear revealed beneath; her exposed stomach is a tanned camber where her blouse has rucked, its flimsy material clinging faithfully to the curves of her breasts.

'You were going to tell me, Guv...'

She speaks languidly, with eyes closed, but nonetheless she seems to know she has his attention.

'... what it was you'd been thinking about?'

Skelgill jerks back from his avid study and hurriedly takes a gulp of tea, as though all along he has been drinking purposefully. He swallows, and then he clears his throat.

'The other night – Thursday – at *The Yat* – we never managed to finish the conversation.'

'Aha?'

'Aye – well, it was the sex thing, actually.'

DS Jones opens one eye. Skelgill can have a blunt way with words, especially when he is feeling tongue-tied, and she can be excused for wondering which direction the conversation is about to take. However, he must sense her anticipation, for he quickly clarifies his position.

'I mean – what you said about the killings.'

DS Jones is silent for a moment, eyes again shut.

'I wondered if it were that.' Her tone is a little flat.

Skelgill brings up his knees and clasps his arms around them, and stares directly ahead across the lake.

'If you're right, assuming we've got victims who aren't connected – it suggests they've been preyed upon.'

'Aha.'

'So what would be the possible scenarios?'

DS Jones remains in sunbathing mode. She runs her tongue slowly around her lips.

'It wouldn't be the first time a working girl has despatched a client, Guv.'

Skelgill frowns.

'But how did she do it?'

There is another pause before DS Jones speaks.

'If the customer were into certain sexual practices? You did touch on that, Guv. We kind of got off the subject.'

Skelgill shifts rather uncomfortably.

'But why would you let someone throttle you without putting up a fight?'

'Apparently on the point of blacking out the intensity of orgasm is much greater.'

DS Jones's analysis comes without hesitation or discomfiture – perhaps it is easier from behind the veil of her closed lids, distanced as she is by her disembodiment. Skelgill, on the other hand, appears frozen, either out of embarrassment, or he is held in the grip of the image she conjures. Then he turns to stare at his companion, and for a moment his eyes are wild and seem to be feasting upon her lithe form, supine and vulnerable as it is. The silence prompts her to open her eyes, and she responds with an expression that might be a wave of alarm mixed with an undercurrent of delight. There is a momentary standoff before Skelgill regains his composure and speaks as though nothing has passed between them.

'How would we begin to investigate this?'

DS Jones is silent for a moment.

'What about *Streetwise*, Guv?'

'Come again?'

Now she glances at him in a rather doe-eyed manner, as though she is politely suggesting he is being disingenuous.

'*Streetwise*.'

'Obviously I'm not, Jones.'

She concertinas smoothly into an upright position, mirroring Skelgill's rowing pose. She reaches for her tea, and takes a tentative sip.

'It's the website sex-workers use to advertise their services.'

'That's a new one on me.'

Again she gives him something of an old-fashioned look. She rolls sideways, for a second or two exposing the smooth curves of her buttocks. She slides her phone from a back pocket.

'I'll show you, Guv – if there's enough signal.'

Skelgill has finished his tea, and while DS Jones is tapping away at her mobile he occupies himself by aiming small stones at the *Kelly Kettle*, which stands askew a few yards beyond them. Cleopatra has curled up in a depression in the shingle, but she raises her nose, perhaps assessing whether this is a game in which she should become involved. Shortly, DS Jones passes the handset to Skelgill.

'There you go, Guv – that's just a random girl. One of forty-seven thousand profiles that are live on the UK site today.'

Skelgill blinks and shifts the screen back and forth until it is legible. (His focal length is clearly longer than he will publically admit.) He spends several moments silently browsing. He becomes still, his breath hissing between clenched teeth. His complexion retains its warm hue.

'Doesn't leave much to the imagination.'

'See the menu on the left-hand side, Guv – it lists all the services she's willing to provide.'

Skelgill shakes his head forlornly.

'I don't know what half of these things mean. What's *tea-bagging*, for Pete's sake?'

DS Jones suppresses a chuckle.

'I don't think it involves a *Kelly Kettle*, Guv. There's a glossary somewhere on the site.'

Skelgill squints suspiciously.

'How come you're such an expert, Jones?'

'It was part of the last block of training modules at police college. Prostitution has gone online big-style, Guv.'

'I can see that.'

Skelgill flicks about, perusing the girl's profile to the extent that is possible on an unsuitable small screen.

'This one's got BDSM listed under her likes.'

'Most of them do, Guv.'

'Oh?'

'I think they tick pretty much all the boxes – I imagine it's to maximise income.'

Skelgill twitches as though a fly is bothering him.

'I don't suppose we can search for death by strangulation?'

DS Jones giggles.

'I guess they wouldn't be that up-front, Guv – but we can find everyone who's advertising in the area – even down to which town they work from.'

'Really?'

'Yeah – look, I'll show you.'

She takes back the mobile and quickly taps in the requisite instructions.

'Sixty-nine in Cumbria.'

Skelgill throws her a doubting glance.

'Coincidence, Guv.'

Then she types again.

'Mostly Carlisle. But twelve in Penrith. Three in Kendal. Two in Keswick.'

'Keswick? I don't believe it.'

'That's what it says, Guv.'

'Does it give addresses?'

DS Jones grins patiently.

'On a lot of these profiles, Guv – they won't even show their faces. I expect you get the address when you phone to make an appointment. Not everyone advertises all the time. And they regularly change their identities – clients like new girls, apparently.'

She watches Skelgill closely, but he is implacable in response to this statement.

'That girl you just showed me – it says she's got over two hundred ratings. What's that all about?'

'The punters – to use their terminology – leave ratings. They can sign up as members and get ratings themselves from the escorts. And they can request to be contacted about services on offer.'

Skelgill blows out his cheeks and ruffles the hair at his temples.

'No wonder the missus goes ballistic when she finds this stuff on the husband's home computer.'

DS Jones shrugs her shoulders in an ambivalent gesture.

'I reckon most of these profiles will be fake, one way or another, Guv – people set up false identities just like they do on the other social networking sites. And they'd use an anonymous email address via one of the free providers.'

Skelgill still looks somewhat bewildered.

'You call this social networking?'

'Thing is, Guv – that's exactly what it is. Just a bit more single minded.'

Again she eyes him minutely, gauging his reaction. But perhaps he senses her closer attention, for he rises and trudges down to the water's edge. Cleopatra rouses herself and trots after him, in case a stick-chase is in the offing. But Skelgill stands broodingly looking out across the surface. There is a ripple now, and for the moment the sun has disappeared. Behind him DS Jones shivers, and indeed she lets out an involuntary complaint. She wraps her cardigan about her shoulders. After a minute Skelgill turns and calls back to her.

'Are there blokes on this site?'

For a second she appears a little coy.

'Girls, guys – and everything in between that's legal.'

Large drops of rain are beginning to fall and imitate the rises of feeding trout. Instinctively, Skelgill is compelled to watch for a moment, until he satisfies himself that their source is not piscine. He turns and strides purposefully up the beach.

'We have to consider this.'

'Think we should call in the specialist unit, Guv?'

Skelgill turns his back to her. Then he kneels and begins collecting up the debris of their camp. He glowers, and silently – though rather forcibly – he jams the various items of picnic paraphernalia into his bag. DS Jones seems to sense that she has touched a raw nerve; she collects the enamel mugs and takes a couple of paces towards the shoreline.

'Shall I rinse them, Guv?'

'No need – I'll sort this lot when I get back.'

She hands over the mugs.

'You were right about the Lakes, Guv.'

'What's that?' Skelgill's expression is still one of disquiet.

'The rain, Guv.'

He glances skywards, and then regards DS Jones, as if he has only now noticed the change in the weather. He sweeps his *Barbour* jacket from the shingle and raises it to shoulder height.

'I'd offer you mine, but you'd look ridiculous.'

DS Jones grins rather helplessly.

'I should have listened to you, Guv.'

Skelgill patiently unfastens a side-pocket of his rucksack. Then with a flourish he pulls out her pink cagoule.

'Recognise this?'

'Aw, Guv – my hero!'

She jumps forward enthusiastically, perhaps pleased to be able to give him a positive stroke, and mitigate her *faux pas*. Skelgill reluctantly manufactures a grin.

'All part of the service.'

'You might not be streetwise, Guv – but no one beats you when it comes to being countrywise.'

Skelgill hauls on his backpack and gives her a sideways look.

'Aye, well – let's just keep this *Streetwise* business between ourselves, eh?'

And he marches away along the shingle.

17. GREAT END

Monday morning

'It's the same rope, Guv.'

Skelgill is grim faced. His eyes are bloodshot and their lower lids swollen. His hair is plastered across his brow and rainwater drips from the tip of his nose. Perhaps it is a trick of the light, a combination of the inclement conditions and insufficient sleep, but he looks haggard beyond his thirty-seven years.

'It's another middle section, Guv – you can see it's been cut at both ends.'

But still Skelgill does not reply. Indeed he seems to have little time for the corpse that DS Leyton inspects, down on one knee on the rocky slope. Instead he stares disdainfully at the angry mountain rising up before them, six hundred feet of slick black cliffs that defy ordinary passage and embody the melancholic conditions. Indeed, the lightning flashes emanating from the scene-of-crime photographer's camera serve only to emphasise the forbidding gloom. This is Great End, a mecca for climbers and scramblers, the most northerly outlier of the Scafell Pike massif and monumental guardian of Borrowdale, a locus where Wainwright was prompted to note that *'sunshine never mellows this grim scene but only adds harshness'*.

'Any ID?'

'Pockets are all empty, Guv. No ring or watch. Big scar over the right eyebrow.'

Skelgill bites systematically at his cheek, his eyes narrowing to mere slits.

'When they found Mallory – seventy-five years after he'd fallen to his death – he had a name-tag sewn into his gabardine jacket. Imagine – climbing Everest in a gabardine jacket.'

159

'Nothing that I can see, Guv.' DS Leyton, uncomfortable on his haunches, huffs and puffs and seems not to notice the idiosyncrasy in his superior's remark. He rises to his feet with a grunt and hitches up his waterproof over-trousers. 'I don't like to interfere too much before the SOCO boys have finished. Alright, Guv?'

Skelgill has turned his back, and is gazing vacantly across the mist-wreathed slopes that tumble from their present stance to a small body of water set amidst undulating grass-covered moraine. DS Leyton struggles across the slippery scree to stand beside him.

'Another one of those little lakes, Guv.'

'Tarns.'

'Sorry, Guv – tarns.'

'Sprinkling Tarn.'

DS Leyton nods briefly to acknowledge Skelgill's naming of the dark pool, its surface reflecting the charcoal of the lowering sky.

'Could that be a connection, Guv?'

'In what way?'

'Three dead bodies – three tarns.'

Skelgill sighs contemptuously.

'This is the Lakes, Leyton. What do you expect?'

DS Leyton folds his arms defensively, tucking his hands into his oxters.

'I realise that, Guv – but we've got to find something, soon.'

Skelgill remains silent, and distracted. DS Leyton's plaintive appeal paraphrases the words of the Chief, a biting rebuke telephoned earlier while they were in transit, and which now must seem to Skelgill to echo accusingly about the bleak fellside, and not just in the privacy of his head.

'What's this called, Guv? This mountain.'

Skelgill continues to stare unblinkingly, and his reply is gruffly extruded from jaws set firm.

'Great End.'

'Not for him, eh, Guv?'

'What, Leyton?'

'Not a great end, Guv.'

*

'I thought I did pretty well, Guv – I reckon I'm getting the hang of this hill-walking malarkey.'

Skelgill initially glowers at DS Leyton, but then something about the latter's indefatigable naivety penetrates his desolate mood and he relents with a suppressed, and ironic, laugh.

'Well – let's just hope for some more murders, Leyton – you'll be fit enough for a Bob Graham before the summer's out.'

'Steady on, Guvnor – careful what you wish for.'

This remark may be variously interpreted, but presumably DS Leyton refers to the deaths rather than his dubiously improving athletic prowess. Any such elaboration, however, is pre-empted by the arrival of their breakfasts in the form of the celebrated Cumbrian fry, accompanied by a large chipped teapot to replenish their mugs.

'Actually, Leyton – I think my wish has just come true.'

Skelgill has temporarily commandeered – with the proprietor's blessing – the somewhat antediluvian farm café at Seathwaite. If there can be a happy coincidence under such circumstances, it is that the hillside eatery is the nearest point of vehicular access to Great End, the site of the discovery of the third and latest victim's body. This was almost literally stumbled across at just after six a.m. by a group of climbers from Wasdale Head, and Skelgill and DS Leyton were on the scene – by car and foot – some ninety minutes later. Skelgill had lingered there for perhaps only ten minutes – and thus it is now around nine a.m. The farm track branching from the Borrowdale to Buttermere road has been sealed off, and emergency services vehicles have swollen the ranks of half-a-dozen or so cars left overnight by hill-users; folk who may be wild camping, or alternatively have hiked through to lodge in Eskdale, Langdale or Wasdale. Any such walkers, returning with breakfast in mind, are for the moment disappointed, and find themselves detained in a barn for interviews as possible witnesses – a task that DS Jones has been summoned to coordinate.

Skelgill still bears the visible (and perhaps invisible) scars of what DS Leyton must suspect has been a late night and a few too many pints with his mountain rescue mates. But, as Gladis's cooking begins to work its magic, at least his boss's black mood shows signs of dissolving. On this basis, he ventures a question that is perhaps designed further to ease the atmosphere.

'Like one of my sausages, Guv? The missus forced a round of toast on me – no way I'll eat all this.'

Skelgill accepts the offered morsel with a nod.

'Cheers.'

'Good grub they do here, Guv.'

'The best.'

'I should maybe bring the family on a nice day – spot of lunch – bit of a stroll – now I know the ropes. What would you recommend?'

Skelgill glances up from his plate. Most people like to demonstrate their knowledge when it comes to giving directions, and he is no exception. He points with his knife held in his left hand, and sweeps it to and fro to indicate the path beyond the building.

'Past this place is the main route to Scafell Pike – that's why it's so popular – most of the Three Peaks crowd come this way.' He pauses to take a swig of tea. 'But that's a bit of a trek for young kids. It's a good mile over a rocky plateau from Great End. Probably your best bet's to carry on to Esk Hause, then turn back along the ridge, over Allen Crags and Glaramara – brings you down into Borrowdale village.'

'I'll have to buy the map, Guv – so you can mark it out for me.'

'Don't waste your money – I'll lend you one. If you buy anything, buy a *Wainwright* – book four you'd need.'

'Right, Guv – will do.'

The storm that has ravaged Skelgill's features appears to be subsiding, but now DS Leyton risks a reversion. Rather ostentatiously he checks his wristwatch, and taps its face meaningfully.

'The description ought to be going out on the news any minute, Guv.'

Hearteningly, Skelgill nods without scowling, though he is preoccupied with loading an improbably large forkful of fried foodstuffs, and does not look up.

'Let's just hope someone who's missing him listens to *Radio Cumbria*, Guv.'

'Someone has to.'

'It would fit the pattern, Guv – what with Harris and Seddon both being from hereabouts.'

Skelgill opens his improbably large mouth and devours the forkful, leaving DS Leyton to continue his speculation.

'And this new one – he's no hillwalker, neither, Guv. Dressed like he's set off for church and gone and got himself lost. Could have been asleep, for the way he's lying there – apart from the rope, obviously.' DS Leyton absently aligns some baked beans on his plate. 'Can't believe we keep finding 'em, Guv – reminds me of when it rained fish in London when I was a nipper.'

Skelgill swallows urgently. Any sentence containing the word fish is liable to win his attention.

'What are you talking about, Leyton?'

'Straight up, Guv – one of 'em fell in our back yard – flounder, my old ma reckoned it was, fresh out of the Thames estuary.'

'Sure it wasn't the neighbour having a laugh?'

'No – it was in all the papers, Guv – and it rained frogs in the nineties – you must have heard about that?'

Skelgill frowns suspiciously.

'Supposed to be to do with a tornado, Guv. Sucks 'em up in a waterspout and drops 'em down somewhere else. That's the only explanation.'

Skelgill shakes his head ruefully.

'I've stopped wondering how the bodies get there, Leyton – I just want to know why.'

DS Leyton puffs out his cheeks in a show of solidarity.

'Reckon he was dumped there overnight, Guv?'

'Had to be – Great End was crawling with scramblers yesterday – I passed by myself on a practice run.'

For a moment DS Leyton looks a little wide-eyed – perhaps at the notion that Skelgill so casually visited the location they (or at least he) just laboured to and from.

'Apparently there's folks turning up at the bottom of the lane, Guv – giving PC Dodd some grief because we've closed it.'

Skelgill purses his lips.

'They'll have to wait – though I shan't shut off Gladis's trade any longer than I need to. I reckon once we've identified the owners who've parked overnight we can open it up. There'll be walkers coming through from all directions – we'd need a small army to close off the fells.'

'What did the farmer and his missus say, Guv?'

Skelgill is a long-term friend and – during his youth – was an informal charge of the Hope family, and thus he has already discussed nocturnal events with the couple, Gladis and her husband Arthur.

'They were up at the crack of dawn – heard nothing in the night and the first vehicle to arrive this morning was one of ours – PC Dodd. This job was done in the small hours again, Leyton. Thing is, even if Arthur had been disturbed by an engine, he'd probably just reckon it was someone doing the Three Peaks.'

'Talking of engines, Guv...'

DS Leyton, whose seat backs on to a partially open sash window, twists around to steal a look at an approaching vehicle, its presence announced by a throaty roar.

'Guv – that's DI Smart's motor.'

Skelgill hackles begin to rise.

'What does he think he's doing here?'

DS Leyton peers through the narrow gap between sash and frame.

'He's got DS Jones, Guv – he must have given her a lift.'

Skelgill leans forward over the table, so that he too can get a view and confirm DS Leyton's observation. He is just in time to see DS Jones emerge from the extravagant sports coupé and unfurl a collapsible umbrella. As she does so, DI Smart scuttles around the car and joins her, placing an arm around her shoulders so that he can share the intimate protection afforded by its small canopy. Skelgill sits back down, his demeanour blackening by the second. A few moments later the new arrivals enter the old-fashioned parlour, its atmosphere thick with damp over-garments and the cloying haze of fried food seeping from a kitchen hatch. DS Jones comes first, looking suitably sheepish, and immediately steps aside to admit DI Smart. Ostentatiously he brushes raindrops from his shoulders and glances about disparagingly.

'Not exactly *The Ritz*, Skel – you're like a pig in shit, mate.'

Even by DI Smart's standards, this slur seems designed to wound, a thrust that might invite the observer to wonder what authority gives him such nerve. He takes a few paces around the small room, and slides a paper napkin from a table setting and uses it to dab some flecks of farmyard mud from his trendy pointed shoes. He is informally attired, wearing slim designer jeans and a black zip-up cardigan, and he draws attention to this outfit when Skelgill fails to respond to his opening gambit.

'I'm on a day's leave, Skel – but I'd called in to drop off a report for the Chief – heard Emma needed a *ride*.' He drawls the last word and then pauses to leer salaciously in her direction. 'Saves the Force a few bob, eh?'

He laughs cynically. That his motivation is altruistic is unlikely to ring true with his reluctant audience. DS Jones is still loitering near the entrance, looking as though she wishes she weren't there at all. DI Smart fixes his weasely stare upon Skelgill.

'Murderer's giving you the run-around, eh, Skel? All these places he keeps leaving bodies – I hear you're thinking of naming a hill-race after him.'

He cackles at his own joke.

'It's no laughing matter, Smart.'

DI Smart seems vaguely affronted by Skelgill's unwillingness to play along. His demeanour hardens and he brushes his hands over his slicked-back hair.

'Chief's certainly not laughing, Skel – I had a bit of a pow-wow with her earlier.' He takes another turn about the room, disdainfully squinting at the pictures and flicking at the seventies' curtains. He knows he has their attention. 'I reckon she buys my theory, Skel.'

Skelgill is bristling, his face colouring red from his cheekbones down.

'And what's that, exactly?'

'Sex killings, obviously.'

Skelgill shoots an accusing glance at DS Jones, who stiffens like a rabbit caught in the headlights. But DI Smart can observe this interchange, and all she can do is to gaze imploringly at Skelgill. There might be the faintest shake of the head, a tremor through her shoulder-length locks, but she is unable to utter the words that would deny she has been persuaded to confide her own notion, perhaps en route.

Skelgill reverts to DI Smart. 'Why *obviously*?'

'You've got a homophobic psychopath on your hands, Skel – it's got all the hallmarks.' DI Smart pulls out a chair and sits astride it, facing the back. 'I told the Chief – this'll have its roots in the gay community in Manchester – my home turf, mate.'

Now Skelgill seems to recognise DI Smart's strategy – he is making a play for the case.

'It's a local affair, Smart.'

DI Smart shrugs indifferently.

'Suit yourself, Skel – but I think you'll find I'm being lined up – for when your country lane peters out.'

Skelgill's patience must be wearing dangerously thin. As a man of few words but volatile temper, at this juncture his subordinates can be excused for hunkering down. DI Smart's offensive tactics might be *de rigueur* – most probably he lacks the empathy to appreciate his foul expertise in finding a chink in an opponent's armour and winkling away at it with his stiletto wit –

but to do so in Skelgill's own backyard, so to speak, is certainly risking the incendiary moment.

But such an eventuality does not come to pass, for the shrill ring of DS Leyton's mobile suddenly releases the tension. And immediately that the sergeant responds to the call, it becomes clear from his reaction that there is significant news. He leans towards Skelgill and places a hand on his forearm.

'Possible ID on the body, Guv – farm labourer from over Threlkeld way.'

Skelgill glances at DI Smart; perhaps there is a hint of triumph in his narrowed eyes. He rises decisively.

'Jones – I'll take you over to get started on the witnesses.'

He nods at DS Leyton to indicate they are to depart.

DI Smart remains seated and again casts about the small room.

'I think I'll stay for a breakfast, Skel – leave you local chaps to it.'

As DS Jones pulls open the door into the hallway, she almost collides with Gladis, overbalancing and apparently on her way to clear empty plates. Skelgill grins with satisfaction and winks resolutely at the elderly lady. Then he calls back over his shoulder to DI Smart.

'We've had the last of the breakfasts, Smart – the delivery can't get through until I open the cordon.'

*

With DS Jones briefed accordingly, Skelgill joins DS Leyton, who is waiting in his car, having earlier chauffeured Skelgill down from their meeting point in Keswick.'

'That's DI Smart away, Guv.'

'Good riddance.'

'What do you want to do now, Guv – fetch your motor?'

'Aye – then you get back to your desk and finish these vehicle checks. I'll call in at Threlkeld and catch up with you and Jones later.'

'Roger, Guv.'

As DS Leyton decelerates at the bottom of the farm track, Skelgill winds down the window to speak with the uniformed constable. The rain has now abated and he appears in reasonable spirits.

'Alright, Dodd.'

'Sir?'

'What did DI Smart say when he came through?'

'Asked me if I ever thought I'd get a car like his, sir.' The constable sounds more than a little vexed.

Skelgill nods.

'Dodd – anyone who wants past – take their details and tell them they can go to the café for breakfast – but no further for the next hour.'

'Right, sir.'

Rather than draw away, however, PC Dodd lingers beside the car.

'What is it, Dodd?'

'Er... how's the dog, sir?'

Skelgill squints, clearly taken by surprise.

'She's fine – I've got a dog walker looks after her.'

PC Dodd nods enthusiastically. Again he exhibits a curious reluctance to end the conversation. Finally, however, he steps back, but not without sticking up a supportive thumb to the senior officer.

'We know you'll crack it, sir.'

A very brief and barely perceptible expression of gratitude flickers across Skelgill's severe features, before his normal self-control is restored.

'Aye – like Mallory climbed Everest.'

He winds up the window and the car pulls away, leaving PC Dodd looking suitably puzzled by this cryptic remark.

18. KNOTT HALLOO FARM

Monday, mid-morning

'So it was the sheepdog that alerted you, sir?'

'Well, my wife actually, Inspector. She noticed the beast roaming about. She'd spotted it yesterday and hadn't thought too much about it, but it was still there this morning.'

'What times would that have been, sir?'

'Around nine both days – we have a couple of Herdwick lambs we've been keeping an eye on in the holding paddock behind Walter's cottage.'

'So would that be unusual, sir – for the dog to be out on its own?'

'I should say so, Inspector. In any event it prompted Lucinda to try the back door – and the place was locked up. Walter would only do that if he went away – but he certainly wouldn't have left the collie to its own devices.'

'Was he in the habit of going away, sir?'

'Not especially – occasionally he'd cycle down to the pub in the village – oh, by the way, his bicycle isn't here.'

Skelgill nods, his brow creasing as he assimilates this new information.

'Could the dog have escaped from the cottage, sir?'

The man raises a hand to his chin and rubs the short tawny beard that merges seamlessly into swept-back hair and gives him a lupine appearance. Of roughly an age with Skelgill, medium height and slim build, he is neatly groomed, and sports the familiar country uniform of heavy-soled antiqued leather brogues, smart corduroy trousers (in this case a rather flamboyant purple) and a well-matched Tattersall shirt. His nails are carefully manicured, and Skelgill's gaze lingers on fingers that are slim and callus-free; these are not characteristic of a typical Lakeland farmer. Then again, nor is the clipped public school accent.

'I don't believe so, Inspector. I'll show you around – but when I looked myself I didn't notice any open windows.'

'When did you last see Mr Barley, sir?'

The man hesitates, and turns to stare rather hopefully down the track that leads away from the farmstead.

'Ah – well, Inspector – I was at the Winterton Show all weekend – over in Lincolnshire – travelled up this morning, you know?'

'So your wife was the last person to see him?'

The man nods and in a rather agitated manner checks his wristwatch.

'She said she'd be back by now – she popped down to Keswick for a meeting with our land agent – we're looking at a property over towards Howtown.'

'Ullswater.'

'That's correct, Inspector.'

Skelgill for a fleeting moment appears irked by what – to him – is the superfluous ratification of his remark. He returns to the matter in hand.

'It's important we piece together his movements, sir. Can you think where else he might have cycled to – did he have any friends, for instance?'

Again the man rubs his beard for inspiration.

'Not that I know of, Inspector. Certainly nobody ever came up here to see him, as far as I'm aware. He was jolly sedentary in his habits, now I think about it.'

'Does either of the names Lee Harris or Barry Seddon mean anything to you, sir?'

The man delays his reply, but he holds Skelgill's gaze, as if he is trying to read a clue from the detective's expression. Then he shakes his head slowly.

'He worked for you, I take it – Mr Barley?'

170

That they are conversing in the past tense as far as Walter Barley is concerned reflects an earlier telephone discussion between one of Skelgill's constables and the farmer, which on the basis of physical description appears to confirm, provisionally at least, the identity of the deceased. Now the man looks a little alarmed, as though the idea of an employer-employee relationship confers a degree of responsibility for the tragedy.

'Oh, no – no, Inspector. He hadn't worked at all since before we arrived – he was in receipt of some sort of invalidity benefit. Though one wouldn't know it to look at him.'

'But it's your property – the cottage?'

'That's correct, Inspector. I mean, technically, he was our tenant – but we didn't charge him rent – a bit of an anachronism – stems from the deal that Lucinda's pater struck when he bought the place. Walter came as part of the fixtures and fittings.'

'How did that happen – if you don't mind me asking, sir?'

'Not at all, Inspector. I met Lucinda up at Oxford. Her father had his family pile in Somerset – Lucinda's elder brother is the Earl now – and he was looking for a bit of a project for her. This place came on the market – I had been schooled locally and knew the area – so that perhaps helped things along. Along with the farm there was an outdoor adventure business based here. A barn burnt down and they lost all their tackle – quad bikes and whatnot – the whole enterprise went bust. So his Lordship got the place for a song – but part of the arrangement was that Walter Barley would be able to stay on in perpetuity. I believe he was injured trying to fight the fire.'

Skelgill nods as this tale unfolds, his expression one of careful attention, as if the details fill gaps in his own incomplete knowledge of events.

'But he was just a worker here at the time?'

'So I understand, Inspector. One assumes the former owner took pity on Walter on account of his injuries – in the line of duty, so to speak.'

'What became of him – the owner?'

'I believe he left the district, Inspector – the original selling agents may know – the same ones we use – *Pope & Parish* in Keswick.'

Skelgill bows his head to indicate he has noted this fact.

'And you and your wife have run the farm since then, sir?'

For the first time the man glances rather uneasily away. He casts his eyes across the misty fellside that rises beyond the farmhouse.

'Since 1997 in Lucinda's case, Inspector. She was a couple of years ahead of me at Oxford. I didn't come down until ninety-nine.'

Skelgill follows the man's gaze. What little of Blencathra that is visible beneath the cloud base is a patchwork of bracken and grass, with no livestock to be seen.

'Predominantly sheep is it, sir?'

The man turns to Skelgill, his features still a little strained.

'Not on a commercial scale, Inspector. Lucinda tinkers – we have some rare breeds. She has – you see – well... a private income.' He digs his hands into his trouser pockets, and jangles coins, as though this is a symbolic act to reflect his inferior position. 'My main line is in farm machinery – that's why I was over at the Winterton Show – then I'm due at the *Great Yorkshire* later in the week.'

'What kind of equipment do you deal in, sir?'

The man looks a little surprised that Skelgill is showing an interest. He gestures towards a rather ramshackle barn, its sides tiled with rusting sheets of corrugated iron.

'I can show you, if you would like. I import a weed-wiper from New Zealand. Damn good piece of kit. You can tow it behind a quad. Ideal for these hill farms that want to clean out their rough grazing. Targets the likes of ragweed and thistles – leaves the grass intact – doubles the viable acreage.'

Skelgill nods, a faintly bemused expression creasing his features as the man unconsciously launches into his sales spiel.

'I perhaps ought to have a look around the cottage, first – if you don't mind, sir.'

'Oh, naturally, Inspector – my apologies. Let me take you. Want to ride down in the Defender?'

'I'm fine to walk, sir – if you are.'

'Certainly, Inspector.'

They set off downhill along the farm track, passing more large sheds where weed-wipers are presumably stored. Outside the first of these is parked a navy-blue long-wheelbase Land Rover, with a trailer attached and goods covered by a tarpaulin – a set-up that lends credence to the farmer's story.

'You mentioned you were at school in the area, sir?'

'Oakthwaite, for my sins.'

Something about Skelgill's reaction must betray his recent connection with the eminent establishment. The farmer glances at him apprehensively, and clears his throat to speak.

'Rum deal over old Querrell, Inspector – though I appreciate you're probably bound by protocol to keep mum.'

'That's about it, I'm afraid, sir.' Skelgill nonetheless looks as though he would like to elaborate. 'You knew him, I take it, sir?'

'Who didn't, Inspector? Querrell *was* the school – heart and soul of everything the place stood for. I hear they've gone all international under the new regime.'

Skelgill nods, but perhaps decides he doesn't have anything to add. They walk on in silence for a minute, and when they reach the cottage the farmer leads the way around to the rear of the building. He produces a key from his pocket and unlocks the back door, leaving the key in position. Skelgill steps forward – not impolitely, but sufficiently so as to make his intention clear.

'If you don't object, sir – I'd rather go in alone.'

'Of course, Inspector.'

'Sir, when you entered earlier – did you disturb anything?'

The man shakes his head decisively.

'No, Inspector – all I did was have a scout around – just to check that Walter wasn't here. Lucinda had heard the appeal for information on the wireless – but she couldn't find her key and had to wait until I arrived back. She called me just as I reached Threlkeld, so I stopped by the cottage as I was driving up. I couldn't have been inside for more than a minute. In fact, it crossed my mind that I probably shouldn't contaminate the scene, so it's really just door handles that I touched where necessary.'

'Excellent, sir. And did anything strike you as unusual?'

Now the farmer reverts to the rubbing of his beard.

'I honestly can't remember the last time I went beyond the kitchen, Inspector. Maybe it was a couple of winters ago to help with a burst pipe? Walter led his own separate life. But certainly nothing struck me as odd – the place is all jolly shipshape as far as one can see.' He glances somewhat cautiously at Skelgill. 'Obviously – to your trained eye it might look entirely different.'

Skelgill produces a modest smile.

'I shouldn't bank on it, sir.'

Now from beyond the cottage a sound begins to grow – it is the rumble of wide tyres and the roar of an engine, eight cylinders that announce an important arrival.

'That'll be Lucinda, Inspector.'

The vehicle passes and Skelgill gets a glimpse of a new-plate Range Rover that bounces up the hill track, rather too fast for the conditions, crashing through potholes and spraying water and mud. The two men exchange pained glances.

'Do you have children, sir?'

There is a noticeable intake of breath before the man replies.

'No – we don't, Inspector.' Now the hint of a sigh. 'Thankfully.'

Skelgill diplomatically turns towards the door.

'I perhaps ought to hold onto the key for the time being, sir.'

'Be my guest, Inspector.'

The man gestures with an outstretched palm, and then begins to step away.

'I'll let Lucinda know you'll be up shortly, shall I, Inspector?'

'Thank you, sir.'

*

We don't see salesmen on Mondays.'

An ironic smile threatens to crease Skelgill's severe countenance as he takes his leave of Knott Halloo Farm. Perhaps these words reverberate, or perhaps it is the raised voices that now reach him by some circuitous means – an open window at the rear of the substantial property? Preeminent in this cacophony is the far-carrying war cry of Lucinda, whose terse reception had him misidentified as an unwelcome representative of a feedstuffs supplier. Now he pauses beside his car to listen for a moment, but it appears that the content of the domestic disagreement is unintelligible, for he shakes his head and climbs into the driver's seat.

He has not learned a great deal from the highly-strung lady of the house. While her answers to his questions have not exactly been evasive, certainly the junior officer who will be despatched to take a full statement will have their work cut out to achieve a definitive version. Lucinda's rambling and slightly hysterical account of her movements since Friday – whilst her husband was away – is full of minor contradictions and selective memories. It seems she leads a lively social life, and spent her weekend very much in the mode of society butterfly, flitting from champagne lunch to afternoon *Pimm's* party to evening cocktail bash. Skelgill declined to inquire as to how she managed to conduct herself from one to the next. In the end, he has settled for what he must consider to be the most telling piece of information, which is that she cannot recall having seen Walter Barley since before lunch on Friday... '*...or was it Thursday, now?*'

Skelgill slows the car to a gentle crawl as he approaches the cottage, henceforth untied of its tenant. As he had been led to expect, his search has revealed little. There were no signs of a forced entry, or a burglary, or even a struggle – never mind a murder. 'Jolly shipshape' was an accurate description. He paid particular attention, however, to a scullery area, where the sheepdog formerly had its living quarters (it now appears to have taken up residence with two chocolate Labrador bitches in the main house). Both food and water bowls were empty, and the litter tray showed signs of use – though the determination of approximately how recently exceeded Skelgill's ambition.

A more straightforward observation was the distinct absence of any communications equipment, apart from a telephone. No computer, no modem, no router, no wiring. This may not be considered unusual, except that in answer to Skelgill's question about how Walter Barley catered for himself, Lucinda had indicated that his groceries were delivered – which rather suggests he ordered them online. This, of course, can be achieved via mobile phone – though that is perhaps unlikely for a man of Walter Barley's generation. Nevertheless, he was not known to haul large bags of provisions from the local village store, dangling from the handlebars of his bicycle.

Perhaps prompted by this particular reflection, Skelgill knocks his gear lever into neutral and allows the car to rumble slowly past the cottage. It begins to gather speed, and from time to time he is obliged to brake to control its progress. He continues in this manner for some minutes, and in due course the long estate quietly rolls into Threlkeld. He seems to be in no hurry – indeed it might be a fuel-saving experiment – and he waits for the vehicle to decelerate naturally, where the road levels out at a bus stop outside the first of the settlement's public houses. There is just enough momentum for him to slew into the car park and grind to a halt on the gravel. He sits in thought for a minute, before locking the car and wandering casually across to enter the hostelry.

About forty minutes later Skelgill reappears and, leaving the village in a westerly direction, joins the A66. The first flush of weekend holidaymakers is arriving in the north Lakes from the M6 junction at Penrith. Eschewing a couple of overtaking opportunities, he settles into the steady stream of cars, their rear windscreens jammed with holdalls, duvets and bulging plastic shopping bags. After two miles he swings off at the A591 exit signposted for Keswick and Windermere. It is the former that proves to be his destination, and he follows the general flow of traffic through the town, to park free of charge in a supermarket car park. From here he goes on foot, more briskly now – his regular pace – side-stepping clusters of cagoule-clad visitors who suspiciously eye the heavens and mutter doubting comments

176

about the likelihood of the rain holding off. Skelgill strides the length of Main Street, passes the Moot Hall, and veers off along the narrower St John's Street, with its century-old picture house. Here he promptly disappears into the Edwardian offices of *Pope & Parish*, Chartered Surveyors & Land Agents.

Skelgill introduces himself to the matronly receptionist in his official capacity, and these credentials produce an immediate response that sees him shown through into one of the partner's offices. There is a small brass plaque on the door marked *Reginald Pope, MRICS*.

'Chief Inspector Skelgill to see you, sir.'

Skelgill does not trouble to correct his unauthorised promotion. Instead he reciprocates the hand that is extended across a heavily cluttered desk, by a diminutive if plump elderly man, who rises to greet him with a broad grin. He indicates in a friendly manner that Skelgill should take a seat.

'Thank you for seeing me without an appointment, Mr Pope.'

The man starts, and throws up both hands in a gesture of regret.

'Ah – my apologies – I'm *Parish* – just borrowing my partner's computer. If it's Pope you want, I'm afraid he's away at our Hawick branch, they're having some difficulties over the Scots missives regarding a converted chapel – but I can arrange an audience by telephone?'

Behind round-lensed spectacles there is a natural twinkle in the man's bright blue eyes, and this is perhaps just sufficient to leave Skelgill in doubt as to whether there was an intended pun (or two) in the man's explanation. He plays a straight bat.

'We're trying to trace the seller of a property – a transaction we believe your firm may have handled, sir. Knott Halloo Farm, above Threlkeld.'

Again the man reacts in an animated fashion, an expression of some surprise sweeping across his features, and his left arm automatically reaching out to slide a protective palm over a manila file that nestles among the papers that lie before him.

'I think you may be ahead of me on this one, Chief Inspector – I must confess.'

He stares evenly at Skelgill, though now there is surely a little upward twitch of the eyebrows. Skelgill in turn frowns quizzically.

'I've just come from there, sir – I'm talking about when the farm was sold towards the end of the nineties.'

'Aha, I see, Chief Inspector – let me think now.'

The man retracts his hand and brings it together with his other in the manner of prayer. He lowers his chin onto his fingertips and closes his eyes for a moment, as though he is willing some faded dossier to slip from the dusty shelves of his memory. Then his eyes spring open and his face lights up with an expression of some glee.

'Stewart – Maurice Stewart! If I recall – I dealt with it myself. Had a son called Clifford – he ran some sort of adventure centre from the farm.'

Skelgill looks relieved.

'Would you by any chance have a forwarding address, sir?'

'Quite possibly, Chief Inspector – though I am afraid our records from that era are not computerised – Pope actually keeps all the archives with his *Châteauneuf-du-Pape*.'

'I'm sorry, sir?'

'In his wine cellar, Chief Inspector.'

'Of course, sir.'

'I could probably have it for you first thing in the morning?'

'That would be excellent, sir – though after all this time the likelihood is they'll have moved on anyway.'

'Where there's faith, there's hope, Chief Inspector.'

Skelgill shifts and straightens uncomfortably in his seat.

'Do you recall anything of the people themselves, sir – or perhaps any of their associates? I can tell you that we're investigating the suspicious death of a former farmworker – Walter Barley – you may have heard the news on the radio this morning.'

The man nods to indicate the affirmative. He moulds his features into an expression of helpful concern, though he begins to shake his head.

'It was all conducted pretty much at arm's length, Chief Inspector. And my memory is wearing a little thin.' He rubs the balding crown of his head, as if to emphasise this deficiency. 'Our instructions were to find a buyer fast. If I remember correctly, there was a business liquidation involved, due to a fire – I imagine the creditors would have been camped out all around the elder Mr Stewart once they realised he was going to be in funds from the sale of the property.'

Skelgill's eyes narrow a little, as though his mind is homing in on an emerging possibility.

'There was a rumour of arson, sir – though it never became a police matter.'

Parish frowns and now more definitively shakes his head.

'If one were owed money it would not make a great deal of sense to destroy one's debtors' assets. Repossession is the norm, Chief Inspector.' He resettles his glasses, which have travelled about halfway down the bridge of his nose. 'And if it had been an inside job, to coin the vernacular – to claim against the insurance – then the limited company would have remained solvent.'

Skelgill nods pensively. There is irrefutable logic in what Parish says. He glances about the small office; the walls are mainly lined with bookshelves, though interspersed by certificates of professional competence – albeit these pertaining to Reginald Pope. His gaze comes full circle and falls upon a pile of glossy sales particulars that lie close to him.

'They mentioned at the farm that they were looking at a place over at Howtown – are they planning to move, sir?'

'Oh, no – I shouldn't think so, Chief Inspector.' Parish speaks slowly, as though he is only for the first time contemplating this possibility – although perhaps he is conscious that there is client confidentiality to consider. 'The Howtown property is going to auction in lots – so there will be parcels of land, potential holiday cottages, a main house – even a breeding flock. And there's a nice bit of lake frontage.'

Skelgill's body language must transmit a degree of interest, for the land agent's finely tuned antennae immediately twitch.

'Do you sail, Chief Inspector?'

'Angling's my bag, actually, sir.'

'Good heavens – a man after my own heart – what's your particular calling, if I may inquire?'

Skelgill looks like he is caught on the horns of a minor dilemma – it is in his hands to allow the conversation to drift away from the case.

'Pike mainly, sir – up at Bass Lake.'

The look of expectation that occupies Parish's countenance fades slightly.

'Ah – I was hoping you might give me some advice on choice of flies.'

'For which water, sir?'

'I have a little mooring on Ullswater – only get out occasionally – and I can never work out which naturals I ought to be using. I know one is supposed to slit the belly of the first trout to discover what they're feeding upon – but how, pray, does one catch it in the first place?'

Skelgill does not react to the latest ecclesiastical reference, and instead leans forward with a pragmatic air.

'I shouldn't worry too much about that, sir – just stock up on a few traditional wets – *Peter Ross, Invicta, Kate McLaren* – *Bloody Butcher's* always pretty lethal, any time of year.' Skelgill imitates the action of a gentle cast. 'Or if there's a bit of a breeze and you want to fish loch-style – casting ahead of your drift – use a team of three – say a *Blue Zulu* on the bob, a *Solicitor* on the middle dropper, and a *Black Pennel* on the point.'

Nodding eagerly, Mr Parish scribbles down these names on an envelope that lies nearest to him on the desk.

'A *Solicitor* – there's not such a thing as a *Land Agent* is there Chief Inspector?'

Skelgill chuckles.

'It's a relatively new Scottish fly, sir – word is it's doing really well on the middle dropper. It's good and shiny and sometimes that's just what you need to rouse a fish.'

'It rather feels like you are being more help to me than I am to you, Chief Inspector.'

'Not at all, sir, always happy to talk about fishing.'

'Well – I realise it's a tad early, but I normally have afternoon tea and scones brought in – perhaps you would join me – or would that be holding you back from your investigation, Chief Inspector?'

Skelgill affects what he must calculate is a sufficiently convincing act of being torn between duty and necessity.

'If it's no trouble – that would be very nice – I haven't managed any lunch yet. But I shouldn't like to distract you, either, sir.'

'Not at all, Chief Inspector – please stay, with my blessing. Would you prefer tea, coffee, hot chocolate, perhaps?'

'Whatever's easiest, sir – I'm quite catholic in my tastes.'

As Mr Parish rises to summon refreshments, Skelgill's remark causes him to perform a minor double take, and a mischievous grin breaks out across his lips.

'Touché, Chief Inspector!'

'It's just plain Inspector, I'm afraid, sir.'

*

'Leyton, I'll need to postpone the meeting with you and Jones.'

'Right, Guv – I'll tell her. What time until?'

Skelgill pauses before replying. He is facing the window of a shop in Keswick's main thoroughfare – though it is not his own reflection that distracts him, but the array of fishing tackle laid out before him.

'Er – tomorrow morning, probably – I'll text you both.'

'Oh – righto, Guv.'

'Leyton – Walter Barley might have left the property on his bike – rusty black *Raleigh* boneshaker with *Sturmey-Archer* three-speed gears – get a description circulated – just in case it's not already at the bottom of Derwentwater.'

'Sure, Guv.'

'Anything from Herdwick, yet?'

'Nothing in writing, Guv – I just rang down to him – his assistant says he's doing the PM now – I managed to get her to cough that death occurred at least two days before the body was found.'

'That could be *Friday*, Leyton.'

'I know, Guv – I suppose it fits the pattern, though. Do 'em in and dump 'em later.'

'Eloquently put, Leyton.'

'Sorry, Guv – you know me – call a spade a spade, and all that.'

Skelgill stoops down and peers closely through the plate-glass at a colourful selection of lures arranged in a budget-priced fly-box.

'See if you can find anything on a Maurice Stewart or his son Clifford – previous owners of Knott Halloo farm – sold it in 1997 – where they are now, what they're up to – might have had money problems.'

'Will do, Guv.'

There is a silence as Skelgill further scrutinises the angling fare on offer.

'Anything else, Guv?'

'I'll be in touch, Leyton.'

Skelgill terminates the call, and advances purposefully into the store.

19. SCALES TARN

Monday evening

Jonathan Otley's *Guide book: A Concise Description of the English Lakes, 1823,* is not one to which Skelgill habitually turns, although as he fly-casts doggedly across the mirrored surface of his present location it is a source of reference he might ostensibly do well to heed. 'Scales Tarn, on the east end of the mountain Saddleback, is an oval piece of water covering an area of three acres and a half, its two diameters being 176 and 124 yards, its depth 18 feet; *and uninhabited by the finny tribe.*'

This assumes, however, that Skelgill is here to *catch* such a creature.

When rational analysis has run its course – or perhaps more accurately has become so overloaded by information as to reach a logic-defying log jam – Skelgill can be observed to default to one of his regular displacement activities. Rather like ironing clothes or mowing the lawn, or peeling vegetables or flannel rag quilting, there are some low-intensity, rhythmical tasks that seem to preoccupy one's superficial consciousness and thus facilitate deeper contemplation: 'feeling' for an answer, rather than thinking about it. The poet A.E. Housman was renowned for compositions that 'came to him' whilst taking long country walks, often after a pint of ale at lunchtime. It is said he would bemoan those occasions when he returned home 'empty handed', so to speak, and was obliged to 'think up' the poem for himself!

In Skelgill's case, angling is not generally a pursuit to which he turns in such circumstances. His obsession with the sport, and his fiercely competitive nature, soon sees him entirely immersed in the prospect of outwitting whatever species lurks tantalisingly beneath the water in question. War is declared and all possibilities of subconscious reflection are banished. This might, however, explain why he is prospecting in the 'uninhabited' Scales Tarn – since there are no fish, there can be no such distraction, only the habitual going through the motions.

A related idiosyncrasy in Skelgill's behaviour is his propensity to disappear from the official radar. Admittedly, more often than not his superiors are unaware of such instances, unlike his closer colleagues, who are accustomed to his unannounced abandonment of his post – and the requirement to hold the fort until he reappears. If challenged, Skelgill has a robust defence. He takes few holidays and draws no distinctions where conventional nine-till-five working is concerned (much to the despair of these same long-suffering subordinates). The notion of separate 'police time' and 'Skelgill time' is not one that he recognises. When he set off earlier, it might have appeared to be going fishing in 'police time' – but he would simply argue he is solving the crime, and point to his incontrovertible strike rate. And should he stop 'solving' at five p.m.?

Of course, this unilateral construct would hold little water in the face of a disciplinary tribunal, and a vague appreciation of his renegade attitude among the powers-that-be might go some way to explain his continued designation as 'plain' Inspector.

The improvement in the weather has been continuous during the day, and now the sky has cleared and there is a bare hint of breeze. As early evening advances, the sun drops behind the great bulk of Blencathra (or *Saddleback*, as Otley referred to it), and – while the 'finny tribe' remains conspicuous by its absence – another biting order of fauna begins to make its presence felt: the *Diptera*, largely represented by the Lake District's local variety of Highland midge.

Skelgill employs several modes of protection against this near-invisible menace. A mosquito-hat is one, its full-face veil providing an effective barrier – though equally an impediment to good vision, and certainly to the consumption of any food or beverage. A second is a proprietary brand of cosmetic skin softener, a handy spray that has remarkable deterrent properties with none of the unpleasant insecticides found in most dedicated repellents. Skelgill dislikes the latter concoctions for their ability to corrode fishing line, and their vile taste. Third – and his preferred option for more than just its ability to discourage bugs – is his *Kelly Kettle*. This battered contraption, which is basically a water-filled chimney sleeve, can be fired up in such a way as to produce a robust cloud of smoke. Under calm conditions, such as currently prevail, Skelgill can sit contentedly cocooned, rather like a cuckoo-spit bug, obliging the tiny vampirettes to seek out other fisherman (or sheep) from whom to obtain their blood meal.

Right now there are neither human nor ovine alternatives available, and thus the defenceless Skelgill is forced to beat a retreat and return to camp. Out of respect he has chosen the opposite bank of Scales Tarn from that where Lee Harris's body was found a week ago. He shows no sign that the time spent in the repetitive act of cast-and-retrieve has prompted a solution to percolate from the depths of his mind and bubble at the surface of his consciousness. Though something has drawn him back to this particular locus, rather like a hopeful dog that keeps returning to a spot where it once found a juicy morsel.

Kneeling, he unpacks the *Kelly Kettle* and, as he must have done in identical fashion on hundreds of similar occasions, begins methodically to build a little lattice of kindling. He is about to sprinkle this structure with methylated spirits (an unnecessary, but safe and effective accelerant), when he stops and rewinds the cap of his *Sigg* bottle, leans it against his rucksack, and gets to his feet. Arms folded, brows knitted, he trudges broodingly back to the water's edge. Here he lingers, staring at the calm pool; if he is bothered again by the no-see-ums he does not show it. Reflected before him, a heron beats purposefully overhead, without deviation, confirmation if any were needed that there is no aquatic fare on offer here. Then there is the grey spine of Sharp Edge, mirrored eerily like a stegosaurian monster at rest beneath clear waters. Skelgill stoops down and scrapes up a handful of pebbles, which he casts high in the air. With a rat-a-tat-tat splash the leviathan disappears; ripples form, enlarge and, after a few moments of elegant integrity, intersect to create a sudden maelstrom, as if a small shoal has just surfaced in unison.

This phenomenon seems to be the catalyst for Skelgill to snap out of his dwam. Purposefully he yanks his phone from his hip pocket and scowls at the screen. He shakes the handset and waves it about – but to no avail – his provider does not serve this rocky corrie. He trudges back to his camp and crams the various items of gear into his rucksack. Hauling this onto one shoulder he picks up his fishing rod and sets off around the tarn. When he reaches the little outfall whence Scales Beck tumbles down to meet the Glenderamackin five hundred feet below, instead of following a similar course towards civilisation, he swings left, and northwards, and climbs the path for Sharp Edge.

He is about halfway across the arête when he hears the first incoming text – the network has found him. Carefully he wedges his rod and backpack into suitable crevices, and then he swings a leg so he is sitting astride the crest, aping Wainwright's safety-first *à cheval* method.

Retrieving his mobile from his pocket, he dials DS Jones.

There is no reply. He cuts the call as it transfers to voicemail. He is facing Blencathra; a group of walkers is silhouetted against the powder blue of the evening sky, stick figures that seem with exaggerated slowness to traverse Atkinson Pike. If they plan to cross Sharp Edge, they are ten minutes or so from his position. He looks at the handset, at DS Jones's contact details, as if he is trying to decide whether to try calling again, or use some other means; she will have been off duty a good hour or more by now.

Skelgill watches the walkers; they begin to descend, one by one dropping from sight beneath the skyline, blending with the dusky hill. He turns his attention back to his mobile phone, and makes a second call.

A young woman answers; there is lively pop music playing in the background.

'Hello?'

'Liz?'

'Aha?'

'It's, er... Dan – from Cumbria. The funny looking one – with the daft dog.'

'That's not how I remember things.'

The Welsh lilt gives her voice an engaging cadence.

'Aye, well – the dog's not so daft, I grant you.'

The woman laughs, though a little nervously, and there is a pregnant pause, rather like the one they shared in the flesh at this location. After a moment it is the woman who speaks.

'Well – how are you?'

'I need to see you.'

'Sure.'

There is a further pause, while the ball seems to rest in Skelgill's court. But as before it is left to her to make the running.

'When?'

'Tonight.'

Skelgill's terse response is phrased as a statement rather than a question.

'O-kay.' Her enunciation hints at anticipation tinged with apprehension. 'Where are you?'

'Virtually the same spot that we first met – give or a take a rock or two.'

'But – that's hours away.'

'Nothing my car can't solve.'

'So – what time – do you think?'

'By midnight?'

'I'll have the cocoa on.'

Skelgill hesitates, as though he is about to comment on this particular beverage.

'Liz – there's something I have to tell you.'

*

The route from Penrith to Penarth – Skelgill's journey barring a quick detour here and there – is almost exclusively by motorway. Slicing down England's western flank, it runs parallel with much of the 160-mile-long Welsh border, only dipping into

Cymru for the last thirty minutes or so. While the island of Great Britain comes in size-wise between Michigan and Minnesota, Wales is more of a match with the state of New Jersey, and – as Skelgill once put it to a bemused American tourist who had mistakenly found his way into the Lakes when seeking Snowdonia National Park – it is a small country that punches above its weight in rugby, singing, and beautiful women.

While it seems possible that at least one of these attributes influences Skelgill's motivation, in the early part of the journey, at least, other more pressing needs preoccupy him. Having called briefly by his own residence, he stops for fuel and provisions at a petrol station, and then – in a manner of speaking – pins back his ears. By the time he has driven on the motorway for half an hour, he has committed enough moving traffic offences to lose his otherwise clean licence.

The catalogue of misdemeanours at the wheel would include eating, drinking, texting and internet browsing, feeding treats to a dog, and – not least – speeding, combined with minor incidents of road rage. Ironically, he decelerates to avoid becoming prey to a mobile speed camera, housed in a police van parked on a bridge near the Kendal junction, and flashes his main beam liberally, should the operator be a colleague with whom he is acquainted. Once he has passed beneath, however, and regained his illicit cruising velocity, a related thought must strike him – for he quickly snatches up his mobile and calls DS Leyton's number. It is now past nine o'clock, so – quite reasonably – his sergeant's phone rings through to voicemail; Skelgill is obliged to leave a message.

His chosen path skims past the cities of Liverpool, Manchester, Birmingham and Bristol. As signs for these conurbations come and go, and the traffic thins out, dusk settles into incomplete summer darkness, a deep violet blue beyond stroboscopic motorway neon. Skelgill nods into a trancelike state, his breathing slow and regular, his eyes glazed and unblinking. Behind him Cleopatra, spread along the seat, dreams fitfully, perhaps of small brown mammals.

Yet, as is the way with all long journeys, it comes to an end with a sudden and contrasting finality. Guided by the satnav app on his mobile phone, Skelgill steers his way briskly through the almost-deserted streets of Penarth – itself these days more or less a suburb of the Welsh capital – and slows to an abrupt halt outside a neat three-storey, end-of-terrace house on the hillside overlooking the winking lights of the marina in Cardiff Bay. The sound of his arrival draws the flicker of a curtain, and – by the time he has secured the car and left sufficient ventilation for the dog – the front door is open. A slim figure strikes a feline pose, an inviting shadowy profile against the subdued hall light. Skelgill grins a little sheepishly as he first stretches and then trots up the steps.

'It's a long way to come to see my etchings.'

'That's one way of putting it.'

'I keep them upstairs.'

'Don't I get my cocoa?'

20. POLICE HQ

Tuesday morning

As DS Leyton is about to enter Skelgill's office he notices, through the small gap between the jamb and the door, left a fraction ajar, that his superior is asleep. Slumped over his desk, Skelgill snores quietly. DS Leyton peers curiously for a second or two, twisting his head sideways so as to obtain a binocular view. He coughs in an exaggerated fashion, but Skelgill shows no sign of response. The sergeant is hampered by brimming mugs of tea, one in each hand, and thus is unable to knock. He could of course push through, but that would expose him to whatever mood in which Skelgill chooses to wake. Instead, he backs away and does a careful about-turn. He begins to retrace his steps in the direction whence he came, but at this moment DS Jones appears hurriedly from around a corner of the corridor; loaded with papers, she is heading for the same meeting.

'Ah, Emma – do us a favour, girl – hold these a mo, will you?'

DS Jones looks a little perplexed, but nonetheless she obligingly tucks the papers under one arm and takes the proffered mugs. Relieved of his burden, DS Leyton digs in his hip pocket for his mobile phone. He quickly dials a number, and listens until the call goes through. Satisfied, he winks at DS Jones, replaces the handset in his pocket, and takes the two teas from her. Then he leads the way back towards Skelgill's office. As they approach the door Skelgill's mobile can be heard ringing, and then Skelgill himself scrabbling about and cursing colourfully when he evidently knocks the item onto the floor. As they enter he is retrieving it from beneath his desk, banging his head in passing. He emerges and struggles into his seat, glaring at the handset and paying no heed to the new arrivals.

'You phoning me, Leyton?'

'Here's your tea, Guv.'

DS Leyton is a paragon of innocence, standing as he is with a mug held out in each hand.

'I just got a call from you.'

DS Leyton shrugs.

'Must be my back pocket, Guv – the missis was saying these trousers are getting too tight – I reckon she deliberately shrinks everything in the wash as an excuse to keep me on starvation rations.'

He slides both mugs of tea across the desk for his superior's consideration, and grins self-effacingly about the room. DS Jones looks suitably amused – though this may be due to DS Leyton's clever ruse, rather than the anecdote about his waistline. Skelgill, however, is not so amenable. He rubs his eyes with the backs of his hands and displays all the signs of having gone without a night's sleep – not least it must be evident to his subordinates that he is still wearing yesterday's clothes.

'We need to find Maurice and Clifford Stewart.'

There is a silence as DS Leyton and DS Jones digest this short sentence, and begin to realise it is all Skelgill has to say on the matter.

'We're doing the usual checks, Guv.' DS Leyton folds his arms defensively as he speaks. 'I've already tried that *Parish & Pope* crowd – but they're not answering their phone yet. There's a recorded message that says they open at nine-thirty – I'll give them another call as soon as we've finished here, Guv.'

Skelgill suppresses a yawn.

'What else have we got – top-line – of importance?'

The two sergeants exchange glances. DS Leyton nods to indicate that DS Jones should speak first.

'Main thing is time of death for Walter Barley. Confirmed as Friday afternoon around five p.m. Same cause as the other two; no additional injuries.'

There is a silence, as Skelgill seems to wrestle with the validity of this information. He stares at DS Jones for a moment, but then turns his sights upon DS Leyton.

'What about you, Leyton?'

'Possible sighting of Barry Seddon, Guv – the door-to-door team have found a woman who thinks she saw him in Penrith around noon on the day he disappeared.'

Again Skelgill is mute for a moment. He picks up the nearest mug of tea and more or less drains it in one gulp. He wipes his mouth on his sleeve. Then he glances from one colleague to the other.

'Anything else?'

DS Leyton takes it upon himself to reply.

'I've put in a request like you suggested, Guv – to see if we photographed any motorbikes speeding on the day Lee Harris was killed. Should get a report by twelve. '

DS Jones leans forward in her chair.

'Won't that information be computerised?'

DS Leyton is about to answer, but Skelgill holds up a hand to quieten him.

'Jones – think bike – on the motorway, the cameras shoot head-on.'

DS Jones taps her glossy crown – now she remembers that for reasons of pedestrian safety British motorbikes do not carry front number-plates, and thus are effectively invisible to such speed traps.

'Of course, Guv.'

'Not that he was likely to have any plates.' Skelgill combs back his unruly hairdo with the fingers of both hands. 'What we're looking for is a photo of a biker matching the description of Harris – at least it might give us a clue to where he went.'

'It's a nice idea, Guv.'

Skelgill does not acknowledge DS Jones's compliment, though he picks up instead on the leading point she has raised.

'So Walter Barley died at most five or six hours after he was last seen.' He grimaces with sour dissatisfaction. 'If Lady Lucinda's memory can be trusted.'

DS Jones extracts Skelgill's account of his farm visit from the sheaf of papers balanced on her lap.

'She said she didn't notice the sheepdog until Sunday, Guv?'

Skelgill squints blearily.

'I'm surprised she noticed it all, given the alcoholic haze she inhabits.'

DS Jones scans the details to refresh her mind.

'Could there be something fishy going on up there, Guv?'

'Such as?'

'Well – you mention she called at the estate agents – what if they *are* planning to sell Knott Halloo Farm and they wanted Walter Barley out of their hair?'

Skelgill scrutinises her, but then his attention wanes and for a few moments he stares vacantly at the surface of his desk. It is only with a sudden jolt that lucidity waxes once more.

'Jones – Walter Barley was murdered by the same person who killed Lee Harris and Barry Seddon.'

DS Jones raises her hands in a helpless gesture.

'I just wondered, Guv – if the explanation about the dog wasn't quite the truth.'

'In what way?'

'Well – say the woman – Lucinda – went into Walter Barley's cottage while he was out.'

Skelgill frowns, ready to point to an obvious shortcoming – but DS Jones continues.

'If the dog escaped past her and ran off – she might have lied about having lost her key – to make it seem like it couldn't have been her who entered the cottage.'

Skelgill puts his hands behind his head, interlocking his fingers. He leans back and closes his eyes, but after a moment he seems to think the better of this action – as if he might succumb to the allure of sleep – and visibly rouses himself. He reaches for the second mug of tea that DS Leyton has delivered (an act of thoughtfulness as yet unrecognised).

'If only dogs could talk, Guv.'

Skelgill scowls at DS Leyton's interjection, though the sergeant is not deterred, and he leans forward with a finger raised in the air.

'Oh, Guv – yeah – one other thing about Walter Barley – I got a shout as I was coming up – no mobile phone contract in his name, but there *is* a live broadband supply to his cottage.'

Skelgill folds his arms, as though this information troubles him.

'There was no gear in there at all, Leyton – not even a double phone socket.'

The three sit in silence for a while. Skelgill's eyelids droop with increasing frequency. It is DS Jones who speaks first.

'What if that was why Lucinda went into the cottage, Guv – to remove all the communications equipment?'

Skelgill screws up his face in a gesture of disagreement.

'Then why tell me she thought Barley ordered his groceries online?' He shakes his head. 'This is a blind alley.'

Now DS Leyton rallies pugnaciously to his fellow sergeant's cause.

'But Lee Harris had no gear neither, Guv – and he'd got broadband, too. And the only phone we've found is Barry Seddon's – and that could be because he locked it in his van and hid the key. Something's amiss, Guv.'

Again there is a period of uneasy silence. Eventually Skelgill speaks, though rather unenthusiastically.

'Remind me – what was the computer situation with Barry Seddon?'

DS Leyton looks a little exasperated. 'If you remember, Guv – we didn't find anything at his cousin's place.' He is generous with his use of 'we', given that it was Skelgill who surreptitiously searched upstairs. 'She didn't mention stuff missing. And there's nothing in the follow-up report.'

'Give her a call, Leyton – that Hilda – find out whether Seddon had a laptop or whatever.'

Skelgill glances at DS Jones to find her already regarding him intently; as he absorbs her gaze it is as if she is willing some thought upon him – perhaps one as yet unshared.

Skelgill shrugs his way out of the metaphysical embrace and turns to face DS Leyton.

'What about the push-bike?'

194

'Nothing as yet, Guv.'

Skelgill cranes around to look up at the map pinned on his wall.

'Concentrate on Keswick. Barley couldn't have gone much further than that – and it's on the way to Borrowdale.' Then he flings his hands apart. 'But there's no real logic – given he was lying dead somewhere for more than two days.'

'We're checking all the obvious places – I'm expecting a report back mid-morning – if that's okay, Guv...?'

Skelgill's concentration has drifted again, as though there is some parallel discussion running in his mind that keeps distracting him from the matters at hand – compounded no doubt by his obvious tiredness. But then his office door opens by about a foot and the stoat-like countenance of DI Alec Smart insinuates itself into the gap. Skelgill is suddenly alert.

'Morning campers – alright, are we?'

Out of dutiful loyalty to their present direct report, DS Leyton and DS Jones do not reply, though they are both obliged by weight of rank to return amenable glances. Skelgill is the only one to speak.

'Smart.'

The single word is a plain identification, lacking friendly undertones. But DI Smart appears not to detect any latent hostility.

'Message as I'm passing, Skel – Chief wants to see you – as soon as you've got a minute.'

Skelgill nods grimly.

'We're right in the middle of something.'

'I should stick an exercise book down your trousers, Skel – I reckon you're in for a bit of a spanking.'

He cackles salaciously and leers at DS Jones, brazenly taking in her crossed legs and elevated hemline.

'See you later, alligator.'

The farewell seems to be aimed exclusively at her.

Skelgill waits until the door has been closed and then, one after the other, drains the dregs of tea from his two mugs. He rises and brushes at his crumpled shirt, which has escaped from his trousers.

'Jones – I want you to pick up these various leads.' He holds out his left hand and cocks first a thumb, followed by successively raised fingers as he counts. 'One – the Stewarts. Two – the speed camera files on Harris. Three – Seddon's cousin Hilda. Four – Barley's bike. Five – any more forensics that come up.'

'No worries, Guv.'

DS Jones exudes a confident efficiency that reflects her reputation – she does not need to be asked twice to do something. In contrast DS Leyton looks a little bewildered; perhaps he fears an unofficial demotion is taking place, and that he is somehow being scapegoated for the pressure that is building up on his superior officer.

'What about me, Guv?'

Skelgill strolls towards the door and inclines his head to indicate DS Leyton should follow.

'I need a bacon roll and a double espresso – and I'm brassic till payday.'

'But what about the Chief, Guv?'

'What about her?'

'But... Smart said...'

'Since when did I start taking orders from Smart?'

'No, Guv – not yet, Guv.'

*

'Fifty-nine, Ullswater Place, Guv.'

DS Leyton's reply is in answer to Skelgill's question about their destination – for once the inspector is at the wheel; it seems he wants to leave no trace of his presence at police headquarters.

'That's near the supermarket, Leyton – we crossed the end of it when we walked up Scotland Road.'

'Right, Guv.'

'Was he seen actually in the street itself?'

'I think so, Guv – want me to check the notes?'

DS Leyton makes as if to lean into the back seat of the car to retrieve his faux leather zip-up document wallet.

'Leave it – we'll be there in two minutes.'

Skelgill's favoured transport café is just a short distance from the location, and within his predicted time they pass the supermarket where Barry Seddon's pick-up was found.

'I suppose it *would* be near here, Guv.'

'Aye.'

DS Leyton watches through the passenger window – then suddenly he swings round to face Skelgill.

'You Stupid Boy!'

'Skelgill throws him a perplexed glance; as if he does not quite get what game his sergeant is playing.

'We're in the money, Guv!'

'Come again?'

'We just passed the bookies, Guv – the old lady who gave us the tip – *You Stupid Boy* – it romped that race on Friday – eight lengths. I forgot to tell you – I checked the papers at the weekend.'

'How much?'

'About forty nicker each, Guv – plus the stake money.'

Skelgill purses his lips in contemplation of this windfall.

'I could get a decent new reel for that.'

What he doesn't state is whether he is including in his calculation the ten pounds he 'borrowed' from DS Leyton for his share of the bet.

'Your fishing tackle shop's just opposite Bettoney's, Guv.'

'Might have to pay a quick call when we're done here, Leyton.'

His use of the adverb *here* reflects their arrival at the junction with Ullswater Place. He turns flamboyantly into the narrow street, where those residents that own cars observe a sensible convention of parking only against the left-hand kerb. DS Leyton ducks towards the windscreen.

'Your side, Guv – far end, by the look of it.'

Indeed number fifty-nine is the third-last house in the long terrace. There is no space opposite, and Skelgill steers onto the area of weed-ridden hard standing that fronts a rank of poorly maintained garages.

'Doesn't look like these are in use.'

'Nah – you'll be fine here, Guv.'

They climb out of the car and survey the scene. Opposite the lock-ups is a patch of waste ground, overgrown with creeping thistles and stinging nettles. It is bordered by the modern larch-lap garden fencing of newly built housing, and there is a tarmac footpath between two properties that provides pedestrian access into this estate. An elderly man wanders past, carrying plastic shopping bags branded in the name of the supermarket.

'Handy short-cut, Guv – saves going all the way round to reach the main road.'

Skelgill nods. He locks the car and sets off back along Ullswater Place.

'What's the lass's name?'

'Kelly Smith, Guv – age twenty – local girl.'

Skelgill approaches the property and rattles the letterbox. Clearly audible from within is the distressed wail of a small child, and he has to repeat the action a couple more times before he raises a response. When the occupant does finally open the door she is cradling an infant in one arm, and awkwardly trying to support a feeding bottle with a crooked hand.

'Police, love – you were expecting us, I believe.'

The young woman is tall and attractive, with wide, high cheekbones and pale unblemished skin; though her lack of make-up and damp long dark hair suggest she has not made any special efforts for their benefit. She wears an all-black outfit of ballet pumps, tight leggings and a low-cut vest top. She steps back to admit the officers. There is something of the bashful schoolgirl about her, waiting outside the Head's office for a reprimand of unknown severity.

'Aye, come in – sorry about the mess.'

She lowers her gaze as they squeeze by, whereas in contrast the closely matching pair of large brown eyes of the baby knowingly observes their passage. In the absence of any instructions to the contrary, Skelgill leads the way directly ahead into a small, shabby kitchen, where there is a *Formica*-topped table and four chairs, plus a high chair. On the table is a baby changing mat with a sealed-up disposable nappy and a tube of cream. Nostrils twitching, Skelgill takes the initiative and at arm's length rather gingerly lifts the mat down onto the floor, as DS Leyton eyes him with some amusement.

'Alright here, love?'

The girl nods a little apprehensively. She seems quite shy, and does not offer them tea or coffee – although perhaps this is a generational failing, such protocols somewhere having slipped from convention. Instead she concentrates on keeping the baby sucking at its bottle, which – given the din it was making a moment earlier – is perhaps a better use of her abridged domestic skills.

'We won't detain you a minute, love – can I call you Kelly?'

Again she nods rather than speaks.

'You've identified a person whose movements we've been trying to trace.' (At this she looks even more fearful, as if upon her youthful say-so the outcome of some great legal case hinges.) 'I'd just like you to tell us again what you saw, Kelly.'

She shifts in her seat and juggles the baby into a more stable position. In doing so she presses it against her bosom and emphasises the shadow of her cleavage between the milky flesh of the exposed tops of her breasts. DS Leyton pointedly averts his gaze, to flick through his notebook, though Skelgill seems not so easily deterred.

'It weren't much.' She shakes her head, though perhaps this is simply to displace strands of hair that have fallen across her face. 'I were just pushing the buggy along and he were coming towards me.'

'What made you notice him?'

'He were smoking – and I don't like the baby near smoke – she had a bad chest infection all winter and right up to last month.'

'And what happened?'

'It's a double-buggy I've got – it takes up all the pavement – and I were a bit late and I remember thinking I was in the way – then he moved off the kerb to let me past.'

'Did either of you speak?'

'I just said thanks – he didn't answer me.'

'How did he seem?'

'I thought he were a bit old to be wearing a hoodie – he had the hood up, like.'

'What about his behaviour, I mean – did he appear happy or sad or relaxed or worried?'

The girl looks up from the baby. Her own large dark eyes flick between Skelgill and DS Leyton, as if she is searching for some cue from real faces that will help her answer this question.

'Probably he were just thinking – like you do when you're walking about.'

Skelgill nods pensively.

'After he passed you – did you see what he did?'

She shakes her head.

'I didn't look back.' Her body language is suggestive of some culpability, and she huddles protectively over the baby. 'I had no reason to suspect owt – that I should watch him, like.'

'Not to worry, love – that's our job.' Skelgill reassuringly indicates to himself and DS Leyton. 'Can you remember where in the street you passed one another?'

'I'd only just gone out – maybe five or six doors down.'

Skelgill nods encouragingly.

'And you didn't see him pay any attention to a particular house?'

At this she shakes her head decisively.

Skelgill glances at DS Leyton, who is taking ponderous notes in his neat though elementary hand.

'And the time, Kelly – you told our constable it was twelve o'clock? That's very precise.'

Suddenly her eyes brighten, as though this is something about which she is more confident.

'I have to collect Jordan – her brother.' She nods towards the baby. 'He's at nursery, mornings nine till twelve – and like I said

I were a bit late last Monday because I'd had to wake Jade. It's only two minutes round the corner but they like you to be there before twelve.'

'And you weren't?'

'It were just – like – a minute to – when I left here.'

There is a large, rather cheap-looking clock on the kitchen wall, and Skelgill follows the girl's glance up to this. He checks it against his own watch and nods, seemingly satisfied.

'This man, Kelly – he was a complete stranger to you?'

Again there is a hint of self-reproach that clouds her expression, a little vertical crease forming between the curves of her eyebrows.

'There's lots of folk use that ginnel – since they built them new houses. And we've only been here since February.'

Skelgill nods, and manufactures an understanding smile. Then he places his palms flat on the table in a gesture of conclusion, and pushes himself to his feet. Immediately the girl's shoulders relax and she gazes benignly at the baby, who has now drained the bottle and dozes contentedly. Skelgill, too, seems intrigued by this vision.

'Amazing what a drop of gin can do, eh?'

The girl glances up at him – perhaps she is not sure if he is joking, although there is a conspiratorial glint in her eye, as though he has hit upon some mother's secret.

'I must try it on my sergeant some time.'

He steps away from the table, followed by DS Leyton, who grins and tries to look suitably sheepish. Skelgill drops his voice to something of a whisper.

'Thanks for your help, Kelly – you've been very cooperative – we can see ourselves out, love.'

*

'Nice kid, Leyton.'

'Difficult not to cop an eyeful, though, eh Guv?'

'Behave, Leyton – anyway, I meant the baby.'

DS Leyton glances suspiciously at Skelgill, whom he must have noticed was not entirely unmoved by the spectacle of the young woman's breasts; in any event, Skelgill is surely the last person to comment favourably about a baby.

'Where are we going, Guv?'

Skelgill has set off in the opposite direction from where their car is parked.

'The bookie's – you stupid boy – round the corner.'

'But – Guv – we put the bet on at Bettoney's.'

Skelgill shrugs off this protest.

'To say thanks.' He grins back at DS Leyton. 'We might even scrounge a cuppa – seeing as Kelly didn't put the kettle on.'

DS Leyton, who has fallen a couple paces behind, scuttles to catch up. He fails to appreciate Skelgill's self-indulgent irony.

'What do you reckon he was doing in this street, Guv?'

Skelgill shakes his head.

'Your guess is as good as mine, Leyton – I need to look at a map to see why you might use that ginnel.'

'Thing is, Guv, the parking's free – and I bet there's always spaces. If you were visiting a house on that new estate and didn't want to leave your motor outside, this would be a handy spot.'

'So?'

'So why park at the supermarket?'

Skelgill nods pensively, and remains in silent thought for a few moments; plainly the parking conundrum troubles him: it might be highly significant, or it could be of no importance whatsoever. He stops and looks about. Certainly DS Leyton is correct in that about half of the available kerbside is currently clear of vehicles. This is not an affluent postcode, and car ownership is evidently patchy; indeed, the modest and dated models on display reflect the limited means of local residents. The red brick back-to-backs have seen better days, and in places weeds spring from cracks in the walls. Skelgill notices a family of starlings, slick iridescent adults and their drab loutish juveniles, picking over litter and discarded cigarette ends in the gutter.

'What about the door-to-door checks in this street, Leyton?'

DS Leyton puffs out his cheeks and shakes his head dejectedly.

'Not a great strike rate, Guv – it's not so easy finding folks at home – especially this time of year. Spoken to about two-thirds of 'em so far.'

Skelgill nods grimly.

'We should redouble our efforts here – especially the high numbers – and then that estate.'

'Definitely, Guv.'

They round the corner of Ullswater Place; the bookmaker's shop is just half a minute further, towards the supermarket. Their opening of the door sets off an electronic alert, and the proprietor – the elderly Scotswoman – glances around in surprise; perhaps it is still a little early for her trade to begin. She is busy in the customer area, rearranging the jars of pens and stacks of betting slips. Along with a reel of masking tape and scissors, on a central table there are two copies of the *Racing Post* that she must be about to display page-by-page upon the walls. Though her features remain implacable she recognises the detectives.

'I hope ye put that bet on.'

Skelgill grins.

'Aye, we did, love – though we're keeping it quiet – don't want you overrun by CID.'

'You'd be surprised by how many I ken already.'

Skelgill raises his eyebrows in mock disapproval, and then his gaze casually falls upon a half-drunk mug of tea that also rests upon the table. The woman follows his eyes.

'Like a wee brew?'

'If you've got a minute.'

She grins, rather toothlessly, it must be said, and inclines her head towards the newspapers.

'Aye – nae bother – but see those papers – just the job for big fellas like youse, eh?'

Skelgill chuckles. Though he stands only a couple of inches above average height, and Leyton a similar measure below, it is plain that the diminutive woman must strain to perform this daily task – presumably with the aid of one of the plastic chairs reserved for punters.

'It's a deal. Come on, Leyton – you're the one supposed to have bookie's blood in your veins.'

While the detectives set about working to their strengths – DS Leyton patiently separating and tearing the sheets and Skelgill rather roughly taping and affixing them – the woman disappears through a door beyond the security screen.

'Imagine if the Chief came in and found us doing this, Guv.'

'Imagine if the Chief came in, full stop, Leyton – I think the moral high ground would be ours.'

'Right enough, Guv.' He clears his throat and evidently decides to take this opportunity to raise a question that has surely been nagging at him. 'Think she *is* threatening to pass it over to DI Smart, Guv?'

Skelgill stiffens in the act of stretching a taped page across its designated space. Certainly there is no hiding from the fact that they have no clear line of enquiry, while the case threatens to spiral out of control – if it has not done so already. Right now he is putting off the evil moment when he must confront his superior virtually empty handed. Perhaps it is an apposite metaphor that sees him presently pinning faint hopes upon a distempered wall. He sets his jaw determinedly.

'It's the classic Smart wind-up.' But his tone does not carry much conviction. 'Anyway, less talk of the Chief.'

'Sorry, Guv.' DS Leyton turns back to the table and peels off the next page. 'Here's the start of Wolverhampton, Guv – evening meeting on the all-weather, mostly handicaps, two-year-olds.'

Skelgill frowns suspiciously, as if he suspects DS Leyton knows more about the sport of kings than he has hitherto revealed. They finish the wallpapering just as the woman returns with their hot drinks, her own mug convivially recharged. She places a small round tray on the table and casts about to assess their handiwork.

'That'll pass – call in every morning, if you like.'

'Give us a few more tips like that last one and we might.'

The woman begins to drag a couple of chairs towards the table, but DS Leyton dodges across to intercept. When they are all seated, Skelgill scratches his head in an apologetic though rather affected manner.

'One of our boys probably came in showing you a couple of photos.'

The woman nods over her mug.

'Aye – the chap you showed me, and a younger yin I didnae ken.'

Skelgill nods and sips his tea, more decorously than is his habit. He looks at DS Leyton, and then at the document wallet that lies beside him on the table. But before he can speak the woman perhaps guesses his line of thought.

'I hear on the radio there's been another.'

Skelgill scowls and nods reluctantly, then indicates with a hand gesture, snapping his fingers.

'Leyton – the picture. Barley.'

DS Leyton raises his eyebrows doubtfully, but Skelgill's stare is fierce and he does as commanded. He unzips the folder and flicks through its contents until he finds the enlarged photograph – a photocopy in fact – of Walter Barley. He hands it to Skelgill, who in turn places it before the woman. Immediately she shows a reaction.

'Aye – he were in on Friday.'

'What?' The detectives utter this in unison.

'*You Stupid Boy* – he put two-fifty on it.'

'Pounds?' This is DS Leyton – now wide-eyed at the prospect of a bet of this magnitude. As the woman nods in the affirmative, he shakes his head. 'Cor blimey – a string of ponies.'

Skelgill is unmoved by DS Leyton's cockney outburst.

'Did he come back to collect his winnings?'

The woman shakes her head. Behind the thick spectacles, there might just be a hint of guilty jubilation in her shrewd eyes.

'You'll have a record of the time the bet was placed?'

'I will – but I can tell ye – it was eight minutes before the off – eight minutes to four.'

'Did he leave straight after?'

The woman chuckles.

'With me right behind him.'

'How do you mean?'

She now gives Skelgill a rather schoolmarmish look over the top of her glasses.

'Two hundred and fifty pounds at seven-to-two – I had five minutes to lay it off. You've never seen me move so fast to Bettoney's.'

Skelgill's eyes are hawkish in their concentration.

'Did you see which way this man went?'

'Aye – when I came out of the shop, he wis jus' going round the corner intae the next street – Ullswater Place.'

21. FOLLOW-UP MEETING

Tuesday afternoon

'Well, Guv – how did it go?'

Skelgill is tight-lipped as he re-enters his office, and gives no indication as to the outcome of his showdown with the Chief. DS Leyton and DS Jones, expectant and fearful, though evidently not in equal measure, are literally on the edge of their seats.

Skelgill rather self-consciously rubs his hands together and contrives a cheesy grin.

'Leyton – at risk of offending the lady present – I'm pleased to report I've still got me knackers.'

He glances at DS Jones, who flashes him a look of exaggerated relief.

DS Leyton, however, leans further forward, his features still heavily creased.

'But what about the case, Guv?'

Skelgill drops theatrically into his chair.

'I appreciate your concern for my well-being, Leyton.' His tone is liberally laced with sarcasm. 'The bad news is you're still answering to me.'

DS Leyton lets out an audible sigh of relief. He paddles back into a more upright sitting position.

'Thank crikey for that, Guv – I'd as soon as strangle myself as work for DI Smart.' He turns quickly to DS Jones. 'No offence, Emma – I know you get on with him.'

DS Jones raises her palms in protest, though her sculpted cheekbones immediately colour beneath her tan. She glances apprehensively at Skelgill, who is assessing her objection through narrowed eyes.

DS Leyton perhaps realises he has created this little moment of friction; he claps his hands together enthusiastically.

'So our lucky trip to the bookie's was in the nick of time, Guv?'

Skelgill turns to DS Leyton.

'*Planned* trip to the bookie's, Leyton.'

'The Chief's not daft, Guv.'

Skelgill might wish to contest this view, but to do so would contradict the wisdom of her present decision. He shakes his head in an ambiguous fashion.

'It's a cushy number up there in the ivory tower, Leyton.'

'The press are having a field day, Guv – I don't envy her that.'

Skelgill shrugs languidly.

'We've got until close of play Thursday, by the way.'

DS Leyton looks alarmed. He shakes his head and his heavy jowls follow suit, a fraction delayed.

'Not even three days, Guv – we still need a big break.'

Silently, DS Jones jolts forward an inch or two, like a sprinter on the cusp of a false start. Her sudden movement attracts the gaze of her colleagues.

'I might have a couple of *small* breaks, Guv.'

Skelgill regards her blankly, as though he is wondering what she could mean.

'Shall I go through the points in your order, Guv?'

'Fine.'

Skelgill, though fortified by various caffeine shots and no doubt the adrenaline of having to face the Chief, is again showing symptoms of fatigue. It is doubtful he can remember the items, let alone in what sequence he listed them. Undeterred, DS Jones refers to her notepad.

'The Stewarts, Guv – previous owners of Knott Halloo Farm. No trace yet of the son, Clifford – but I think I've tracked down the father, Maurice.'

'To where?'

'Galloway, Guv – a kind of nursing home – I'm just waiting on absolute confirmation from the DC who's following it up.'

'How did you find him?'

Again she consults her notes.

'The agents – *Pope & Parish* – they provided the address of a company that was dissolved shortly after the sale – not much more that a PO Box here in Penrith. So that was a dead-end. Next I tried the National Farmers' Union – in case they'd stayed in agriculture. Lots of Stewarts – especially in Scotland – but I couldn't get a match.'

DS Jones glances up at Skelgill, to see that his attention is flagging.

'Then I phoned my uncle.'

This left-of-field statement prompts a response from her superior.

'Your uncle?'

'The one who worked as a gardener at Oakthwaite School, Guv?' Her intonation suggests this question is rhetorical, and she continues without pause. 'I figured he'd be roughly contemporary with Maurice Stewart – and it turns out he knows of him indirectly. My uncle heard at a family gathering a few years back that Stewart had gone to this old folks' place – it was through a distant relative who had some connection there.'

'Where in Galloway?'

'Near a village called Glenlochar.'

Skelgill's concentration rachets up another notch, albeit from a low base.

'Loch Ken.'

'Sorry, Guv?'

'Glenlochar is beside Loch Ken – I've fished it a few times for pike – got snapped up by a monster once – potential Scottish record, I reckon – wouldn't mind having another dash at that.'

Skelgill appears to drift off into a little reminiscence; it seems more likely the subject matter is planning for pike than the practicalities of an interview over the border in Galloway.

'Shall I move onto the second point, Guv?'

He nods forwards; it is hard to tell if this is his approval to proceed or a relapse caused by an attack of sleep. But when DS Jones hesitates, he utters a confirmation.

'Aye – go on.'

DS Jones lifts her pad and from the loose papers beneath it she separates two identical colour photocopies. The content is a facsimile of a photograph taken by a police speed camera. It features a motorcyclist hunched over his handlebars, bent into the headwind, and clearly wearing a black leather jacket, blue jeans, and black pointed biker-boots. The overprinted data read *104 mph*, along with the date and time of the offence. She hands one sheet to each of her colleagues.

'That's him, Guv!' DS Leyton flaps the photograph in the air. 'It's the same outfit he had on – definitely.'

Both sergeants look eagerly at Skelgill. He is gazing blearily at the page.

'Surprised that heap would do a ton.'

'It's him, Guv – he was coming up to Penrith – just like the others!' DS Leyton is jubilant; he rises and takes a turn about the office. 'The *Milky Bars* are on me!'

He rattles the loose change in his pocket and disappears into the corridor. Though Skelgill's preference is for a steaming mug of canteen tea, the nearby machine is often called upon for reasons of convenience. There is also an adjoining snacks dispenser. DS Leyton reappears cradling three plastic cups protectively in his large stubby fingers. He passes them around and then deals chocolate bars from his jacket pocket.

DS Jones holds up her copy of the picture.

'It certainly looks a good match, Guv – under the circumstances it would be a big coincidence. And less than an hour before the earliest possible time of death.'

Skelgill seems reluctant to become carried away. He stares again at the image, munching introspectively for a few moments before he opines.

'It's a Honda, that's for sure.'

'That places all of them in Penrith, Guv.' DS Leyton is still excited. 'We can really narrow this wild goose chase down, Guv.'

'All we know, Leyton, is that he came up the motorway. He might have been heading for John O'Groats.'

Skelgill looks at his wristwatch and gestures to DS Jones that she should continue with her findings.

'What was the next point?'

'Barry Seddon's *iPad*, Guv.'

Skelgill squints suspiciously.

'How do you know he had an *iPad?*'

'I phoned his cousin, Hilda – like you asked, Guv.'

'Where was it kept?'

'That's the point, Guv – it's gone – it's been taken away.'

'What are you talking about, Jones?'

'On the day after Barry Seddon went missing – on the Tuesday – before anyone knew he was dead – someone came to the house to collect his *iPad* for repair. Either she'd forgotten about this, or it just didn't occur to her to mention it to you.'

'Have you traced the supplier?'

DS Jones looks up, a hint of alarm in her eyes.

'I think the murderer took it, Guv.'

Skelgill folds his arms, but does not reply.

'A young guy in his twenties called – smartly dressed – in a suit, with a briefcase – said it was arranged that he was to collect a laptop.'

'You said *iPad.*'

'Exactly, Guv – that's what you'd expect someone to have, isn't it? But Barry Seddon didn't have a laptop or broadband.' She brushes back locks of hair that fall across her face as she bows to read her notes. 'There was some discussion and they agreed it must be a mistake and that Seddon must have wanted his *iPad* repaired – so the guy took that away. Hilda Seddon sounds like she has no clue about this kind of thing – it would be easy to bluff her – she just handed it over – no paperwork, no mention of the firm's name, nothing.'

'Cor blimey, Guv – the sheepdog!'

This loud interjection is from DS Leyton.

'Sugar rush, Leyton?'

'Who let the dog out, Guv? What if it were the same geezer – took away Walter Barley's computer gear? Opens the door and the dog does a runner. You'd be happy with that if you were burgling.'

Skelgill purses his lips and nods grudgingly.

'Thing is, Guv – Barry Seddon hid his keys under his van – so the killer impersonated a computer repair bloke. But he'd have the keys to Barley's and Harris's joints.'

Skelgill permits himself a wry grin.

'According to the old lady across the yard it was the witches that came for Lee Harris.'

'I bet it *was* a hen party, Guv – this gent's too clever to get spotted like that.'

Skelgill turns to DS Jones.

'You got a description?'

'Top-line, Guv – there's been so much going on in the past couple of hours – there's still more to tell you. I thought we should probably interview Hilda Seddon and get a proper identikit done.'

Skelgill considers this and nods his approval.

DS Leyton crushes the wrapper of his chocolate bar in a raised fist.

'Guv – the killer must be getting rid of all their comms gear so we can't track him down.'

Skelgill watches with interest as DS Leyton tosses the ball of paper at the waste bin and misses. He looks as though he would like a shot himself, but as he casts about for his own wrapper it has disappeared.

'Don't jump the gun. Leyton – for all we know a whole pile of valuables has been stolen – and Hilda's computer man might yet turn out to be bona fide.'

There is a moment of silence as they perhaps all row back a little from the edge of the whirlpool of elation that these findings have stirred up. DS Jones slides out another page from her sheaf of documents.

'This is potentially a small fly in the ointment, Guv – we've found Walter Barley's bicycle.'

'How's that a problem?'

'It was in Keswick – like you guessed, Guv.'

Skelgill frowns, though at the same time he manages to look pleased with himself.

'Where and when?'

'Reported lunchtime today – dumped in the River Greta below the footbridge into Upper Fitz Park. It had a flat front tyre. We don't know when or how it got there.'

'Plenty of folks use that bridge – someone must have seen something.'

DS Jones looks torn.

'I've got it on the action list, Guv – but when I heard about your four o'clock sighting of him I figured it was a lesser priority. I didn't want to pull any resources away from the door-to-door checks in Penrith.'

Skelgill strokes the bridge of his nose with the fingers of both hands, concealing a yawn between his palms.

'Fairy snuff.'

DS Leyton is looking up at the map behind Skelgill.

'Think he met someone in Keswick?'

DS Jones nods encouragingly.

'I was wondering if he caught the bus to Penrith.'

At this suggestion Skelgill shakes his head vehemently.

'If he were getting the bus, there's a stop at Threlkeld – all he'd have to do was freewheel down the hill from the farm to the village – no need to bike four miles to Keswick.'

'Maybe the bike was nicked, Guv?'

Skelgill yawns and slumps back into his chair.

'You always think the worst of people, Leyton.'

On this note of light relief they all laugh, and there is a pause for sips and slurps of tea, more the latter in Skelgill's case. Covetously he eyes DS Jones's untouched chocolate bar; she notices his interest.

'You're welcome to that, Guv.'

Skelgill obliges without further negotiation. As DS Leyton looks on forlornly, his boss tears open the wrapper and takes a bite, then waggles the remaining portion in his female colleague's direction.

'Dare I ask if there is anything else, Jones?'

'Your last point was the forensics, Guv.' She traces a line on her notepad with her finely manicured nails. 'I've spoken with Dr Herdwick – he said he's still mystified at the lack of injuries – but that he thinks all three bodies could have been kept wrapped in some kind of plastic sheets – he's getting extra tests done.'

Skelgill seems to become distracted by this information, and stares without expression at the wall between his two sergeants while chewing rhythmically. After a few moments his eyelids begin to droop, and DS Leyton – as if trying to make himself more comfortable – scrapes his chair loudly on the floor. The sound penetrates Skelgill's drowsy reverie, and he rouses himself and checks his watch once again.

'Jones – have you got those details for the nursing home?'

'I'll ring down and chase them, Guv – they should be ready.'

Skelgill stands up and reaches for his jacket. It is approaching the end of their shift, and DS Leyton coughs rather nervously.

'What it is, Guv – I've got my youngest's end-of-term show at five-thirty.'

Skelgill regards DS Leyton implacably.

'No probs, Leyton – I was planning to go on me tod.'

DS Jones, watching Skelgill expectantly, looks a little deflated. Rather peremptorily, she gathers up her papers and rises to her feet.

'I'll get you that info, Guv. I'll email it to you straight away.'

As DS Jones slips behind him, DS Leyton cranes his neck to watch her depart. Then he shakes his head in silent admiration and leans covertly towards Skelgill.

'No wonder they call her *Fast-track*, eh, Guv?'

Skelgill thumbs the lapels of his jacket.

'Aye, well – she just needed pointing in the right direction, Leyton.'

DS Leyton nods tactfully and takes his own leave.

Skelgill gathers his personal belongings and effects a swift retreat from the building. However, once car borne, rather than

make for the nearest motorway junction he h
Penrith on the A6. After a few minutes he turn
road into a lane, and shortly from the lane in
concealed track that enters a small copse, where he
halt. He switches off the engine, rounds the car and re-e
the passenger door. Then he winds back the passenger sea
maximum extent, stretches out his legs, and promptly falls
asleep.

R

The region of Galloway is three times the size of the Lake District, and yet it attracts only a fraction of the visitors. This is curious on the face of it, given the proximity of the two areas, and their marked similarities. Where Lakeland has its meres, dales and becks, Galloway boasts lochs, glens and burns in equal measure. Indeed, Galloway offers crowd-free hillwalking that Cumbrian outdoors folk can only dream of, and its highest peak, The Merrick, a slumbering giant at the heart of a great wilderness, is a match for its much-trodden English counterparts across the shimmering Solway Firth.

Quite what makes Galloway so forsaken a land (statistically, at least) is hard to fathom. Skelgill's present journey is perhaps ninety minutes, by good roads. Why few among the holidaying hordes invest such modest time to discover the history, culture and wildlife of this ancient realm is something of a mystery.

Skelgill's route, in fact, turns out to be rather more convoluted, for he takes a detour to Aspatria, to spend five minutes with Hilda Seddon. Ironically, this small Cumbrian town lies on the beeline that notionally joins Penrith and Castle Douglas (the nearest substantial settlement to his destination), but the interposing estuary means he must retrace his tracks in order to enter Scotland. It is approaching seven p.m. as he skims over the Esk at Metal Bridge, and such is his level of concentration that he omits his habitual sideways glance to check the state of the tide. He flashes across the border at well above the speed limit, and is obliged to brake abruptly when suddenly he becomes aware of the fast-enlarging exit sign for Gretna, its kitschy factory outlets, and the A75 west.

Clouds have been the order of the day, and now that they darken the landscape with a premature sense of dusk, perhaps the contrast between Galloway and Lakeland becomes more stark. Where the Lakes has its verdant oakwoods, soft and inviting, hugging the contours and blending into the fellsides, Galloway is a manmade patchwork of midnight-green conifer plantations, whose angular margins challenge aesthetics and slice across bog and scree like the arbitrary borders of African countries. Such austerity is amplified in the names of many natural features: Loch Doon, Long Loch of the Dungeon, The Black Water of Dee, Murder Hole, Rigg of the Jarkness, and the Range of the Awful Hand. And where Lakeland towns are thronged with colourful cagoule-clad visitors, who spill chattering from quaint freshly painted pubs adorned with overflowing hanging baskets, an air of melancholy hangs over Galloway; by comparison its villages appear deserted, their buildings in less-than-pristine repair, eaves slowly dripping with black rain; while beyond in the swirling mists mingle the ghosts of Covenanters, lamenting their tragic risings.

Yet in this isolation resides Galloway's appeal. It has long been a haven for those seeking solitude and seclusion – the creative and the meditative – and among its farming and foresting inhabitants moves a significant population of artists, artisans and aspiring adherents of various obscure faiths and orders, tenaciously eking a living off the beaten track. Skelgill's destination – Glenlochar Castle Retreat – has provenance in this regard; now a private retirement home, it was formerly the base of a Buddhist community – a group that departed at the turn of the century when planning permission for a proposed human-waste power generation plant was denied by the local authority. In any event, despite its name, a fortified role has never been one of its functions, although during the war it was occupied as a training centre for the construction of Bailey bridges on nearby Loch Ken.

Thus, as Skelgill turns into the winding driveway, crowded by straining banks of rhododendrons, he ought not anticipate some grand edifice in Scottish Baronial style. Instead, rounding the final bend, he encounters the incongruous car crash of two social classes, two properties juxtaposed. By far the grander, on the left, is constructed in the Greek Revival style of the mid 1800s, in local greywacke with red sandstone quoins, jambs, lintels and sills; a low-slope hipped slate roof; and a massive central porch, its columns, door and cornicing painted white, and surrounded by long three-over-six sash windows that create the impression of a vacant multi-eyed countenance with an oversized mouth. Standing flush against this building – admittedly in the same severe stone – is a graphically contrasting traditional Galloway farmhouse, also of two storeys (though these much lower), the three dormers of its upper floor jutting from the steep gabled roof, their angled rake edges and those of the porch beneath clashing jauntily with the horizontal lines of the main house.

Architecture does not rank high among Skelgill's interests – or even disturb his general sentience – but as he kills the engine he stares at the distressing agglomeration. After a minute he emerges into a fine drizzle that thickens the air and dampens the crunch of his feet on the gravel. He approaches the ostentatious portico and is about to mount its fan of worn steps when, to his right, the front door of the smaller property opens. A cheery-looking woman of late middle age, medium height and stout build, alerted presumably by the dull slam of his car door, leans out and beckons for him to come.

'This way, duck – the reception's all shut up for the night.'

She steps back to admit him, only at the last second extending a hand, as if she is unsure how to greet a policeman.

'Veronica – duty housekeeper – I'm on until six in the morning.'

'Skelgill, Cumbria CID. I believe you spoke with one of my colleagues.'

The woman nods eagerly, closing the door and ushering Skelgill ahead of her into a surprisingly wide hallway furnished with a small settee and an easy chair, and a coffee table angled between them.

'You're here to see Maurice – he's expecting you – he's just finishing off his supper.' She pulls on the back of the chair, an action suggesting that he should sit. 'Would you like a cup of tea and a wee cake while you wait – you'll have had a long journey?'

'Don't mind if I do – if it's no bother?'

'Och, you just sit yourself down – I shan't be a wee minute.'

His acquiescence seems to have an endearing effect. She beams widely and bustles away. Skelgill lowers himself into the seat, an amused smile creasing the corners of his mouth: she has an English accent of a Midlands nature – but, in the way of many an incomer to a foreign region, she has adopted some of the local vernacular, if not quite the pronunciation. Presently, from what must be a small staff kitchen, emanate the promising rumble of a boiling kettle and the ring of a tin – and perhaps the sound of slicing, several times repeated. Indeed, Skelgill is not disappointed when she reappears bearing a well-stocked tray of refreshments, comprising a large steaming mug of tea and a reserve pot, milk and sugar, and a stand with three slices each of carrot cake and Victoria sponge. There is only one side plate.

'You not having some yourself?'

'Och – no, I've got to watch my figure.'

She smoothens the sides of her dress as she settles upon the settee and helps Skelgill to his first slice; there is no doubt that, with just a few inches trimmed off here and there, her now matronly curves would once have turned heads. Skelgill might empathise with the mismatched challenge of idling away long nightshifts, and only a tin of cakes for company.

'You're not Scottish?'

'We're from West Bridgford.'

Skelgill nods as he chews.

'Nottingham.'

'That's right, duck – not many people up here know that.'

Skelgill cocks his head to one side.

'Probably not many people up here have fished the Trent.'

'Och – so that's how you know.'

Skelgill raises his eyebrows in affirmation as he takes a gulp of tea.

'You said *we*?'

'My husband, Bill – he's the handyman, does the grounds as well – it'll be four years this September we moved up – we've got a little cottage down by the loch. Bill likes his fishing, too.'

Skelgill nods, perhaps wrestling with the temptation to become sidetracked.

'What's the set-up here – as regards your patients?'

The woman's eyes seem longingly to be following the movements of Skelgill's side plate, with its diminishing portion of Victoria sponge. Skelgill notices this and changes tack.

'Why don't you get yourself a mug and a plate – if Mr Stewart is going to be a few minutes – I'm in no rush.'

'Are you sure, duck?'

But in asking this question she is already rising to her feet and heading for the kitchenette. Returning, she sighs with relief as she makes herself comfortable once more. Skelgill watches with interest as she opts for the sponge, as if he has a little wager with himself resting on this outcome.

'It's just a gentleman's retirement home – nothing fancy – for those who'd struggle to manage on their own. Though we don't provide medical care, so they have to move on if a condition becomes a problem.' She takes a bite of cake and then, holding one hand over her mouth out of politeness, quickly adds, as if for the official record, 'We're all first-aid-trained, of course.'

Skelgill nods encouragingly.

'And Mr Stewart – was he here before you came?'

The woman nods.

'About seven years, I think he's been.'

'Does he have any visitors?'

Now she shakes her head, and finishes her next mouthful before she replies.

'None at all – but he's got a mobile phone – we have to buy him top-up vouchers in Castle Douglas when he's running low.'

'Do you know who he speaks with? We're trying to trace his son, Clifford.'

Again there is the cake-induced delay.

'He's quite secretive, you see – keeps to himself, even among the other chaps – and we've only got eight residents altogether at the moment.'

She leans forward a little conspiratorially, although at first Skelgill must assume she wants a second helping of cake, since he lifts the remaining selection for her consideration.

'Och, I shouldn't, you know.'

Skelgill grins at her disarmingly.

'Thing is – I'll eat it all, if you won't – and I'm not sure that's a good idea either.'

'Well, just a wee slice then, to help you out.'

This *wee* can only be intended euphemistically, since none of the surviving slices could remotely be described as ungenerous. She opts for the last piece of Victoria sponge, which seems to satisfy Skelgill as he helps himself to carrot cake. The woman resumes her confidential pose, and speaks in something of a hushed tone.

'What I was going to say was – and you'll see for yourself – he's a bit strange.'

'In what way?'

'He spends most of his time studying horses – he gets that racing newspaper delivered every day – and he likes to watch the races on the television – when the others will let him.'

'Does he place bets?'

'Not that I know of – I mean he doesn't leave here.'

'What about online betting?'

The woman shakes her head decisively.

'I know you can do it with computers these days – but we don't have any – not even for the staff. My Bill says good riddance – it's one less thing to go wrong.'

'Could he bet by phone?'

The woman considers this, but again shakes her head.

'I'm not sure he's got a credit card – he pays us in cheques and cash.' She gazes at her empty plate for a moment. 'He receives regular mail though – thick envelopes that come recorded – he must get his money sent through the post.'

Skelgill does not respond immediately. Perhaps he is trying to work something out, and is disguising these mental calculations as the process of savouring the carrot cake.

'Excellent, this – did you bake it yourself?'

The woman looks pleased and nods with affected modesty.

'Wait till I tell my sergeant – he'll be cooking up an excuse for us to come back.'

Now she chuckles and perhaps even blushes with pride. Skelgill resumes his stealthy interrogation.

'Veronica – you said he was *strange* – the business with the horses – that's not so unusual is it?'

She nods, recognising that there is an unfinished part to her explanation.

'It's more Maurice himself, really – it's like... well, sometimes he's not quite there – except that you can't help thinking he's putting it on.'

'What – as if he's acting a bit daft in order to be evasive?'

She nods enthusiastically.

'That's exactly it.'

Skelgill grimaces.

'I must admit – it's a tactic I use myself often enough – sometimes I don't even know I'm doing it – according to my boss, anyway.'

She smiles at his little joke. Skelgill casually prods at the crumbs on his plate.

'Veronica – you probably know him better than anybody – do you think I can trust what he says?'

She has been swift to answer most of Skelgill's questions, but now she wavers. She leans back in her seat, brushing crumbs from her lap and keeping her eyes on her hands as she interlocks her fingers; she appears undecided.

'Possibly – but I shouldn't stake your job on it, if I were you, duck.'

Skelgill nods pensively, and reaches for another slice of carrot cake.

*

Skelgill has been guided through the smaller property into the adjoining main house, and now he enters the day room alone. There are five elderly men comfortably seated around a large television, from which blares a popular soap opera – though on reflection not *that* popular, since they all appear to be sleeping. Two others click dominoes at a card table in one corner; neither looks up as he advances and then exits the lounge through double doors that lead into a large conservatory. Mercifully, the glazing is efficient, and the strident cockney angst is excluded once he closes the doors behind him. The conservatory itself is pleasantly furnished with wicker settees and matching low tables; healthy looking houseplants spill from hanging baskets; beyond the glass there is a view down to the loch, though the misty dusk precludes much detail. Seated in a wheelchair and bent over a desk and facing the same outlook, is a schoolboy-like figure, though closer inspection reveals him to be bald, but for a few wisps of hair forming a crescent at the back of his skull. Maurice Stewart is making notes as Skelgill approaches, and shows no sign that he detects the latter's presence. A small transistor radio beside him emits the chatter of a sports talk-station. Skelgill takes a slight detour, and grabs the top of a wicker chair, which he drags with him.

'Yu've come through at last, then.'

The man, who seems to have knowledge of Skelgill's earlier arrival, speaks in a Cumbrian accent, and without glancing up. As Skelgill positions his seat at forty-five degrees to the desk, Maurice Stewart switches off the wireless set and with some effort manipulates the wheelchair around to half-face him.

'Mr Stewart – thanks for sparing the time – I waited until the all-weather meeting at Wolverhampton was finished – I figured you'd be following it.' He grins affably. 'Besides, your housekeeper bakes a mean carrot cake.'

The man regards Skelgill with a mixture of scepticism and guarded interest – the former presumably because he knows his visitor is a detective, and the latter perhaps because it must be rare for him to be engaged in terms that acknowledge his pet subject, let alone with some apparent know-how thrown in.

While he is formulating a response – if indeed he is – Skelgill presses home the small advantage he might just have gained.

'There was a horse I fancied in the last race – *Danny's Girl*, it was called.'

Skelgill says this casually, though with such intonation to suggest he is interested in the outcome. Maurice Stewart glances briefly at the neat piles of papers arranged on the desk, and then turns back to Skelgill.

'Aye, well – she din't run, she were withdrawn – so yer saved yerself a few bob there.'

Skelgill looks a little surprised.

'You wouldn't have advised it?'

The man shakes his head. He has a long bulbous nose, a white chin-curtain beard, and brown eyes hazy with a hint of glaucoma. These features, together with his heavy brow and furtive demeanour, create a striking resemblance to a proboscis monkey. Whether of the wise variety or not, remains to be seen, but for the moment he certainly holds his peace, obliging Skelgill to continue.

'I reckoned I had a reliable tip on that – in the bookie's this morning.'

The man shifts slightly but still does not comment. Though Skelgill is to some extent playing a game of blind man's buff, he is at least on firm ground – the filly bearing his own name caught his eye whilst he voluntarily posted up the race cards earlier.

'Same person as gave me *You Stupid Boy* at Newmarket last Friday.'

Now Maurice Stewart shows signs of interest.

'Aye, well – yer did alright there. What did yer get?'

Skelgill is straining the sinews of his gambling knowledge. He is obliged to guess the gist of this question.

'Four to one.'

The man nods. It is evidently the correct answer. He swivels for a moment and picks up the sheet of lined foolscap on which he has been working. He glances cursorily at the page and then shows it to Skelgill.

'Nine to two were available.'

He indicates with a bony index finger, tipped with a long brown nail, cracked and curved like a devil's toenail fossil. There are several matching columns of handwritten figures in jerky black biro, perhaps a hundred pairs of numbers in all. The meaning of the first column is not clear, but the second clearly holds a record of the odds, written in the traditional style – 11/4, 2/1, 13/8 and so on. The nail traces a shaky course down the page, almost to the very bottom of the last column, where the figures *9/2* are written. At the top of the sheet is the heading *'Naps & Next Best'*. Skelgill takes hold of a corner of the page to get a better look; perhaps to his surprise the man releases it to him and slumps against his wheelchair with a small groan of discomfort. Skelgill likewise sits upright and scrutinises the page, frowning in an informed fashion and nodding from time to time. He must be racking his brains for some intelligent comment, but now the man is more forthcoming.

'Yon figures in red are the losers.'

Skelgill scans the page for a second time, a puzzled expression clouding his features.

'There aren't any in red.'

The man throws back his head and cackles jubilantly, though the laughter quickly disintegrates into a chaotic bout of phlegmy coughing that culminates in him spitting profusely into a handkerchief wrestled from (and returned to) a trouser pocket. Skelgill watches implacably through this ostensibly disturbing episode; it seems he senses no distress. When calm is restored, he hands back the page of winners.

'That's some system you've got, Mr Stewart.'

The man smirks, though there is perhaps the glisten of pride in his dark eyes – unless this is the product of tears that welled up during the coughing fit.

'Aye, happen I've cracked it, eh lad?'

Skelgill folds his arms and shakes his head in admiration.

'How do you do it – I mean, without revealing your formula?'

The man squints and picks at the back of his head with two hands, as though he is removing a tick.

'I've got all me filters, twelve of 'em – usual things like bloodline, trainer, jockey, form, weight, going.' He gestures towards a folded copy of the *Racing Post* that is arrayed with the other materials on the desk. 'Official ratings, handicaps, tipsters' predictions, odds ratios.'

He yawns without covering his mouth, revealing unnaturally white dentures top and bottom. Skelgill checks his wristwatch; it is true that the evening is wearing on and quite likely the old man is tiring.

'Sounds impressive.'

But Maurice Stewart scoffs.

'That's nowt – anyone can get that information.'

Skelgill tips his head to one side.

'But surely the skill is knowing what to do with it?'

The man shrugs dismissively. He leans out of his chair and stretches for a single sheet of paper, this one covered in printed data, with many columns of tiny figures set against horses' names. He passes the page to Skelgill who, after a couple of moments' scrutiny, looks up inquiringly. It seems this is a satisfactory response.

'Time horses – that's what it's all about, lad – time horses.'

Skelgill again nods deferentially.

'You must make a fortune, Mr Stewart.'

The man's response is an abbreviated version of the cackle-and-cough routine, although this time thankfully not requiring the hanky.

'I don't bet, lad.'

Skelgill inhales as if he is about to speak, but in reaching to return the page his gaze drifts beyond Maurice Stewart and he notices a budget-edition mobile phone resting on the far corner of the desk. The man follows Skelgill's eyes – and instead of replacing the data-sheet in its allocated space, he slides it casually over the handset. He hesitates for a moment before he settles back to face the detective. Now he yawns again, more laboriously this time.

'Any'ow, lad – thee din't come to discuss horses – yon Morag'll be along to pack us off ter kip soon.'

Skelgill holds up a palm in acknowledgment, and then joins both hands together between his knees and assumes a more business-like though still affable posture.   Whether he has detected the subtle change in his antagonist's demeanour is difficult to gauge.

'Mr Stewart – the main purpose of coming to see you is to ask about your son, Clifford.'

'Why – what's he bin up ter?'

Immediately there is the cackle, perhaps with a more manic flourish than before.   The apelike eyes seem to glint with amusement.

'Oh – it's nothing like that, sir – it's just that we have reason to believe he might be in danger.'

For a fleeting moment the man's features seem pained, though the reaction could equally be one of contempt.

'Danger, eh?'

'It's essential we trace him, you see, sir.'

'*Cliff Edge.*'

There is a sense of wistful nostalgia conveyed in this short expression, with each word being separately emphasised.

'I beg your pardon, sir?'

'Cliff Edge – that's what he called himself – *Dangerous Cliff Edge.*   He liked that – being the star turn.   Lock up your daughters, here comes Dangerous Cliff Edge.'

Skelgill inches closer.

'Do you mean when you had the outdoor activity centre – and the climbing wall? At Knott Halloo?'

'Aye, he were a reet good climber were our Cliff.'   The man makes a throaty rattle, as though he is agreeing with himself by agitating the catarrh lining his trachea. 'Cliff Edge. Ha!'

'Do you know where we can find him, sir?'

The man pitches forward and pinches the end of his nose between the thumb and forefinger of one hand.   Whether this is intended as a confiding gesture it is hard to discern, but his reply suggests such.

'No one knows where to find Cliff.'

227

In his enunciation there is a hint of triumph – the accent upon *no one* – as if Clifford's whereabouts is a long-held secret in which only he shares and he is flaunting this accomplishment before Skelgill. Suddenly he jerks back upright and again there is the unnerving laughter.

'Including yourself, sir?'

Now the man shrugs indifferently; he does not seem inclined to answer verbally.

'When did you last see him?'

Maurice Stewart yawns once more, and closes his eyes for several seconds. Skelgill stares at him with concern, perhaps trying to assess whether he is overcome by sleep. Then the eyes disconcertingly spring open.

'See who?'

'Your son Cliff, sir.'

'What about him?'

'Has he been in touch with you lately?'

The man sways in his chair; he has an intoxicated air.

'He speaks to me – don't they all, eh?'

Once more there is the spluttering cackle and cough. But now a movement attracts Skelgill's attention. It appears that the staff are shepherding their clients off to bed. A woman unfamiliar to Skelgill – skinny and plain looking, asexual in her uniform of beige smock and matching trousers, dark hair wrung into an ascetic top knot – bangs open and fastens back the interconnecting doors. This must be the aforementioned Morag.

'Time to turn in, Mr Stewart – cocoa's already in your room.'

She shoots a severe glance at Skelgill, a clear signal that his presence is now no longer desired – at least as far as she is concerned. Perhaps her shift ends once she has packed away the inmates and, rather like a barmaid trying to clear a pub of its laggards who loiter long after last orders, maybe she too undergoes the closing-time transformation from hospitable to hostile. The television through in the day room has been silenced, and she extinguishes the lights in the conservatory. Skelgill rises, but takes the opportunity to step across to the windows, now that the internal reflection has been eliminated.

Leaning over, he presses his forehead against the glass and peers out into the darkness, but in his eagerness to see outside he upsets a vase and only just manages to catch it before it tumbles onto the tiled floor. He re-settles it carefully and makes an apologetic mimed gesture – the woman briefly looks askance, but she is more concerned with wrenching round the wheelchair and aiming it at the ramp up into the lounge.

'He in't out there, lad!'

Maurice Stewart calls back over his shoulder, seemingly amused by Skelgill's antics. Skelgill quickens his stride to catch up, and attempts to offer his assistance with the chair – but the silent orderly makes it clear with her nearest shoulder that she requires no help. Skelgill keeps pace and twists around to make eye contact with her charge.

'Mr Stewart – is there anyone we could ask – who'll know where Clifford might be?'

The simian features of the old man seem to fill with malevolent glee.

'Dig all yer like – yer'll not find Cliff.'

*

Skelgill turns left out of the driveway of Glenlochar Castle Retreat, between square sandstone columns topped by eroded eagles that seem to lurch ominously in the red glow of his tail lights. He changes up into second gear – but no more – and perhaps fifty yards further on he stops alongside a field entrance on the right. Emerging from the vehicle, pulling in his head in tortoise-fashion against the intensifying rain, he puts his shoulder to the rickety wooden gate. It swings easily enough at first, though jams against the uneven ground at the perpendicular. Nonetheless, he returns to the car and manoeuvres it through the gap and swings it hard against the dry-stone wall. Now it is out of sight from the road. Then he clambers into the central passenger section, and drags various items of wet-weather gear from the cargo compartment. In the restricted space there follows a limited struggle, accompanied by unrestrained swearing.

But two minutes later he tumbles out clad in wellingtons, leggings, and his dubiously impermeable combination of threadbare *Barbour* and sagging *Tilley* hat. He locks the car, checks his powerful flashlight against the palm of one hand, hauls the gate back into its closed position, and sets off in the direction whence he came.

He has obviously decided that the driveway is the most practical route of approach. This seems wise given his meagre knowledge of the surrounding terrain – there could be bogs, bogles, or fields full of bad-tempered *Belties* – and, now that night has fallen, beneath the heavy cloud cover visibility is almost non-existent. Somewhere, teenage tawny owls, recently fledged, call insistently for fast food; though tonight they may be disappointed. Indeed, the darkness is intense. Neither the country lane nor the driveway is illuminated, and it is no coincidence that sparsely populated Galloway is home to Britain's first dark sky park. Skelgill feels his way rather drunkenly along the centre of the gravel track, straining to see the tips of his fingers – though naturally unwilling to employ his torch.

And just as well – for about halfway to his destination he is almost caught unawares as headlights suddenly illuminate a bend only thirty yards ahead. Skelgill is hemmed in by the tall banks of seemingly impenetrable rhododendrons – but this is a familiar Lakeland species and, trusting to this knowledge, he covers his face with his arms and throws himself against the hedge just as the bright beam swings after him. The shrubs yield and then spring back into place; he disappears from view and the car rumbles past at a constant velocity. If the driver has anything, it can only have been fleetingly, at best a dark form passed off as a roe deer – or perhaps more wishfully as the wandering spirit of a Covenanter abroad – not a sight that most folk would stop to investigate on such an inauspicious night.

Skelgill immediately pokes his head out from the bushes. The vehicle is an old mini of some description, and through the rear glass of the car, silhouetted against the illuminated foreground, the driver's distinctive hairstyle is recognisable as that of the orderly, Morag; and there is a second female in the passenger seat. Skelgill fights his way into the open and rearranges his attire, which has twisted during his temporary flight. Brushing twiggy debris from his hair he realises he has become separated from his hat. He decides it is safe to use the flashlight. He trains the beam on the foliage, but then notices the missing item lying flat upon the gravel – a condition caused by the hat having been run over. Phlegmatically he punches it back into shape and jams it firmly down upon his head, then raises the collar of his jacket to optimise his waterproofing.

He sets off again in darkness. Perhaps he feels more confident for this episode – certainly it would appear that the evening shift has departed, and only the night staff (solely Veronica?) will remain. And when the property comes into view he is able to get his bearings. Both houses have porch lamps, and from some of the upstairs windows a pale glow is cast. But Skelgill is wary of triggering an intruder light, and he keeps his distance as best he can. He heads right, and takes a wide loop around the smaller structure before making a dash across a well-tended lawn to the rear corner of this building. Rabbits scatter silently before him.

Now he edges cautiously along the back wall, ducking beneath windows as he passes. Reaching the last of these before the junction with the main house, he pauses. From the darkness within there is the homely flicker of a television; peering around the window frame, Skelgill can see that the set is positioned against the far wall of the room. Secure in the knowledge that the watcher will thus be facing away from him, he allows himself a complete view of the interior. Sure enough, there is the back of Veronica's head. She is comfortably accommodated on a broad settee, with her legs stretched out and her slippered feet supported on a round pouffe. Next to this is a coffee table, upon which there are the tea things familiar from earlier, now supplemented by the addition of a capacious pink cake tin.

Skelgill grins and moves on. Still hugging the building he swiftly finds his way around the jutting profile of the conservatory, to the point opposite Maurice Stewart's desk.

Briefly he probes with the flashlight to satisfy himself that nobody is lurking in the darkened extension. Then he prises open the window he unfastened during his clumsy episode with the vase. Leaning in, almost overbalancing, he can just reach the desk. Deftly, he removes something and slips down onto the grass, hunching over so as to shield the item from the steady rain. Gripping the torch between his teeth, a mad grimace tearing at his features, he yanks out his mobile phone and begins methodically to take photographs.

23. KNOTT HALLOO FARM

Wednesday morning

'Early bird gets the worm, eh, Danny, lad?'
Skelgill produces a wry grin as he leans over to shake the hand of the man clambering into the passenger seat of his car.

'Not for long, Jim.'

'How's that?'

Skelgill hands over a grease-stained brown paper bag; simultaneously he nods in the direction of the burger van.

'Look at his tax disc.'

'Shouldn't you be doing something about that, Inspector?'

Skelgill nonchalantly takes another bite and makes a scoffing sound through his nose.

'Marra – I'm working on a triple murder case – about to be quadruple if I don't get my finger out – I can't go round nicking folk for their road tax.'

'S'pose not, lad.'

Skelgill holds up his own half-eaten roll.

'Anyway, what's that saying – about cutting off your nose to spite your face?'

The man nods agreeably.

'Decent burgers, Danny.'

'Leyton – one of my sergeants – sniffed it out.' Skelgill shakes his head. 'If only he had half the nose for crime.'

'Which I take it is where I come in – is this my tea, by the way?'

Skelgill indicates and the man extracts one of two polystyrene cups from the centre console.

'Thanks for meeting up – I shan't delay you for long.'

'Don't worry, Danny – now I'm behind a desk I'm on flexitime – you might just have to buy me another one of these, that's all.'

'I'll keep it brief – had to raid the post office to pay in the first place.'

'Let's have it, then.'

The man – some fifteen years the senior – is an employee of Cumbria Fire Service. Once leader of the mountain rescue group to which Skelgill belongs, an accident curtailed his climbing days in both capacities. He is a large man, well over six feet, with tight grizzled curly hair, a strong jaw and small blue eyes that twinkle beneath blond brows.

'You've read about the murders?'

The man nods but remains efficiently tight-lipped.

'I'm investigating a connection to Knott Halloo Farm – one of the victims lived in a cottage on their land. There was a fire, going back the best part of twenty years – I vaguely remember it, but I was at that age where... well, I suppose local news wasn't my main priority.'

'You mean you're not at that age any more?' The elder man chuckles and nudges Skelgill. 'I thought you were the Lakes' answer to *Peter Pan*?'

Skelgill grins sheepishly.

'Aye, well – I have my moments. Ask my boss.'

The man shakes his head sympathetically.

'Well, some of us are old enough to remember – as it happens.'

Skelgill's eyes narrow.

'Did you attend?'

'Aye – though not in the first instance. That summer there was a spate of forest fires – dashing about like blue-arsed flies we were. Caused a delay in getting a tender up to the farm – it was beyond saving by the time our lads got there. But it was an isolated unit – fair old size, like – so there was no risk to the rest of the property, and the immediate surroundings were rough grazing. I was the investigating officer.'

'Was there much left to investigate?'

Jim shakes his head.

'Razed to the ground. It was basically a big wooden barn – some kind of climbing and activity centre – with various timber constructions inside, plus they stored the mechanical equipment in there – if I recall there was quite a little fleet of quad bikes, plus the fuel in jerry cans – that's what caused it – leaking petrol vapour built up and probably the heat of an engine took it past its flashpoint – or could have been a spark off a battery. There was a pile of hay, too – the place must have gone up like a tinder box.'

'So foul play wasn't suspected?'

The man shrugs.

'Situation like that – you could never say *never*... but not on the face of it.'

Skelgill looks uneasy.

'I seem to remember there being stories of arson – I mean, this would have been in the years after – vague gossip over a pint.'

The fireman shakes his head.

'As I recall, they weren't insured – which ruled out the usual suspects.'

Skelgill nods several times, to indicate he has considered this possibility.

'What about malicious arson?'

'Thing is, Danny – like I say – you can't rule it out – but when all it would take is to kick over a petrol can that's already standing there and chuck a fag-end on it – there's no way of telling. The blaze destroyed everything – even all the metal was melted.'

'What about injuries – it's been suggested to us that this guy – the murder victim – was apparently hurt trying to fight the blaze?'

Jim rubs his jutting chin reflectively.

'I'd need to dig out the report, Danny – but I'm pretty certain there was nowt. With a barn of that size and design – whacking great doors – even if there's folk inside when the fire starts, it's

235

unlikely they wouldn't get out. Happen yon laddo was trying to rescue some of the kit – must have been worth a few bob.'

Skelgill nods, albeit a little reluctantly.

'I was rather hoping you'd have heard something off the record.'

'Aye, there's no fun in the facts, Danny. You know how the rumour mill gets going, especially in these parts.' The man cocks his head to one side and winks at Skelgill. 'I even hear talk you've had your whites back on.'

Skelgill's high cheekbones take on a faint tinge of pink.

'It was a three-line whip; I had no choice.'

'Word is you skittled Carlisle cops singlehanded.'

Now Skelgill affects a modest simper.

'That just proves your point about the rumour mill, Jim.'

'Aye, well – we could do with a bit of help from you, if the old back's mended – still plenty of games left this season, lad.'

The man might have hung up his climbing boots, but he still turns out for the mountain rescue cricket eleven, as well as providing honorary services that include club secretary, groundsman and chairman of selectors – though with limited resources and frequent injuries, the latter role is more a job of rustling up eleven fit men.

'Happen I'll give you a buzz once this case is sorted, Jim.'

The man grins.

'So how long's that going to be – next spring?'

Skelgill throws him a wide-eyed glance.

'You must be joking – if the Chief is to be believed, either I crack it by tomorrow night or I'm on gardening leave.'

The man ponders this statement, pursing his lips and nodding supportively.

'Course – you could always make that *cricketing* leave.'

*

'Morning, Guv – are you on your way in?'

Skelgill is drinking a second cup of tea, and for once has his phone on hands-free as he heads along the A66.

'Just had a meeting, Jones – next stop Knott Halloo Farm.'

'Oh, right, Guv.'

DS Jones might be optimistic of being apprised on Skelgill's interview with Maurice Stewart; however nothing seems to be forthcoming.

'Er... a few more developments to update you on, Guv – including about the farm – well, the farmer, at least.'

'I'm all ears.'

'We've checked his alibi – he was definitely exhibiting at the agricultural show in Lincolnshire, from midday on the Friday until it closed on Sunday evening. Just him and a young female assistant were staffing the stand.'

'So where's the story?'

'He told you he drove back on the Monday, Guv.'

'Aye.'

'On the Sunday night he stayed at a hotel near Lincoln with his wife.'

'Hold your horses, Jones – his wife was at some posh cocktail party at the Sharrow Bay on Sunday night.'

'I know, Guv.'

Skelgill is silent for a moment.

'You've not met his wife, have you?'

'No, Guv.'

'Jones – if you had, all might become clear.'

'I see, Guv.'

'I'll bear this in mind when I speak to him.'

'Sure, Guv.'

'What next?'

DS Jones hesitates as she presumably refers to her notes.

'Walter Barley's bike, Guv – a small boy was seen shoving it off the bridge and running away back towards the town – seems like DS Leyton might have been right.'

'Got a description?'

'It's from an old lady, Guv – walking her dog in the park – quite a distance off. Aged about twelve, brown hair, white trainers.'

'There's two hundred kids in Keswick fit that description.'

'I know, Guv.'

'What about the time?'

'Just before five – Friday afternoon.'

'Barley was probably dead by then.'

'I've asked PC Dodd to make inquiries up at Threlkeld, Guv – I figured the bike was most probably taken from the farm, or – like you said – from near to the bus stop. That would narrow down the number of twelve-year-old boys – there's only a hundred or so houses in the entire village.'

Skelgill is nodding, though he does not seem overly enthused by this information.

'Okay.'

DS Jones perhaps senses his disinterest, and her disembodied voice takes on a note of urgency in an effort to raise the tempo of their conversation.

'Next thing, Guv – Leicestershire police have traced Lee Harris's biological mother – Janet Atkins.'

'Aye?'

Skelgill's inflection suggests this subject has struck more of a chord.

'She's not in a good way – drinking, that is. The report doesn't say much – but I just spoke to the WPC who interviewed her. She said there was nothing concrete she could put in writing, but she felt the woman was holding out on her.'

'In what way?'

'The official line was that Lee Harris was fostered out because of the alcoholic father – but she got the impression that Lee himself was the problem.'

'Linda Harris said Lee was starting to misbehave – that's why they took the action.'

'Sure, Guv – it's just a point of subtle emphasis, I suppose. Apparently Janet Atkins kept repeating that he wasn't a *bad boy* – in the way that mothers do when they know the opposite.'

Skelgill takes a sip of tea and gazes up at the fells to his left. The cyclonic spell is continuing – indeed the remnants of an Atlantic hurricane have been responsible for the overnight downfall. But now the warm front has passed and a clear, dry day is promised. Lakeland vegetation is reaching its summer peak, and the roadside verges hang heavy with the creamy blossom of meadowsweet. Skelgill lowers his window to admit whatever mixture of natural aromas will come his way.

'Love and marriage.'

'Sorry, Guv?'

DS Jones sounds nonplussed.

'Love and marriage – it's what they call meadowsweet. Nice scent, until you crush the flower.'

'Right, Guv.'

Skelgill does not elaborate upon the train of thought – if indeed there is one – that has brought him to this cryptic destination. Meanwhile, DS Jones, who might be wondering whether he refers to Lee Harris's family circumstances – or in fact if there is some hidden message for her – waits expectantly. She might at least reasonably anticipate a modicum of praise for her diligent work: another late finish and an early start to glean the latest developments for her capricious boss's delectation. After a lengthy pause, Skelgill's approbation – if it can be classified as such – is characteristically oblique when it comes.

'Has Leyton done any work?'

DS Jones is suitably diplomatic in her reply.

'He's at his desk now, Guv – shall I transfer you?'

'Aye – and keep me posted – I don't know when I'll be with you.'

'Sure, Guv – I'll put you through.'

The line is silent for a few moments – perhaps longer than it might take for a call to be transferred between two colleagues who sit within sight of one another – and thus sufficient for Skelgill to suspect there is some collusion before he is reconnected.

'Morning, Guv – how's it going?'

Skelgill does not reply directly, but instead gets directly down to business.

'What's the latest on the door-to-door inquiries?'

There is a silence, during which it can be imagined DS Leyton practises various facial expressions.

'Just getting it up on my screen, Guv – here we go. We've moved onto the new estate, fanning out from that walkway – last night we got the last few missing ones in Ullswater Place.'

Skelgill sucks in air between his teeth, rather in the manner of a reformed smoker.

'I take it I'd have heard if we'd identified an obvious strangler in the street.'

'It's all looking above board, Guv. Mostly elderly folks, scattering of young couples, a few girls sharing, three single mothers – like that Kelly we saw – but no single males – at least not under pension age. Then again, how old was Dr Crippen?'

'Crippen didn't climb mountains.'

'Fair point, Guv.'

Skelgill is silent for a moment as he concentrates on an overtaking manoeuvre.

'Leyton – get someone round all the bookmakers in Kendal – see if anyone recognises Lee Harris, and whether there's a record of bets he's placed.'

DS Leyton sounds a little unconvinced, but knows better than question his superior. Instead his voice takes on a more animated note.

'By the way, Guv – turns out that bookie, the Scotchwoman, she lives in Ullswater Place with her old ma – suppose it's not surprising seeing as she's been there so long – handy for her work, like.'

'Aye, suppose so.'

*

Strictly speaking Knott Halloo Farm is not Skelgill's next stop, since he makes a short detour to collect a joyous Cleopatra from his dog walker, who has a vet's appointment (or, at least, the lupine Sammy does). In due course, however, he motors up through Threlkeld and continues until he passes the late Walter Barley's cottage. He halts beside one of the barns, alongside the navy-blue Defender belonging to the farmer, and where an open door suggests its owner might be found. Beyond, Lucinda's

Range Rover appears to be absent from the main house. Skelgill fastens Cleopatra onto her baler-twine leash before permitting her to leap from beneath his tailgate.

'Ah, Inspector – it's a fine morning.'

The farmer has been attracted by the sound of Skelgill's approach, and emerges from the barn wiping his hands on an oily rag.

'Sorry to disturb you, sir.'

'Oh, it's no trouble whatsoever – I'm just getting a couple of demonstration models tidied up for the *Great Yorkshire*, Inspector. Killing a bit of time, if truth be told.'

'When does it kick off?'

'Trade day tomorrow, then open to the public through until Sunday.'

'You'll be taking the wife, I imagine, sir?'

The man hesitates just long enough to suggest that Skelgill's innocently aimed question has struck its target. A flicker of alarm darkens his usually bright countenance, and he reaches for the comfort blanket of his neatly trimmed beard.

'Oh, no, Inspector – she's not really keen on that kind of thing – all the standing around – and then we have our livestock here to take care of.'

The two men hold one another's gaze – although it is not an equal contest. Where Skelgill's is keen and penetrative, the other's anticipates a second salvo.

Skelgill clicks his fingers in a self-reprimanding manner.

'Of course, sir – I was forgetting that. Your rare breeds.'

There is palpable relief in the man's demeanour.

'So, er... how may I help you this morning, Inspector?'

Skelgill waves a hand vaguely towards the slopes of Blencathra.

'I just wondered if I might have a bit of a poke around – stretch the legs – I've got the dog today, you see, sir.'

'I do indeed, Inspector – an impressive creature she is, too.' He bends on one knee to make her acquaintance. 'Is she a police dog?'

Skelgill grins at this prospect.

'Let's say she's on probation, sir.'

He perhaps thinks the better of explaining Cleopatra's true provenance, given this man's connection to her former home.

'She's a friendly girl – though you wouldn't want to get on the wrong side of her, I should venture.'

'That goes for a few females I could name, sir.'

The man glances up, a wounded look about his countenance.

'Tell me about it, Inspector.'

Skelgill squats down on his haunches and joins in the patting of the dog; it seems there is some comradely rapport between the two men.

'What I had in mind, sir – if I could see the site of the climbing barn that burnt down – then I thought I might give her a bit of a run up the fell – if you could put me right as to where you've got stock loose.'

'Certainly, Inspector – we'll go now, shall we?'

They set off on foot, passing the farmhouse and following a continuation of the main track through a small copse, to the point where it stops at a wooden gate. There are sheep grazing in this enclosure – regulation Lakeland Herdwicks, their thick grey coats ready for shearing. The animals seem unperturbed as the two men and (more significantly) a dog amble through. The line of the track is just visible, and takes them to an exit gate onto unfenced rough pasture. For a minute or so the gradient steepens, but as they pass between small bluffs, the ground levels and widens into a flat area the size of a large gym hall, with an almost vertical wall of chiselled rock rising on the uphill side.

'I think originally it must have been a quarry, Inspector.'

Skelgill's gaze slowly scans in an arc from left to right – but, apart from the uncharacteristically even ground, there is little to suggest a substantial building once stood on the site; nature has long seen to that. He perhaps appears disappointed, for the man speaks again, apologetically.

'I'm afraid there's not a lot to see – and it's not an area we ever use – just keep the odd bit of equipment up here from time to time.'

Skelgill nods, his features contemplative.

'It's a good distance from the nearest water supply – not the easiest place to put out a fire.'

'I imagine not, Inspector – I really don't know whether they would have tried to get the tenders up the track, or run hoses from the farm.'

Skelgill looks at him intently.

'My sources indicate the barn was pretty far gone by the time the fire bridge arrived, sir.'

The man nods benignly. He has regained his normal easy-going manner.

'I shouldn't be surprised, Inspector.'

'Did Walter Barley ever speak about the incident, sir?'

The man puts his hands into the pockets of his corduroys and taps at a loose rock with the toe of a brogue. He shakes his head.

'I can't recall that he did, Inspector – he was pretty cagey altogether, if truth be told – he wasn't one to pass the time of day.'

'How did you hear about his injury being connected to the fire, sir?'

The man rubs his chin-stubble with the knuckle of a forefinger.

'I'm honestly not sure, Inspector – it's going back quite a bit, of course, and when we took over here his tenancy was a *fait accompli* – Lucinda may have mentioned it to me in passing, but we just treated him as the reclusive neighbour down the road.'

Skelgill is about to respond, but Cleopatra suddenly decides there is something of interest in a nearby patch of bracken; she catches him off guard and to keep his balance he lurches in her desired direction. The attraction turns out to be a dead rabbit, desiccated and long picked over by crows, though its honeyed, musky odour must be a cornucopia of pleasure to a canine snout. When Skelgill turns he sees that the farmer has also moved away; he is down on one knee examining a patch of grass, perhaps three yards square, cropped short by extant herbivores. As Skelgill approaches he begins to pull at some protrusion in one corner.

'Cliff?'

Skelgill steps nearer.

'Cliff Edge?'

The man does not react. For a few seconds he continues tugging at whatever it is, but then he looks around in surprise.

'I'm sorry, Inspector – I was distracted – you said something – about a *cliff?*'

A sudden look of alarm occupies Skelgill's face, and his cheekbones redden, like a schoolboy who has blurted out a confession to a blissfully ignorant master when none was needed.

'Oh, I... er...' He indicates with a thumb over his shoulder to the rock face that borders the site. 'I was thinking... they perhaps used that cliff edge as a natural climbing wall – as well as having an artificial one in the barn.'

The man gazes helpfully past Skelgill.

'Oh, yes – I'm sure that's quite likely – not that it's anything I know much about, Inspector.' Still on his haunches he wipes his hands, and then for illustration purposes pats the end of what appears to be a thick iron link sticking out of the turf. 'My chain harrow, Inspector – I wondered where it had gone.'

Skelgill, recovering his composure, squints at the object.

'What – it's *buried?*'

The man struggles to his feet, looking a little sheepish.

'Well – yes – it has become somewhat overgrown. I remember I towed it up here after the last time I used it.'

'Must have been a while ago, sir?'

The man thumbs his beard.

'Probably five years, now you mention it, Inspector. We have a field down towards the village that we used to sow with oats. I ought to give that another go next spring.'

'Want a hand pulling it out? I reckon we could manage it.'

'Oh, no, no – no need, Inspector – thanks all the same – I shall bring up the Defender some time and attach it to the winch. No point in putting out one's back unnecessarily.'

Skelgill, perhaps subconsciously, stretches his spine; there is an old injury that wouldn't be thanking him for his offer of assistance.

'Well – I oughtn't keep you if you're off to Yorkshire later, sir – I'll perhaps just give the dog a bit of a run, if you don't object.'

'Be my guest, Inspector – we don't have any stock on this part of the fell – so she can roam freely.'

*

Though Cleopatra is off the leash, she seems content to stick close to Skelgill as he works his way up the hillside, picking a winding course that finds the easier going. Although there is no trodden path, a firm, dry route is indicated by patches of montane flora, dwarf species that thrive in the fast-draining loam: tormentil, heath bedstraw and wild thyme, miniature meadows of yellow, white and purple, a kaleidoscopic blur beneath the feet. Overhead, in contrast, an azure sky is unblemished by cloud or bird; the clouds will come this evening; the birds less predictably – mid-mornings on such summer days deserve a break, when foraging began six hours ago at dawn.

An abrupt roar has Skelgill turning on his heel to gaze out across the broad dale to the south: an RAF Tornado, silent ahead of its wave of noise, rends the vista, like an artist's knife cutting an unsatisfactory landscape canvas. The eye at first is attracted to the apparent location of the sound, but the fast jet is always several degrees in advance, not easy to spot against the dun fells. He tips a wing at Blencathra, then banks westwards to seek the Irish Sea, beyond Skelgill's horizon, yet only seconds away by supersonic means.

Skelgill watches the modern marvel out of sight, then turns to approach a work of more rudimentary technology. As the gradient steepens, weathered rocks become prominent among the grass and heather, cracked and pitted and encrusted with ancient lichens and mosses, monochromic in their dotage. Blending naturally into this grizzled patchwork is a doorway into Blencathra. Hand-chipped three hundred years ago, the angular entrance to an adit appears black in the bright sun at Skelgill's back. There is no approach path; it is as if the miners who hewed this rough portal kept going and never came out, swallowed by the mountain. Today not even sheep have seen fit to beat a track to its shelter.

He calls in the dog and loops the lead through her collar. Obediently, she walks to heel as he ducks into the mouth of the tunnel. Skelgill might wonder what bantam ancestors of his toiled here – if they worked unbowed they must have stood a good half-foot shorter than he. His discomfort is compounded by the lack of a torch – even his mobile phone is still clipped in place to the dashboard of his car. He faces velvet blackness until his pupils adjust from bright sunshine. As such, with his free hand, he fumbles blindly in the void before him, like a subterranean creature would use its antennae.

Though never a caver himself, he is no stranger to this underground world; boyhood dares concerned these places, and his mountain rescue team is summoned likewise on occasion, and trains for all eventualities. In such circumstances he would be fully equipped with helmet, harness, rope and head-torch. Abreast of the horror stories, therefore, his caution is to be expected. Cleopatra, however, knows no such trepidation, and moves ahead in investigative fashion. Of course, her rod-rich retinas endow her with six times the night-vision of her companion, and perhaps sensing this Skelgill lets out a few turns of the leash from his wrist. Where his forbears held forth a canary, he follows a four-legged friend.

In the classical manner, the adit bores horizontally into the hillside, a speculative shot uncannily aimed at pockets of rare metal ores, deposits that had lain undisturbed for millions of years, gathering interest. As Skelgill's eyes begin to adjust to the lack of light, any gains are offset by the intensifying darkness as he explores further from the entrance. The roof and walls of the passage begin to crowd in, and he opts to run his free hand along the uneven ceiling, as a precaution to warn against a jutting rock.

But it is no such solid protrusion that he encounters – instead something altogether more unearthly – as clammy webbed fingers grasp his palm. What *Gollum*-like creature can this be? He jerks back with a cry of shock. There is a flutter in the air – and perhaps a tiny guttural breath. It is a bat. Minding its own

246

business, it has found its beauty sleep rudely interrupted by Skelgill's clumsy fumblings. It beats about for a couple of seconds, and then apparently heads deeper into the tunnel. Cleopatra, momentarily alarmed by Skelgill's reflex squawk, switches quickly into hunting mode – unlike her master, she can hear the tiny winged mammal's cries of indignation. She darts forward and – in succumbing to this instinct – takes a leap in the dark that is very nearly her last, for just ahead of them lies an invisible abyss. But one further feature of canine biology delays this undesirable outcome: where two legs would have seen her plummet to her doom, instead only her front paws initially slide over the edge of the shaft. In this hiatus, the length of baler twine attached to Skelgill's wrist provides a temporary lifeline. Skelgill, after first recoiling from the bat, is now yanked forward in a manner that must seem like the take of a pike to break all records; a take of the kind that catches him blithely off guard, perhaps as he inattentively retrieves after the last cast of the day. As such, what can only be learned behaviour – but which for him has become as good as instinct – kicks in, and he, in a manner of speaking, strikes. This action holds the dog fast – so long as the baler twine will remain intact. Skelgill drops to his knees, and with an angler's aplomb he winds in the line in short sharp jerks as he crawls towards her, all the time maintaining the tension. Then with one sudden lunge he slides his free hand down the line and grabs her collar. Cleopatra might weigh fifty pounds, and Skelgill might have a latent back injury, but adrenaline is a remarkable substance, and he hauls the dog one-handed over his shoulder and deposits her on the cave floor behind him. He unravels the leash from his wrist and casts down the free end. At this juncture no one can really blame poor Cleopatra for making a bolt for the light at the end of the tunnel.

Skelgill remains on his knees. He turns back to face into the darkness. Cautiously he slides along on his hands until he reaches the edge of the pit. There is nothing to see – it is just a marginally blacker pool that spreads across the dark width of the passageway. Skelgill tuts in self-reprimand; he knows the dangers of these dank places, that their eighteenth century architects were prone to sink shafts seemingly at random. He fumbles about and finds a loose stone. Then he tosses it like a coin, with a flick of his thumb. He counts – one, two, three... *splash*. Somewhere between one hundred-and-fifty and two hundred feet, and who knows what beneath the water? He backs well away before he rises, cautiously raising his hands above his head to feel his way. Now, however, his eyes are functioning with greater efficiency, and in any event there is the light that filters in from the narrow portal. Cleopatra's silhouette paces to and fro, eager to greet her rescuer, oblivious to his role in her near downfall.

As much as Skelgill was blinded by the darkness when he entered the cave, the glare of the sun must now seem like a dizzying explosion of light, in which the universe turns white and the stellar blossoms of the bedstraw blend into one all-enveloping Milky Way. Indeed, he clears the mouth of the tunnel and sways across to a grassy hummock, upon which he sinks gratefully. He grins affectionately at Cleopatra, who joins him and settles down, her death-defying episode as quickly forgotten as her last meal. Skelgill casts about as though he is missing his *Kelly Kettle* – which, of course, he is. Then he notices the twine trailing from the dog's collar, and unfastens the loop and absently winds it into a loose hank.

While he is doing this, his gaze falls upon the wrist of his right hand, the one around which he had anchored the lead. There are red welts and strangled creases in his weathered skin. At first his expression is one of mild annoyance. But as he continues to regard the injury, a realisation settles upon his countenance: one of great concern and yet equally magnificent illumination. Shocked, for a moment he sits upright and stares unseeing across the dale. Then a determination sets in. He rises and, with a click of the fingers to the dog, sets off at a trot down the fellside.

24. CLIFF EDGE

Wednesday afternoon

'Hello?'

'Er... is that *Mary?*'

The man seems to have a mild speech disorder; he pronounces the 'r' in Mary as a 'w'.

'Aha.'

'Oh, I er... I was reading your profile... on *Streetwise.*' Again there is the substituted letter.

'Aha.'

'Is it convenient to talk?'

'Ja.'

Despite her assent, the woman sounds disinterested. Her Eastern European accent does not reflect her quintessentially English pseudonym.

'I was thinking of making an appointment.'

'Is sixty for half hour. One hundred one hour.'

'Okay.'

'You want come now?'

'Oh... er, no – I was wondering about tomorrow – I wanted to ask you...'

But the woman has hung up.

The man returns his attention to his computer screen. He exits the profile of 'Mary' and returns to a menu page, with thumbnail photographs and abbreviated descriptions – a kind of small ads section for sexual services. He scrolls up and down and then selects one of the dozen or so images. Now he reaches again for the phone, activates the speaker, and taps in the next number. There is a prolonged period of ringing and, once the call is answered, a few seconds in which female and male voices can be heard in the background.

'Hiya.'

She follows the convention of not answering by name.

'*Belle?*'

'That's right, darling.'

The woman sounds a little breathless.

'Is it a bad time just now?'

'Not at all, darling – I was just saying cheerio to my last gentleman.'

The man hesitates, perhaps momentarily disconcerted by the image of this prosaic detail.

'I'm phoning – about an appointment – and to ask a few things.'

'Ask away, chuck.'

The *chuck* – perhaps a careless lapse from the more intimate 'darling' – is suggestive of Mancunian origins, though her accent is hard to discern. Her voice has a note of maturity that does not exactly correlate with her youthful and likely airbrushed photographs.

'It says on your profile – in your likes – it mentions bondage.'

'That can be arranged – on you, that is.'

'Oh – of course – what exactly do you – er, offer?'

The woman sounds accustomed to dealing with nervous prospects; she makes an exaggerated purring sound in the back of her throat.

'I've got lovely metal handcuffs – same as the police use – for your wrists *and* your ankles – and a policewoman's outfit – my gentlemen seem to like the short skirt and suspenders when they're being – *arrested.*'

Now she laughs salaciously.

'Well, er – I...'

'I can pretend to be a policeman, if that's what you prefer – the *truncheon*, you know?'

The man's mouth is dry, and before he can construct a reply the woman speaks again.

'When did you want to *come?*'

'I, er... was thinking of tomorrow – which area of town are you?'

'In the new motel by the M6 – I've got a late checkout until one, so my last appointment will be at twelve – unless you just want the half-hour, darling?'

'Twelve is fine.'

'It's a hundred and thirty for the hour.'

'Okay.'

'What name was it, darling?'

'Oh, it's er... Cliff.'

'See you tomorrow at twelve then, Cliff.'

As soon as the call is ended the man returns to the online menu. He browses for a while, clicking to and fro between various profiles. Eventually he settles upon one featuring a shapely blonde described as being in her early twenties – though a veil of hair cleverly obscures her face. Again he engages his speaker function and types in the number. This time the call is answered almost immediately.

'Hello.'

Once more the voice has an older ring to it than might be expected from the girl pictured.

'Is that Anna?'

This time it is the woman that hesitates before she replies.

'You want an appointment?'

'I was hoping...'

'I'm fully booked this week.'

Her voice lacks the warmth of the previous respondent. Her accent may be local, though it is relatively neutral.

'You were recommended to me...'

'Who by?'

'I don't know if they'd want me to mention their names – it's some of my old pals – connected through *Streetwise*.'

Again he pronounces the word with difficulty.

'Are you a member?'

'I've been away – for a long time – I've just come back to the area – I've only got a couple of ratings – you were recommended to me, you see.'

'What's your nickname? We only see members with positive feedback.'

'Mine is positive – if you want to check it – search under ... *Cliff Edge*.'

The woman does not reply. It is possible that she too is looking online – perhaps silently upon a tablet. After a few moments she speaks, and now for the first time there is a note of enthusiasm in her tone.

'What did you have in mind?'

'I noticed on your profile page it says you provide bondage.'

'That's not on us, you realise?'

'When you say *us*...?'

'It's a two-girl service.'

'Oh, right.'

'Are you looking at *Streetwise* now?'

'I am, yes.'

'Click on the tab that says *Duo*.'

There is a pause as the man does as she suggests. Now before him there are lurid images of the blond posing provocatively with a considerably taller, though no less alluring, brunette. They are advertised as sisters, Anna and Alanna. After a few moments he exhales heavily.

'That's exactly the kind of thing.'

'Have you done it before?'

The man, though apprehensive, manages a nervous chuckle.

'I think you could say I know the ropes.'

Again there is the speech impediment, and he pronounces the final word as *wopes*. The girl gives the impression that she is listening intently, her breathing now audible down the line.

'Can you just hold on a second, honey – while I check my sister's diary?'

'Sure.'

After perhaps as long as a minute, she comes back on the line.

'When were you thinking of?'

'Are you free tomorrow, about midday?'

'Yes, we can manage that.'

'Ok, then – I'd like to go ahead.'

'That's you booked in, honey.'

'How about the address?'

'Will you be coming by car?'

'I guess, so.'

'Do you know Penrith, honey?'

'Reasonably.'

'There's a big supermarket on Scotland Road.'

'I think I remember that.'

'You can park there – it's free. Cross towards the town centre – there's a phone box. Call us from that number – then we'll know you're not a time-waster.'

'Okay.'

'Then we'll give you the address – you can walk from there.'

'Perfect.'

As soon as they end the call the man resumes his perusal of the *Duo* page. On reflection he might note that the woman never mentioned the price.

25. CRUNCH TIME

Thursday morning

DS Leyton and DS Jones, who have not actually laid eyes on their superior for the best part of two days, assemble timeously in his office for an eleven o'clock debriefing. Of Skelgill, however, there is no sign. The sun slants intermittently through the dust-streaked glass of the window, as cloud that brought overnight rain progressively breaks up; DS Jones moves to adjust the blinds accordingly. DS Leyton places a mug of tea on Skelgill's desk: a precaution to save him being immediately despatched for the same, before a meeting can begin.

After about fifteen minutes – during which the two officers first exchange pleasantries but then begin to share their concerns over the impending deadline for producing tangible progress in the case – there is suddenly an unfamiliar scrabbling sound as something approaches rapidly along the corridor. Enter Cleopatra, dragging her leash. Nosing open the door, she appears delighted to see both of the detectives, and dodges to and fro, uncertain of how to divide her affections between them. (It must be said, DS Leyton is a less-willing recipient.) Skelgill enters a moment later, carrying a worn roll of carpet and the bottom half of a round green bait box that still has a scattering of blowfly pupae stuck to its inner wall.

'Change of plan – I need you to look after Cleopatra for a bit. Stick her in the corner – she'll be fine – you can take it in turns to work in here.'

DS Leyton, in particular, looks alarmed at this prospect – and recoils as Skelgill drops the rank-smelling rug onto his lap and hands him the improvised drinking bowl.

'Dog walker's got an emergency – took Sammy into the vet yesterday – got him x-rayed – turns out he's swallowed an entire cob of sweet corn – needs an op.'

DS Leyton now grimaces, perhaps thinking through the corollary of ingesting such an item.

'Leave you to it – got to get to the bank – catch up this afternoon.' Skelgill is already heading out of his office, when an afterthought strikes him. 'She'll need a walk shortly – visit to the ladies' – if you know what I mean?'

He winks and is gone, swiftly closing the door to thwart any prospective canine escape bid.

DS Leyton pushes the rug unceremoniously onto the floor. Cleopatra approaches and sniffs at it rather despondently. DS Jones, though shaking her head, looks amused.

'I could do without this, Emma – I've got to meet the door-to-door team at twelve over on that new estate.'

DS Jones stands up and relieves him of the drinking bowl.

'Why don't I come with you? I could give the dog a bit of a walk – there's that big green in the middle of all the houses.'

DS Leyton glances at Cleopatra, who seems to know she is the subject of the discussion and cocks her head on one side, as if she keenly is awaiting his decision.

'Kills two birds with one stone, I suppose.'

'It's better than keeping her cooped up in here. And my team are going to be busy for the next hour or so. I can leave them to it.'

DS Leyton nods decisively.

'Let's do it.' Cleopatra butts his knee and he reaches out to give her a tentative pat. 'You're not such a bad old girl, are you?'

DS Jones inspects the bowl, and grimaces as she notices its unsavoury contents.

'I'll just go and rinse this and get her a drink.'

But as she reaches to open the door someone from outside beats her to it. It is DI Smart. He smirks at the female officer and casts a patronising nod at the still-seated DS Leyton. Then his gaze falls distastefully upon the Bullboxer, who is cautiously sniffing at the toe of his nearest shoe.

'I heard Skelly had his dog in – what is this, an amateur bloodhound?'

Before either of Skelgill's sergeants can fashion a reply in his defence, DI Smart speaks again.

'Sooner this larking about's over the better for all of us – when's his meeting with the Chief?'

DS Leyton fidgets uncomfortably.

'Close of play today, sir.'

'Tidy – well, on Friday we can start with a clean sheet.' He takes a step back, frowning, evidently irritated by the dog's interest in his footwear. Then he reaches down and brushes at the trousers of his designer suit – although Cleopatra has made no contact with them. 'Tell you what – to kick things off, I'll treat you to a curry – a good old Ruby Murray eh, Leyton? Get the professional show on the road.'

DS Leyton nods without enthusiasm. DS Jones is looking stone faced.

'Won't be Manchester standard, I'm afraid – but beggars can't be choosers, eh?'

And with this – arguably double-edged observation – he slides out of the office and pulls the door to behind him.

DS Leyton can't help himself from letting go an expletive.

'Excuse my French.'

DS Jones shrugs. She seems pensive.

'I wonder where he has gone.' She refers to Skelgill. 'He didn't seem too concerned about the meeting with the Chief.'

'Maybe he's having lunch with her – he was swanky by his usual standards – salaries go in today – perhaps he's treating her – trying to win her over?'

The detectives each look at one another – there is an exchange of unspoken thoughts. They both shake their heads. Then DS Leyton adds a caveat.

'You know the Guvnor, Emma – anything's possible.'

*

The man parks as directed. It is quite likely that he selects the exact spot in the supermarket lot where Barry Seddon left his pick-up just ten days ago. He vaults easily over the perimeter wall and jogs across the road through a gap in the traffic. Some distance off there is a red telephone box. As he approaches he digs in his pocket for change, and then checks his watch. The kiosk is empty, but he waits a minute or so until it is precisely ten to twelve. Then he taps out a number stored on his mobile phone.

'Hello?'

It is the same voice that answered yesterday, although there is perhaps an apprehensive note, even in the single word of acknowledgement.

'It's Cliff – you said to call from here to get your address.'

The girl seems to be listening for his distinctive pronunciation. There is a pause before she replies.

'Thirty-seven Ullswater Place. We'll be ready in ten minutes.'

'Okay, shall I –?'

But the woman has rung off.

The man replaces the receiver in its cradle and exits the booth. Ullswater Place is barely two minutes' brisk walk away. He stands for a moment and looks about rather aimlessly, like someone who has missed a bus and is mentally unprepared for the wait. The morning is blustery, though mild, with scattered clouds and bursts of bright sunshine. He notices a family of swallows resting on a telegraph wire, jabbering excitedly amongst themselves. Then he seems to have an idea, and sets off purposefully back past the supermarket and crossing towards the arcade of shops. Here he slows his pace, and considers each outlet thoughtfully as he passes. They appear quiet – indeed the bookmaker's has a handwritten sign on its door saying 'Back Soon' – though giving no indication as to when that might be. Reaching the corner, he turns into Ullswater Place. Now he consults his wristwatch again: it is five to twelve. He walks the length of the street, on the side of the odd numbers, reaching the row of garages. Turning, he slowly retraces his steps, all the way to the corner, en route stepping off the narrow kerb to enable an old woman pulling a shopping caddy to have right of way. One more about turn and he makes his final half-lap of the stretch of pavement. Arriving at number thirty-seven he knocks and is promptly admitted. At a house opposite, net curtains twitch.

*

While DS Leyton stands surrounded by an attentive cluster of clipboard-bearing uniformed police officers, DS Jones strolls unobtrusively at the far side of the large central grassy area thoughtfully designed for residents of the new housing scheme. There is a fenced-off play zone, where a couple of bored-looking mothers are exercising their boisterous pre-school children, and – at alternate intervals around the perimeter path – benches and waste bins, some of the latter specifically designated for dog owners. DS Jones, though armed with a polythene carrier bag from the supply in her colleague's car boot, as yet has not had to avail herself of this facility. There are also young saplings ringing the small park, although several appear the worse for wear, vandalised in keeping with the general background haze of graffiti that has colonised most flat surfaces like some inarticulate urban lichen.

Despite the grass being damp, and in need of a cut, Cleopatra seems more content to walk on this than the path, which has dried in the light wind. Being a female of her species, she shows scant interest in the invisible doggy messaging that has been layered upon the various upright obstacles thoughtfully provided by human planners for canine convenience. But she is none the less alert to her surroundings, and deals short shrift to any others of her kind who dare brazenly to inspect her hindquarters. She is not a dog to be trifled with.

Following one such incident she suddenly stiffens, turning to face into the breeze. Her ears are pricked and she strains at the leash. DS Jones appears bemused, as there is no one – human or canine – to be seen; at least not until an elderly lady with a wheeled shopping bag emerges from a fenced walkway between two houses, and continues around the far side of the green (ignored by the dog). Then Cleopatra is obliged to fend off another unwanted advance, and by the time she has made clear her displeasure, whatever raised her interest appears to have passed. DS Jones glances across to DS Leyton – he is still preoccupied with his debriefing, so she sets off on another lap of the oval. Perhaps the polythene bag will soon be called upon.

*

The man – having requested that he keep on his boxer shorts (initially, at least) – is now spread-eagled upon a PVC sheet in the small dimly lit room on the first floor at the back of the terraced house. The remainder of his clothes are laid over an easy chair, itself draped in a decorative woollen throw. His valuables rest upon a nightstand beside the double bed.

The blonde woman in the dominatrix outfit works assiduously, systematically tightening the bands that restrain him, rather in the perfunctory manner of a truck driver strapping down a load of timber. The wide *Velcro* cuffs grip his wrists and ankles, yet as she stretches the sinews of his joints, they make little if any impression into his flesh: just the job to avoid taking home telltale signs of an illicit hour's activity – if indeed one is *going* home.

The subdual completed to her satisfaction, the woman turns to the various accessories arranged on the bedside table. She selects a black rubber ball-gag and, as the man opens his mouth to protest, pops it into place and reaches behind his head to secure its straps. Now she stands back to admire her handiwork.

'Time to fetch Alanna.'

Throughout this preparatory procedure, her expression has been businesslike and aloof. But now her features soften and – despite her stated intent to the contrary – she does not move away. Instead she regards the man with a certain desirous curiosity. Then she turns and picks up a bottle of oil. She flips open the lid and, reaching over him, in an almost experimental fashion squirts a jet of liquid in a zigzag pattern, working from his chest, down to – and in fact carelessly over – the fabric of his close-fitting boxer shorts. Carefully she re-seals and replaces the bottle. Now she begins to smooth the oil over his well-formed pectorals, dwelling on his nipples with the heel of her hand. Gradually she moves her attention to his abdominals – he has a distinct six-pack and no obvious fat – and thence slides her fingers slowly and deliberately beneath the waistband of his underwear. So far the man has not reacted – despite her attention to his impressively toned muscles, he has not moved one of them. But now his body visibly tenses, and for the next few moments he closes his eyes as the woman explores freely.

Suddenly there is a single tap on the door. It might have been a draught – but the woman reacts instantly, withdrawing her hand and stepping back from the bed. She picks up a small towel and, wiping away the oil, she bustles around the bed. The man watches dumbly as she opens the door a fraction, and then steps back to admit a tall brunette, similarly attired.

This second woman – 'Alanna' – is considerably taller, certainly younger, though she has an altogether different build; when it comes to feminine curves, it is the elder that has the advantage. As she enters the room she pauses to slide a small bolt, before turning to take in the scene before her. She notices the glisten of the oil in the candlelight, and perhaps more than that.

'What's going on?'

There is an accusing note in her voice, which is throaty in tone.

'Just teasing him.'

The blonde – 'Anna' – looks a touch abashed.

'Time for teasing's over.'

The brunette steps forwards purposefully, and clambers onto the bed, kneeling between the outstretched legs of the man. As she gains her balance, in her right hand she brings into his line of sight a length of climbing rope, wound into a coil. He eyes this keenly, and makes an unintelligible sound through the gag.

'Clifford.'

For a moment this is the only word she says. She stares acutely at his strained features.

'It's been a long wait, Clifford.'

Again there is a stifled response.

'I probably wouldn't know you if we passed in the street. Maybe we have. I was too young to remember much at all. But there are some things you never forget. I wonder if you remember me, Clifford.'

The woman drops the rope and with both hands rips back her long dark wig. Beneath is short-cropped blonde hair. Then she gestures to the blonde, who passes her the hand towel. Roughly she wipes away her crimson lipstick, and much of the make-up from her face. Then she tears open her black PVC basque and tosses it aside. Beneath is a distinctly male torso.

'You liked little boys, didn't you, Clifford?'

The man seems fascinated, staring, transfixed – at the moment stunned by the revelation.

'You liked the girls – you liked my sister, especially – but really you preferred the boys. You and your disgusting friends.'

Now the young man – for that is what he is – holds up the rope close before his captive's eyes. The man seems to be gulping, swallowing the saliva that must be building up behind the gag.

'But your pals have gone, Clifford – we've seen to that – they took our bait – just like you have. Fancy choosing your old nickname – *Cliff Edge*.'

The young man begins to wave the coil of rope to and fro, close to the older man's face.

'We've saved the best until last – the ringleader. Now it's your turn to feel powerless – unable to resist – how do you think that felt – not daring to tell?'

He giggles rather manically, and glances at the blonde; she looks on implacably.

'Not that you'll be able to tell – we don't take prisoners – at least, not for long – you've made us what we are, Clifford.'

He slips off the end of the bed and moves around to one side. Seen now as an overtly masculine figure, half-naked yet wearing women's thigh-length boots and a matching black PVC thong, he is like a demonic satyr in a distorted burlesque version of a Greek drama. He shakes out the rope from its coils and slides one end beneath the man's neck, then growls with satisfaction as his sister pulls several feet through and they exchange the loose ends. Then the pair crowd over their victim. Gradually they draw in their respective sections of the rope until it begins to tighten around his neck, compressing his prominent Adam's apple.

Now, for the first time, the man begins to protest. His limbs are stretched to the extent that his whole body is immobilised – resistance as such is futile – all he can move is his head, but turning it from side to side serves little purpose other than to create painful friction against the tightening rope. Instead, he resorts to what limited vocal options are available to him – unintelligible moans as they might be. And yet, they appear to win him a moment's respite, for the young man releases the tension upon the rope and nods to his sister to do likewise.

'What is it, Clifford – trying to say sorry? It's a bit late for that.'

But nevertheless he reaches behind the man's head and rips open the strap that retains the ball-gag; he drags the object from the man's mouth.

'I'm a police officer! – let me go! – my colleagues are on their –'

Before the gasping man can complete the final phrase his captor jams the gag back into his mouth, forcing it crudely between his bared teeth with both thumbs. He sneers malevolently.

'Nice try, Clifford – but it's only you that likes a little bit of *wope*, isn't it *Cliffowd*?'

As he imitates the man's distinctive speech impediment, and then places the stress on his name, he gives the rope a sharp tug, catching his sister unaware, and dragging the man's head to one side. If she has experienced a fleeting doubt, he does not allow her to dwell upon it. With malign intent he stares across his supine victim until – as if she is under some hypnotic spell – she takes up the slack.

'Last one, sis – and then we've done it.' The muscles of his arms contract as he tightens his grip. 'Goodbye Clifford Stewart.'

But it is not *Goodbye Clifford Stewart*, for the man about to die really is a police officer, by the name of Detective Inspector Daniel Skelgill.

At this moment, there is a faint sound from beyond the bedroom door. Perhaps the rattle of a letterbox as the midday mail is delivered. The assassins pay no attention to this, immersed in their gruesome ritual, their eyes fixed snakelike upon their victim. There is a louder sound and the blonde girl glances up. Her brother shows no sign of response – he is yet too engrossed in the task. But then, all in a rush, there is the clump of rapid footsteps on the stairs, the rattle of the bedroom door – which of course is bolted from within – and then an almighty crack as it flies open and simultaneously the athletic figure of DS Jones follows through with the karate-style kick that has broken it down. The door swings around and slams against a mirror, sending shards scattering about the room. The two siblings release the rope and back away on either side of the bed. DS Jones takes in the scene and cries out the name of her boss. A second later, DS Leyton, preceded by Cleopatra straining violently at her lead, lurches into the room, his boots heavy on the bare boards. The young man bends down and picks up a shard of the mirror, he steps towards the two police officers, wielding it like a knife.

'Drop that – and get down on the floor!'

DS Leyton's command, peppered as it is by a string of East End superlatives, stops the young man in his tracks, but he shows no sign of obeying the command.

'You've got three seconds, sonny boy! – then I release the pit-bull! – when I give the code word, she'll rip out your throat!'

The man glances down at the dog – certainly she is straining hard and apparently preparing to spring in his direction.

'Drop it – and get down! Three! Two! One–'

And at the count of one the man does as ordered. Whether it is from fear of what fate is about to befall him (for he cannot know that Cleopatra's only interest is in leaping upon the bed to greet her master, whose scent she detected so frustratingly from the park only a few minutes earlier), or because the realisation strikes home that the captive cannot be their intended victim; either way, he yields.

'And *you* – down – flat on the floor!'

DS Leyton points to the blonde woman, now almost exhausting his lexicon of oaths for stressful situations; more easily defeated, she obeys compliantly.

DS Jones leaps onto the bed and reaches frantically over Skelgill's unmoving torso; his eyes are closed and saliva drains like a departing life force from one corner of his purple lips.

'Guv, Guv – oh, please no, Guv!'

She rips away the gag and the rope and slaps his cheeks. There is no response.

'Guv – please, Guv!'

There are tears streaming down her face but her training kicks in and she defaults immediately to first aid mode. Kneeling upright she places the heel of one hand upon his breastbone and prepares to begin compressions. Then his eyes flick open.

'What kept you two?'

'Guv!'

DS Jones looks like she is about to slap him again, but then she grabs his face roughly between her hands and bends over and plants her lips upon his – mouth to mouth, but not as the British Police First Aid Manual defines it.

'Sergeant Jones – *cuffs*!' DS Leyton ends this sentence with a final useful phrase that shocks his colleague back to the reality of the situation – he means they must restrain the suspects.

DS Jones clambers off the bed and pulls her handcuffs from her belt. Quickly she secures the young man, and then rounds to repeat the procedure with the girl, taking DS Leyton's proffered handcuffs. That done, she turns to unfasten Skelgill's bonds – these are easily removed – although only if one has a free hand. Skelgill sits up, wiping his lips.

'Back-up?'

'On the way, Guv – I radioed just before we entered. Be here any second, I reckon.'

Skelgill now demonstrates just how quickly a man can get dressed, especially when he knows uniformed police officers are about to burst upon a somewhat compromising situation. He pockets his personal belongings and socks, and jams on his shoes. Meanwhile DS Leyton has ordered the detainees from the room, and driven them ahead of him down the stairs. Cleopatra sits patiently, and now Skelgill squats down to stroke her behind the ears. He tugs at his shirt – the oil is making it stick, and seeping through in darker blotches.

'How did you find me?'

DS Jones perhaps suffering a sudden ebb of adrenaline, sits to face him, lowering herself onto the end of the bed. She grins and slowly shakes her head. He is incorrigible – his life just saved and it is business as usual.

'The bookmaker, Guv – the Scottish woman. She lives across the road. She'd popped back to help her old mother with something – the mother spotted you walking up and down the street and thought you were a suspicious character. She called her daughter to the window – she recognised you and saw you come in here. Then a male she didn't recognise – the young guy I guess – looked out of the door a minute or so later – he seemed to be checking that the street was all clear – then the curtains at the front of the house were pulled to. DS Leyton had given her his card. She phoned us – we were in the park just through the ginnel. DS Leyton was briefing his team – I was walking Cleopatra. As luck would have it.'

Skelgill nods pensively.

'What made you break in?'

DS Jones flashes him a bashful glance.

'Maybe women's intuition?'

Skelgill grins ruefully.

'More likely you're picking up my bad habits.'

26. THE TAJ MAHAL

Friday evening

That Skelgill has offered to treat his trusty lieutenants to a Friday night feast, signing off the week in style, ostensibly owes itself to a celebration of a job well done, and – though he has played down the *bare* facts, so to speak – to thank them for their timely intervention at thirty-seven Ullswater Place. *Ostensibly*. With Skelgill, however, nothing is ever that simple. Indeed the seasoned (and thus cynical) observer might also ascribe certain ulterior motives to his generosity, such as delivering 'one in the eye' to his rival DI Smart, and – not least – the excuse to partake in the virtually unlimited amount of food that always seems to be a feature of an Indian meal.

And there is one last pudding to be proved in the eating – whether Skelgill has remembered his wallet.

The past thirty hours have been something of an expedition for both sergeants – as if the great uncharted river they have been navigating has suddenly flowed majestically into its delta. The final outcome – its imminent confluence with the ocean – is no longer in doubt, but the myriad of channels and connections that have opened up for investigation has almost been overwhelming. The arrest has raised as many questions as it has answered.

Skelgill, on the other hand, has for long periods kept a low profile, paddling away on his own canoe 'to get his head round his report'. Today he reappeared just before five p.m. with what looked suspiciously like fisherman's sunburn across his cheekbones.

In these respects, the relaxed early-evening gathering at the Taj Mahal provides the perfect opportunity for the three colleagues to catch up and share their findings. DS Leyton, having dipped his nose in the froth atop a pint of chilled Indian lager, begins in typically self-deprecating style.

'I couldn't have been more wrong, Guv – at the start – thinking it was some crackpot randomly picking off his victims.'

DS Jones glances sympathetically at her fellow officer.

'The thing is – they did appear totally unconnected.' She turns to Skelgill, who sits facing her across the table. 'That was amazing how you made the link, Guv.'

Skelgill averts his eyes; perhaps he detects an underlying note of inquiry in DS Jones's congratulatory remark. He snaps a poppadum into two and then carefully pushes the pieces together on his plate to give the impression of an undamaged whole.

'We talked about getting a break – well we got one, but I just didn't know it at the time.' He takes a tentative sip of his own lager, and pulls a disapproving face before swallowing a second larger mouthful, as if washing down the unpleasant taste with more of the same is the best remedy. 'I rescue a holidaymaker's kid up at Sharp Edge – give the mother a hard time – she claims she used to come up as a schoolgirl – when she was a member of the outward bound centre – her and her mate had a crush on the instructors – but she didn't mention any names, and so there's no story at this point.'

Now he jabs at the poppadum with stiffly spread fingers and causes irreversible damage.

'Until Walter Barley cops it – in ritual style with a climbing rope. Suddenly there's a connection of a sort – Barley used to be a labourer at a farm where a climbing barn burnt down. Okay – it's nearly twenty years later that he's murdered, but then we hear he had some involvement at the time of the fire.'

Skelgill begins to scoop up sweet mango chutney and sour lime pickle. He eats it swiftly before continuing with his monologue.

'Then I remembered that Liz –' (he hesitates for a second, as though using her first name is some small *faux pas*) 'Mrs Williams – the little girl's mother – said she had a scrapbook and photographs.'

More poppadum-and-pickles goes the way of the previous.

'It was a shot in the dark – but there it was – a kind of team photo taken in the barn, the kids and the adults – the quad bikes were lined up in front of the climbing wall – and all the folk sitting on them or clinging to ropes in various positions. From teenagers down to primary school age.'

Now Skelgill systematically breaks the remaining pieces of poppadum into little pieces. He looks up and glances from one colleague to the other.

'We have to trace all those kids.'

There is a sombre moment as both sergeants nod gravely. After a respectable silence, DS Jones's curiosity gets the better of her.

'How did you manage to get the photograph, Guv?'

'What?' Skelgill scratches his head absently. 'It must have been Monday night I went down to Wales.'

There is the unasked question of how he was able to contact 'Mrs Williams'. It appears Skelgill's account will skirt around this detail.

'She remembered Clifford Stewart and Walter Barley by their first names. Okay, so we'd have expected to find them in this photo – but there were two other adult males in the picture.'

Skelgill signals to a waiter for more poppadums.

'I drove back through the early hours – holding my breath all the way to Hinckley. I knocked-up that poor woman Linda Harris at the crack of dawn. But, sure enough – she identified Lee Harris – he'd have been about eighteen at the time. She showed me a picture of him not much younger. Then she even made me a bacon cob, Leyton.'

DS Leyton grins in a relieved manner.

'We thought you were a bit cream-crackered on Tuesday, Guv.' He glances at DS Jones. 'Either that or we were boring you something rotten.'

'There's never a dull moment when you're around Leyton.'

'I'll take that as a compliment, Guv.'

Skelgill produces a wry smile.

'Then I took the photo to Hilda Seddon and she picked out Barry Seddon. So I'd got a connection between the victims –

and that confirmed my suspicion that Clifford Stewart would be next – but I still had no real idea of what they'd been up to – why they were being targeted. Liz mentioned in passing that the 'Walter' character had a bad case of wandering hands, but that was as far as it went – and she just shrugged it off as par for the course back in those days.'

Now Skelgill is pensive for a few moments. Perhaps without realising, he has lapsed back into the familiar in referring to Liz Williams by her first name. He looks up at DS Jones, who is watching him with interest.

'Seems like she was one of the lucky ones. Jones – your team will need to pick this up with her.'

DS Jones nods, and appears satisfied by this act of delegation.

But DS Leyton is looking puzzled.

'So, Guv – Clifford Stewart and Walter Barley, I get – like you say, they were based on the farm. But how did the other two become involved?'

'Think about it, Leyton – for example, what piece of kit would you need to build and service a climbing wall?'

DS Leyton holds up an index finger to indicate his sudden enlightenment.

'You mean scaffolding, Guv?'

'Exactly – and it doesn't come cheap. Even full-time builders hire scaffolding – so Seddon must have had the contract for Knott Halloo Farm – would have made regular maintenance visits. Meanwhile Lee Harris is the local itinerant Honda expert – in the photo, all the quad bikes were Hondas. He must have drifted up north with the travelling fair, and thereafter stuck around plying his trade – probably had regular jobs at the adventure centre – service and repairs. Settled in the area after it went bust – as we know, was working down at Kendal most recently.'

Skelgill drinks some more of his lager.

'So that connects all of our four victims – if you count Clifford Stewart as a victim – to Knott Halloo Farm. Given it burnt down not long after, and they appear to have dispersed as a group, I figured it was a fair bet that it was someone from that era that was after them. Then you have to ask why? And why the rope? To be honest – I only got the answer to that when it was round my own neck. An eleventh-hour confession, you might say.'

The two sergeants exchange a look of alarm, but DS Leyton tactfully steers the conversation away from this particular precipice.

'Talk of confession – they ain't singing yet, Guv – but we're starting to fill in the gaps.' He takes a sip of lager like a conference speaker realising his mouth is dry. 'Their real names are Jason and Kaye Lamb – brother and sister – though both adopted – looks like the biological parents may have been travellers. They grew up mainly in the Penrith area. She's apparently been working as an escort around Cumbria for quite a few years, under a string of aliases. He's been living in Manchester – early indications are that he's been involved in the transvestite scene down there, roughly the same line as his sister. We think we've located him on a couple of dodgy websites. She's now thirty-one and he's twenty-six – take that back to the time of the fire and she'd be thirteen and him just eight. There's a record of them being taken into care not long after – followed by some troublesome fosterings. Pair of them kept running away and eventually when they were old enough they just disappeared off Social Services' radar.'

DS Jones is listening intently. She turns her glass of sparkling water so that the brand logo is facing away from her.

'Guv, there's an ironic parallel with Lee Harris. I've been speaking again with the liaison officer who contacted his real mother. She's had another chat with her. She's still a bit cagey, but reading between the lines, Lee Harris was being abused and he started mimicking the behaviour – targeting his little sister. That's probably what drove the mother to get him out of the household. Might have saved the sister – but looks like it was too late as far as young Lee was concerned – his path was laid out. Start as a victim – then pass it on.'

DS Leyton turns to DS Jones. 'What advice do you reckon they'll get?' He knows she has been focusing upon this aspect.

270

'I spoke with the Crown Prosecutors this afternoon – they're pretty certain the Lambs will plead guilty once we place the facts before their legal representatives. The circumstantial evidence is already piling up. We rushed through the forensic tests on the debris collected around the property – there's traces of Barry Seddon's DNA on a cigarette end, and of Walter Barley's DNA on a piece of chewing gum. There's also a patch of engine oil that exactly fits the composition of the oil stain beside Lee Harris's flat. It's like each of them left a calling card outside number thirty-seven. Then there's a fibre match on all their clothing – from an unusual mohair blanket that was draped over a chair in the bedroom. We're still doing tests on Jason Lamb's car – but it looks like they moved the bodies as we'd thought, the next night after each murder, straight from the front door into the waiting car – it's barely two yards – wrapped in PVC sheets like the one that was on the bed when we broke in.'

She glances apprehensively at Skelgill, but his gaze remains steely.

'So there's already probably enough there, Guv – without even resorting to the confession they made to you.'

'Unwitnessed.'

The two sergeants appreciate Skelgill's reticence when it comes to the finer details of how he unmasked the criminals. DS Leyton now chips in supportively.

'And we've got the last piece of rope, Guv – that alone, it's enough to hang 'em.'

They all chuckle at this timely intervention, and sit back in their seats as their generous selection of starters arrives. Skelgill has overseen the ordering; he is especially partial to the establishment's seekh kebab, and glances about anxiously until he sees that there are sufficient portions. He takes one such item, and slides the salad from the plate to make room for more important fare. Meanwhile DS Leyton continues the dialogue.

'How long do we reckon they've been planning all this for?'

Skelgill looks grim-faced as he considers this question.

'Probably two decades, Leyton.'

'Seriously, Guv?'

But now Skelgill shrugs.

'Maybe they'll decide to tell us, Leyton.'

DS Jones takes a small sip of mineral water.

'I've been wondering if they were influenced by the wave of celebrity cases in the last couple of years. When you think about it, what they actually did wouldn't take a lot of organisation. The crux was luring their victims to Ullswater Place.'

DS Leyton is nodding, though he still appears doubtful. However, DS Jones continues.

'The girl could easily have been seeing one or more of them as clients. If she'd surfaced with an alias – what, ten years after the events at the farm – they'd not recognise her. And, let's face it, we know these guys all shared a common interest.'

DS Leyton leans forward a little.

'Do you think they were still acting as some kind of ring?'

Skelgill puts a second kebab on hold to interject.'

'I reckon anything like that ended with the fire at Knott Halloo Farm – but probably there was a bond between them. And then there's the gambling connection through Maurice Stewart. The numbers I got from his mobile suggest he was supplying Harris, Seddon and Barley with tips. So if they were sharing betting information – who knows what else?'

DS Jones looks animated – she holds up a palm like an eager student.

'The computers, Guv – I think there could be more to the thefts than covering their tracks.'

'Aye?'

'Once they got hold of them, they'd be able to impersonate their victims – access their address books and send emails or social messages pretending to be them. For instance, that old lady in Kendal – what if the 'witches' she saw *were* the Lambs stealing Lee Harris's laptop on the Saturday night after they'd killed him? On the Sunday they could have contacted Barry Seddon, pretending to be Harris – recommending he try their services. They could have sent the same kind of messages to Walter Barley and Clifford Stewart. That might explain how they managed to get them to come in a cluster.'

Skelgill is listening with interest, though he raises a hand in a cautionary manner.

'Aye, well – hold your horses as far as Clifford Stewart is concerned – remember that was me.' He frowns with disapproval as he discovers the samosa he is eating is one of the vegetarian batch that DS Jones requested. 'But then again – I did tell them I was acting on a referral from old pals – and that helped to do the trick.'

'So, you could be right, Emma.' DS Leyton regards his colleague with admiration. 'If only we can find where they've dumped all the phones and computer gear, we might get the answer. We're trying to identify the owners of those lock-ups – before we start breaking in to 'em. That's where my money is.'

DS Jones grins modestly. She rises and passes dishes to her colleagues before serving herself a small helping of tandoori chicken accompanied by mixed salad. Skelgill's plate – and to a lesser extent that of DS Leyton – looks like it holds an entire main course.

DS Leyton begins to speak, but simultaneously biting into a parcel of uncertain composition he is taken unawares by its spicy nature and is forced to dive for his cooling beer. The others look on in amusement. He mops his brow with his serviette and makes an attempt to appear composed.

'What I don't get though, Guv – the Lambs took the risk of warning off their next victim – once the deaths hit the news.'

Skelgill shakes his head, simultaneously tearing at an unyielding chapatti.

'Aye – but think of the timing, Leyton. Harris you can forget – he was first. But Seddon was killed on the same day we found Harris's body – Monday. We didn't release the names until the Thursday night. Barley was murdered the next day, Friday. Aye, he must have missed the news – or decided he was going ahead anyway – we didn't give out details of how they were killed, other than apparent climbing accidents. He had no reason to make the sinister connection.'

DS Leyton purses his lips and nods slowly in acceptance of this logic.

'But they still thought they'd reel in Clifford Stewart, Guv?'

'Aye – well, who knows how they were going to play that one. But I reckon they were getting over-confident. Probably thought we hadn't got a clue – so time was on their side.'

DS Leyton is nothing if not persistent when it comes to ironing out the wrinkles in the modus operandi of the suspects. Again a thought clouds his features.

'Thing is, Guv – why go to all the trouble of displaying the bodies like they did – surely the reason would be to strike the fear of God into the next victim? From what you've pointed out, there wasn't even time for that – apart from Clifford Stewart.'

Skelgill waves an acknowledging fork at DS Leyton, indicating he has the solution to this conundrum.

'It's a good question, Leyton – and a lot of trouble to go to. I carried an equivalent weight up to Scales Tarn – thankfully I did, else I'd never have met Liz – Williams.' (He adds the surname under scrutiny from DS Jones.) 'It's do-able, but a killer – excuse the pun. But Jason is obviously a fit young lad.'

DS Leyton nods in agreement.

'Actually, Guv – one of the reports on him mentioned he was a promising fell-runner as a youth and that they were trying to encourage that.'

Skelgill indicates with an open palm that this bears out his point.

'A fit young lad – but also a *disturbed* young lad. We don't know what happened to these kids – but we do know that places like Sharp Edge were used to scare the living daylights out of them – to control them. Liz Williams actually joked about it when she told me – but it must have been terrifying for those they'd singled out for special treatment.'

DS Jones is staring hard at Skelgill.

'So, Guv – do you think in some way it was about taking back control?'

Skelgill is eating again, but he shakes his head decisively.

'I go along with the idea of it being a message – but not to their next target for murder, nor us. I reckon it was a signal to all their fellow victims.'

DS Leyton regards Skelgill intently.

'How do you mean, Guv?

Skelgill stares back squarely.

'What's the biggest frustration in the case of the unmentionable disc jockey?'

'That he died before he could be punished.'

'Exactly. And if Lee Harris had died in a motorbike accident, and Barry Seddon had fallen off his scaffolding, and Walter Barley had been savaged by a sheep... you get my drift?'

The two sergeants nod in silence. Skelgill continues.

'But when they're found murdered – *executed* – with a climbing rope around their necks, and then dumped at a particular landmark – a place that strikes fear into your own heart – if you'd been a victim and you heard that on the news – think about it.' He pauses for dramatic effect, and then bangs his fist hard on the table. 'Justice has been done.'

Again there is a hush as they each consider the possibility that the terrible retribution wreaked by the Lambs has some underlying sense of twisted righteousness – unproven as any such misdemeanours by the murder victims may yet be.

'But what about Clifford Stewart, Guv – we've still got him to find? We can't let him escape justice.'

Skelgill's features crease into an expression of distaste.

'I suspect he already has done, Leyton.'

'How's that, Guv?'

'I believe he died in the fire. I reckon if we find anything of Clifford Stewart it'll be a bunch of charred bones down the mine beyond Knott Halloo Farm.' Skelgill folds his arms and glares angrily. 'Maybe Maurice Stewart will come clean – or maybe he's half-cracked and not capable of speaking sense. But I think that fire was a deliberate act.'

'Set by whom, Guv?' DS Jones is the first to speak.

Skelgill squints into the shadowy middle distance of the intimately lit restaurant. It is steadily filling up, though the patrons are mostly local couples and there is a subdued air about the place.

'Your guess is as good as mine, Jones. Maybe there was a falling out. Maybe it was Maurice Stewart who uncovered what was going on – blamed it on his son. Maybe Clifford did it and it went wrong – perhaps he actually committed suicide. Maybe even it was an angry parent.'

DS Leyton methodically folds his cutlery onto his plate.

'So that would mean it was hushed up, Guv?'

'Aye – and that fits the facts. There was no insurance claim. The Stewart family – whatever was left of them – abandoned the area like rats from a sinking ship. Walter Barley got a cottage for life out of it – for keeping mum, perhaps.'

'But what about Clifford Stewart, Guv – I mean his death going unnoticed?'

Skelgill shrugs.

'If his body was removed from the scene and he was never reported missing – who was to know he'd not gone away? The fire brigade got there too late – they were up to their necks in forest fires and were content to sign it off as spontaneous combustion caused by petrol fumes.'

DS Jones leans forward.

'And, Guv – the Lambs – they wouldn't know Clifford was dead.'

Skelgill nods slowly.

'I told them I'd been away for a long time. They didn't question that.'

'You must have been the icing on the cake, Guv.'

Skelgill raises his eyebrows in a self-conscious gesture. But before his embarrassment can be compounded white-jacketed waiters arrive in synchrony to clear the table of debris. The detectives now sway from one side to the other, like diners on a rolling cruise ship, to enable the staff to reach past them. As this task is completed, DS Leyton glances at his wristwatch and places his hands on the table as if he is about to rise.

'If you don't mind, Guv – my pass-out is about to expire – I've got to meet the mother-in-law off the nine o'clock from Euston.'

Though he winks at Skelgill, his superior looks alarmed.

'What about your dinner – we've only had the starters?'

'Guv – I'm stuffed already – and, anyway – I've got a cunning plan.'

'Such as?'

'Well – you know what I told you about DI Smart threatening to bring us here – talking this place down – and gloating about the case?'

'Aye.'

'I thought maybe if we left a nice doggy-bag on his desk for him to find first thing on Monday morning – he'd blame you, of course, Guv.'

Skelgill seems amused – though such a sentiment must be tinged with the regretful prospect of good food going to waste.

'Fair enough, Leyton – we'll see what we can do, eh, Jones?'

This statement appears to leave a window ajar should he opt to raid the now-superfluous order.

DS Leyton climbs to his feet and slips his jacket from the back of his chair. He reaches inside and pulls out his wallet. He extracts a generous wad of notes and is about to lay them on the table when Skelgill stands up and intervenes.

'Put that back, Leyton – this is my treat.'

'You sure, Guv?'

Skelgill waves away DS Leyton's protests.

'I told you it was – besides, I'm flush.' He resumes his seat looking pleased with himself. 'There was one other thing I got from Maurice Stewart, though he doesn't know it – the winner of the two-thirty at Lingfield this afternoon.'

DS Leyton grins widely and shakes his head.

'Blimey, Guv – I hope you didn't back it at the Scotchwoman's shop.'

Skelgill shakes his head.

'No – but I told her.' He chuckles. 'Between us I reckon we cleaned out Bettoney's.'

'Nice one, Guv.'

DS Leyton does not appear to bear any resentment for not being let in on the hot tip. With a parting wave, and a word of thanks to the effusive manager at the door, he takes his leave. There is a proud glint in Skelgill's eye as he watches his sergeant lumbering bravely off into the night, to an uncertain fate.

'Impressive arrest you two made.' The tone of Skelgill's voice suggests he could almost be talking to himself. 'He's as soft as putty – but you'd want him alongside you in a tight corner.'

DS Jones is leaning forward across the table, her own dark eyes glistening in the flicker of the candlelight. She appears fascinated by her boss's rare display of fraternal affection – although her next statement perhaps belies her underlying emotions.

'I still can't believe you did it, Guv.'

Skelgill frowns dismissively.

'Well – if you recall, *Miss* Jones – it was a little bird not so far from where I'm sitting that told me all about *Streetwise* in the first place.'

DS Jones gives him an imploring look, as if she means to suggest it is one huge leap from such knowledge to the radical approach he clandestinely adopted. Skelgill casually swallows the last of his lager and waves for refills.

'You know, the more I thought about Barry Seddon's last recorded movements – the more I felt they had the hallmarks of someone paying a visit to – how shall I put it? – a lady of ill-repute.'

DS Jones feigns concern – perhaps that he would easily recognise such signs.

'I didn't imagine you'd take it so seriously, Guv. How *did* you convince them you were Clifford Stewart?'

'I suppose I had their momentum on my side – I was giving them what they wanted – so they didn't look too closely.' He runs his fingers through his hair. 'Liz – you don't need to worry about her, by the way – she told me that Clifford couldn't pronounce the letter 'r' – he said *wope* instead of rope. Then there was his old nickname I got from Maurice Stewart – Cliff

Edge – I used that to create a profile on *Streetwise* – got myself a couple of ratings –'

DS Jones suddenly chokes on her water, and Skelgill has to leave his seat to thump her on the back.

'It's not what you think, Jones.'

Temporarily incapacitated, she is unable to reply, and dabs tears from her eyes with her napkin.

'I made up a couple of girls' profiles – then I used their accounts to give me ratings. Took a good few hours burning the midnight oil – but in the end I was quite impressed with my computer ingenuity. Got a bit confused with all the passwords, though.'

DS Jones is shaking her head.

'And are these ratings available to read online, Guv?' Now her lips form into a suggestive pucker.

Even in the semi-darkness of the restaurant, Skelgill's cheeks visibly colour.

'I've, er – closed down the accounts – I got them on a free trial period.'

DS Jones allows him to stew for a moment. Then she relents.

'That was a crazy risk you took, Guv.'

Skelgill leans closer across the table, his voice lowered.

'I had to get the evidence. Until they told me what they were up to – their motives – I still hadn't really put it all together – let's face it, I could have got it completely wrong – it might have been the service exactly as advertised on *Streetwise*. As it was I made three other appointments – in the process of trying to find an escort based in the right area. And this pair had a clever system – you had to call them from a nearby phone box. That's one reason there was no helpful number left on Barry Seddon's mobile.'

DS Jones reaches for her glass and wraps her fingers around its base. Her hand is just an inch or so from Skelgill's.

'You could have said something, Guv – for your own safety – I would have kept quiet if some daft theory of yours never came to anything.'

Skelgill compresses his lips and inhales slowly through his nose. In a grateful gesture, he brushes his knuckle against her fingers, but then sits back in his seat. He shakes his head at his own stupidity.

'My mind was jumping about all over the place – I even got completely side-tracked at the eleventh hour and tested out the farmer at Knott Halloo – in case *he* was Clifford – he thought I was crackers when I started calling him Cliff Edge.' Skelgill tuts to the heavens at his folly. 'But then I returned to my original theory – that Clifford really had disappeared from the face of the earth – I had a look in the old mine behind the farm. Cleopatra nearly fell down a shaft – I just about cut off my hand breaking her fall – then I was thinking if I used a wide tape for a handle, the baler twine wouldn't dig in to your skin.'

DS Jones raises her eyebrows.

'The restraining straps that leave no marks.'

'Another little piece in the jigsaw. I guessed I had that coming to me – but I'd banked on being able to tell them who I was – that their game was up – I thought at worst they'd abandon me and do a runner. I hadn't bargained for the gag.'

'Or the oil?'

Now he simpers rather sheepishly.

'All in the line of duty, Jones.'

DS Jones's expression breaks into an impish smile.

'I'm tempted to remind you of a statement you made in your office after seeing the Chief, Guv.'

Skelgill remains poker faced.

'All in good working order.'

'Nice boxers, by the way – and at least they were on the right way round.'

Now Skelgill meets her gaze with an intensity of his own – but then abruptly he jerks bolt upright in his seat.

'What is it, Guv?'

'*Boxers* – you've just reminded me – Cleopatra's in the car – I'd better check her before they bring the main course – in case we're a while – she's probably starving.'

DS Jones casts about the restaurant as if she desires to attract the attention of a waiter – but at this moment the staff appear to be otherwise occupied behind the scenes.

'I was thinking, Guv – since DS Leyton wants his meal packed up.' She hesitates for a second before continuing. 'We could get the rest of it as a takeaway?'

Skelgill, who has risen to his feet, wavers for a moment. Then he nods once.

'Okay – I'll go and sort the bill – you stick your head round the kitchen door – your powers of persuasion are greater than mine.'

A couple of minutes later they leave together and stroll across the car park towards Skelgill's estate. Dusk is falling and Cleopatra is not obviously visible. Then DS Jones spots a movement to the rear.

'She's in the back section, Guv.'

Skelgill lifts the tailgate. DS Jones involuntarily recoils – there is a sudden sharp stink of fish. Cleopatra sits innocently on the flatbed, her head cocked to one side.

Skelgill appears alarmed. He reaches past the dog and retrieves the empty lower half of a partially gnawed plastic sandwich box.

'Oh, no – disaster.'

'What is it, Guv?'

'She's eaten all my dead-baits!'

DS Jones laughs heartily, and after a moment Skelgill is forced to join in.

'I think I'd better keep the takeaway food in the front, Guv.'

Skelgill concurs.

'Aye – the little devil, eh? I was thinking of giving her some of Leyton's chicken tikka masala – but she can forget that now.'

He closes the tailgate and they round to their respective doors. DS Jones holds up the brown paper carrier bag containing their meals.

'Shame DS Leyton had to go, Guv – that's considerate of him, looking after his mother-in-law.'

Skelgill stares uncomprehendingly across the roof of the car. Then he breaks into a grin.

'Jones – he's not picking up his mother-in-law – that was what's called making a diplomatic exit.'

***

Next in the series...

TEN LITTLE FISHES

By the time Detective Inspector Skelgill becomes the tenth person to be stranded on secluded Grisholm (*Pigs' Isle* in Old Norse) where a writers' retreat is taking place, one of the assembled literati is already dead.

Though natural causes may provide the explanation, a second 'accidental' death and a raft of curious experiences convince Skelgill that a cold and calculating killer is at large. But where is his evidence?

Set around Derwentwater in the English Lake District, this traditional whodunit sees Skelgill striving both to fathom the mystery *and* convince his superiors that it is not merely his imagination at play.

'Murder on the Lake' by Bruce Beckham is available from Amazon

FREE BOOKS, NEW RELEASES, THE BEAUTIFUL LAKES ... AND MOUNTAINS OF CAKES

Sign up for Bruce Beckham's author newsletter

Thank you for getting this far!

If you have enjoyed your encounter with DI Skelgill there's a growing series of whodunits set in England's rugged and beautiful Lake District to get your teeth into.

My newsletter often features one of the back catalogue to download for free, along with details of new releases and special offers.

No Skelgill mystery would be complete without a café stop or two, and each month there's a traditional Cumbrian recipe – tried and tested by yours truly (aka *Bruce Bake 'em*).

 To sign up, this is the link:

https://mailchi.mp/acd032704a3f/newsletter-sign-up

Your email address will be safely stored in the USA by Mailchimp, and will be used for no other purpose. You can unsubscribe at any time simply by clicking the link at the foot of the newsletter.

Thank you, again – best wishes and happy reading!

Bruce Beckham

Made in United States
North Haven, CT
07 January 2024

47167855R00157